# NOMINATING MAGAZINES

The Atlantic Monthly, 8 Arlington Street, Boston, Massachusetts 02116

Cosmopolitan, 224 West 57th Street, New York, New York 10019

Esquire, 2 Park Avenue, New York, New York 10016

The Georgia Review, University of Georgia, Athens, Georgia 30602

Harper's, 2 Park Avenue, New York, New York 10016

Mademoiselle, 350 Madison Avenue, New York, New York 10017

The Missouri Review, Department of English, 231 A & S, University of Missouri, Columbia, Missouri 65211

Ms., 119 West 40th Street, New York, New York 10018

The North American Review, 1222 West 27th Street, Cedar Falls, Iowa 50614

The Paris Review, 45-39 171st Place, Flushing, New York 11358

Playboy, 919 North Michigan Avenue, Chicago, Illinois 60611

Ploughshares, Box 529, Cambridge, Massachusetts 02139

Redbook, 959 Eighth Avenue, New York, New York 10019

Seventeen, 850 Third Avenue, New York, New York 10022

Shenandoah, Box 722, Lexington, Virginia 24450

Tendril, P.O. Box 512, Green Harbor, Massachusetts 02041

TriQuarterly, 1735 Benson Avenue, Evanston, Illinois 60201

Vanity Fair, 350 Madison Avenue, New York, New York 10017

# THE
# EDITORS'
# CHOICE

VOLUME IV

# THE EDITORS' CHOICE

## VOLUME IV

### COMPILED BY
### GEORGE E. MURPHY, JR.

A BANTAM/WAMPETER PRESS BOOK

BANTAM BOOKS
TORONTO · NEW YORK · LONDON · SYDNEY · AUCKLAND

THE EDITORS' CHOICE, VOLUME IV
*A Bantam Book / January 1988*

*Windstone and accompanying logo of a stylized W
are trademarks of Bantam Books, Inc.
This was published simultaneously in hardcover and trade paperback.*

**Library of Congress Cataloging-in-Publication Data**
(Revised for vol. 4)

The Editors' choice.

"A Bantam/Wampeter Press book."
1. Short stories, American. 2. American fiction—
20th century. I. Murphy, George E. (George Edward),
1948–
PS648.S5.S34  1985    813'.01'08    84-24157
ISBN 0-553-34176-6 (U.S. : pbk. : v. 1)
ISBN 0-553-34221-5 (U.S. : pbk. : v. 2)

ISBN 0-553-34466-8

*Published simultaneously in the United States and Canada*

*Bantam Books are published by Bantam Books, Inc. Its trademark, consisting
of the words "Bantam Books" and the portrayal of a rooster, is Registered in
U.S. Patent and Trademark Office and in other countries. Marca Registrada.
Bantam Books, Inc., 666 Fifth Avenue, New York, New York 10103.*

PRINTED IN THE UNITED STATES OF AMERICA

FG      0 9 8 7 6 5 4 3 2 1

**COMPLIMENTS OF BANTAM BOOKS**

666 FIFTH AVE. NEW YORK N.Y. 10103 · 212-765-6500

EDITOR'S CHOICE VOLUME IV
Compiled by George E. Murphy
Pub Date: January 1, 1988

Hardcover:
ISBN 0-553-05241-1 $17.95 288 pp.

Tradepaperback:
ISBN 0-553-34466-8 $8.95 288 pp.

Following the first three volumes of The Editor's Choice, comes THE EDITOR'S CHOICE IV. As in the the first three volumes, the stories in this collection have been voted best among contemporary writing by America's editors from such magazines as The Paris Review, Esquire, Harper's, Seventeen, TriQuarterly, and The Atlantic Monthly. The writers this year include Margaret Atwood, Russell Banks, Sue Miller, and Thomas McGuane and newcomers such as Gail Galloway Adams, Robert Cohen, and Amy Herrick.

Contact:
Sally Williams
Elizabeth Chapman

# CONTENTS

# INTRODUCTION

❦

God, I love this job.

The tarpon were running in the harbor and my friend, Bob Reiss was on the phone. He and John-John and Walley were headed out for Cuban-mix sandwiches and bait.

"Can I be at the Marina in an hour? Are you kidding? See you there." I said.

Already dressed and showered, and with the marina only five minutes away, I figured I'd get another story or two read and took my mug of coffee out to the back deck. The story was Tim O'Brien's "The Things They Carried" from *Esquire*. I found myself in Vietnam looking into Lt. Jimmy Cross's backpack and the accumulating weight of his love letters, Rat Kiley's comic books and illustrated New Testament, Ted Lavender's tranquilizers—all the small and idiosyncratic talismans against that alien environment.

When I started "The Middle Man," Bharati Mukherjee's nomination from *Playboy*, I was jerked into the present, to Nicaragua. I was watching Maria, the only woman among a band of Contras, mistress to an enigmatic American soldier of fortune. She was wise, sensuous, and powerful in a world of contraband and deceit.

I thought to myself, "After four years, these stories are still getting better."

As I reached for Gail Galloway Adams' "Inside Dope" from *The North American Review*, I heard an outboard engine and a voice yelled, "Where the hell were you?"

It was Reiss in his Red Sox hat, standing against a row of rods in a 20-foot Mako.

Looking at my watch, I said, "Sorry. Why didn't you just phone?"

"George, we called ten times!"

I headed inside to get my sunglasses and drop the stories back on my desk. As I did so, I glanced at the beginning of Rachel Pastan's "Underground" from *The Georgia Review:* "It was, apparently, a small dinosaur, only five feet high . . ."

Reading a little further wouldn't hurt, I thought. What a great story! Here was this sleepless college girl, Lisa, wandering around her dormitory basement every night, opening doors and making bizarre discoveries.

Outside I thought I heard an engine start and a voice shout, "So long, George." But I had started to lay the stories out in neat little piles on the coffee table. There was Bandit, the unforgettable bird dog in Tom McGuane's "A Man in Louisiana," from *Shenandoah*. And the three beautiful, coveted, and pseudo-debutante Abbott sisters in Sue Miller's story from *Mademoiselle*. Stories by Elizabeth Tallent, Mary Gordon, Margaret Atwood, Russell Banks.

I put on my sunglasses and went outside to an empty dock. That's friends for you.

I thought as I continued reading through the afternoon, story after wonderful story, how these gems were not just coming from the big national magazines but also from a wealth of small literary periodicals around the country. I was reminded of an article in a recent *Library Journal* citing statistics on how much award-winning fiction is being published in these increasingly important literary journals. I looked at the names new to me which I'm sure we'll all be seeing again: Todd Leiber, Leigh Alison Wilson, Richard McCann, Amy Herrick.

I thought of the increasing attention being paid to the short story in recent years: The American Book Award going to Bob Shacochis's collection *Easy in the Islands;* the return of short story collections to the bestseller list; even the institution of new prizes, like the Dungammon Foundation's annual $25,000 Rea Award to a writer of short fiction.

At the end of the afternoon, Reiss called to gloat. The tarpon *had* been running. I pictured these silvery fighters leaping from the green waters of the gulf and I pictured my friends hauling prize after prize into the boat for the photo of proof—only to toss them back and watch them dive toward the bottom of the harbor.

Ordinarily, this would have bugged the hell out of me but something else was troubling me. I could only include eighteen stories in the collection from the more than fifty that had been nominated. Funny, tragic, powerful, moving stories that made me wish this collection could be three times larger.

My job is to toss them back too, to say no when my heart is crying run it, print it!

God, I hate this job.

> —George Murphy
> The Houseboat "Sea Dog"
> Key West

# THE
# EDITORS'
# CHOICE

## VOLUME IV

# GAIL GALLOWAY ADAMS
# INSIDE DOPE

## FROM THE NORTH AMERICAN REVIEW

§

THIS IS A STORY about being in love with a man named Billy Lee Boaz, only he's called Bisher, don't ask me why. You need to know what he looks like because Bisher is a type, if men don't recognize, at least the women will. First, a Boaz is not big. Five feet six inches is about as tall as is allowed, and they are dark with black hair and eyes, real tanned skin, and bodies just as trim and tight as their lips are wet and loose. They have bandits' faces, with bright shiny eyes that gleam in a dashboard's light, white teeth that do the same, and they are as good in bed as they are in working on the engines of a Pontiac. They don't do sports except sometimes if the high school is small enough you'll see them on the football line digging in like baby buffalo; stamina and spite keep them there against all odds. They usually aim their every action to rewards, and the mean variety end up in the service yelling at shaved-head recruits and being fussy over lockers. The civilian ones are good-natured boys, then men, who smile a lot. They are the kind, who when they come down to breakfast in clean white T-shirts and starched khaki pants, freshly showered, shaved, come smiling into the kitchen. Their hair is always cut the same, "some

1

off the back and sides, just barely trim the top," and around each ear is pared an arch the color of their palms, their soles, and underneath their underwear. They're jittery men too, jiggling change as they stand, walking forward lightly on their toes, slumping back hard into their heels, and somehow you are always aware of them from the navel down. Although they do nothing with their hands and arms to indicate their lower parts, still, the itch of lust is in the air. When they love you they are given to coming up and getting push-up placed with you against the wall, then they lean down to lick your throat. Before you gasp they unroll a pack of Luckies tucked like a second bicep in their shirt, and light one in a dramatic way: scratching the match against their thigh, snapping it in two with a nail, or deliberately letting the flame burn into their fingerpads. They are also the kind of men who groan when it feels good, and Bisher, who was my brother-in-law, had all these qualities.

But of course, and finally, Bisher is different and that's why I'm telling about him. Bisher was, and is, a genius. Everyone attests to that, even the principal who threw him out of school. Bisher works, and has for years, at the Standard Shell station and wears a blue blouse with his name embroidered on his chest, an oval with a red satin stitch of Boaz, Bill right over his heart, and he's the one who taught me to call a work shirt "blouse." "More uniform," he grinned, explaining that in the army they call them blouses instead of shirts and "no one ever called dogfaces feminine." Then he folded in the sides of cloth like wrappings on a gift, and tucked them in his pants. I remember that was the summer I was fifteen, and I sat on the shag rug, listening to, watching, and admiring Bisher.

My sister Ellen married Bisher at the end of her junior year in high school and there's no need to go into what that did to our family. First, everyone almost died, then they cried from March to June, and finally, when my parents realized those two would not give up, they were wed under my father's guiding prayers, and we all gave thanks that one of the two— probably Bisher—had the sense to hold off babies for a while. In towns like ours as soon as a marriage was announced, countdown began. People bought layettes the same day they bought a plate for the bride's table setting. After a return from a honeymoon in "Gay Mehico," Ellen and Bisher made our third floor home. The room had been ours, mine and Ellen's, I mean, and was really two rooms with a long hall in between, a sink curtained off at one end, and a toilet in a closet near the stair. "Deluxe," Bisher said the day he moved in. "I'll add this to my list of ten best spots to stay from here to Amarillo." Ellen blushed to see him standing there amidst our pink stuffed bears and faded rag rugs. I moved reluctantly down to a room which was used once or twice a year for visiting missionaries, more often for making costumes for the church's plays. With Bisher upstairs our lives took on new rhythms and new ways.

My dad did not, of course, like Bisher, but being a Christian thought he should and tried to talk to his new son-in-law each day. "Well, young man." Dad would clear his throat. "Well, Billy Lee."

"Call me Bisher, sir," said Bisher. So Daddy would nod, and ask, "Have a good day?"

"Yes, sir." Bisher'd reply as snappy as an ensign in starched pants, then he'd wink at me, and purse his lips at Ellen, which made me giggle and her blush, then both snicker. My mother always caught these triad exchanges, saw us, her daughters, as traitors, and would draw her lips together and pale. She absolutely hated, detested, despised Billy Lee. She refused to call him Bisher, forbade my father to, cursed "that Boaz," his family, his pets, and malign chance that put him here in this town when he should have been in Houston getting mugged. "Just trash," she'd mutter, "nothing but trash. I never thought I'd raise my Ellen to marry trash."

I would sit on a high stool in the kitchen waiting for Momma to finish washing the dishes I was to dry, and listen to her tirades against Bisher, and wonder why he made her feel that way. "It's lust, nothing but lust," she'd said once, then flushed, slapped me on the arm right where I was picking a scab off a mosquito bite, and yelled at me to get upstairs to my room and stop hanging around minding everybody's business, which I thought wasn't fair. But as I moped my way up to the room beneath the bed where Ellen and Bisher now slept, I knew then, as now, that no matter what my mother said, I was on my sister's side, and Bisher's. And I also knew that I would love that short dark boy until the day I died.

Bisher was able, finally and always, to get around my mother as he got around everyone. He won her over in the end, for all the time she was dying, the one person she ever wanted to see was him. "Where is that scamp?" she'd ask. "He worries me to death." She'd pull at the collar of her bed jacket, push at her limp hair, and say, "I wouldn't care to see him again." The door'd creep open and Bisher's face would appear, dark and shiny as mischief. "Got a minute, madame?" he'd whisper, letting his eyes look shyly everywhere except at her until she'd say, "Come on in, you're letting air out to the hall." Then, Bisher'd slip in the room so quick if you didn't know better you'd think he made his living as a second story man, or maybe he was a meter man gone bad, and gone to bed with the lady of the house. But like everybody else he touched, he touched our mother, made her do things she'd never dreamed of. He taught her to smoke on her deathbed. We could hear her gasp for breath, and laugh between puffs and coughs. "Oh, Lord," she'd say, or pray, with stammering breath, "this is so wrong," and then would peer closely at the end of her Camel to see if it would contradict. "Look here," Bisher'd command, and she'd watch him fill the room with smoky rings. She learned that too. It was disconcerting to creak open the door to check and see if she was resting well, and catch her lying there, propped up on ruffled pillows, head tilted back to the ceiling, her mouth a perfect "o" as it puffed out those rings until they circled her like Saturn's do. Now I understand that that was one of Bisher's secrets. He's the kind of man who'll take you to a raunchy honky-tonk, if you want to go, and all night while you are sipping 3.2 beer, his feet would be tapping yours under the table, and he'd be winking or nudging at you as if to say, "Why aren't you bad?" He let you play it fast, but safe, and you were grateful to him for it.

I wouldn't say that Bisher's what they call a "good old boy." He's not; at least I don't think he is. For although he works on cars and engines and loves them, he doesn't care for guns. He has one, everybody does, but his hangs behind the door forgotten as a worn-out coat. "I never liked hunting much," he'd said one night in the kitchen when we were helping Momma skin rabbits a church elder had brought. Dumped out of a gunnysack onto the floor, their blood-splotched fur filled the room with thickness. Ellen, pregnant with her first, ran to throw up; Momma murmured, "Oh, Lord," and even Daddy, who preached of death as a new beginning, looked distressed. "Let's make them look like meat," Bisher said, "then they won't trouble us as much." He'd heaped them in a plastic tub where they hung limp as coronation trim to be sewed on, then took them to the porch, beheaded, skinned, saved their lucky feet, buried all the innards, and put them pale and shimmering into a pot with seasonings. "No, I never cared for hunting," he said thoughtfully when all that had been done. "Because I always thought just before I shot," he paused, looked apologetically at my father, "what if it's true we're born again, and in another body, say like, a deer? Why I couldn't shoot a deer to save my life, 'cause every time, I'd remember Lewis Moon, and how he liked to run before he died. Why, what if Lewis was that deer? Excuse me, sir." My daddy muttered, "Quite all right," and hurried out to write up a lesson for the Senior Sunday School with two main themes: Number I: Do we need to hunt our animal friends? and Number II: Beliefs on coming back to life that Christians should put right on out of their heads.

But what made Bisher unique was that he was a genius, and how he got to be one is legend in our town. Others have tried his trick since, just to end up laughingstocks when they have failed. There has been only one other acknowledged genius in this whole county, and George Shapland was never any fun like Bisher. He was always tucked up in a book which Bisher said "just proved he wasn't a natural genius. Not that there is a thing wrong with books. It's just that they don't have no place." George graduated from high school at age fifteen after having proved the geometry teacher wrong, and having settled the history teacher in his place (both were coaches so shouldn't be blamed for being soft in hard subjects), and then he went to State Tech where he took a double load of everything and made friends with others like him who cluttered up cafeteria tables with maps and measuring instruments. Later it was rumored he became a monk. But Bisher's genius wasn't like George's ordinary kind, for Bisher's brain was pure, and how he brought it to the attention of the authorities was genius enough.

A new teacher came to teach English and the Romance tongues, and one week into French, Bisher's genius was revealed. Called on to read a page of Lesson II, Bisher balked at his desk, slumped into his heels, and said in French he'd rather not. The rest of the students didn't know what he said, thought it was filth, and that was why the teacher gasped, then said, "You read it, you canard." When Bisher quacked and waddled to the front the others didn't know what was going on. They now thought Bisher was making bathroom gestures, sounds. He jumped on the teacher's desk, then barely looking at the text, he read Lesson II, skipped on to IV, ending up with Number XII, and he answered all the questions too. The other students still thought he was Danny Kaye-ing them, making Frenchy sounds, making fun of French, so they were laughing at his ooo-la-la's, but meanwhile the teacher had caught on to Bisher's brain, and stood there listening to him reel off syllables like DeGaulle. When Bisher finished a rundown of the hardest, longest words in the index, translating them all, a silence fell upon the room. "Is he right?" whispered a semibright boy, and the teacher numbly nodded her head. When she did, Bisher, who was still standing on the desk, now holding the book across his chest in a Napoleon stance, suddenly, without a sideways glance, hurled that text out the window, splintering all the glass. At the crash, he jumped to flee the room, the teacher in pursuit behind, screaming, "My boy, my boy, my dear dear boy," in French. Bisher got kicked out of school about ten minutes later even though the teacher intervened, claiming (it was the first time) Bisher's genius. The principal would hear none of this. "Don't let me hear of this boy's genius. I call it fits myself. There's at least ten idiots in the institute can reel off dates and times better than this Billy Lee "Bisher" Boaz boy. And as for this last—this French episode—why, I don't know." He shook his hands from the wrist as if that limpness signified Paris and all its decadence. Then he threw Bisher out, saying the reasons were breaking windows and the backs of books, and disrespect for a foreign land. Once expelled, Bisher was stripped, not only of the lessons he already knew, but of all the offices he held, which, though many, were not various. He was the sergeant-of-arms for every club from Future Nurses to the Lindbergh Boys. He had more pictures in the *Cattle Call* annual than anybody but the Snowball Queen, but that year he was officially excised, and every organization picture had an oblong blank that once was Billy Lee. He signed those anyway with Greek signs.

The second reason he was a genius was inside dope. What that means is that Bisher knew something about everything—he really did. Like all smart men, he'd claimed to have read the dictionary from A to Z, and was always threatening to start in on the Britannica. In every conversation Bisher had things to add, and always they were interesting. He was like those columns in the newspaper called "Ask Mr. Tweedles" where people write in to ask "What are warts made of?" and "Why are tulips bulbs?" That is what Bisher Boaz could do too; not only explain warts in scientific terms, he could tell you about all the different kinds of warts, from plantars on your feet to venereal on your you-know-where. But unlike a Tweedles, who had to stop at column's end, Bisher didn't. If you showed the slightest bit of interest, as I did since my hands were always covered with warts, seed pearls of them ringing my fingers, grits of them on my fingertips, he'd tell you how to make them go away. Every night press half an onion and some lemon juice on your palms, then put your hands in gloves so the acid would start to eat away those knobs. Salt and hot water rags might work, but not as well, and he'd heard from a sailor that in Madagascar, the natives called warts "woolies" and smeared them with corn meal and lard and exposed them to the sun. "Are you sure, Billy Lee," my momma questioned, "he didn't get that mixed up with cooking techniques?" "No, ma'am," said Bisher, "no siree. And Old Man Allison—he spits on pennies, then ties them to your hands." I shivered to think of wet copper staining my hands green, melting my flesh.

But warts were just one of the things that Bisher knew, could do. For instance, he knew names, real names of movie stars—Bernie Schwartz for Tony Curtis, Judy Garland/Frances Gumm. "Archie Leach, now that's a laugh," he'd laugh. "Imagine, Cary Grant!" He knew the made-up names of every level down to grip, and watching a movie with Bisher could be a chore. "Bobby Raymond's his real name," he'd whisper when the villain appeared. "Hers is Susie Moore," when the girlish victim smiled at death. "Oh, boy," he'd crow, then clap his hands, "Old Lyman Harkney's playing that soda jerk," and even when the story was spoiled by these outbursts you didn't mind, but wanted to see Old Harkney make a comeback shake. You wanted to know Norma Jean Baker by her real name even when Bisher would argue against that change. "Now why? Norma Baker is a good star's name. Norma Talmadge made it. Baker sounds so clean, so why'd she change? Brought her nothing but bad luck, poor kid. Did you know she had a round white bed?" He knew political nicknames too, and was the first person I ever knew to call FDR Frankie Dee. Bisher said, "His own family did that in the confines of their room. The missus, that's Eleanor, I've heard she called him F. Dee Dee."

And Bisher knew the names of things, like knots. He never tied a shoelace, his or his kids', without telling you just what it was: "Half-splice, granny circle, mariner's wheel," whatever design he'd chosen for that day. Once he'd macraméd his oldest boy's laces halfway down, naming each loop and twist as he taught the child to tie. It was the same with ties. "Windsor, Crown, Full-Dress, or Brummel Bunch," he'd say, and later, when my dad was old, unable to sort out the ends of his own, Bisher was always there on Sunday mornings "to arrange cravats." "A Fanchon Loop?" he'd ask as my dad would nod, then watch in the mirror, as Bisher, shorter, hidden behind him, deftly moved the material into wings. Names of tools, nails, brads, a half-lug screw, a soft-headed angle iron, all these are in my memory, along with others I never try to find in hardware stores. All are "inside dope" and fun to know. You can see why children always loved him, wanted to go with him to the Dairy Queen to hear him order "Dope and Dodos two by two," or "Adam and Eve on a Raft with a side of down." My daughter loves her hamburgers "dragged through the garden," and she'll eat almost anything if Uncle Bisher says it is a "meal with a story behind it."

I am married to a man who is as different from a Bisher Boaz as any man can be. My Mel is tall, lean, pale, wears wire-rimmed glasses, and is a chemist with hair thinning at the crown. He was appalled at tales of Bisher until he met him, fell under his spell as hard as anyone. When those two are together I love my Mel more as he tries to slouch his frame down half a foot, and bounce tough in Bisher's stride. It can't be done, but

I love him for the trying. Bisher knows what he's about with Mel, teasing, making frogs on my husband's arm, and laughing, scuffling out a foot to kick Mel in the rear. "Break your behind, my old Max. You ain't nothing but a hoked-up cook." He nicknamed Mel "Max" the second day they'd met. "He has a look of Maximilian Schell, or the Emperor of Mexico." My husband, immensely pleased, laughed, betrayed himself with a blush. He's wanted a nickname all his life, not just Mel; a shortened version of your plain name is not enough. Years ago at a summer camp, he'd tried to start a nickname on his own. Tall and awkward at first base, he'd chatted up his teammates, addressed himself as "Stumpy," encouraged the others to do the same, but Stumpy didn't stick. Until Bisher's baptism, my Mel remained just what he was, a two-syllable Jewish boy good at math and "chemicals." As Max he expands in blue jeans that fit rather than cling oddly to his waist, and the whole-of-him is revved up by Bisher, he's sparked. He starts making lists, and listing things as "Number 1."

Oh, Bisher's lists . . . he has one for everything: ten famous redheads, five deadly Arizona snakes. When my daughter squeals, tumbles backwards on the grass, hurling her legs over her head to show cotton bloomers with a ruffled hem, I know if Bisher were here he'd have her on a list. "Want to hear a list of five famous women who showed their private pants in public places? Number 1: Marilyn Monroe on a hot-air grate in New York City, 1956." And the names remain, for Bisher nicknamed everyone. Ellen had a dozen or more but "Mistress Mellow" was the one she liked the best. I was "Grits" because "You love 'em, you're full of 'em, and your warts feel like 'em." Far from being insulted I loved that name, signed Grits to papers until I was married. My mother was "Miz Matty Mustard," my dad was "Mr. Chaps." Every friend that Bisher had was changed, renamed. Frail Danny Sells became "Dan, the Panic Man" who tried feats like hanging from a window ledge at noon, while C.C. Collins, a druggist in his daddy's store, was called "Chuckles Capistrano, that fine chap," and he grew to specialize in oily giggling. Bisher had nicknames for every pet he met. "Here Wolf," he'd coax and our old collie Fred would try to growl, and then he'd croon, "Hey Big Rufus Red," as he stroked our orange-striped tomcat Sam. But what I always loved the best was to listen to Bisher talk about all the places that he'd like to have been. He knew those nicknames too, and the way that the natives said them, like New-pert News, and San Antone. I loved the ones that ended in a liquid "a": Miama, Cincinnata, Missoura; or when he'd give you a choice of pronunciation, say between Nawlans and New Orleens. My favorites always were the "Sans": Peedro, San Jo, Frisco, and San Berdoo.

I have often wondered what it would be like to make love to Bisher, or one of his type, and even, on occasion, have worked myself into a frenzy over this. In those early days I watched Ellen with a discerning eye that only sisters have, to see if what she and Bisher did "showed." On her it did. She was and is a woman who is lush, not fat but full, and her skin glows. A man would have to want those deep wide breasts, those soft round thighs that show you she is a natural blonde. Sometimes I wonder who it was I envied most: Bisher sinking into her to be subsumed; or Ellen having him with all life's energy.

But for all my dreaming, I am aware that Ellen's not had an easy time of it with Bisher being like he is. It's a funny thing that there are men who zero in on a woman that they want, as the only thing in life they'll ever want, and once she's got, and though she's loved, they start to roam. My husband sees Bisher's episodes as excess energy or misdirected compassion; Bisher's attempts to help some poor girl out. Beginning with advice, he always ends in bed. It is assumed that Ellen realizes that these lapses don't signify, that she is secure in her position of Number 1. The problem is that it never works that way. She still cries her eyes out over each new blonde, and each year I settle down to write a letter telling her that once again all will be well, that Bisher will behave, realize the error of his ways, not to pack her bags and move out here to us, not to storm the honky-tonk, not, whatever else she does, to go to the hussy's house to fight it out with her. Above all, I write, just be calm, you've been through this before. Take up guitar, I urge. You've always had a pretty voice, you like to sing, Bisher likes to hear you sing (not that that matters, I say with an exclamation mark), and that will turn your thoughts away from what is going on at Ruby's Watering Hole this year. Just get through it, Ellen, one more time. You know you are his everything. And all my love. Then, because I know Bisher would be hurt, and oddly enough, so would Ellen if I left it out, I add, P.S. Give our love to Bisher but hold off giving it to him for a while.

It always seemed to me that the love story of my sister and Bisher should have high drama in it: a shooting outside The Broken Spoke with Boaz slumping down, wounded in a limb, to be lifted into the back of a pickup truck and jolted into town to have the lead removed. I've pictured that scene a thousand times: Ellen in a cotton dress, shivering in the air-conditioned corridor, waiting for a word about her man, and, at the other end of that linoleumed aisle, a swinging door, behind which sits the hussy who has caused it all. She's a brassy blonde, wearing stretch pants and patent go-go boots, but close up, to complicate things, her eyes are tired and vulnerable. It would be her ex-husband, released from Huntsville on a 2-10 who shot Bisher down, and that man's now cuffed and crying in the city jail. But even as good a character as Boaz was, he couldn't make his fate a better story, and I always find the ending sad the way it petered out. Finally it was just what you'd expect anyone to do—not a Bisher Boaz genius with all his sweet teenaged love. It was just one blonde too many, and too trashy, and then it wasn't bearable any more. Ellen couldn't even laugh, as she'd once done, at the tales of woe they'd tell Bisher and he'd repeat to her as to why he'd got involved. Although he'd hardly aged, remaining just as trim as his boyhood self, he "was older now, and should know better, should think of the kids, should consider her," now wider, heavier, her tolerance covered over by both knowledge and flesh. So they were divorced, like one out of every four, and within the year my sister married a widower who was a vet, wore pastel polyester leisure suits, and had chains dangling on his exposed chest (he is another type who deserves a story of his own). But he seems to love Ellen about as much as he does Samoyeds, and she seems quite content. As for Bisher, within a month he'd married his latest blonde craze who promptly hung up her dancing pumps, let her hair go back brown, and started in making meringue pies with too much tartar in the gelatin.

On our first visit since the divorce Mel said he wanted to

go see Bisher and I could come if I thought Ellen would not mind, but he meant to go anyway. At breakfast Ellen said she didn't mind, that she saw Bisher almost every day or so to discuss the kids, or just to talk. Pouring coffee for us, she flushed, glanced at the empty place where the vet would sit except he had to attend the birth of puppies, and said, "You know that Bisher. He's always got the inside dope on everyone."

We drove out to see Bisher at his station, and I stayed in the car because it was so hot out there on the concrete where Mel and my ex-brother-in-law were sparring, making plans to go fishing on the coming Saturday. Then, suddenly, Bisher was walking over to the car. Smiling, he leaned into the window frame and said, "Give me a kiss, sweet Grits," and offered me his sweet wet lips. I inhaled that old smell of him: sweat and nicotine and gasoline and the lotion of Old Spice and Lava Soap and began to cry. "Oh, Bish," I blubbed, and he said, "Now, Grits, don't cry." As he massaged my shoulder blade, I heard him say, "Got a brand new list of five dark men who married blondes and then went wrong. Number 1: Joe DiMaggio." Then we three laughed. That night in bed beside Mel, knowing Ellen and her new man, whose hands smell of Lysol and dog hair, are just down the hall, I wondered again of sex and love and Bisher. How can she bear it, I thought, to know somewhere not far away he is in bed, in love with someone else who listens to his whispering of words like Frisco, Nawlins, San Berdoo?

Leaving town, we swung by the station to beep good-bye to Bisher. As we honked, drove off and left him standing on the platform next to the pumps I saw he didn't wave.

"The Arapahoe Indians invented waving bye. Did it backwards to their own faces," was the first piece of inside dope he'd ever told me. And so Bisher never waved good-bye, instead he bobbed his head. Now, this morning, he nodded us away as if to say it was his energy that moved the engines of our lives.

# MARGARET ATWOOD

# THE WHIRLPOOL RAPIDS

FROM REDBOOK

∽

THERE ARE SOME WOMEN who seem to be born without fear, just as there are people who are born without the ability to feel pain. The painless ones go around putting their hands on hot stoves, freezing their feet to the point of gangrene, scalding the lining from their throats with boiling coffee, because there is no warning anguish. Evolution does not favor them. So too perhaps with the fearless women, because there aren't very many of them around. I myself have known only two. One was a maker of television documentaries, and was one of the first to shoot footage in Vietnam. There would be the beach and then the line of jungle with the soldiers advancing toward it, and in front of them, walking backward, would be this woman. Providence appears to protect such women, maybe out of astonishment. Or else, sooner or later, it doesn't.

I'm told the fearlessness goes away when these women have babies. Then they become cowards, like the rest of us. If the baby is threatened they become ferocious, of course, but that is not out of the ordinary.

The other woman I knew, and still know—her luck has held—is Emma, who has always intrigued me. I think of Emma as a woman who will do anything, though that isn't how she thinks of herself. The truly fearless think of themselves as normal.

This, as far as I've been able to tell, is how she got like that.

When she was twenty-one, Emma nearly died. Or so she was told, and since four of those with her actually did die, she had to believe it. At the time she hadn't felt anywhere near dead.

It was a freak accident, and the fact that she was there at all was an accident too, the result of a whim and of knowing someone. Emma always knows a lot of people. The person she knew for this occasion was a man, a boy really, about her own age. He didn't qualify as a boyfriend; he was just one of the group she'd hung out with the previous year, at the university. In the summers he worked for a travel agency, a good one that specialized in organizing out-of-the-ordinary tours: bicycle trips through France, African game parks, that sort of thing. This boy, whose name was Bill, was one of the tour leaders. Because of his prowess with bicycles he had well-developed leg muscles, clearly visible that day, as he was wearing shorts and a T-shirt. It may have been these bicycle muscles that saved him, in the event.

Emma did not have bicycle muscles. At that time she had good biceps, though, the result of lifting heavy trays. She was working as a waitress in the coffee shop of a tourist motel in Niagara Falls. The motel had a neon sign outside that showed two entwined hearts, and even had a bridal suite, wallpapered in red.

This place reflected the vulgarity of the town itself, its transience, it's tinsel-and-waxworks tawdriness, fitting contrast to the notion of Eternal Love, which, despite the jokes she's made about it at various times in her life, Emma has never ceased to believe in.

At that point she wasn't thinking of love, but of making enough money to get her through her last year at the university. Niagara Falls was a good place for that: The satiated tip well. If she had been elsewhere, none of this would have happened.

There was nothing remarkable about Bill; he was merely one of those agents of Fate who have intruded on Emma's life from time to time and then departed from it, mission accomplished. Like many fearless people, Emma believes in Fate.

Bill was a nice boy; nice enough so that when he ambled into Emma's coffee shop one day and told her that he wanted her body, Emma took it as a joke and did not resent it. Really he wanted her to come on a test run, he said. The travel agency he was working for was doing a pilot project on a new kind of tour: down the Whirlpool Rapids below Niagara Falls, on a big rubber raft. They'd done the run nine times so far, and it was perfectly safe, but they weren't ready to open the tour to the public until they'd had one more test. It was only travel agency people and their friends going, he said, and they were short of bodies: There had to be a full contingent for the thing to work; they needed forty people for the weight and balance. It struck him as the kind of thing that might appeal to Emma.

Emma was flattered by this image of herself, and readily accepted it as a true one: a physically brave young woman, a bit of a daredevil, willing to put on a life jacket at a moment's notice and sit on a large inflated platform of rubber and swirl down the dangerous Niagara Whirlpool Rapids. It would be like roller coasters, which she'd always found compelling. She would join the ranks of those who had, in the past, wished to challenge Niagara Falls: the tightrope walkers, and those who'd had themselves bolted into padded barrels and flung into the river above the drop; even the suicides, whom Emma lumped in with the challengers, because if you were not in some way gambling, why not just use a gun? In all of these attempts, it seemed to Emma, there was an element of religious trial. All of these people were flinging themselves on the mercy of something or other. Certainly not just a river. *Save me, Lord; show me I'm important enough to deserve it.* This, Emma thought, looking back on it afterward, was what had prompted her: a desire to risk the self that was really a form of arrogance.

Emma said yes at once, and arranged for her next day off to coincide with the tenth rubber-raft test run. On the morning of the day, which was a Monday, Bill picked her up from the run-down frame house she rented with three other girls and drove her across the Rainbow Bridge to the launching site, which was on the American side. It turned out afterward— some reporter dug it up—that the Canadian officials had refused permission to launch the raft on their side, considering the enterprise too hazardous. But even if Emma had known this it probably wouldn't have stopped her.

The raft was black and enormous, and seemed, resting at its moorings, very stable. Emma was given an orange life jacket, and buckled herself into it, helped by Bill. Then they scrambled on board and found seats at the front end. They were among the first to arrive, and had to wait for the others. Emma began to feel slightly let down and to wonder why she'd come. The raft was too big, too solid; it was like a floating parking lot.

But once they'd moved out into the current, the rubber surface under her began to ripple, in large waves of contraction, like a giant throat swallowing, and spray came in upon them; and Emma knew that the rapids, which had looked so decorative, so much like cake frosting from a distance, were actual after all. There were some dutiful thrilled noises from the other passengers, and then some genuine noises, less thrilled. Emma found herself clutching Bill's arm, a thing she wouldn't ordinarily have done. The sky was an unnatural blue, and the shore—dotted with the white-clad or pastel figures of tourists, which appeared static and painted, like a design on wallpaper— was very far away.

There was a lot of talk later about why the tenth run should have failed so badly, after the other nine had gone without a hitch. Some attempts were made to pin it on the design of the raft; others said that, owing to an unreasonable amount of rain during the preceding week, the water level had been too high and the current far swifter than usual. Emma could not remember wondering why, at the time. All she saw was the front of the raft tipping down into a trough deeper than any they'd yet hit, while a foaming wall of water rose above them. The raft should have curved sinuously, sliding up the wave. Instead it buckled across the middle, the front half snapping toward the back, like the beak of a bird closing. Emma and Bill and the other people in the front row shot backward over the heads of the rest, who were jumbling in a heap at the bottom of the V, now submerging. (Emma didn't exactly see this at the time; she deduced it later. Her impressions were of her own movement only, and of course it was all very fast.)

Something struck her on the side of the head—a foot in a boot, perhaps—and she was underwater. Later she learned that the raft had flipped and a man had been trapped underneath it and drowned, so it was just as well that she had been flung clear. But underwater she did not think. Something else made her hold her breath and struggle toward the surface, which she could see above her, white and silver—so her eyes must have been open. Her head rose up, she gasped air and was sucked under.

The water tumbled and boiled and Emma fought it. She was filled almost to bursting with an energy that came from anger: *I refuse to die in such a stupid way* was how she formulated this afterward. She thinks she shouted, at least once: *No.* Which was a waste of breath, as there was nobody around to hear her. There were rocks, and she collided with several and was bruised and scraped, but nothing more hit her head. After what seemed like an hour but was really only ten minutes, the current slowed and she found she could keep her head above the water and actually swim. It was hard to move her arms. She propelled herself toward the shore, and, finally, dragged herself up onto a small rocky beach. Her running shoes were gone. She must have kicked them off, though she couldn't remember doing it; or maybe they had been torn off. She wondered how she was going to get over the rocks without shoes.

The sky was even bluer than it had been before. There were some blue flowers also, weeds of some kind, cornflowers, growing among the rocks. Emma looked at them and did not feel anything. She must have been cut; her clothes were certainly ripped and there was a lump on the side of her forehead, but she didn't notice any of this at the time. Two people, a man and a woman, in summery clothes, came sauntering toward her along a path.

"What country am I in?" Emma asked them.

"Canada," said the man.

They walked past her and continued their stroll, as if they did not notice anything unusual about her. Probably they didn't. The news of the accident had not yet reached them, so they didn't realize there had been one.

Emma, in her turn, did not find their behavior out of place. That's good then, she thought to herself. She wouldn't have to go back over the bridge and through Immigration, which was lucky, because her purse had been swept away. She began to walk upstream, slowly, because of her bare feet. There was an unusual number of helicopters around. She thumbed a lift to the motel—she doesn't know why she elected to go there instead of to her house—and by the time she got there, the accident had been on the news and everyone thought she was dead.

She was taken to the hospital and treated for shock, and interviewed on television. Her picture was, briefly, in the papers. Bill came to see her and described his own experience to her. He had reached a point, under the water, at which he had given up, and the water had become very peaceful and very beautiful. This was how Emma realized that she herself hadn't been at all close to death. But Bill's bicycle-muscled legs had kicked by themselves, like a wounded frog's, and brought him back.

For a while Emma felt closer to Bill than she did to anyone, but this feeling passed, although they still send each other Christmas cards. There was never any possibility of a romance: They were, after the accident, too much like twins, and then too much like strangers. Intimacy brought about by shared catastrophe can only go so far.

Emma has told me that she learned several things from this experience. One of them was that many more people than she'd thought would have known about her death, had it occurred, and been affected by it in some way; but they wouldn't have been affected very deeply or very long. Soon she would have become just a name, the name of a woman who had died young, in a tragic accident, some years ago. It was for this reason, perhaps, that Emma never had any of those wistful longings for death, those flirtations with the pale horseman, that afflict so many women in their twenties. She never thought to herself, a little hopefully, a little melodramatically, that maybe she wouldn't see thirty, that some unspecified but graceful disease would carry her off. Not her. She was determined to live, no matter what.

Nor was she ever tempted, after that, to give up anything—a man, an apartment, a job, even a vacation—in the mistaken conviction that by doing so she would be helping along the happiness of others. Because she found out early how very little difference she makes in the general scheme of things, she has clenched her teeth, ignored whimpers and even threats, and done what she liked, almost always. For instance, none of her friends will go to auctions or bargain sales with Emma anymore: She tends to get what you wanted. And at least four marriages have been trashed by Emma, who had decided in every case that the man wasn't right for her after all. Women who believe in Eternal Love develop such habits.

As you might expect, Emma has frequently been called selfish and unfeeling. I think it has been to her credit that on these occasions she has not trotted out the story of her near-death by drowning as a justification for her dubious behavior.

But the most obvious effect of the accident on Emma was her strong subsequent belief—it amounted to an article of religious faith—that she was invulnerable. She didn't merely feel this, she knew it, as firmly as she knew that her hand was her hand. She had been thrown into the Whirlpool Rapids of Niagara Falls and had lived; therefore nothing could touch her. She walked in a bubble of charmed air, which at times she imagined she could almost see, shimmering around her like mist; like, in fact, the mist that rose from the falls themselves.

Little by little this belief faded. It was strongest right after the accident, but evaporated year by year, until by now nothing is left of it but a faint phosphorescence. Her friends call it optimism, this conviction of hers that everything will work out for her somehow.

What Emma has become, finally and after many false starts, is an insurance investigator for an airline company, a job that takes her to some strange locales and is more hazardous than you might think. Emma is always getting free cases of champagne, which she returns, or death threats, which she doesn't. I myself keep up with her through the postcards she sends, from places like Zaire. When I see her, once or twice a year, I find myself looking at her skin. The rest of us are beginning to wrinkle, but for some reason Emma is not. It must be that small injection of death, that early dose of mortality, that has rendered her immune.

RUSSELL BANKS

# MY MOTHER'S MEMOIRS, MY FATHER'S LIE, AND OTHER TRUE STORIES

FROM VANITY FAIR

∾

MY MOTHER TELLS me stories about her past, and I don't believe them, I interpret them.

She told me she had the female lead in the Catamount High School senior play and Sonny Tufts had the male lead. She claimed that he asked her to the cast party, but by then she was in love with my father, a stagehand for the play, so she turned down the boy who became a famous movie actor and went to the cast party with the boy who became an obscure New Hampshire carpenter.

She also told me that she knew the principals in Grace Metalious's novel, *Peyton Place*. The same night the girl in the book murdered her father, she went afterwards to a Christmas party given by my mother and father at their house in Catamount. "The girl acted strange," my mother said. "Kind of like she was on drugs or something, you know? And the boy she was with, one of the Goldens from Catamount? He just got drunk and depressed, and then they left. The next day we heard about the police finding the girl's father in the manure pile—"

"Manure pile?"

"She buried him there. And your father told me to keep quiet, not to tell a soul they were at our party on Christmas Eve. That's why our party isn't in the book or the movie they made of it," she explained.

She also insists, in the face of my repeated denials, that she once saw me being interviewed on television by Dan Rather.

I remembered these three stories recently when, while pawing through a pile of old newspaper clippings, I came upon the obituary of Sonny Tufts. Since my adolescence, I have read two and sometimes three newspapers a day, and frequently I clip an article that for obscure or soon forgotten reasons attracts me; then I toss the clipping into a desk drawer, and every once in a while, without scheduling it, I am moved to read through the clippings and throw them out. It's an experience that fills me with a strange sadness, a kind of grief for my lost self, as if I were reading and throwing out old diaries.

But it's my mother I was speaking of. She grew up poor and beautiful in a New England mill town, Catamount, New Hampshire, the youngest of five children of a machinist whose wife died ("choked to death on a porkchop bone"—another of her stories) when my mother was nineteen. She was invited the same year, 1933, to the Chicago World's Fair to compete in a beauty pageant but didn't accept the invitation, though she claims my father went to the fair and played his clarinet in a National Guard marching band. Her father, she said, made her stay in Catamount that summer, selling dresses for Grover Cronin's Department Store on River Street. If her mother had not died that year, she would have been able to go to the fair. "And who knows," she joked, "you might've ended up the son of Miss Chicago World's Fair of 1933."

To tell the truth, I don't know very much about my mother's life before 1940, the year I was born and started gathering material for my own stories. Like most people, I pay scant attention to the stories I'm told about lives and events that precede the remarkable event of my own life. We all seem to tell and hear our own memoirs. It's the same with my own children. I watch their adolescent eyes glaze over, their attention drift on to secret plans for the evening and weekend, as I point out the tenement on Perley Street in Catamount where I spent my childhood. Soon I, too, will be living in exile, retired from the cold like my mother in San Diego, alone in a drab apartment in a project by the bay, collecting Social Security and wondering if I'll have enough money at the end of the month for a haircut. Soon all you'll have of me will be your memories of my stories.

Everyone knows that the death of a parent is a terrible thing. But because our parents usually have not been a part of our daily lives for years, most of us do not miss them when they die. When my father died, even though I had been seeing him frequently and talking with him on the phone almost every week, I did not miss him. Yet his death was for me a terrible thing and goes on being a terrible thing now, five years later. My father, a depressed, cynical alcoholic, did not tell stories, but even if he had told stories—about his childhood in Nova Scotia, about beating out Sonny Tufts in the courtship of my mother, about playing the clarinet at the Chicago World's Fair—I would not have listened. No doubt, in his cynicism and despair of ever being loved, he knew that.

The only story my father told me that I listened to closely, visualized, and have remembered, he told me a few months before he died. It was the story of how he came to name me Earl. Naturally, as a child I asked, and he simply shrugged and said he happened to like the name. My mother corroborated the shrug. But one Sunday morning the winter before he died, three years before he planned to retire and move to a trailer in Florida, I was sitting across from my father in his kitchen, watching him drink tumblers of Canadian Club and ginger ale, and he wagged a finger in my face and told me that I did not know who I was named after.

"I thought no one," I said.

"When I was a kid," he said, "my parents tried to get rid of me in the summers. They used to send me to stay with my Uncle Earl up on Cape Breton. He was a bachelor and kind of a hermit, and he stayed drunk most of the time. But he played the fiddle, the violin. And he loved me. He was quite a character. But then, when I was about twelve, I was old enough to spend my summers working, so they kept me down in Halifax after that. And I never saw Uncle Earl again."

He paused and sipped at his drink. He was wearing his

striped pajamas and maroon bathrobe and carpet slippers and
was chain-smoking Parliaments. His wife (his third—my mother
divorced him when I was twelve, because of his drinking and
what went with it) had gone to the market as soon as I arrived,
as if afraid to leave him without someone else in the house.
"He died a few years later," my father said. "Fell into a
snowbank, I heard. Passed out. Froze to death."

I listened to the story and have remembered it today
because I thought it was about *me,* my name, Earl. My father
told it, of course, because it was about *him,* and because for an
instant that cold February morning he dared to hope that his
oldest son would love him.

At this moment, as I say this, I do love him, but it's too
late for the saying to make either of us happy. That is why I
say the death of a parent is a terrible thing.

After my father died, I asked his sister Ethel about poor
old Uncle Earl. She said she never heard of the man. The
unofficial family archivist and only a few years younger than
my father, she surely would have known of him, would have
known how my father spent his summers, would have known
of the man he loved enough to name his firstborn son after.

The story simply was not true. My father had made it up.

Just as my mother's story about Sonny Tufts is not true.
Yesterday, when I happened to come across the article about
Sonny Tufts from the Boston *Globe,* dated June 8, 1970, and
written by the late George Frazier, I wouldn't have bothered
to reread it if the week before I had not been joking about
Sonny Tufts with a friend, a woman who lives in Boston and
whose mother died this past summer. My friend's mother's
death, like my father's, was caused by acute alcoholism and had
been going on for years. What most suicides accomplish in
minutes, my father and my friend's mother took decades to do.

The death of my friend's mother reminded me of the
consequences of the death of my father and of my mother's continuing to live. And then our chic joke about the 1940s film star
("What ever happened to Sonny Tufts?"), a joke about our
own aging, reminded me of my mother's story about the senior
play in 1932, so that when I saw Frazier's obituary for Tufts,
entitled "Death of a Bonesman" (Tufts had gone to Yale and
been tapped for Skull and Bones), instead of tossing it back in

the drawer or into the wastebasket, I read it through to the end, as if searching for a reference to my mother's having brushed him off. I learned that Bowen Charlestown Tufts III, scion of an old Boston banking family, had prepped for Yale at Exeter. So that his closest connection to the daughter of a machinist in Catamount, and to me, was probably through his father's bank's ownership of the mill where the machinist ran his lathe.

I had never believed the story anyhow, but now I had proof that she made it up. Just as the fact that I have never been interviewed by Dan Rather is proof that my mother never saw me on the television in her one-room apartment in San Diego being interviewed by Dan Rather. By the time she got her friend down the hall to come and see her son on TV, Dan had gone on to some depressing stuff about the Middle East.

As for Grace Metalious's characters from *Peyton Place* showing up at a Christmas party in my parents' house in Catamount, I never believed that either. *Peyton Place* was indeed based on a true story about a young woman's murder of her father in Gilmanton, New Hampshire, a village some twenty-five miles from Catamount, but in the middle 1940s people simply did not drive twenty-five miles over snow-covered back roads on a winter night to go to a party in a decrepit farmhouse owned by strangers.

I said that to my mother. She had just finished telling me, for the hundredth time, it seemed, that someday, based on my own experiences as a child and now as an adult in New Hampshire, I should be able to write another *Peyton Place*. This was barely two months ago, and I was visiting her in San Diego, an extension of a business trip to Los Angeles, and I was seated rather uncomfortably in her one-room apartment. She is a tiny, wrenlike woman with few possessions, most of which seem miniaturized, designed to fit her small body and the close confines of her room, so that when I visit her I feel huge and oafish. I lower my voice and move with great care.

She was ironing her sheets, while I sat on the unmade sofa bed, unmade because I had just turned the mattress for her, a chore she saves for when I or my younger brother, the only large-size people in her life now, visit her from the East. "But we *weren't* strangers to them," my mother chirped. "Your father knew the Golden boy somehow. Probably one of his local drinking friends," she said. "Anyhow, that's why your father wouldn't let me tell anyone, after the story came out in the papers, about the murder and the incest and all—"

"Incest? What incest?"

"You know, the father who got killed, killed and buried in the manure pile by his own daughter because he'd been committing incest with her. Didn't you read the book?"

"No."

"Well, your father, he was afraid we'd get involved somehow. So I couldn't tell anyone about it until after the book got famous. You know, whenever I tell people out here that back in New Hampshire in the forties I knew the girl who killed her father in *Peyton Place*, they won't believe me. Well, not exactly *knew* her, but you know—"

There's always someone famous in her stories, I thought. Dan Rather, Sonny Tufts, Grace Metalious (though my mother can never remember her name, only the name of the book she wrote). It's as if she hopes you will love her more easily if she is associated with fame.

When you know a story isn't true, you think you don't have to listen to it. What you think you're supposed to do is interpret, as I was doing that morning in my mother's room, converting her story into a clue to her psychology, which in turn would lead me to compare it to my own psychology and, with relief, disapprove. (*My* stories don't have famous people in them.) I did the same thing with my father's drunken fiddler, Uncle Earl, once I learned he didn't exist. I used the story as a clue to help unravel the puzzle of my father's dreadful psychology, hoping no doubt to unravel the puzzle of my own.

One of the most difficult things to say to another person is I hope you will love me. Yet that is what we all want to say to one another, to our children, to our parents and mates, to our friends, and even to strangers.

Perhaps especially to strangers. My friend in Boston, who joked with me about Sonny Tufts as an interlude in the story of her mother's awful dying, was showing me her hope that I would love her, even when the story itself was about her mother's lifelong refusal to love her and, with the woman's death, the absolute removal of any potential for that love. I have, at least, my father's story of how I got my name, and though it's too late for me now to give him what, for a glimmering moment, he hoped and asked for, by remembering his story I have understood a little more usefully the telling of my own.

By remembering, as if writing my memoirs, what the stories of others have reminded me of, what they have literally brought to my mind, I have learned how my own stories function in the world, whether I tell them to my mother, to my wife, to my children, to my friends, or, especially, to strangers. And to complete the circle, I have learned a little more usefully how to listen to the stories of others, whether they are true or not.

As I was leaving my mother that morning to drive back to Los Angeles and then fly home to New Hampshire, where my brother and sister and all my mother's grandchildren live and where all but the last few years of my mother's past was lived, she told me a new story. We stood in the shade of palm trees in the parking lot outside her glass-and-metal building for a few minutes, and she said to me in a concerned way, "You know that restaurant, the Pancake House, where you took me for breakfast this morning?"

I said yes and checked the time and flipped my suitcase into the backseat of the rented car.

"Well, I always have breakfast there on Wednesdays—it's on the way to where I baby-sit on Wednesdays—and this week something funny happened there. I sat alone way in the back, where they have that long, curving booth, and I didn't notice until I was halfway through my breakfast that at the far end of the booth a man was sitting there. He was maybe your age, a young man, but dirty and shabby. Especially dirty, and so I just looked away and went on eating my eggs and toast.

"But then I noticed he was looking at me, as if he knew me and didn't quite dare to talk to me. I smiled, because maybe I did know him—I know just about everybody in the neighborhood now. But he was a stranger. And dirty. And I could see that he had been drinking for days.

"So I smiled and said to him, 'You want help, mister, don't you?' He needed a shave, and his clothes were filthy and all ripped, and his hair was a mess. You know the type. But something pathetic about his eyes made me want to talk to him. But honestly, Earl, I couldn't. I just couldn't. He was so dirty and all.

"Anyhow, when I spoke to him, just that little bit, he sort of came out of his daze and sat up straight for a second, like he was afraid I was going to complain to the manager and have him thrown out of the restaurant. 'What did you say to me?' he asked. His voice was weak but he was trying to make it sound strong, so it came out kind of loud and broken. 'Nothing,' I said, and I turned away from him and quickly finished my breakfast and left.

"That afternoon, when I was walking back home from my baby-sitting job, I went into the restaurant to see if he was there, but he wasn't. And the next morning, Thursday, I walked all the way over there to check again, even though I never eat breakfast at the Pancake House on Thursdays, but he was gone then, too. And then yesterday, Friday, I went back a third time. But he was gone." She lapsed into a thoughtful silence and looked at her hands.

"Was he there this morning?" I asked, thinking coincidence was somehow the point of the story.

"No," she said. "But I didn't expect him to be there this morning. I'd stopped looking for him by yesterday."

"Well, why'd you tell me the story, then? What's it about?"

"*About?* Why, I don't know. Nothing, I guess. I just felt sorry for the man, and then because I was afraid, I shut up and left him alone." She was still studying her tiny hands.

"That's natural," I said. "You shouldn't feel guilty for that," I said, and I put my arms around her.

She turned her face into my shoulder. "I know, I know. But still—" Her gray eyes filled, her son was leaving again, gone for another six months or a year, and who would she tell her stories to while he was gone? Who would listen?

# CHARLES BAXTER
# SURPRISED BY JOY

## FROM TENDRIL

∽

## 1

BECAUSE THEIR PSYCHIATRIST had recommended it, they both began to keep journals. Jeremy's was Woolworth stationery drab, and Harriet's was sea blue with the words *A Blank Book* printed in gold script in the upper right-hand corner. Thinking that pleasant images would relieve the tone of what was to follow, she sketched a wren in flight, a Victorian lamppost, and an ash tree on the first page. Then she changed her mind and blacked the drawings out. There weren't any drawings in the book Jeremy used. His writing was tiny and defiant. His first sentence, which was undated, read: "Benson told us it would help if we wrote down our thoughts, but I don't have any thoughts, and besides, the fact is that I don't feel like writing a goddamn thing." That was the end of the first entry.

One night Jeremy came home and found all the silverware—knives, forks, spoons, gravy bowls, and ladles—lined up according to type on the living room carpet in front of the hide-a-bed sofa. Harriet said she wanted to do an inventory, to make sure the place settings were all present and accounted for. She threatened to count all the dishes, and all the books. A week later when he arrived home she was standing on her head with her legs crossed and her knees positioned against the wall. He put down his briefcase, hung up his coat, and sat in his chair. "So," he said. "What's this?"

"An article I read says it helps." Upside down, she attempted a smile.

"Standing on your head."

"Yeah. Think about it: the brain under stress needs more blood, the cerebral cortex especially. The article says that when you stand up you feel an instant of physical exhilaration." She closed her eyes. "The plumber came out this morning. The faucet's fixed."

"Physical exhilaration." He turned away from her to stare out at the street, where two children were roaring by on their Big Wheels.

"They say you'll feel better."

"Right. What article did you say this was?" He didn't wait for her to answer. "It sounds like *Parade* magazine. How much did the plumber charge? God, I could use a drink. I have the most amazing willpower." He glanced at her. "Did you cry a lot today?"

"No. Not much. Not like last week. I even did two full baskets of laundry. After lunch, when the plumber was gone, that was hard. For about ten minutes I couldn't help it and locked myself in the bathroom and then I wrote in the journal. Gretchen called and invited me into her weaving class. Do you think I should? It seems so dull and womanish. How was your day?" She tumbled backward, stood up, and looked at him with an experimental, unsteady smile.

"Do you feel exhilarated?" She shrugged. He said, "The usual. The black box." He rose, went to the kitchen for a beer, and clomped down the stairs to the basement, where he played his clarinet while watching television with the sound off. His music consisted of absentminded riffs in eerie unrelated keys.

They had brought their child home to a plain three-bedroom brick bungalow of the type referred to as a "starter house" for young married couples. Its distinguishing characteristics were those left by the previous owners. Jeremy and Harriet had never had time to redecorate it; as a result, their bedroom was covered with flocked jungle orange wallpaper, the paint in

Harriet's sewing room was oyster gray, and the child's room had been painted blue, with two planets and four constellations mapped out on the ceiling with phosphorous dots and circles. At the time, their child was too little to notice such things: She gurgled at the trees outside and at the birds that sang in the shrubbery below her windowsill.

This child, Ellen, had been born after many difficulties. Harriet had had a series of ovarian cysts. She ovulated irregularly and only when provoked by certain powerful hormonal medications that left her so forgetful that she had to draw up hourly schedules for the day's tasks. She had the scars to prove that surgical procedures had been used to remove her enlarged ovaries piece by piece. The baby had been in a troublesome position, and Harriet had endured sixteen hours of labor, during which time she thrashed and groaned. Jeremy watched her lying in her hospital gown, his hands pressed against her lower back, while her breathing grew louder, hoarse and rhythmical. Their Lamaze lessons proved to be useless. The lights glared overhead in the prep room and could not be dimmed. In its labors her body heaved as if her reproductive system were choking in its efforts to expel the child. Her obstetrician was out of town on vacation in Puerto Vallarta, so the delivery was finally performed by a resident, a young woman with a short punk hairdo and whose purple fingernail polish was visible through her surgical gloves.

The oyster-gray paint and the phosphorous planets in the house suited Ellen, who, when she was old enough to toddle, would point at the stars on the ceiling and wave at them. At this time she could not pronounce her own name and referred to herself as "Ebbo" or, mysteriously, as "Purl." On a spring morning she climbed from the crib onto the windowsill in pursuit of a chickadee singing outside. Cheered by the sun, Harriet had left the window open to let the breeze in. Ellen pushed herself past the sill and managed to tumble out, breaking the screen. She landed on a soft newly tilled flower bed next to a bush. When Harriet found her, she was tugging at flower shoots and looking pleased with herself. She said, "Purl drop." She shrugged her right shoulder and smiled.

They latched the screen onto a stronger frame and rushed

around the house looking for hazards. They installed a lock on the basement door so she wouldn't tumble downstairs, and fastened shut the kitchen sink's lower cabinet so she wouldn't eat the ElectraSol. She lived one day past her third Christmas, when for the first time she knew what a Christmas tree was and could look forward to it with dazed anticipation. On Christmas day she was buried up to her waist in presents: a knee-high table complete with cups and saucers, Bert and Ernie finger dolls, a plastic Fisher-Price phonograph, a stuffed brown bear that made sounds, a Swiss music box, a windup train that went around in a small circle, a yellow toy police car with a lady cop inside, and, in her stocking, pieces of candy, gum, a comb, and a red rubber ball her mother had bought at Kiddie Land for twenty-five cents.

On December twenty-sixth Jeremy and Harriet were slumped in the basement, watching Edmund Gwenn in *Miracle on 34th Street* for the eighth or ninth time, while Ellen played upstairs in her room. They went through three commercial breaks before Harriet decided to check on her. She hadn't been worried because she could hear the Fisher-Price phonograph playing a "Sesame Street" record. Harriet went down the hallway and turned the corner into Ellen's room. Her daughter was lying on the floor, on her side, her skin blue. She wasn't breathing. On her forehead was blood next to a bright cut. Harriet's first thought was that Ellen had been somehow knocked unconscious by an intruder. Then she was shouting for Jeremy, and crying, and touching Ellen's face with her fingers. She picked her up, pounded her back, and then felt the lump of the red rubber ball that Ellen had put in her mouth and that had lodged in her throat. She squeezed her chest and the ball came up into the child's mouth.

Jeremy rushed in behind her. He took Ellen away from Harriet and carried her into the living room, her arms hanging down, swinging. He shouted instructions at Harriet. Some made sense; others didn't. He gave Ellen mouth-to-mouth resuscitation and kept putting his hand against her heart, waiting for a pulse.

Later they understood that Ellen had panicked and had run into the edge of the open closet door. What with the movie and the new phonograph, they hadn't heard her. The edge of the door wasn't sharp, but she had run into it so blindly that the collision had dazed her. She had fallen and reached up to her forehead: A small amount of blood had dried on her hands. She had then reached for her stuffed raccoon; her left hand was gripping its leg. She was wearing, for all time, her yellow Dr. Denton pajamas. In the living room, waiting for the ambulance, Harriet clutched her own hands. Then she was drinking glass after glass of water in a white waiting room.

Their parents said, oh, they could have another, a child as beautiful as Ellen. Her doctors disagreed. Harriet's ovaries had been cut away until only a part of one of them remained. In any case, they didn't want replacements. The idea made no sense. What they thought of day and night was what had happened upstairs while they were watching television. Their imaginations put the scene on a film loop. Guiltily, they watched it until their mental screens began to wash the rest of the past away.

For the next two months they lived hour to hour. Harriet grew to hate the sun and its long lengthening arcs. Every day became an epic of endurance, in which Harriet sat in chairs. Harriet's mother called every few days, offering excruciating maternal comfort. There were photographs, snapshots and studio portraits, that neither of them could stand to remove. Nature became Harriet's enemy. Living trees broke open into pink-and-white blossoms in spring. Harriet wanted to fling herself against the trees. She couldn't remember what it was about life that had ever interested her. Every object in nature habitually referred to her daughter. The world began a vast and buzzing commentary to keep her in cramps, preoccupied with Ellen, who had now irresistibly become Purl. The grass no longer grew up from the ground but instead stood as a witless metaphor of continuing life. Dishes and silverware upset her, unaccountably. She couldn't remember who her friends were and did not recognize them in the street. Every night the sky fell conclusively.

Jeremy had his job, but every evening, after seeing about Harriet, he went straight down to the basement where the television set was. He played his clarinet, drank beer, and watched "Hogan's Heroes" and the local news until it was time for dinner. He opened the twist-top beer bottles and drank the beer mechanically, as if acting on orders. After overhearing the music he played, Harriet began to call it "jazz from Mars," and Jeremy said, yes, that was probably where it came from. He paid attention to things at work; his music could afford to be inattentive.

He came upstairs when dinner was ready. This meal consisted of whatever food Harriet could think of buying and preparing. They didn't like to go out. They often ate hot dogs and A&P potato salad, or hamburger, or pizza delivered by the Domino's man in a green Gremlin. Jeremy sometimes fell asleep at the dinner table, his head tilted back at the top of the chair, and his mouth open, sucking in breaths. Harriet would drape one of his arms around her neck and lower him to the floor, so he wouldn't fall off the chair while asleep. They had talked about getting chairs with arms to prevent accidents of this kind; they both assumed they would spend the rest of their lives falling asleep at the table after dinner.

They started seeing Benson, the therapist, because of what happened with the Jehovah's Witnesses. In mid-May, the doorbell rang just after dinner. Jeremy, who this time was still awake, rose from the table to see who it was. Outside the screen door stood a red-haired man and a small red-haired boy, eight or nine years old, both of them dressed in nearly identical gray coats and bow ties. The father was carrying copies of *The Watchtower*. The boy held a Bible, a children's edition with a crude painting of Jesus on the cover. Leaving the screen door shut, Jeremy asked them what they wanted.

"My son would like to read to you," the man said, glancing down at the boy. "Do you have time to listen for a minute?"

Jeremy said nothing.

Taking this as a sign of agreement, the man nodded at the boy, who pushed his glasses back, opened the Bible, and said, "Psalm forty-three." He swallowed, looked up at his father, who smiled, then pulled at the red silk bookmark he had inserted at the beginning of the psalm. He cleared his throat. "Give sentence with me, O God," he read, his finger trailing horizontally along the line of type, his voice quavering, "and defend my cause against the ungodly people; O deliver me from the deceitful and wicked man." He stumbled over "deceitful." The boy paused and looked through the screen at Jeremy. Jeremy was watching the boy with the same emptied expression he used when watching television. His father touched the boy on the shoulder and told him to continue. A bird was singing nearby. Jeremy looked up. It was a cardinal on a telephone wire.

"For thou art the God of my strength," the boy read, "why hast thou put me from thee? and why go I so heavily, while the enemy oppresseth me?"

For the first time, Jeremy said something. He said, "I don't believe it. You can't be doing this." The father and the boy, however, didn't hear him. The boy continued.

"O send out thy light and thy truth, that they may lead me, and bring me unto thy holy hill, and to thy dwelling."

Jeremy said, "Who sent you here?" The father heard the sentence, but his only reaction was to squint through the screen to see Jeremy better. He gave off a smell of cheap aftershave.

"And that I may go unto the altar of God," the boy read, "even unto the God of my joy and gladness; and upon the harp will I give thanks unto thee, O God, my God."

"You're contemptible," Jeremy said, "to use children. That's a low trick."

This time both the boy and his father stared in at him. Harriet had appeared and was standing behind Jeremy, pulling at his shirt and whispering instructions to him to thank them and send them on their merry way. The father, however, recovered himself, smiled, pointed at the Bible, and then touched his son on the head, as if pressing a button.

"Why art thou so heavy, O my soul?" the boy read, stuttering slightly. "And why art thou so disquieted within me?"

"Stop it!" Jeremy shouted. "Please stop it! Stop it!" He opened the screen door and walked out to the front stoop so that he was just to the right of the father and his boy. Harriet crossed her arms but otherwise could not or did not move. Jeremy reached up and held onto the man's lapel. He didn't grab it but simply put it between his thumb and forefinger. He aimed his words directly into the center of the father's face.

"Who sent you here?" he asked, his words thrown out like stones. "This was no accident. Don't tell me this was an accident because I'd hate to think you were lying to me. Someone sent you here. Right? Who? How'd they ever think of using kids?" The bird was still singing, and when Jeremy stopped he heard it again, but hearing it only intensified his anger. "You want to sell me *The Watchtower*?" he asked, sinking toward inarticulateness. Then he recovered. "You want my money?" He let go of the man's lapel, reached into his pocket, and threw a handful of nickels and dimes to the ground. "Now go away and leave me alone."

The stranger was looking at Jeremy, and his mouth was opening. The boy was clutching his father's coat. One of the dimes was balanced on his left shoe.

"Go home," Jeremy said, "and never say another word about anything and don't ever again knock on my door." Jeremy was a lawyer. When speeches came to him, they came naturally. His face in its rage was as white as paper. He stopped, looked down, and hurriedly kissed the boy on the top of the head. As he straightened up, he said softly, "Don't mind me." Then, mobilized, Harriet rushed out onto the stoop and grabbed Jeremy's hand. She tried smiling.

"You see that my husband's upset," she said, pulling at him. "I think you should go now."

"Yes, all right," the father mumbled, blinking, taking the Bible from his son and closing it. The air thickened with the smell of his aftershave.

"We've had an accident recently," she explained. "We weren't prepared."

The man had his arm around his son's shoulders. They were starting down the walk to the driveway. "The Bible is a great comfort," the man said over his shoulder. "A help ever sure." He stopped to look back. "Trust in God," he said.

Jeremy made a roaring sound, somewhere between a shout and a bark, as Harriet hauled him back inside.

Benson's office was lodged on the twentieth floor of a steel-and-glass professional building called The Kelmer Tower. After passing through Benson's reception area, a space not much larger than a closet, the patient stepped into Benson's main office where the sessions were actually conducted. It was decorated in therapeutic pastels, mostly off-whites and pale blues. Benson had set up bookshelves, several chairs, a couch, and had positioned a rubber plant near the window. In front of the chairs was a coffee table on which was placed, not very originally, a small statue of a Minotaur. Benson's trimmed mustache and other-worldly air made him look, Jeremy said, like a wine steward. He had been recommended to them by their family doctor, who described Benson as a "very able man."

Harriet thought Benson was supposed to look interested; instead, he seemed bored to the point of stupefaction. He gave the appearance of thinking of something else: baseball, perhaps, or his golf game. Several times, when Jeremy was struggling to talk, Benson turned his face away and stared out the window. Harriet was afraid that he was going to start humming Irving Berlin songs. Instead, when Jeremy was finished, Benson looked at him and asked, "So. What are you going to do?"

"Do? Do about what?"

"Those feelings you've just described."

"Well, what am I supposed to do?"

"I don't think there's anything you're supposed to do. It's a choice. If you want me to recommend something, I can recommend several things, among them that you keep a journal, a sort of record. But you don't have to."

"That's good." Jeremy looked down at the floor, where the slats of sunlight through the venetian blinds made a picket fence across his feet.,

"If you don't want my help," Benson said, "you don't have to have it."

"At these prices," Jeremy said, "I want something."

"Writing in a journal can help," Benson continued, "because it makes us aware of our minds in a concrete way." Harriet cringed over Benson's use of the paternal first-person plural. She looked over at Jeremy. He was gritting his teeth. His jaw muscles were visible in his cheek. "Crying helps," Benson told them, and suddenly Harriet was reminded of the last five minutes of "Captain Kangaroo," the advice part. "And," Benson said slowly, "it helps to get a change of scene. Once you're

ready and have the strength and resources to do it, you might
try going on a trip."

"Where?" Harriet asked.

"Where?" Benson looked puzzled. "Why, anywhere. Anywhere that doesn't look like this. Try going someplace where
the scenery is different. Nassau. Florida. Colorado."

"How about the Himalayas?" Jeremy asked.

"Yes," Benson said, not bothering to act annoyed. "That
would do."

They both agreed that they might be able to handle it if it
weren't for the dreams. Ellen appeared in them and insisted on
talking. In Jeremy's dreams, she talked about picnics and hot
dogs, how she liked the catsup on the opposite side of the
wiener from the mustard, and how she insisted on having someone
toast the bun. The one sentence Jeremy remembered with total
clarity when he woke up was "Don't *like* soggy hot dogs." He
wouldn't have remembered it if it didn't sound like her.

She was wearing a flannel shirt and jeans in Jeremy's
dream; in Harriet's she had on a pink jumper that Harriet had
bought for her second birthday. Harriet saw that she was
outgrowing it. With a corkscrew feeling she saw that Ellen was
wearing a small ivory cameo with her own—Harriet's—profile
on it. She was also wearing a rain hat that Harriet couldn't
remember from anywhere, and she was carrying a Polaroid
photograph of her parents. Harriet wondered vaguely how
dead children get their hands on such pictures. In this dream
Harriet was standing on a street corner in a depopulated European city where the shutters were all closed tight over the
windows. Near her, overhead in the intersection, the traffic
light hanging from a thick cable turned from green to amber to
red, red to green, green to amber to red. However, no cars
charged through the intersection, and no cars were parked on
the street. A rhythmic thud echoed in the streets. Leaves mold-
ered in the gutters. Harriet knew that it was a bad city for
tourists. In this place Ellen scampered toward her down the
sidewalk, wearing the pink jumper and the rain hat, the photograph in her hand, the cameo pinned near her collar. She
smiled. Harriet stumbled toward her, but Ellen held out her
hand and said, "Can't hug." Harriet asked her about the hat,

and Ellen said, "Going to rain." She looked up at the bleary sky, and, following her lead, so did Harriet. Flocks of birds flew from left to right across it in no special pattern, wing streaks of indecision. Clouds. Harriet gazed down at Ellen. "Are you okay?" Harriet asked. "Who's taking care of you?" Ellen was picking her nose. "Lots of people," she said, wiping her finger on her pant leg. "They're nice." "Are you all right?" Harriet asked again. Ellen lifted her right shoulder. "Yeah," she said. She looked up. "Miss you, Mommy," she said, and, against directions, Harriet bent down to kiss her, wanting the touch of her skin against her lips, but when she reached Ellen's face, Ellen giggled, looked around quickly as if she were being watched from behind the shuttered windows, reached both hands up to her mouth, and disappeared, leaving behind a faint odor of flowers.

"Such dreams are common," Benson said. "Very very common."

"Tell me something else."

"What do you want me to tell you?"

"Something worth all the money we're paying you."

"You sound like Jeremy. What *would* be worth all the money you're paying me?"

"I have the feeling," Harriet said, "that you're playing a very elaborate game with us. And you have more practice at it than we do."

"If it's a game," Benson said, "then I do have more practice. But if it's not a game, I don't." He waited. Harriet stared at the giant leaves of the rubber plant, standing in the early summer light, torpid and happy. Jeremy hadn't come with her this time. The Minotaur on the coffee table looked inquisitive. "What is the dream telling you about Ellen, do you think?"

"That she's all right?"

"Yes." Benson breathed out. "And what do you have to worry about?"

"Not Ellen."

"No, not Ellen. The dream doesn't say to worry about her. So what do you have to worry about?"

"Jeremy. I don't see him. And I have to worry about getting out of that city."

"Why should you worry about Jeremy?"

"I don't know," Harriet said. "He's hiding somewhere. I want to get us both out of that city. It gives me the creeps."

"Yes. And how are you going to get out of that city?"

"Run?" Harriet looked at Benson. "Can I run out of it?"

"If you want to." Benson thought for a moment. "If you want to, you will run out of it." He smoothed his tie. "But you can't run and pull Jeremy at the same time."

After Jeremy's dream, she no longer served hot dogs for dinner. That night she was serving pork chops, and when Jeremy came in, still in his vest but with his coat over his shoulder, she was seated at the table, looking through a set of brochures she had picked up at a travel agency down the block from Benson's office. After Jeremy had showered and changed his clothes, he was about to take a six-pack out of the refrigerator when he looked over at Harriet studying a glossy photograph of tourists riding mules on Molokai. "It says here," Harriet announced, "in this brochure, that Molokai is the flattest of all the islands and the one with the most agricultural activity."

"Are you going on a quiz show? Is that it?"

She stood up, walked around the dining room table, then sat down on the other side. She had a fountain pen in her hand. "Now this," she said, pointing with the pen to another brochure, "this one is about New Mexico. I've never been to New Mexico. You haven't either, right?"

"No," Jeremy said. "Honey, what's this all about?"

"This," she said, "is all about what we're going to do during your two weeks off. I'll be goddamned if I'm going to sit here. Want to go to Santa Fe?"

Jeremy seemed itchy, as if he needed to go downstairs and play a few measures of jazz from Mars. "Sure, sure," he said. He rubbed his eyes suddenly. "Isn't it sort of hot that time of year?"

She shook her head. "It says here that the elevation's too high. You can stay in the mountains, and it's cool at night."

"Oh." Then, as an afterthought, he said, "Good."

She looked up at him. She stood and put her hand on his face, rubbing her thumb against his cheek. "How's the black box?" she asked. She had recently started to wear glasses and took them off now.

"How's the sky?" he asked. He turned around. "The black box is just fine. I move around it, but it's always there, right in front of me. It's hard to move with that damn thing in your head. I could write a book about it: how to live with a box and be a zombie." He reached for a beer and carried it to the basement. She could hear the television set being clicked on and the exhalation of the beer bottle when he opened it.

2

The flight to Albuquerque took four hours. Lunch was served halfway through: chicken in sauce. The stewardesses seemed proud of the meal and handed out the trays with smug smiles. Jeremy had a copy of *Business Week* in his lap, which he dropped to the floor when the food arrived. For much of the four hours he sat back and dozed off. Harriet was closer to the window and dutifully looked out whenever the captain announced that they were flying over a landmark.

In Albuquerque they rented a car and drove north toward Taos, the destination Harriet had decided upon, following the advice of the travel agent. They stopped at a Holiday Inn in Santa Fe for dinner. Appalled by the congestion and traffic, they set out after breakfast the next morning. As they approached the mountains, Jeremy, who was driving, said, "So this is the broom that sweeps the cobwebs away." He said it softly and with enough irony to make Harriet wince and to pull at her eyebrow, a recent nervous tic. The trip, it was now understood, had been her idea. She was responsible. She offered him a stick of gum and turned on the radio. They listened to Willie Nelson and Charlie Daniels until the mountains began to interfere with the reception.

In Taos they drove through the city until they found the Best Western motel, pale yellow and built in quasi-adobe style. They took showers and then strolled toward the center of town, holding hands. The light was brilliant and the air seemingly without the humidity and torpor of the midwest, but this atmosphere also had a kind of emptiness that Jeremy said he

wasn't used to. In the vertical sun they could both feel their
hair heating up. Harriet said she wanted a hat, and Jeremy
nodded. He sniffed the air. They passed the Kit Carson museum, and Jeremy laughed to himself. "What is it?" Harriet
asked, but he only shook his head. At the central square, the
streets narrowed and the traffic backed up with motoring tourists. "Lot of art stores here," Harriet said, in a tone that
suggested that Jeremy ought to be interested. She was gazing
into a display window at a painting of what appeared to be a
stick-figure man with a skull face dancing in a metallic vulcan-
ized landscape. She saw Jeremy's reflection in the window. He
was peering at the stones on the sidewalk. Then she looked at
herself: She was standing in front of Jeremy, blocking his view.

They walked through the plaza, and Harriet went into a
dime store to buy a hat. Jeremy sat outside on a bench in the
square, opposite a hotel that advertised a display of the paintings of D. H. Lawrence, banned in England, so it was claimed.
He turned away. An old man, an Indian with shoulder-length
gray hair, was crossing the plaza in front of him, murmuring an
atonal chant. The tourists stepped aside to let the man pass.
Jeremy glanced at the tree overhead, in whose shade he was
sitting. He could not identify it. He exhaled and examined his
Seiko angrily. He gazed down at the second hand circling the
dial face once, then twice. He knew Harriet was approaching
when he saw out of the corner of his eye her white cotton pants
and her feet in their sandals.

"Do you like it?" she asked. He looked up. She had
bought a yellow cap with a visor and the word "Taos" sewn
into it. She was smiling, modeling for him.

"Very nice," he said. She sat down next to him and
squeezed his arm. "What do people do in this town?" he
asked. "Look at vapor trails all day?"

"They walk around," she said. "They buy things." She
saw a couple dragging a protesting child into an art gallery.
"They bully their kids." She paused, then went on. "They
eat." She pointed to a restaurant, Casa Ogilvie's, on the east
side of the square, with a balcony that looked down at the
commerce below. "Hungry?" He shrugged. "I sure am," she
said. She took his hand and led him across the square into the
archway underneath the restaurant. There she stopped, turned,

and put her arms around him, leaning against him. She felt the sweat of his back against her palms. "I'm so sorry," she said. Then they went up the stairs and had lunch, two margaritas each and chicken in hot sauce. Sweating and drowsy, they strolled back to the motel, not speaking.

They left the curtains of the front window open an inch or so when they made love that afternoon. From the bed they could see occasionally a thin strip of someone walking past. They made love to fill time, with an air of detachment, while the television set stayed on, showing a Lana Turner movie in which everyone's face was green at the edges and pink at the center. Jeremy and Harriet touched with the pleasure of being close to one familiar object in a setting crowded with strangers. Harriet reached her orgasm with her usual spasms of trembling, and when she cried out he lowered his head to the pillow on her right side, where he wouldn't see her face.

Thus began the pattern for the next three days: desultory shopping for nicknacks in the morning, followed by lunch, lovemaking and naps through the afternoon, during which time it usually rained for an hour or so. During their shopping trips they didn't buy very much: Jeremy said the art was mythic and lugubrious, and Harriet didn't like pottery. Jeremy bought a flashlight, in case, he said, the power went out, and Harriet purchased a keychain. All three days they went into Casa Ogilvie's at the same time and ordered the same meal, explaining to themselves that they didn't care to experiment with exotic regional food. On the third afternoon of this they woke up from their naps at about the same time with the totally clear unspoken understanding that they could not spend another day—or perhaps even another hour—in this manner.

Jeremy announced the problem by asking, "What do we do tomorrow?"

Harriet kicked her way out of bed and walked over to the television, on top of which she had placed a guide to the Southwest. "Well," she said, opening it up, "there *are* sights around here. We haven't been into the mountains north of here. There's a Kiowa Indian pueblo just a mile away. There's a place called Arroyo Seco near here and—"

"What's that?"

"It means Dry Gulch." She waited. "There's the Taos

Gorge Bridge." Jeremy shook his head quickly. "The D. H. Lawrence shrine is thirty minutes from here, and so is the Millicent A. Rogers Memorial Museum. There are, it says here, some trout streams. If it were winter, we could go skiing."

"It's summer," Jeremy said, closing his eyes and pulling the sheet up. "We can't ski. What about this shrine?"

She put the book on the bed near Jeremy and read the entry. "It says that Lawrence lived for eighteen months up there, and they've preserved his ranch. When he died, they brought his ashes back and there's a shrine or something. They *call* it a shrine. I'm only telling you what the book says."

"D. H. Lawrence?" Jeremy asked sleepily.

"You know," Harriet said. "*Lady Chatterley's Lover.*"

"Yes, I know." He smiled. "It wasn't the books I was asking about, it was the *quality* of the books, and therefore the necessity of making the trip."

"All I know is that it's visitable," she said, "and it's off State Highway Three, and it's something to do."

"Okay. I don't care what goddamn highway it's on," Jeremy said, reaching for the book and throwing it across the room. "Let's at least get into the car and go somewhere."

After breakfast they drove in the rented Pontiac out of town toward the Taos ski valley. They reached it after driving up fifteen miles of winding road through the mountains, following a stream of snow runoff, along which they counted a dozen fishermen. When they reached the valley, they admired the mountains and accommodations but agreed it was summer and there was nothing to do in such a place. Neither blamed the other for acting upon an unproductive idea. They returned to the car and retraced their steps to the highway, which they followed for another fifteen miles until they reached the turn for the D. H. Lawrence shrine on the Kiowa Ranch Road. Jeremy stopped the car on the shoulder. "Well?" he asked.

"Why do we have to *decide* about everything?" Harriet said, looking straight ahead. "Why can't we just *do* it?"

He accelerated up the unpaved road, which climbed toward a plateau hidden in the mountains. They passed several farms where cattle were grazing on the thin grasses. The light made the land look varnished; even with sunglasses, Harriet squinted at the shimmering heat waves rising from the gravel.

Jeremy said, "What's here?"

"I told you. Anyhow, the description isn't much good. We'll find out. Maybe they'll have a tour of his inner sanctum or have his Nobel Prize up in a frame. The book says they have his actual typewriter."

Jeremy coughed. "He never won the Nobel Prize." Harriet looked over at him and noticed that his face was losing its internal structure and becoming puffy. Unhappiness had added five years to his appearance. She saw, with disbelief, a new crease on his neck. Turning away, she glanced up at the sky: a hawk, cirrus clouds. The air conditioner was blowing a stream of cool air on her knees. Her gums ached.

"Only two more miles," Jeremy said, beginning now to hunch over the wheel slightly.

"I don't like this draft," she said, reaching over to snap off the air conditioner. She cranked down the window and let the breeze tangle her hair. They were still going uphill and had reached, a sign said, an elevation of nine thousand feet. Jeremy hummed Martian jazz as he drove, tapping the steering wheel. With a small shock Harriet recognized the hummed riff from one of Jeremy's Charlie Parker albums. The little dirt road went past an open gate, divided in two, one fork going toward a conference center indicated by a road marker, the other toward the house and shrine. They came to a clearing. In front of them stood a two-story house looking a bit like an English country cottage, surrounded by a white picket fence, with a tire swing in the backyard, beyond which two horses were grazing. They were alone: There were no other cars in sight. Jeremy went up to the door of the house and knocked. A dog began barking angrily from inside, as if the knocks had interrupted its nap. "Look at this," Harriet said.

She had walked a few steps and was looking in the direction they had come from; in the clear air they could see down the mountain and across the valley for a distance of fifty miles or so. "It's beautiful," she said. Jeremy appeared from behind her, shielding his eyes although the sun was behind him. "What're you doing that for?" she asked.

"You have dark glasses. I don't."

"Where's the shrine?" she asked. "I don't see it anywhere."

"You have to turn around. Look." He pointed to the

picket fence. At its north corner there was a sign that Harriet had missed:

## SHRINE ☞

"That's very quaint," she said. "And what's this?" She walked toward the fence and picked a child's mitten off one of the posts. Mickey Mouse's face was printed on the front of the mitten, and one of his arms reached up over the thumb. She began laughing. "It doesn't say anything about Mickey Mouse in *Fodor's*. Do you think he's part of the shrine?"

Jeremy didn't answer. He had already started out ahead of her on a path indicated by the black pointing finger. Harriet followed him, panting from the altitude and the blistering heat, feeling her back begin to sweat as the light rained down on it. She felt the light on her legs and inside her head, on her eardrums. The path turned to the right and began a series of narrowing zigzags going up the side of a hill, at the top of which stood the shrine, a small white boxlike building that, as they approached it, resembled a chapel, a mausoleum, or both. A granite phoenix glowered at the apex of the roof.

"The door's open," Jeremy said, twenty feet ahead of her, "and nobody's here." He was wearing heavy jeans, and his blue shirt was soaked with two wings of sweat. Harriet could hear the rhythmic pant of his breathing.

"Are there snakes out here?" she asked. "I hate snakes."

"Not in the shrine," he said. "I don't see any."

"What do you see?"

"A visitors' register." He had reached the door and had stepped inside. Then he came back out.

She was still ten feet away. "There must be more. You can't have a shrine without something in it."

"Well, there's this white thing outside," he said breathlessly. "Looks like a burial stone." She was now standing next to him. "Yes. This is where his wife is buried." They both looked at it. A small picture of Frieda was bolted into the stone.

"Well," Jeremy said, "now for the shrine." They shuffled inside. At the back was a small stained-glass window, a representation of the sun, literalized rays burning out from its center. To their left the visitors' register lay open on a high desk, and above it in a display case three graying documents asserted that the ashes stored here were authentically those of D. H. Lawrence, the author. The chapel's interior smelled of sage and cement. At the far side of the shrine, six feet away, was a roped-off area, and at the back an approximation of an altar, at whose base was a granite block with the letters DHL carved on it. "This is it?" Jeremy asked. "No wonder no one's here."

Harriet felt giddy from the altitude. "Should we pray?" she asked, but before Jeremy could answer, she said, "Well, good for him. He got himself a fine shrine. Maybe he deserves it. Goddamn, it's hot in here." She turned around and walked outside, still laughing in a broken series of almost inaudible chuckles. When she was back in the sun, she pointed her finger the way the sign had indicated and said, "Shrine."

Jeremy stepped close to her, and they both looked again at the mountains in the west. "I used to read him in college," Harriet said, "and in high school I had a copy of *The Rainbow* I hid under my pillow where my mother wouldn't find it. Jesus, it must be ninety-five degrees." She looked suddenly at Jeremy, sweat dripping into her eyes. "I used to have a lot of fantasies when I was a teenager," she said. He was wiping his face with a handkerchief. "Do you see anyone?" she asked.

"Do I see anybody? No. We would've heard a car coming up the road. Why?"

"Because I'm hot. I feel like doing something," Harriet said. "I mean, here we are at the D. H. Lawrence shrine." She was unbuttoning her blouse. "I just thought of this," she said, beginning to laugh again. She put her blouse on the ground and quickly unhooked her bra, dropping it on top of the blouse. "There," she said, sighing. "Now that's better." She turned to face the mountains. When Jeremy didn't say anything, she swung around to look at him. He was staring at her, at the brown circles of her nipples, and his face seemed stricken. She reached over and took his hand. "Oh, Jay, sweetie," she said, "no one will see us. Honey. What is it? Do you want me to get dressed?"

"That's not it." He was staring at her, as if she were not his wife.

"What? What is it?"

"You're free of it." He wiped his forehead.

"What?"

"You're free of it. You're leaving me alone here."

"Alone? Alone in what?"

"You know perfectly damn well," he said. "I'm alone back here." He tapped his head. "I don't know how you did it, but you did it. You broke free. You're gone." He bent down. "You don't know what I'm talking about."

"Yes, I do." She put her bra and blouse back on and turned toward him again. His face was a mixture of agony and rage, but in the huge sunlight these emotions diminished to small vestigial puffs of feeling. "It's a path," she said. "And then you're surprised. You get out. It'll happen to you. You'll see. Honestly."

She could see his legs shaking. His face was a barren but expressive landscape. "Okay," he said. "Talk all you want. I was just thinking—" He didn't finish the sentence.

"You'll be all right," she said, stroking his back.

"I don't *want* to be all right!" he said, his voice rising, a horrible smile appearing on his face: It was a devil's face, Harriet saw, and it was radiant and calm. Sweat poured off his forehead, and his skin had started to flush pink. "It's my pleasure not to be all right. Do you see that? My *pleasure*."

She wiped her hands on her cotton pants. A stain appeared, then vanished. "You want that? You want to be back there by yourself?"

"Yeah." He nodded. "You bet. I feel like an explorer. I feel like a fucking pioneer." He gave each one of the words a separate emphasis. Meanwhile, he had separated himself from her and was now tilting his head up toward the sky, letting the sun shine on his closed eyelids.

She looked at him. In the midst of the sunlight he was hugging his darkness, his new home, his loyalty. She stepped down the zigzag path to the car, leaving him there, but he followed her. Once they were both in the car, the dog inside the ranch house began its frantic barking but stopped after a few seconds. She took Jeremy's hand and scanned the clouds in the west, trying to see the sky the way he did, but she couldn't.

All she could see was the land stretched out in front of her, and, far in the distance, all fifty miles away, a few thunderheads and a narrow curtain of rain, so thin that the light passed straight through it.

# ROBERT COHEN

# THE SCIENTIFIC METHOD

FROM PLOUGHSHARES

෨

1949. I AM ALREADY six years old and no stranger to adversity when my mother shakes me awake one September morning and tells me we are leaving Los Alamos and moving to Santa Fe. Instinctively, I sniff her breath for liquor. But there is only the sour musk of coffee and, from her armpits, another smell, slightly floral, which I know to be something she exudes on her own, some essence. Whether other people—my father, for instance, who is already gone; he normally leaves at daylight— notice this smell, or associate it, as I do, with unhappiness and self-doubt, I'm not sure. I am only six, after all. There are limits to my understanding.

For instance, I do not entirely comprehend the need for my parents to separate. True, they do not get along very well. But from my scattered observations of life on the Hill, most couples get along no better, except at the parties, where there seems to be a great deal of hugging and kissing and pronounce- ment of affection. It is only afterward, when the ties get loosened and the shoes come off and the bedroom door is left carelessly ajar, that the fights start up.

There was a party just last night, in the McNultys' apartment below ours, and from the sound of things it was quite a wingding. Through the floorboards came occasional whoops of laughter, a good deal of jazzy music, and some syncopated stomping I took to be dancing. Lying in bed, I could, from long habit, picture my father tinkling moodily at the piano, his gaze abstracted, as one or another of his colleagues endeavored to loosen him up with some bawdy jokes; and my mother, drink in hand, laughing a bit too loudly in the kitchen, straining her neck forward a little too far to catch some wisp of gossip from the women she privately despised. To blot out the picture, I began to whistle through my teeth along with the music.

"Maybe you should close your eyes, lovey," said Mrs. Burke, peering in at me from the doorway. My mother's sole confidante, she is a solidly built, white-haired matron given to sarcasm, hot drinks, and fat novels. She appears to have no great fondness for me, or for children in general. In some people, the capacity for private amusement is so great that the demands of social discourse merely serve as the backdrop for their own idiosyncratic passions. Mrs. Burke takes me in stride; she performs the duty of baby-sitting with a kind of gallant geniality indistinguishable from boredom. I perceive it as part of a larger strategy directed toward my mother, toward whom she seems fiercely attached. Relative, at least, to my father. "Go to sleep," she urges

"I am asleep," I say. It doesn't feel like a lie, at the time.

A shriek vaults through the floorboards. Mrs. Burke, in the doorway, sniffs in disapproval. "Janet Sommers. That silly bitch."

"Silly bitch," I agree.

It is not so difficult, talking to adults. All you have to do is listen. Mrs. Burke smiles and comes forward to sit at the edge of the bed. "You're all right, lovey," she says. "You've got a future."

Her weight bends the mattress so that I have to prop myself up on one elbow to avoid falling into her lap. As long as I have the ear of a sympathetic grown-up, I decide to clear up something that's been troubling me. "Who's Stalin, anyway?" I ask

Mrs. Burke arches an eyebrow. "Never heard of him."

"Yes you have."

"Why do you want to know?"

"My mom says he's the reason we're staying here," I say. "He had some kind of test, and now we have to stay."

She just sits there, nodding her head like a doctor. "And what did your father say?"

"He said we'd stay anyway. He said he likes it here."

More nods. "Do *you* like it here, lovey?"

I shrug. Were I more precocious, perhaps I'd manage to express the confusion I really feel over the matter. Like, dislike—the truth is, I have no standard of measurement for such things. Aside from one trip to New York to attend my grandfather's funeral, I have had no opportunities to experience any other sort of life. Thus I take my cues from those close to me—specifically, my parents, who appear to be split on the question. I know only one thing for certain: I do not like the split itself. It afflicts us all, individually and as a unit. It has somehow become the overriding fact of my life.

"When's he going to finish that thing, anyway?" She is staring off into the corner of the room, at the hull of the model organ—the spindly wooden frame and the tangled circuit of stretched wire—which has occupied the bulk of my father's evening and weekend attention for as long as I can remember. Lit by a shaft of moonlight, it does not look now to be as precariously balanced or haphazard a construction as it does in the glare of daylight. Suddenly it looks promising, almost "ready to sing," as my father likes to put it. Soon he will teach me how to make music spring up from the wood and the wire. It is kept in my room for a reason, after all: It is meant for me.

We both must have fallen asleep then, because the next thing I know big jowly Donald Burke is looming over the bed, shaking his wife—who lies curled up beside me—gently awake. "Annette. C'mon, pallie. Come on. Atta girl." His big palm massages her shoulder in a tiny circle, as though he is rubbing a spot out of her sweater. His lips purse when he notices me looking up at him. "Hello, sport," he whispers casually. "What'd you do, slip her a mickey?"

I don't know what the hell he's talking about, so I just blink a few times. We've never had much to say to each other, he and I. A metallurgist at the lab, he is a blustery and intimidating fellow, uncomfortable with domestic life, impatient with the modulations required by a situation such as this. And yet, staring up into the enormous solidity of his shoulder, the baggy exhaustion of his eyes, I do not feel sorry to have him in my bedroom. "I hurt my thumb," I announce in a whisper, over his sleeping wife. It isn't exactly true, either. I've merely slept on it, and now it's asleep, tingling and numb. I seem to be turning into quite a little liar.

He stands, crosses around to my side of the bed, and sits Indian-style on the wood floor. "Give me a look." Frowning, he turns the thumb over in his calloused palm, pressing it above the joint. "That hurt?"

"A little."

"Try to bend it."

I bend it quickly, feel no pain, then flex it very slowly a couple of times, to suggest concentration. The floor is dirty, but he doesn't seem to notice. Still holding the base of my hand, he lets out a long weary sigh. "That's good. That's very good, sport. Someday, you know, we'll be able to do a lot more for people and their thumbs. We'll just bring you into the lab when it hurts and fit you for a new one."

"A new thumb?" My brows knit in skepticism. "Where'll you get it?"

"Why, we'll *make* it, sport. Whip it right up, then plug it on like an extension cord."

"Will it hurt?"

He smiles. With the moonlight coming in from the window, I can see the inside of his mouth hovering a couple of feet away. It is a wide, confident thing, his mouth—unlike my father's, which is drawn into a grim line most of the time—but I think I can see the gums pulling back from his lower teeth. "Not a bit," he says. "That's the whole point, you see. Your thumb will be a thing that works perfectly. And not just yours, either. Everybody will have one. Maybe two."

"Where will you put them?"

"Oh, I don't know. You'll be able to take it off when you go to sleep, I guess. Put it in the fridge, next to the Coca-Cola."

"I don't think so," I respond vaguely.

"No?"

Donald Burke pulls himself up so that he is now squatting on his knees. He throws a quick glance toward his sleeping wife, clucks his tongue, and brings his hands up so that they cover his mouth mysteriously. Then he brings them forward in closed fists. I lean close, expectant. When his hands are just below the level of my neck, he opens them and smiles a crooked smile unlike anything I've seen before.

There, cupped in his hands, looking almost blue in the dim light, are his teeth.

I hear myself let out a little yell. So, evidently, does Annette Burke, who turns over, stretches sleepily, and, shaking her wide head to clear it, sits erect. "Hello, pumpkin," she says to her husband. "Fun party?"

He waves his wrist. "The usual. A lot of the new folk, you know. Kept getting the names wrong. I'm no damn good at parties."

"Uh huh," she says, as though she isn't listening.

"Well, you know what I mean."

I examine him closely as he speaks. There they are, snug and white and precisely ordered, right where they belong. Either he is some sort of sleight-of-hand magician, or else I only imagined those were his teeth, or else I am dreaming, and none of this is real, including the conversation going on at this moment between these two people who are not my parents but have somehow come to straddle my bed—in which case, I figure, I should really just relax, lay back, and let their banter carry me through the night without trying to sort it all out; because dreams, when they're occurring, do not imply their shape to the dreamer, and this one feels like it might keep on going in just this manner for an eternity, with the dance music coming up through the floorboards and the light turning everything blue and people passing around the parts of their bodies like pieces of a puzzle—

Dimly, I hear the click of a door.

In the morning, I help my mother load the suitcases and boxes full of kitchen stuff into the Ford. Because she is small, anemic, and by nature disorganized, it takes a great number of trips, with a lot of time spent pausing to regain her strength and composure. She is having a tough morning. It isn't really in her to be resolute, to take more than one step forward without a half step back, and when we are nearly finished I find her sitting at the top of the stairs, smoking a cigarette and looking pensively at the bare walls of the kitchen through the open door. A radio is playing in one of the other apartments—I can hear a weatherman predicting a hot day. Both of us wear long pants and long-sleeved shirts, but it is too late to change, my mother informs me. "Are we forgetting anything?" she asks.

"I don't know."

"Well, let's go see. Let's make sure."

Together we walk through the apartment. It has never been decorated with much care, so we've been able to do a pretty thorough job despite ourselves: The place, furniture aside, looks stripped clean, except for my father's work space and the bathroom, which for some reason my mother refuses to include in her inventory. Perhaps she has left more of herself behind than she thinks. I peek in, and find her everywhere: in the sloppy fold of the towels; the long strands of hair contorted into a Rorschach blot on the drain of the shower; the trace of her damp footprints on the throw rug; the empty pill bottles prescribed by the psychiatrist, who arrived only last year and quickly became so popular with the ladies.

Finally, we go through my room again. My mother snatches an errant sock from the floor of the closet, and some marbles that have found their way under the box springs. While she kneels at the foot of the bed, searching the floor, I wander over to the organ-in-progress and run my finger along the gum-faced plywood of the wind chest. On the workbench beside it are a number of little metal fittings my father has been experimenting with for the ducts. I grab half a dozen of them in my hand and jiggle them softly, feeling the weight of their collisions.

"Ready?" My mother is standing up and looking around one last time, her chest heaving under her shirt. It's funny: I have seen her cry so many times, in the light of so many mornings, that I no longer attribute the sight or sound of it to grief, or an acute pain of any sort; rather, I register it as a tic of expression, an allergic reflex, something to indulge matter-of-factly for a moment and then move on.

As for me, my lack of understanding of consequence is coming in handy: This whole enterprise strikes me as a phase of adventure, an impromptu digression. Building one's future is just like building anything else—the ratio of design to improvisation will vary according to inspiration, materials, and under-lying circumstances. My father's organ, for instance, is already shaping up differently than the sketches he used to labor over anticipated; still, he continues to work through the permutations and possibilities with detachment and patience. He calls this the Scientific Method. Though I grasp it only superficially at best, it is related somehow, I think, to the test Stalin has taken recently, and the reason my father needs to stay at the lab, and it has something to do, probably, with that tall tale Donald Burke told me about my thumb, and god knows what else—but there is no time, just now, to digest it all; the Ford sits outside, loaded with our possessions, and my mother has composed her features into a mask of determination and prag-matism. "Let's go, then," she says, bringing her hands together into a parody of cheer, or prayer. "Before we change our minds."

We go. Passing the new hospital, the new library, the new housing, on a freshly paved road, we are bucking the traffic of history. Four years ago, "the first team," as my father called them, took this route off the mesa, leaving behind a half-formed community coping with its own success, notoriety, and uncertain future. Everything was at once secure and up for grabs, which made it fertile ground for men like my father—gifted, ambitious, dogged; men who, by substituting structure for inspiration, have found themselves able to make those small leaps of craft and status that determine the trajectory of a career. He had begun as an outsider, and he made adjustments; now the place belongs to him. Because he has never expected much in the way of happiness, he will not do much peeking under the rug of his contentment. Nor will he, with his physics and his music, miss us very much. Or at least no more than when we shared the same apartment.

On the drive out of town we pass the new stadium, still under construction, which will be named for one of the men from the lab who was killed in an accident. It is nearly finished. The benches gleam in the sunlight, ascending from the playing field in neat semicircular rows. The symmetry of the place radiates a power as old as the Greeks. As the car rounds a sharp curve, I turn full around on the front seat to watch it recede against the backdrop of the Jemez mountains. My last view is of the stadium's back wall, still incomplete—an assortment of unused girders lean awkwardly against the base, which is littered with candy wrappers, yellowing newspapers, and beer cans from the crew's Friday lunch.

"Sit down, *sheynkeit*," says my mother, "so you don't fly out the window."

I stay right where I am.

"Please, Heschel." She looks over and notices my balled fist. "What's that? What's that in your hand?"

"Nothing." But when I open my hand I find some of the fittings from the organ's wind chest. I do not remember putting them in my pocket before, or grabbing hold of them now. "They're Dad's," I say.

"You shouldn't have taken them. They might be important."

The stadium is out of sight. We wind down the lowest of the finger mesas. The view out the back window is partly obscured by boxes and suitcases, so all I can see are the peaks of the Jemez jutting up from the Valle Grande. My father once told me how the whole thing was formed. A massive explosion, not so different from the one that lit up the southern sky a few years ago. And now Stalin has taken some test over on the other side of the world, and the men are flooding in to work at the lab, to figure out a way to cause an even bigger explosion. You get the feeling, growing up in Los Alamos, that explosions are not entirely terrible things; or possibly, that in what we call the terrible, there are other things going on, cycles of birth as well as death, options opened as well as closed. Reality gets twisted into a variety of shapes: some good, some bad, some too close to call. Volcanoes blow up, then turn to lush hill country. Cities get built, then deteriorate, then revive. People love each other, then stop and move somewhere else. Everything is liquid motion. Matter comes and goes. It's almost musical.

Of course, I am only six at the time, and have not yet begun to think in these terms, but in a childish, visceral way, I have taken a little leap of discovery myself. Winding out of the canyon, away from my father, headed out toward that metropolis of Wild West strangeness called Santa Fe, I finger the fittings of the wind chest and begin to hum.

My mother, hunched forward on the seat so she can see over the dashboard, lets out her breath. Soon she's humming, too, though it is not the same song. She hums what she always hums, "Cheek to Cheek," in the key she always hums in, which my father claims is quite a bit flatter than B-flat.

We arrive in Santa Fe just after noon. The house is on the eastern edge of town, on slightly higher ground than the rest. When we get out of the car, I can see the roof of the cathedral near the square, but the glare from the sun is too strong to identify other landmarks. Everything looks bleached. My mother has already yanked open the trunk of the Ford, but now her attention has turned to the house. "Look, Heschel," she urges, and takes a couple of steps onto the property. "Isn't it beautiful?"

It isn't exactly beautiful, this new house of ours. It has a small, constricted look about it, and after the wood structures of Los Alamos the muddy brown adobe seems primitive, more like an eruption of the earth below it than a willful addition, sculpted by men. The driveway is unfinished gravel, the yard strewn with weeds, rocks, and scrub, and the windows are the size of postage stamps. Still, it *is* a house. I've never lived in a house before, and neither has my mother. A diaspora Jew arriving in Zion for the first time, she actually bends down low to smell the ground in the front yard, sighing with exaggerated relish. "You smell? Isn't it beautiful?"

"Yeah," I say, still standing by the open trunk.

She catches something in my voice, something she has been fearing, or expecting, and looks at me over her shoulder through her hard nut-brown eyes, and for a moment I'm sure she's going to cry. But she doesn't. "Ours," she says, more to herself than to me. It is her customary way of talking.

I reach into the trunk for my suitcase, which is on top because it's so frail and the handle is broken, and when I bring my left hand up to support it from the bottom the organ fittings spill onto the red earth at my feet. It's just as well, I figure. I have my hands full with projects of my own, and the Scientific Method has failed us once already.

# MARY GORDON

# THE DANCING PARTY

FROM MS.

༅

"I KNOW WHY you're in this mood," says the angry wife, "I just wish you'd admit it."

They drive in darkness on the sandy road; she has no confidence that he will find the house, which they have only seen in daylight. And she half wishes he will get a wheel stuck in the sand. She would be pleased to see him foolish.

"I'm in a bad mood for one reason," says the husband. "Because you said to me: Shape up. No one should say that to someone: Shape up."

"I could tell by your face how you were planning to be. That way that makes the other people at a party want to cut their throats."

"Must I sparkle to be allowed among my kind?"

"And I know why you're like that. Don't think I don't. It's because for once the day was shaped by my desires. It's because you watched the children while I swam. For once."

"Yes, it's true, the day was shaped by your desires. But I'm not resentful. Not at all. You must believe me."

"But I don't believe you."

"Then where do we go?"

59

"We go, now, to the party. But I beg you: Please don't go in with your face like that. It's such a wonderful idea, a dancing party."

The house is built atop the largest dune. In daylight you can see the ocean clearly from the screened-in porch. The married couple climb the dune, not looking at each other, walking far apart. When they come to the door, they see the hostess dancing with her brother.

How I love my brother, thinks the hostess. There are no men in the world like him.

The hostess's brother has just been divorced. His sister's house is where he comes, the house right on the ocean, the house she was given when her husband left her for someone else. Her brother comes here for consolation, for she has called it "my consolation prize." And it *has* been a consolation, and still is, though she is now, at forty-five, successful. She can leave her store to her assistants, take a month off in the summer, and come here. She earns more money than her ex-husband, who feels, by this alone, betrayed. She comes, each morning, to the screened-in porch and catches in the distance the blue glimpse of sea, the barest hint, out in the distance, longed for, but in reach. She'd brought her children here: the long, exhausting summers of the single mother. Watched their feuds, exclusions, the shore life of children on long holiday, so brimming and so cruel. But they are grown now, and remarkably, they both have jobs. Her daughters have jobs working in the city. One is here, now, for the weekend only. Sunday night, tomorrow, like the other grown-ups, she will leave. The daughter will be in her car, stuck in the line of traffic, that reptilian creature that will take her in its coils. Exhausted, she will arrive in her apartment in Long Island City. She will wait until morning to return her rented car.

I will not be like my mother, thinks the daughter of the hostess. I will not live as she lives. How beautiful she is and how I love her. But I will not live like that.

She lifts an angry shoulder at the poor young man, her partner, who does not know why. She is saying: I will not serve you or your kind. I will not be susceptible.

She sees her mother, dancing, not with her brother any longer, but with another man. She sees her mother's shoulder curving toward him. Sees her mother's head bent back. Susceptible. Will this be one more error of susceptibility? Oh, no, my mother, beautiful and still so young, do not. Shore up and guard yourself. As I have. Do not fall once more into those arms that seem strong but will leave you. Do not fall.

She leaves the young man now to dance with the best friend of her mother. This woman has no husband, and a child of two. The mother with no husband and a child of two dreams of her lover as she dances with the daughter of the hostess.

The scientist has come without her lover. He has said: "Oh, go alone. You know I hate to dance." She phoned her friend, a man in love with other men. Come dancing with me. Yes, of course, he says. He is glad to be with her; he too is a scientist. They work together; they study the habits of night birds. They are great friends. The lover of the scientist is brilliant, difficult. In ten years she has left him twice. She thinks now she will never leave him.

The daughter of the hostess puts on music that the angry wife, the mother with no husband, and the scientist don't like. So they sit down; three friends, they sit together on the bench that rests against the wall. They look out the large window; they can see the moon and newly lit a square white patch of sea. They like each other; they are fortyish; they are successful. For a month each summer they live here by the ocean, a mile apart. The angry wife is a bassoonist of renown. The mother with no husband writes studies of women in the ancient world. These women, all of them, have said to each other: What a pleasure we are good at what we do. And people know it. The angry wife has said: "You know you are successful when you realize how many people hope you will fail."

And how are you? they ask each other. Tired, say the two, the angry wife, the mother with no husband, who have young children. I would like to have a child, the scientist says. Of course you must, the two say who are mothers. Now they think with pleasure of the soft flesh of their children, of their faces when they sleep. Oh, have a child, they tell the scientist. Nothing is better in the world.

Yes, have a child, the hostess says. Look at my daughter. See how wonderful. The daughter of the hostess has forgotten, for a time, her anger, and is laughing with the young man.

Asks him: Are you going back on Sunday? Would you like a ride? The hostess thinks: Good, good. My daughter will not drive alone. And maybe he will love her.

I am afraid of being tired, says the scientist to her three friends.

You will be tired if you have a child, they say to her. There is no getting around it. You will be tired all the time.

And what about my work?

You will do far less work. We must tell you the truth.

I am afraid, then, says the scientist.

The widow sits beside them. And they say to her, for she is old now: What do you think our friend should do?

The widow says: Two things in the world you never regret: a swim in the ocean, the birth of a child.

She says things like this; it is why they come to her, these four women near the age of forty. She has Russian blood; it makes her feel free to be aphoristic. She can say: To cross a field is not to live a life. To drink tea is not to hew wood. Often she is wrong. They know that, and it doesn't matter. She sits before them, shining, like a bowl of water, colored, just for pleasure, blue. They would sit at her feet forever; they would listen to her all night long. She says: I think that I have made mistakes.

But they do not believe her.

She says: In my day we served men. We did not divorce. I do not think then we knew how to be good to our children and love men at the same time. We had wonderful affairs. Affairs are fine, but you must never fall in love. You must be in love only with your husband.

But only one of them has a husband. He is sitting, drinking, talking to another man. His wife would like to say: Look at the moon, don't turn your back to it. But she is tired of her voice tonight, the voice that speaks to him so cruelly, more cruelly than he deserves. She would like to say: Let's dance now. But she doesn't want to dance with him. Will I get over being angry, she wonders, before the party ends? She hopes she will and fears that she will not.

The widow greets her friend across the room. They have both understood the history of clothes. And so they watched, in the late 1960s, the sensitive and decorative march of vivid colored trousers and light, large-sleeved printed shirts, of dresses made of Indian material, of flat, bright, cotton shoes. So in their seventies they greet each other wearing purple and magenta. As they kiss, the gauzy full sleeves of their blouses touch. Tonight to be absurd, the widow's friend has worn a feather boa. Her husband, her fifth husband, stands beside her, gallant and solicitous for her and for her friend.

The widow says to her old friend, pointing to the four women sitting on the bench: I think they've got it right. Their lovely work.

The friend says: But look, they are so tired, and so angry.

The widow says: But we were tired at that age, and angry. They will have something to show.

Who knows, the widow's friend says, turning to her husband. Dance with me, she says, I think this one's a waltz.

He kisses her, for she has made him laugh. They dance, they are the only ones now dancing with the hostess's daughter and her friends. The music has gone angular and mean, it seems to the four women on the bench. The hostess's daughter thinks: Perhaps, then, I should marry a rich man. I am not ambitious, but I like nice things.

The mother without a husband thinks about her lover. Of his mouth, his forearms, his way of standing with his knees always a little bent, the black hairs on the back of his small hands.

The hostess thinks: Perhaps I will ask this new man to stay.

The scientist thinks: I will live forever with a man who hates to dance.

The daughter of the hostess thinks: I love my mother, but I will not live like her.

The widow thinks: How wonderful their lives are. I must tell them so that they will know.

Her friend thinks: If this man dies I will be once more alone.

The angry wife wishes she were not angry.

Suddenly a funny song comes on. It has a name that makes them laugh: "Girls (Just Want To Have Fun)." The daughter of the hostess claps her hands and says: No men. The women, all of them: the hostess and her daughter, the scientist, the mother with no husband, the angry wife, the widow and her friend, stand in a circle, kick their legs in unison, and laugh. And they can see outside the circle all the men, ironical or bored-looking, the kindly ones amused. They all look shiftless there, and unreliable, like vagabonds. The two old women cannot bear it, that the men should be unhappy as the women dance. The widow's friend is first to break the circle. She takes her husband's hand and leads him to the center of the room. The widow dances with the handsomest young man. The daughter of the hostess walks away. But the four women near to forty sit down on the bench. The angry wife can see her husband's back. His back is turned against her; he is looking at the moon.

# AMY HERRICK

# IN THE AIR, OVER OUR HEADS

## FROM TRIQUARTERLY

ॐ

PERHAPS SARAH TAKES the apartment at this rude and disreputable end of the city as an act of curiosity. In any case, she can't afford much more. She takes the job, although it doesn't pay well, because she wants to be on hand to deliver any possible blows of reason to this dark and ignorant age. She knows she will witness much injustice and she expects to see the miserable and oppressed and mad thrown into dungeons (where they can have time to grow even more miserable and oppressed and mad). She recognizes that *she* is as free as one is granted to be—given the anarchy and disorder that roam the universe like wolves—and she spends the winter training her reflexes to stop on a dime. However, she doesn't sleep well, perhaps because she is not sure how much actual power you get from being free in this great light world.

Early in the spring she is assigned her first murder case. Theresa Maldonado, after eight years of having her nose broken and her teeth knocked out, finally picked up a carving knife one night and marched Luis Maldonado around the kitchen table and stabbed him five times through the heart. Sarah thinks she is ready for this. She, herself, sick of love, of raising hopes and watching them dashed, of jumping around deafened and myopic, kissing people on the mouth and later tripping over things in their darkened rooms searching for her glasses, throws herself with deadly seriousness into this case.

Theresa has a small heart-shaped face with sadness as incurably stamped on it as a postmark. If Sarah can bring in a verdict of temporary insanity, then Theresa will walk away free. Sarah cannot imagine who would not agree that stabbing Luis was as innocent and temporarily insane an act as you're likely to get on this whirling little planet with its rivers of blood.

Throughout the case the jurors sit up and listen to Sarah like daisies in three straight rows, alert and nervous and eager to please. But on the morning when they finish their deliberations, they shuffle back into the courtroom sheepish as a cloud of butchers. They declare Theresa guilty of murder in the second degree.

After this Sarah starts to experience some imbalance of the inner ear, so that even while she is lying in bed the earth seems ready to finish itself off by a small tip and wrench out of orbit. The trillion tiny heartless voices of the stars rush in her ears until she gets up and stands at the window and looks down at the street. She is standing there one night, trying to catch her breath, when the phone rings and it is Robin announcing that she is going to be released from the hospital tomorrow.

Sarah doesn't know what to do. The next day she waits across the street from the hospital in the shadow of the fruit stand, disguised in an old brown trench coat. While she waits, she watches a man with the brightest, drunkest blue eyes she's ever seen going methodically through the garbage cans. He wears two different shoes and stacked on his head are five or six assorted hats. Who could be such a fool as to look for more hats in a world like this? she wonders.

When Sarah looks across the street again, there is Robin with a little suitcase in her hand, slipping quickly out of the arched and ominous doorway and down the shadowed side of the steps. But as soon as she comes to the bottom and hits the sunlight, she stops stock-still as if she were dazzled or stupefied by the sudden brightness. She puts her suitcase down and stands there blinking patiently up at the sky. Her black hair frizzes out around her head as if the last nurse has combed it in a great rush and fury. Sarah couldn't blame this nurse a bit and she stares unhappily from her hiding place at Robin and tries to make up her mind.

When at last she decides, she strides across the street without wasting any more time, almost hungrily. Robin cries out sleepily when she recognizes her and they embrace. Then Sarah pushes her away. "You have exactly a month with me," she says. "Use the time well. After that you're on your own."

"You're the same!" Robin says joyfully. "I talked about you a lot in there, but Carlisle, one of the twins, said you'd forgotten me, just like Martin Burnbauer has forgotten me. Carlisle is in there with his brother because one of them supposedly tried to kill their mother. The doctor told them they couldn't have their street clothes back until they admitted that their mother doesn't really flap around their bedroom at night in the shape of a bat."

"And if you act or talk crazy, you're out like a shot."

"I'm just talking about Carlisle."

"Swell," Sarah says, "because your special assignment is to get real and find a job." Grimly, she takes Robin's pack and, shouldering it, sets off without looking back to see if she's following.

They stop on the way for some groceries and as they are toiling up the bread aisle, they pass a man in faded red sweatpants. His arms are loaded with yogurt.

"Too much dairy," Robin says to him as he passes. "It'll give you mucus."

"Mucus is good for you," the man answers. He has a deep, ponderous voice which conceals at the bottom a not-quite-decipherable message. Sarah feels immediately that something has gone wrong. She cannot bring herself to look at him. He wears a tiny gold earring in the shape of a cello in one ear. He is short, she thinks, and fairly tall. My type. He has those kind of eyes that are blue as chunks of sky. No wait—they're brown as mud. She'd better leave. She rolls away up the aisle with her cart.

When he happens to get on line right in back of them at the check-out counter, Sarah is sure that he must have fallen for

Robin already. It happens all the time. People fall for her like they are jumping out of planes without parachutes, their eyes wide open. They fall down, down through the blue sky and land on the front stoop bearing roses, telephoning in the middle of the night. Gangsters fall for her and drug addicts and the guys who hand out advertisements on street corners. Robin's part in this seems completely innocent and unconscious. Nevertheless, humming like a hand grenade about to detonate, she sets off the celestial bridegroom in most of the people she passes.

And, indeed, when Sarah turns to look at her, she finds her standing there sleepily, completely wrapped up in reading the headlines on the sensational newspapers:

"IS ELVIS REALLY DEAD?"

Sarah sighs and turns away to gaze with relief and boredom at the palatial, orderly press of the supermarket's treasures, so she is completely unprepared when a fat woman cuts in line in front of them. She is tough and pasty looking, but has balanced a disarmingly tiny pink hat on her head. Sarah does not say anything for a moment. Someone can always pull a knife and, further, she is thinking about the fundamental social inequalities and miseries of which such rudeness is the natural consequence. But since it is necessary at all times to define and make justice, otherwise you might as well be dead, Sarah finally says to this lady, "Excuse me, but I believe we were next in line."

The lady turns and looks at her with one of those huge stone faces which are the result of a life of volcanic rage and says, "I'm in a hurry."

"Well, we're not," she says, "but the fair thing to do would be to ask if we minded if you went ahead."

"Life is tough," the lady snorts and turns her huge back away.

Sarah hears her heart hammering hotly just inside the threshold of her ears. She tries to catch Robin's eye for some sign of fraternity, but Robin, it seems, has noticed nothing. She is still reading the headlines:

"DOCTORS SAY HEAD TRANSPLANTS NOW POSSIBLE"

A few minutes later when the time comes for the fat lady

to pay for her groceries, she finds that her wallet has been stolen.

Sarah looks up, startled at the squeal of rage. The transformation is wonderful. The stony flesh turns soft and tremulous. The tiny pink hat bobs frantically as the woman wades through her purse again. The fourth or fifth time the woman is going through her purse, her attention is arrested by something. She stops and slowly draws out a small matted black feather, possibly an old pigeon feather that's been dipped in ink. "Where did this come from?" she demands furiously. "Who put this here?"

No one, of course, answers.

Sarah is somewhat startled at the shiver of delight that darts straight across her pulse like a little fish and then disappears. The fat woman throws the feather down on the counter and jolts and jounces out the automatic door.

Sarah prepares to turn and look at the man in red sweatpants accusingly. She sets her face into a stern and unapproachable glare, but is brought up short. He looks even better than he did a few minutes ago. She takes a few steps backward to keep her wits clear, but seeing him gazing speculatively at Robin, she gets a distinct whiff of some spice scent drifting down from the Baking Needs aisle. Nutmeg, is it? Or More-Grief-to-Come?

That night Sarah watches the street below and listens for Robin in the adjoining room, but can hear nothing except the Midnight Hour Social Club, which has put a loudspeaker into its front window in the hopes of drawing new customers. Every night around twelve this loudspeaker bursts into music. Sarah pushes chewing-gum-like earplugs in her ears and watches the two plainclothesmen who have been staking out the storefront next door for heroin traffic. They stir and stretch themselves in the shadows. In this ruined neighborhood it is a slow, cold spring, but still the grass and meadowsweet, the wild clover and dandelion steadily poke up into the vacant lot so that where the broken glass coldly sparked like a field of stars through the winter, now there is a thin creeping veil of green. She hasn't lost a case in weeks. Not since Theresa Maldonado. She is trying to understand this. Everything turns to gold in her hands. Muggers, car thieves, cat burglars exit gayly from the courthouse and melt away into the innocent crowd. She stands there with her earplugs in her ears trying to figure this out and all that comes to mind is a picture of Theresa as she might be right now, lying pale and still in her dark cell, temporarily released from prison by sleep. At that moment a figure in red sweatpants turns the corner and comes jogging slowly down the street. She sees that it is the man from the supermarket. He is pensive and brooding, a little heavy on the feet. She stares helplessly at his running shoes which, with their outsize, cushioning soles, look like clown shoes to her. As he passes by their window he seems to slow down and look up. She feels a slight burning sensation on her face and the skin of her abdomen, a sweet allergic kind of sensation, like she has eaten one too many strawberries. And she knows that it is nothing much, nothing that won't pass digestively. Still, she is relieved to think that he must be looking for Robin. When he sees Sarah in the window, he falters for just a moment and then raises one hand in greeting, like a traffic cop, perhaps perfectly serene in his faith that this one hand will be powerful enough to keep him from being smashed flat. She watches him as he jogs ponderously down the street and disappears around the corner.

She is up till dawn thinking it out—why the unjust, when the just would do as well? She gazes through her bedroom window and she begins, at last, to believe that in the movements of the clouds, the ups and downs of the sun, the ravings of the birds in the morning, she can see what's going on, that she has started to read some of the secret purposes of nature.

Sarah is not surprised when she comes home one night to find the jogger outside their door on the second-floor landing, playing the cello. She walks by him without a word and lets herself into the apartment.

"Hey!" he calls out to her indignantly as she shuts the door behind her.

Robin is sitting dreamily on a chair in front of the open refrigerator. Every once in a while she leans forward and pulls a little corner off of something and eats it. "Your friend is outside," she says in a muffled voice. "You know, Max, the runner."

"Please don't pick like that," Sarah says. "It makes my skin crawl. Just take something out and eat it. A whole thing of something." Sarah knows that this request will not be honored. Robin needs to pick as a way of getting around her mother, who is now dead. But in order to please Sarah she tries. She slowly carries a whole cantaloupe on a blue-and-white plate over to the sofa and lies down and cuts herself a tiny slice. She takes a rest and after that she eats another tiny slice. In the hallway, Max stops to tune his cello and then starts up again. Sarah shifts her gaze and stares in fascination at the pattern of blue-and-white roses marching around the circumference of the chipped plate. She understands that the noncausally related objects in the area around you will generally confirm the true state of your mind. They might even predict the culmination of things if you know how to pay attention. Sarah imagines that she will be able to read the whole ruthless future here in these roses and she rejoices grimly at the power she thinks she is beginning to muster over all these secret things.

"I hope you looked for a job," Sarah says, certain that Robin has barely moved all day, knowing how easily she is transfixed now by motes of light or little cracks in the wall.

"Actually, I've been very busy, but I can't take just any job, you know. I can't concentrate well and, besides, I have to keep my feet off the ground."

Sarah knows better than to ask why this is so. "Well, then I hope you looked for a job where you can keep your feet off the floor."

"I suppose you mean a paying job. There's lots of ways to get paid, you know. I'd work for certain valuable sorts of information."

Sarah comes and stands behind Robin's head and pulls gently on her long, almost black, hair. "What is it you would consider valuable information?"

Robin looks up at Sarah and says seriously, "Well, for one thing, I'd like to know if there really are accurate records kept of everybody's good and evil deeds and to what use these records are put and I'd also like to know what happens when you die. Though there's other ways to get paid. For instance, Martin Burnbauer, my ex-husband, used to often barter the jewelry he made for things he needed—vegetables or beans. Once he got a wisdom tooth extracted in exchange for a silver bracelet."

Sarah frowns in annoyance and lets go of Robin's hair. "I don't want to hear about that creep, Burnbauer. He's gone now and good riddance. Why do you always want to be talking about him?"

A fat tear, blue against the light of the plate on her chest, slips down Robin's face and dangles clownishly from her chin.

"Oh my God, how can you cry for that worm?" Sarah yells.

"I'm not crying for him!" she shouts. "He wasn't a worm! He rescued me from my mother in the nick of time and he was the moon and the stars to me, but I'm not crying for him anymore. I'm crying because something's been pinching my toes."

Sarah sighs. She checks the floor for any sign of demon hands coming through the linoleum, but can't see any. How had they become friends in the first place? She is irritated by the mystery of this, by what it implies about the limits of what you can know of your own desires and needs. She sits down at the bottom of the sofa by Robin's feet. "But the question is, did you look for a job today?"

Robin is closely examining the air over Sarah's right shoulder. "You think I'm out of my mind, don't you?"

Sarah shrugs. "That's the general idea."

"But you can't imagine what I can see from this vantage point," she says grimly.

Sarah, unable to stop herself, twists her head to see what Robin is staring at. There's nothing there.

"Your friend is out in the hall, you know," Robin says.

"What do you mean, *my* friend?" Sarah says indignantly. "He's no friend of mine."

"I had a very interesting conversation with him through the peephole. His name is Max and he says he was born with a tail."

"Swell."

"But they operated on it when he was a baby and took it off."

"I hope he put it in a glass jar and preserved it."

"I don't know if he did. He didn't tell me that. But we had quite an interesting conversation and he warned me not to fall in love for a while because it might interfere with my convalescence. He said that people who are in love are the most perishable things in the business."

Sarah cuts herself a slice of cantaloupe from Robin's plate and lifts it to her mouth angrily. The cantaloupe is very ripe and has that pungent, gluey taste, reminiscent of love. She thrusts it away from herself. "One of the best things you could do for yourself is to stop talking to strange men."

"You don't need to worry. His squatters were talking about food. You never need to worry when they're talking about food."

"What are you talking about? What squatters?"

"You know what I mean, those invisible things that hang around people's heads. I call them squatters. Max's were talking about food. He's perfectly safe."

"Oh yeah? Well, what about the tail? 'Never trust anybody with a tail' is my motto."

"Don't worry," Robin says.

The last crab apple blossoms in the park give up the ghost to a breeze and Sarah and Robin are sitting quietly listening to the cello when the perfume reaches them a few minutes later. Robin stirs restlessly as if she scented her mother's grave, but Sarah takes it without flinching.

Later in the week the heat drops down over the city like a net. Sarah stands at her bedroom window and watches the street. The Midnight Hour Social Club bursts into music and one of the plainclothesmen stretches and goes off and comes back in a little while with an ice-cream cone. She wonders what propitious moment exactly they are waiting for to make their bust. Whether she feels sorry or not for the poor sniffling junkies she cannot tell. Now there is a slow parade of movement down at the corner and soon Max is galloping forlornly by in a pair of red running shorts.

"Faster!" Sarah yells out to him tauntingly and the plainclothesman, who is licking ice cream off his wrist, looks up at her window suspiciously.

Sarah calls the Midnight Hour Social Club and tells them that their loudspeaker is keeping the whole neighborhood awake and that they should turn it down. They ask if she is the person who called last night. If she is, they say, she should be on the lookout for death. Then they hang up.

On Saturday Sarah cajoles Robin into getting up off the sofa and going with her to the laundromat. As soon as they get there Robin promptly sits down and props her feet up on a box of Cheer. She looks on calmly while Sarah loads the clothes into the machines.

When Sarah is done, she comes over to Robin furiously. "Stop being such a lump! You've got to get up and move around and do more. Don't you understand how unhealthy this is?"

"Don't be silly, Sarah. I move around plenty. I have a whole other life you don't see."

Sarah rolls her eyes at the ceiling. "I'm talking about your body. I'm talking about getting your blood moving. You've got to get out there and look for a job."

Robin smiles. "I'm on top of that, Sarah. Really. I'm thinking about trying to get a job in a nursing home. I've wrestled with a lot of fat, greasy devils and I think I might be able to help people prepare for the big time—dying, I mean."

Sarah pictures Robin going around propping everybody's feet up on boxes and stools. But now Robin is staring fixedly into the back recesses of the laundromat. Sarah turns to follow her gaze, expecting to see nothing, but there is Max. He is explaining to a little boy that he is from outer space and has grown from a benevolent pod. He tells the boy to look inside his ear and see if he can see the blue lights. He says that where he's from, people's heads are full of blue lights, not brains. He leads the boy over to the doorway and points up to the sky where he lives, in case the boy ever wants to visit him. Then he saunters over to Sarah's and Robin's bench and somehow manages to sandwich himself into the space between them.

"Hello, hello. How are you?" he asks, addressing either.

Sarah looks away.

"Sarah isn't sleeping well because of the loud music and I've been plagued by something evil creeping around on the floor lately," Robin says.

"I know just what you're talking about."

Sarah whips around and glares at him, but he seems not to notice. He, too, stares at some invisible spot in the air overhead. His expression is lustful, but kind.

"I found it in my car."

"What?!" Robin shouts.

"It's true. It's true. I know this will sound incredible, but I was driving around late last night and suddenly I had this feeling that there was someone or something inside the car with me."

"Where were you going?" Sarah asks suspiciously.

He looks at her coolly. "That doesn't come into the story. Assume I was joyriding. Assume I was out for a little air or something."

She flushes and drops her gaze to his funny shoes.

"There I was and suddenly I had this feeling there was something in the car with me and I called out, 'Who's there?' —very loudly to put whatever it was on the defensive, but there wasn't any answer. I tried looking over into the backseat, but I couldn't see anything. Finally I panicked and pulled the car over to the curb and jumped out. I waited on the curb for something to happen, but nothing did. I waited a long time, but then finally I walked over to the car and looked inside. There, on the front seat, right next to where I had been sitting, was this watermelon."

Sarah looks up and is startled to find his brown eyes, half closed, fixed on her. "It was inexplicable," he says sternly. "There was no way it could have gotten into the car. But there it was. What was I supposed to do? If it was a joke, it was the worst sort of joke. I opened the door and rolled it across the seat and let it drop onto the pavement. Then I drove away quickly, but I felt claustrophobic and had difficulty breathing as if the car had filled up with smoke."

The way he's staring at her, she gets the feeling he thinks she's the one who did it.

"I hear you're a lawyer," he says blandly. "It must make it hard to sleep at night seeing the wheels of justice turn so slowly. How do you feel about all those murderers and rapists getting off so lightly?"

She stares at him in disgust.

"Oh, oh," he says. "I've offended you."

"I'm a public defender."

"Don't tell me you're one of those guys who thinks everyone's innocent."

"It's probably more to the point to say that I think no one is innocent."

At this moment, one of Sarah's machines bursts open and everything—soapsuds, water, sheets, towels, underwear and socks—comes spilling out onto the dirty cement floor.

Sarah feels this indignity keenly, as if somehow it were her fault, as if this laundry all over the floor spelled out a secret and grave inadequacy, a lack of sexual poise or knowledge of how to talk smoothly at parties.

Max and Robin help her to shove it all back in. Also the little boy helps eagerly, handing up dripping panties and socks, one by one.

Then the man who owns the laundromat comes in, not a nice person, a densely fleshed man, who obviously holds all these furtive humans with their sacks of dirty laundry in great contempt. Sarah knows just what she must do. She marches over to him and tells him what has happened and that he must make sure the catches on the doors are kept in better repair. He looks at her as if she were a juvenile delinquent.

"You didn't shut the door. If you'd shut the door the way you're supposed to shut it, it wouldn't open in the middle of the cycle."

"I banged the door shut. I shut it as shut as you can shut it."

"You banged the door shut? You banged the door?" He advances on her menacingly. "That's why these machines are always breaking down. People like you banging the doors."

"The door wouldn't shut. I had to bang it."

"This is what I mean. If you don't shut the door properly, it will open in the middle of the cycle. This is not the laundromat's responsibility."

"You should get the doors fixed so that normal human beings can shut them."

"Nothing wrong with the *doors*."

Sarah sits down on the bench trembling with rage. Robin

and Max, leaning up against a spinning washer, look like they've noticed nothing.

When Sarah gets up later to load her clothes into the dryer, she shuts the door and before she even has a chance to put her money in the slot, the dryer begins to turn all by itself.

Furthermore, she's not the only one this is happening to. As she looks around the laundromat she sees that people everywhere are discovering that their dryers have been liberated. Stuck in the round window of each one is a black feather.

Suspicious, she looks around for Max and finds that he is standing right next to her. "How is that done?" she asks angrily.

He shrugs. "Oh, it's easy, I imagine. You just stick a little wire strip in the slot. A bobby pin might do it." He smiles at her lazily, first with just the corners of his wily eyes, then more slowly with his wide mouth. "I know a good place to go dancing," he says. "Would you and Robin like to come with me tonight?"

Sarah's not fooled by this. "You can have her all to yourself. I have a brief to write."

But Robin, of course, will not go either. She says she has plans to make and as soon as she gets back to the apartment, she lies down on the sofa and begins to make them.

For a week Sarah does not see Max and she doubts that Robin could be seeing him either, for she appears entirely disabled by her thoughts. When Sarah leaves in the morning, Robin is lying on the sofa staring spellbound at what appear to be ordinary, empty patches of air. When she arrives home in the evening, she is still there as if she hadn't moved all day.

During this week, as the northern half of the planet tips closer to the sun, the streets and sidewalks appear to shudder and shift with heat. But at night, as Sarah stands at her window and looks at the soft black sky speared on the towers and antennas of the buildings, she feels her other heart, the standing-apart, direct-as-gravity one, the one which even in the midst of anxiety and indigestion and disappointment always remains cool and responsive, takes note of beauty and memorizes it, recognizes justice when it comes, she feels that one coming out more and more certainly, like a pale, far star.

She is on her way home from work on Monday night and just passing the Paris Movie Emporium, where couples are welcome, when Max turns the corner in her direction. She tries to go around him, but he grabs her hand and steps up very close as if he were going to steal her purse.

"Well, did you get him off?"

"What?" Sarah says, standing rigidly, ignoring her own hand in his. "What?"

"Don't be funny. You know what I'm talking about. The one you were writing the brief for the night I asked you guys to go dancing. Did you get him off?"

"Oh, him. Yes, I got him off. Did you go dancing?" and, here, she manages to wrench her hand free. She is very relieved, like she has just safely pulled it out of a glass jar filled with bees.

He grabs the other hand. "Don't you ever worry about some of these people getting off scot-free?"

"I've seen many people go to prison who needed something a lot different than several years in a tiny cell to heal them of what ails them. I worry about that a lot more." She takes the other hand back and looks up at the evening sky. It is a clear, darkening green and she has the impression that it is, somewhere, full of stars.

"How's Robin doing?" he asks.

"She leaves in a week. I gave her a month and she has apparently spent that month lying on the sofa. Her time is almost up."

Here he steps forward anxiously and stares into her eyes. She tries to stare back at him without flinching, but feels him poking around in there, searching for God knows what. Afraid that he will look into her heart and see Theresa there in her tiny cell lying on her cot and know how she herself has failed, she closes her eyes and takes a step back.

"You're a real tooth fairy," he said sadly. "What did you want her to get done in one month?"

Sarah is furious, but keeps her composure. "She'll never have any idea of what's going on out there until someone pushes her out. Nothing can get through that fog of hers as long as someone keeps giving her the opportunity to lie on their sofa."

"You don't really know that," he says worriedly. "Sometimes you can't see what friendship is doing for somebody. It works invisibly."

"Ha," she says. "Why, next thing I know you'll be telling me about hardened criminals who suddenly turn into balls of stardust after years of infamy and roll home to make soup for their mothers all because some friend stood by them."

"That wasn't what I meant."

The movie this week at the Paris Movie Emporium is *Schoolgirls' Recess.* As she turns away she sees him staring unhappily at a large poster photograph of a young girl lifting her blue-and-green Catholic school uniform to expose her childish rump.

When Sarah gets home she is surprised to find Robin lying on her back on the sofa grating a carrot over a plate on her stomach.

"What are you doing?" Sarah asks in a threatening voice.

Robin turns to her smiling. Her cheeks are pink with exertion. "I'm making carrotballs for dinner."

"Carrotballs!"

"Martin Burnbauer, my ex-husband, used to make them. They were good, but I can't remember what all the ingredients were so I'll have to improvise."

"Well, I'm not going to eat them, you know. You're just making them so you can wallow in your memories of that creep, Burnbauer."

"Martin was a king."

"He was a creep and a hustler. He exploited and abused you."

"You're misinterpreting things. You didn't like him. I liked him. Besides which, you're not getting enough sleep, which clouds your judgment."

"Those are voodoo carrotballs, aren't they? You probably put some of Martin's leftover hair in there, didn't you?"

Robin laughs.

"I'd like to remind you that you don't have much time left to find some work."

"I've decided to take the test for the fire department."

"The fire department test is extremely difficult and they're very selective. You have to be able to climb hand over hand to the top of a fifty-foot rope and then slide down, plus a lot of other difficult endurance tests."

"No problem," Robin says from where she lies on the sofa. "I'm feeling very strong."

Sarah, reflecting only idly on the injustice that gives Robin so much love and attention and leaves her with carrotballs, is surprised to find the thick stem of her own heart snap and flood. She turns away quickly so Robin will not see, but Robin, quick as a whip, grabs up a pepper shaker from where it is sitting on the floor nearby, and starts flinging clouds of pepper into the air over Sarah. "Take off, you demons!" she shouts. "Don't worry, Sarah, this usually routs them!" Sarah stands meekly, sneezing and weeping, while Robin wages battle.

When Sarah passes by the Paris Movie Emporium the next evening, she notices that the pictures on the billboards have been changed and she looks at them curiously to see what the new movie is to be about. Stuck in the top of one of the billboards is a black feather, and she is taken aback to find that all the new pictures are cutouts from women's magazines: banana-cream pies, brides, babies in diapers.

She and Robin sit out on the stoop that night and, to Sarah's disgust, she finds that all up and down the street, everyone is talking about the Black Feather. On this stoop there is a mother and baby from the third floor and some old ladies who fan themselves with tabloids. On the sidewalk in front of them, four men have just unfolded a folding table and are playing cards.

Sarah is juggling for the baby with an orange, a tennis ball, and a small white leather shoe that has dropped off the baby's foot.

At first the conversation here ranges far and wide as if they could look into a glass ball and see all those tiny, sinister Russians lining the streets of Moscow or as if they could zoom right into the living room of that family where the little boy pushed his sister out the fifth-floor window, but eventually it comes round to the Black Feather.

"He makes Sarah want to spit," Robin says confidentially to the old ladies.

"Why's that?" asks the young mother, listening in.

Sarah lets the objects she is juggling fall to the ground and she glares furiously at everyone on the stoop. "Because these are just childish revenges. If you want to make people kinder and better behaved toward each other you have to make them feel welcome in the world. Revenge just makes everybody dig themselves in deeper."

"Well, I don't know," says the young mother, "sometimes I think it cheers people up and lets them get on with things."

"Oh, boy," says Sarah. "Don't you see this Black Feather guy is probably just making greedier people greedier and dangerous people more dangerous? And he's certainly not doing anything to further his own course of self-improvement."

"How do you know he's a he?" asks one of the old ladies scornfully.

Sarah shrugs, but the baby, reclining on the stoop in a paper diaper, stares up at her with that perspicaciousness of those who speak no language. Blushing, she picks up the orange, the tennis ball, and the baby shoe and begins to juggle again. For a moment, the objects hang shining and suspended in the light of the streetlamp. She sees the plainclothesmen in the shadows staring suspiciously into the air at these flying items.

In the last week Sarah has given her, Robin lies on the sofa counting softly under her breath. Sarah wins three more cases and at night she stands at her window and sees that the city, at heart, is really only constructed out of little dots of light. Toy trains twinkle in the distance around the elevated tracks and disappear. Would I cross that bridge when I came to it? she wonders. That little hammock of fireflies?

By Friday evening she has decided to tell Robin it is time to go. When she gets home Robin is sitting on the sofa with her feet stretched out in front of her on a stool. She is watching them narrowly as if they were an enemy force. Sarah, in the ominous heat, moves around the house irritably, banging and sweeping and dusting.

"Do you remember my mother?" Robin asks. "All she did all day long was squeeze cantaloupes and change toilet-paper rolls and throw out spoiled food. Do you remember what she looked like? Like a big gray squid. That's what's happening to you."

"Oh, I don't think so," Sarah says, distracted by the thought. She insists that Robin get up off the sofa and take a walk with her around the Ukrainian street fair, which is just opening its week of festivities tonight. Before she goes out, Sarah puts on a soft lavender-colored skirt and a white blouse and goes to look at herself in the mirror to see if she does look like a squid. She is taken aback to find that she has entered on one of those unaccountable phases of great beauty and she turns away fast as if she has seen a spook waving at her shyly from a cloud of light over her head.

Robin is in the kitchen inspecting the inside of her sneaker.

"What are you doing?" Sarah asks.

"My shoes feel slippery."

"Well, put some talcum powder on your feet and hurry up about it."

In spite of the heat, there are hundreds of people jammed into the three-block street fair. Stalls lit by strings of colored lanterns line the streets and the summer dark lends to the scene a grim, fairylike purpose. The smoke from the sausages and deep-fried pastries thickens the air. Religious articles lean over the counters and beckon to them—red-daubed and thorny saints, the Virgin Mary posed as if for a graduation picture in her nimbus of light.

At the end of the street is a raised platform skirted with a cloth decorated in twining birds and flowers. The folk dancers twist around in a speeding circle. Against her will, Sarah feels her hopes rise. If she cannot have love, at least she has within her the power to stand up to the anarchy and disorder of the world, to name what is fair and bear it company.

Behind her she hears Robin cry out as if she saw something coming too. When Sarah turns she sees a little boy, perhaps four years old, standing in front of them, stock-still in terror. Obviously lost, he scans the crowd desperately with dark, bright eyes. He seems to feel instinctively, like a bird that has flipped prematurely out of its nest and crashed into the grass, that he had better not move. He whimpers and tries to look around without moving his head. He is dressed to kill with a plastic sword tucked into his black pirate sash and a red bandanna tied around his head.

Sarah is tempted by doubt as she stands there. It seems to her that she sees the expanding and contracting universe replaying this scene, mercilessly, again and again. At last, however, she takes a step toward him. Out of the corner of her eye, she sees Robin step forward too. Before they can reach him, his mother appears.

They know she is the mother because she is holding in her hand a plastic pirate ship. Her pink sundress is too tight and the straps cut into the soft flesh over her breast. She is scanning the crowd desperately and her eyes are strained with fear, but when she sees the child at last, all emotion seems to drain out of her face. It goes dead and white. She rushes over to the boy and grabs his arm and with the back of her hand, slaps his face.

"Didn't I tell you to stay with me?" She slaps him again. "Didn't I?"

The little boy, at the sight of the white, blank face bending over him, closes his eyes. He whimpers each time she hits him but, other than that, stands quite still. The tiny sight of him standing there without resistance drives his mother into a fury and she slaps the side of his head.

"Do you hear me? Do you hear me?"

He nods yes, but doesn't say a word. He is concentrating on some far black sail on the blue horizon.

Sarah hears Robin give a long low hiss, but when all the breath is gone from her lungs, she seems to slump and turn away. Although this scene is taking place right here, off the curb, the space surrounding this mother and child appears theatrically bright and far away, and the great crowd on the street seems to squint and lean forward as if they watched from a high balcony.

Someone has to explain this to me, Sarah thinks. These terrible gaps in the world with no pity in them. How all around the earth tonight there are little rooms noisy with pain where torturers crush their victims' kneecaps and how great a distance we bystanders have to travel before we can open our mouths to say a word.

Sarah sighs and steps toward them. "Excuse me," she says to the woman. "I think maybe you're making a mistake. This little boy was lost and he was looking for you."

The woman stops what she's doing and frowns at Sarah. She writes her off with a glance. "You got any children of your own?" she asks and, without waiting for the answer, turns back to her son. She digs her fingers into his arm and shoves the pirate ship into his hands. His fingers curl around it automatically and he is dragged away.

Sarah stands there furious and mortified. The woman seemed to be implying that she could read a secret truth about Sarah. Some hidden barrenness maybe, or inability to hold a man. She walks back through the crowd, her face burning.

She and Robin wander slowly up and down the street examining the things for sale on the tables. They are standing in front of a table overflowing with a jumble of stuff—spatulas and tablecloths, flea collars and key chains—when Max comes up to them. "Very Ukrainian," he says, picking up a plastic cup filled with assorted screws and nails, six for a dollar.

Robin beams at him, but Sarah tries to freeze him out with an icy stare. He tags along with them happily. Sarah, in a fury, decides to leave them behind in the crowd. She weaves her way in and out of knots of people until at last she finds herself alone, standing in front of a lemonade booth. She buys herself a cup. It is freshly squeezed, with honey and ice, and, as sometimes a food or drink can, for a moment it perfectly answers her thirst and loneliness. Recklessly, she buys herself a second cup and, of course, is suddenly struck with the thought of Theresa imprisoned in this heat without the possibility of such succor. She drops the full, sweet cup into a trash can and turns away.

There, in front of her, is the plump child abuser and her pirate son. The woman is examining a potholder in the light of the streetlamp. The child stands next to her, perfectly still, his face swollen with crying, his eyes straining at some invisible spot up in the shadows.

Sarah turns her gaze away for a moment and so misses what happens in the next few seconds. When a whispering and tittering begins in the crowd behind her, she thinks at first it must be for her, that everyone has noticed her immense sadness, but when she turns she sees that after all they are laughing at the pirate boy's mother, who is suddenly standing there in just her panties, her dress lying in a circle around her feet. She is looking in moonlike bewilderment at the laughing and gaping crowd. It is a difficult sight and Sarah understands why everyone laughs. She thinks how the human nude never lends much glory to the landscape, not like a tiger or a python would, or even an everyday horse, standing in a meadow; it's too soft and hairless a thing, too tipsily bipedal. And this human in particular is so pale and biscuitlike in appearance that the crowd cannot help but be convulsed with hilarity.

But when the woman suddenly understands that she is naked, it becomes a different matter. Before their eyes she seems to blow up into a supernaturally huge and furious figure, a crimson-faced banshee or vampire. She shrieks something foul at the crowd in a strange and hellish-sounding tongue and they fall silent waiting for her to burst into flames.

However, what happens after all is that her lower lip begins to tremble and tears spring into her eyes and she leans over to pick up her dress. When she tries to arrange it back over her shoulders she finds that someone has neatly razored open the shoulder straps and neatly razored a long slit down the back.

Here, a man bends down and picks up the black feather where it has fallen and lain covered by the dress and Sarah groans in shame for everyone. When the man tries to hand it to the woman, she knocks it away and it falls back to the ground. She holds the dress around herself as best she can and hustles the little boy in front of her and out of the crowd.

Max, of course, is leaning against a car watching the scene calmly and Robin is standing next to him. In a minute everyone is laughing and chattering again as if the world was after all just an elephant standing on the back of a turtle, a finite and knowable place. The children, grossly innocent and particularly joyous, pretend to be the fat woman, sketching her breasts in the air and replaying, again and again, her discovery of her nakedness. The adults laugh at the children and the folk dancers swing around very fast. Sarah watches Max closely from the corner of her eye. He looks sleek and content. His eyes are half closed.

She storms over to him in a fury. "And what do you think will happen now?" She watches him carefully for some betraying sign, but he merely opens his eyes a little wider and stares at her in surprise. "Whaddaya mean?" he says.

As his brown eyes meet hers she feels her skin turn pink and then dissolve, no doubt leaving all her internal workings clearly revealed.

"To the child!" she shouts at him and tries to hold his gaze so that he will not look down and see her intestines shining out eagerly. "What do you think will happen to that child now? Why, she'll probably just take him home and beat him up some more, out of pure spite and misery."

He frowns and seems to think this over. "Well, that may be true," he says slowly, "but then, on the other hand, people have to tell each other things, don't you think? You can't be a witness to such things and not speak. If you don't, your heart dries up."

"I have blood in my shoes," Robin says suddenly. She has been shifting miserably from one foot to the other for several minutes now.

"What do you mean?" they both say to her sharply.

"Well, I don't know. I've been feeling something slippery in there all evening and now I've realized it's blood."

"Show me," Sarah orders.

Robin bends down obediently and takes off one of her shoes. She holds it up to the light to show them. "See," she says.

The shoe looks slightly sweaty, but there's not a trace of blood.

Sarah stares at Max as if this, too, were his fault. Then she looks at Robin. "Tomorrow your time with me is up, you know," she says gently. "You've got to go."

When they get back home, Robin goes into her room and shuts the door quietly behind her. Sarah stands at the window in the dark and watches the street. She knows what to expect. She's running it wide open and light, aboveboard. She's getting a grasp of the inner nature of things and a street like this holds no secrets from her. At ten-thirty the plainclothesmen appear to take their places in their doorways. At twelve, the Midnight Hour Social Club's loudspeaker comes on. At twelve-thirty, Max goes by.

At twelve-thirty-five, the moon appears over the vacant lot, silent and critical, white and cool. Sarah greets it sternly, without even blinking. At twelve-forty, to her astonishment, Max comes galloping back up the street with a bouquet of flowers in his arms. Without even thinking about it, she leans way out to stare at him, unable to make head or tail out of the meaning of this.

He stops at the bottom of her fire escape, smiles up at her and grabs hold of the ladder which someone has foolishly left down. The plainclothesmen stare at him sleepily as he climbs up to her window.

"Well!" he says as he jumps, with a thud, into her room.

She takes a quick step backward and finds herself in the dark, out of the light of the streetlamp.

"Why aren't you sleeping?" he asks accusingly.

She is certainly furious at this intrusion, but she also feels caught in a curious tight spot—as if at the very brief space where the tide changes, both helpless and languorous, about to be thrown back up on the beach.

"Insomnia," she says briefly.

"Aaah," he says. "That would explain several things. I suppose the music from across the street doesn't help either, does it?"

She doesn't answer him.

The streetlamp hovers at his back like a pink alien space-ship, so while his outline glows brightly, he is otherwise dark and faceless. She breathes very deliberately, wanting to keep her reflexes sharp, but this plan backfires. The air is filled with an overpowering scent of summer leaves and pollen and her head swims. When, at last, she takes a step forward, she sees that it is because of the big, feathery, plucked-looking bouquet of flowers.

Well, he is surely in love, she thinks wistfully. He is standing there looking smug and yet defenseless, the way you look when you undertake to crawl up out of the sea onto land for the first time.

Sarah hears Robin open her bedroom door and step into the hallway. "Well, go ahead," Sarah sighs. "There she is."

Sarah goes over to the window and looks out. The moon is now riding high over the tenements and the street is caught in its steady, penetrating light. Nothing will escape. It holds everything transfixed with its baleful, white glance. It seems to her she's been standing here looking out this window into the moonlight for a long, long time, when Max, whom she'd thought years gone, says sadly, "You've been misunderstanding me, I think. I brought these flowers for you."

At first these words only get to her in the way small matters do, like flies at a picnic or a shoelace coming undone or someone saying, "Please pass the pepper." And even as she realizes, with a lurch, what they must mean, and even as she is wondering, with that curious thrill with which one wonders such matters, what his kisses will be like, she knows that this will come and this will go, and maybe it will be a sweet matter, but it won't be of much importance.

Sarah is pleased to find herself so lightly snared and she thinks about how not only is the world no longer considered to be a finite place, lodged solidly in the heart of a bright-faced God, it is also no longer considered to be an infinite place, constructing itself endlessly out of an endless variety of chances and accidents. No, nowadays, it's supposedly the organization itself of the world which is so magical, which throws off stars and gases, which creates its own energy and falls into dust and then rises up out of the dust even more terrible and complicated. She is eager to win as much power and influence as she can over the secret nature of these things.

Plainclothesman Number One shakes himself and walks off to get his nightly ice-cream cone. Plainclothesman Number Two saunters over to the vacant lot to take a pee. He wades into the tall grasses and the moment he disappears, a dark figure detaches itself from the shadows below and races lightly across the street toward the Midnight Hour Social Club. This hooded figure, sure of itself and fast, has in its hand a long, pointed instrument and, for a second, Sarah's heart stops, thinking she recognizes Theresa's bloody knife, but then she sees it is a screwdriver.

Sarah wants to yell out some warning, but doesn't dare for fear of adding any more dangers to the situation. And, indeed, in a moment a couple emerges from the club. The hooded figure hesitates only briefly and then steps back into the shadows. The couple is not dancing now, but that they have been dancing recently is easy to tell for their feet skip a little and the man is snapping his fingers. The woman is dressed in a full, red skirt which is only now beginning to deflate slowly. Sarah holds her breath in terror lest they turn around, but their eyes and ears must still be ringing and they walk happily to the corner through the loud music and disappear.

Instantly the hooded figure leaps from the shadows again and dashes toward the loudspeaker, which is propped high in the window just out of reach. It leaps up and stabs the speaker once, twice, three times in the guts with the screwdriver and suddenly the street is silent. The figure pauses for a moment, hand in pocket, then drops a black feather to the ground and turns and races back across the street.

Suddenly Sarah finds herself urgently sleepy and yawns a big yawn. "Did you realize it was her all along?" she asks him irritably. She can barely keep her eyes open.

"Sure," he whispers and now he leans forward and touches her cheek with just the tips of his fingers. They feel cool and smell sweet from the stolen roses and foul from the daisies plucked out of vacant lots. "I saw her take that lady's wallet in the supermarket. Besides, who else could it have been?"

Sarah just manages to reach out and brush his cheek lightly with her sleepy fingers.

In a minute they hear Robin reenter the apartment and close the door to her room.

"You're not really going to throw her out tomorrow, are you?" he asks.

Then, only mildly astounded to find that *this* is the place she gets caught, she says, "No, of course not."

"I knew you wouldn't," he says gently.

She yawns right in his face and, smiling, pushes him out the window onto the fire escape.

Even before he has reached the bottom, she has fallen into bed, knowing that this may be the last holy moment for a long time and that it is not given to her to know just where the next will come from.

She acknowledges grumblingly to whoever hovers in the air over her head that although she may have within her the power to stand up to the anarchy and disorder of the world, she actually has only the most limited authority over that power. It will choose its own times and will behave erratically in accordance with some impenetrable plan. All she can do is be as ready as possible to make good.

Then, turning her face against the cool pillow, she is swept out toward the far morning on a wide, untracked river of sleep.

# JANETTE TURNER HOSPITAL
# THE DOMINICAN SEASON

FROM COSMOPOLITAN

∽

IT'S THAT TIME again, the Dominican Season I call it. They come into my office alone, they have an air half eager, half furtive, they have in their wallets a card with a lawyer's name on it. The Dominicans. (I give them that label privately. I have actually inscribed it on the appropriate folder, a black one, in my vertical file.) November always shakes the Dominicans loose.

I suppose that this is what happens: About the same time winter is humming its first cold notes, all the girlfriends and mistresses in the land turn to their married lovers and raise their soft soprano voices in seductive harmony. Wouldn't it be nice, goes their singing whisper, if we could spend this Christmas together *legally*? And wouldn't it be nice to spend a few days right now under sun and palms, to get away from it all right now, while the last leaves are falling and your wife is applying pressure? And besides, their sweet melody goes, I've heard that in the Dominican Republic, where they serve piña coladas on the beach and where the off-season rates are a steal, I've heard you can get a divorce in twenty-four hours and it's legal here.

Well, who could resist?

Anyway, I can spot them in the first five minutes.

They walk in under the glowing sun-laced octopus logo, SUN WORLD/WIDE WORLD (that's us), they stand in front of my desk, they fidget. Dead giveaway, right there. People planning a normal vacation, adulterous or not, don't fidget. Smile to themselves, yes; smirk, daydream, browse through brochures on paradise. But not fidget. The Dominicans fidget because they've been warned that the whole operation is chancy; the timing might not work, the bribes may be too subtle or not subtle enough, the judge may be off on the circuit-court rounds or just off fishing. And there's also this: Who else plans a tropical vacation in *November*, for God's sake?

Oh, the Dominicans are easy to pick. Take this one walking in now, five feet eleven or so, absolutely nothing special about him, a completely unremarkable man, except that a lick of tow-colored hair keeps falling across his forehead and he keeps pushing it back. As always, this mannerism causes me agitation. (Question: How is it that an intelligent woman, mother of an eight-year-old daughter, successful travel agent, divorced but surviving, emotionally mature, etc., etc., can be unnerved by a meaningless bodily tic? By some total stranger's habit of pushing his hair out of his eyes? Answer: This is a mystery in the same category as the useless existence of the appendix in human beings; or the problem of the emu—why is it called a bird if it can't fly?—or the riddle of the sphinx. Moral: Avoid men in whose presence, for impenetrable but potent reasons, you cannot behave rationally.) Some women, possibly, would consider this man attractive. I won't quibble.

I do not go to the counter immediately. I seem to be absorbed with my computer terminal, the entering of flight numbers and travel dates. The man with the tow-colored hair is not a good waiter. He fidgets. He takes a business card from his wallet and looks at it. (The lawyer's name: S. Barbarra, Santo Domingo. Or possibly W. A. Gualtieri. Or maybe another I don't even know about.) He looks at his watch.

"Can I help you?" I seem to have only just become aware of him.

"Ah, yes." He has a nervous boyish grin that some women might find attractive. Even very attractive. "I suddenly find myself with five days available for some R and R. I, ah, a friend has been telling me there are some great deserted beaches in the Dominican Republic this time of year."

I say dryly, "This time of year, there are great deserted beaches pretty well anywhere."

He laughs. "You have a point. Fact is, the slack periods for an accountant never coincide with the best times for the beach."

An accountant; it figures. I've noticed this before, how Fate is not the impassive blindfolded lady she's supposed to be. Not for a minute. She's malicious, she's devious, she's like that teacher I had in the fifth grade who humiliated me by reading aloud to the class a note I had written (but had no intention of sending) to a boy I was crazy about. That kind of sadism, that's what gives Lady Fortune her kicks.

Perhaps it's because I'm at the five-year mark. All the articles say it takes five years. So here I am like a rat in some sadist's laboratory maze, almost through the experiment, almost at the safety point, and some guy walks into my office and flicks his hair out of his eyes the way Simon did. Grins the way Simon grinned. Even goes so far as to be an accountant. And we're going to pretend Fate is neutral? In this week of all weeks? This week which is five years almost to the day when Simon came in with the papers?

"It'll make Christmas easier for both of us, don't you think, to have it all over and done with? And there's this quick way, a lawyer friend explained it, if I fly to Santo Domingo . . . I just need your signed consent, that's all."

And so, of course, I signed. What else was there to do?

Mostly, I'd say, I've coped extremely well, though I had a very bad month when he remarried. It was the unseemly haste that got me and the bits I picked up from Laura, who naturally had to go to the wedding and who volunteered that Daddy looked so happy. It's tricky, Laura's chatter. I feel it would be as wrong to forbid it as to pry (never even a temptation with me, I so strongly want to know nothing), but I find almost any news unsettling. I just change the subject as quickly and unobtrusively as I can. Anyway, on Sundays he picks her up from a neutral place, my sister's, so I don't have to see him. I haven't now for years, we alternate at school occasions, it's worked okay.

And here I am where it almost doesn't matter. The five-year mark.

"The Dominican Republic," I say to the man in my office. "Yes, there's a place called Juanita de la Mar that I'm sure you'll find convenient. Right on the beach." And close to the judge's private chambers; so I've heard from satisfied clients. This is an esoteric little corner of the travel business in which I happen to be an expert.

"Well," he says, surprised and relieved, "I think that's the very place my friend mentioned."

"I'm sure it is. Our clients find it entirely convenient for their purposes. Reservations for two?"

"Uh—alas, I'm traveling alone on this one."

"Five days in a tropical paradise *alone*?" (Why should they get off scot-free? Make them squirm a little, I say. It evens the score, if ever so slightly.)

Still, usually they take the usurper along for the Dominican fling. He does look uncomfortable, this one. Perhaps he's different from most, who are indecently eager to get on with their rearranged lives.

"Usually," I say (why should I spare him?), "my clients— even though they often have business to attend to while they're in Santo Domingo—usually they manage to take someone along, a wife, a girlfriend." I pause, then toss off, "For some reason, with my clients, it's mostly girlfriends, but girlfriends who have the look of wives-to-be."

"To tell you the truth—" He falters, but thinks better of it. Shrugs and laughs. "Accountants," he says, self-deprecatingly, "even their vacations are dull."

So I make the reservation for Mr. James Whitby, I print out his airline ticket, I reserve his seat, nonsmoking, aisle, 8B. "Long legs," he says, and grins, raking his hair out of his eyes. "Just about kills me if I can't stretch them out in the aisle."

Well, I think after he leaves, it has been noted before: that one may smile and smile and be a villain. And I endow him with a bewildered wife who is even now leaving her infant son with his grandmother for a day or so, just to tide her over a small stint of falling apart. It's no big deal, it happens every day, perfectly decent people find themselves inflicting ghastly damage on others, everyone knows this. Nobody understands it.

Maybe, given a different set of circumstances, I could have done it myself, who knows? I try to rearrange the past mentally, to see Simon drinking too heavily in bars, pushing maudlin confessions across a beer-sloppy table at total strangers. But his wedding interferes, and Laura's artlessly honest comment (such an adorable three-year-old flower girl she had made!): "It was *fun* at Daddy's wedding, and Daddy and Cindy and me danced a dance! When can I visit Daddy and Cindy again?"

I don't try to figure things out, I just stay busy. Sex and love? It's so much easier to unsnarl the timetables of Punjabi railways for adventurous retirees or to plot connections true to the microsecond for jet-restive businessmen.

Still, there are certain aspects I give careful thought to. A single parent with a single child, there are risks, grave risks, no question about it, and the risks are nearly all on the child's side. There's the temptation, for one thing, that the parent will draw too much physical comfort from the child, too many hugs and kisses—and children give so generously, so thoughtlessly. I think about this risk a lot; I'm grateful in many ways (and resent it like crazy as well) that Laura has such good times with her father. And every once in a while, over dinners with reasonably promising men (businessmen, usually; clients whose travel affairs I handle; married, invariably—I'm not crazy, I can only handle the safely unavailable), I drink an extra glass of wine to relax, I accept the inevitable invitation to the hotel room, we have sex. It's okay, sometimes it's even great. Sometimes I actually enjoy it and glow a little the next day. But it's strictly because of Laura, part of a strategy. To keep my hand in, as it were. So I won't turn, well, whatever—bitter, dried up, *peculiar*.

I wouldn't say I have any answers. I wouldn't say I have any useful words of advice for the wife of James Whitby, Dominican. But I've gotten through five years, more or less. It's something. So I don't know why, right now, I should feel so—unstrung or why my hands should be shaking or why I should feel so unbearably restless, so physically restless, that in fact I have to ask Joe to handle everything for the next fifteen minutes (I employ three people, part time, so there's always someone to cover). I find I have to walk around a city block or two.

It's this ridiculous sense of *anniversary*, I conclude. And the aforementioned snicker of Lady Fortune, who gets turned on by playing with mirrors and circles. It's the five-year itch, the last flare-up of the disease before I'm immune. After this, who knows? I might even end up inviting Simon and Cindy in for drinks when they come to collect Laura.

But right now, the itch is bad. It is manifesting itself as a craving, an obsession to understand. To know why and how someone like James Whitby, who is probably ordinarily decent and reasonably sensitive and perfectly kind 99 percent of the time, whose hair falls across his forehead in a particular way (a particular meaningless but devastating way), to understand how such a man can casually undo in a few sordid minutes (I understand that's all it takes, finally) the careful structure of years of intertwined living. Because, after all, any marriage, even one gone sour, is at least that, is at least an architectural wonder whose dismantling, it seems to me, should have—well, at least dignity, a sense of ritual, a touch of the tragic perhaps, maybe even a little pomp and circumstance.

So I pace the block one more time to see if the obsession will pass of its own accord. Then I go back to my desk and make some calls. First to my sister, and yes, she can, and yes, a break in the sun will do me good. The rest I could do backward and upside down.

I book a nonsmoking window seat, 8A. I always do like to see where I'm going.

"Don't I know you from somewhere?" he asks. Perhaps it's his usual opening gambit, though he does seem genuinely perplexed, searching back, pushing that cowlick out of his eyes.

"Lesli Jacobs," I say, raising a sardonic eyebrow, implying that this was clearly what he was after. (A whole week has passed since he walked into my office; who remembers bank tellers, store clerks, travel agents seen a week ago?)

James Whitby looks embarrassed, unfairly accused of improper advances. He stretches his long legs into the aisle. He picks up the folder showing what to do if the plane nosedives into the ocean, and reads it studiously.

Not until the first round of drinks has settled and the lunch is being distributed in its dinky trays does he suddenly turn and say, "Hey! It's just come to me. The travel place. You're the girl who did my tickets."

"Woman," I say primly. "The woman who did your tickets, though I do employ a girl and two young men. It's *my* travel agency. I own it."

"You booked the seat next to me on purpose." His tone is accusatory.

I say coolly, "At the rate I do business, it's difficult enough remembering the customers, let alone their seat numbers. Or do you feel there's some law against travel agents' taking nonsmoking window seats?"

"No, of course not. It's just—such an odd coincidence."

"It's actually rather common for travel agents to check out the resorts they recommend."

He looks sheepish, raking his fingers through that lock of hair. "Put that way," he says, and laughs nervously, "you must think I'm a bit of a—I'm terribly jumpy lately. I really need this break, I guess." He grins. "Drinks on me when we get to Juanita de la Mar? Will that make amends?"

I am about to relent, possibly even to confess, possibly even about to get maudlin about five-year anniversaries, except that his forearm, coming into contact with mine along the divider between our seats, administers such unexpected sensations to sundry nooks and crannies of my body that I find myself sounding like a prim and proper feel-by-numbers businesswoman who is a bit, well—*peculiar*. I sound, in fact, as if I have arrived smack in the middle of that fate which the strategically planned candlelight-dinners-and-sex are designed to save me from.

"Actually," I say, "it *is* a working trip. Collecting data for the Association of Travel Agents. I try not to mix business and pleasure."

The boyish grin surfaces and is quickly checked. He says levelly: "That must surely be rather difficult when your business *is* pleasure."

"You'd be surprised. At least fifty percent of the travel I

arrange is for reasons other than pleasure. This particular assignment, for instance. It's to check out a new service the association is thinking of offering. Would you believe that droves of people fly to Santo Domingo purely to get a speedy divorce?"

"Good grief," he says, and a wavelet of Scotch flings itself out of the thin plastic airline glass.

I raise innocent eyebrows. "That shocks you?"

"Well—" He rearranges his long legs around the stewardess's trolley and insists on intercepting the meal tray and passing it over to me. The maneuver takes all his concentration.

"This divorce gambit," I say, relentless. "We hear the arrangements have to be made in rather unorthodox ways, but the divorce itself is quite legal in the U.S. My job is to find out how it's done, so we can handle the increasing number of inquiries about it."

He is attacking the miniature steak and the pebble-size roast potatoes. He takes what I can only describe as a gulp of red wine. He clears his throat. "To tell you the truth," he says, "that happens to be the very reason I'm making this trip myself."

"No! Are you serious?" I bring the back of my hand dramatically to my forehead. "But that's marvelous. You'll be able to tell me all the details." I turn to him and place my hand on his arm, the light touch of a woman in perfect control of the situation. "Of course I haven't the slightest right—" I bat my eyelashes. "Still, if you didn't mind, it would be enormously helpful."

"Sure," he says awkwardly. "Why not?"

"I suppose this is a great relief? Finishing things off so neatly and quickly?"

"Well, I—" He gulps some more wine. "Yes, I guess it is."

"We're also preparing a profile," I say (this is very therapeutic, watching him bolt down his food and wine as though it will give him a disease if it stays in his mouth more than one second), "of the kinds of people who might use this service."

"Oh?" He looks at me warily. "And what are you finding?"

"Well, when I say we, I mean the association's marketing and research people. I don't really know what they've come up with yet. Not my area. My job is to find out the actual complications—"

He is not the type who gets chatty about private distresses, not even on a plane after drinks, when most people become astonishingly self-revelatory. After a rather lengthy silence, I prod, "This is where I'm hoping you'll help me. With the nuts and bolts of the procedure. The hows. Maybe the whys."

He laughs. "If I knew that—"

For some reason, my palms are sweating. "You're having second thoughts?" For some reason, my sense of balance seems to depend on his answer.

"Doesn't everyone?"

"Apparently not. Some men remarry within days of the final decree."

"Oh, as to that," he says, "there are certain kinds of momentum—" He goes to refill his wineglass, is disproportionately dismayed that the bottle is empty, signals for another, mutters, "Damn, I could do with a smoke if I hadn't quit," and then restlessly slides out from under his tray table, knocks off a fork, strides down the aisle toward the bathrooms.

I breathe in a deep breath of triumph. Enjoy your heartburn, Simon, I say to his restive back. And then realize with a little shock what my thoughts are up to.

Don't push your luck, I think as I stand on my balcony looking out at the palm-beribboned ocean. Settle for small triumphs. Settle for the likelihood that even Simon had uneasy moments. Any day now you'll be able to forgive him. In a month or so, you could meet him for lunch maybe and discuss riding lessons for Laura.

Consider this trip as genuine R and R, I instruct myself, and go for a walk on the moonlit beach. Begin to enjoy things for their own sake again. You haven't gone under, Lesli, you haven't done badly, I'm proud of you. So now that the survival business is behind you, forget revenge, forget blame, *forget.* Open up and enjoy a little.

So I go for my walk. I sink my bare soles into the damp sand, I let the waves froth around my ankles, I climb the dunes, I sit at a table on a patio under palm trees and order a piña colada with an orchid blooming at the lip of the frosted glass. I smooth my long hair back over my shoulders, catch a reflection of myself in the waiter's eyes, feel good.

As I sip, I become aware of the intense pressure of a stare. Out of the corner of my eye, I can see a man two tables away. He is making no pretense at subtlety. The weight of his eyes is like the force of the sun at noon on a Santo Domingo beach. I hear his chair scrape on the patio flags, hear his footsteps, see the shadow. He is at my table. "Mind if I join you?"

The voice, the face. It is Simon, and I am unable to speak.

"I wanted to surprise you," he says. "It was tricky on the plane." I am afraid to look in his eyes. "Look," he says, "I know it was all my fault. Five years of insanity, but it's over now. Can we start again?"

But of course when I lift my eyes, it is just as I feared. There is nothing but a sea breeze moving through the frangipani blossoms. The same tired old fantasy.

"Hey," James Whitby says, tapping me on the shoulder in the murky bar called the Mermaid's Cavern. "You're awfully hard to find. How about that drink we agreed on and a progress report on my adventures with a tropical judiciary?"

Suddenly, I want nothing to do with him, nothing at all. I've been recuperating; long solitary walks on the beach, long swims, I am almost okay.

"It was really brash of me to intrude on your private affairs," I say. "I don't know what I was thinking of. And really, the drink is unnecessary."

"Not at all, not at all. I was behaving damned rudely. Besides, it will be a pleasure."

I get up to leave. "Thank you. But, in fact, I do have another appointment."

"Oh, damn." He looks quite ludicrously disappointed and is raking his fingers through his hair at a furious rate. "I could do with someone to talk to. Get drunk in front of. I tell you, this whole thing is going to drive me out of my mind. Only twenty-four hours left and I haven't even located the judge yet. I've run out of gifts of imported Scotch. I'm going out of my mind."

"Tough," I say, before I have time to censor myself. "A divorce should cost a little."

He looks startled. For whole seconds we stare at each other, and then I turn and walk out of the bar.

I zip closed my suitcase and carry-on, check the drawers one last time. And then the phone rings.

"Lesli? James Whitby. Listen, I know you think I'm a jerk, but this is urgent. Crucial. Our plane leaves in two hours, right?"

"Right."

"Please just hear me out. Just as one human being to another. Will you do that much?" His voice is manic, stretched as tight as violin strings. My mind races: He's been picked up by the island police, charged with bribery. Or with some more obscure, fabricated crime. His panic passes through the receiver like a virus.

"Where are you?" I ask. My heart is yammering in my ears.

"Sandor village. Take a cab eight miles east of the city, go left at the main village intersection, past the big white house, past some fields. It's the house with the rubber tree growing practically all over it, looks like the magic beanstalk."

"I'm on my way."

I don't know quite what I expect: police, terrorists, kidnappers? Some chickens are scratching under the rubber tree; a group of nearly naked children shriek a welcome, swarm on the cab, guide me into the house, past some wicker furniture, into a kitchen dominated by a huge ancient white-and-chrome refrigerator. A woman is seated at the Formica table, writing, a couple of men lounge against a wall, someone sits on the sink counter. James Whitby, who seems charged with high-voltage energy, knocks over his chair as he rises from the table where he sits opposite the writing woman.

"Thank God you got here. If I miss this plane, I can't see Williams and Epstein, Accountants, making any more allowances." He indicates the room with a sardonic sweep of his hand. "The judge's chambers." The gesture ends with a flourish in the direction of the woman at the table. "And the judge." He raises his eyebrows expressively. "At the last minute they inform me I have to have a witness who can vouch for my identity. Her Honor will show you where to sign."

I feel as though I am sleepwalking. I sign as instructed. Her Honor flicks on a cigarette lighter and holds a stick of sealing wax over its flame. A red blob falls on the document and dribbles across it like blood. She presses her signet ring into the blood clot, rises, presents the document solemnly to James Whitby. A bottle of champagne is broken open, poured into paper cups, and passed around.

"My God," James Whitby says shakily, laughing a little. "It's done. I'm divorced."

"Congratulations," I say. "Should I kiss the ex-groom?"

We only just make the plane. In fact, they have to lower the stairway again to let us on. After the first drink, I turn to him and say with the kind of superclarity and distinctness preferred by drunks and nervous wrecks: "That was very, very sordid."

"It was," he agrees.

"But I want to shake your hand." I am very solemn. I shake his hand in the way of a pompous chairman of the board concluding a deal that he is going to deny in the press. "You have released me. You have broken a spell. Anyone capable of snuffing out a marriage in a few seconds like that is not worth crying over."

"You're probably right," he says. "I'm sure you're right."

We drink steadily throughout the flight. We both leave our cars where they are in the overnight lot at La Guardia and take cabs home to our respective addresses.

Two days later, I call my sister.

"I'm cured," I tell her. I mean of the past, which has hung on like a bout of mono for five years. "I'm going to call Simon and suggest he pick up Laura at my place. I'm sort of interested to find out if I even like him, or what."

"That's great," my sister says. "I knew if you gave it enough time—But listen, this means there's a vacuum—the space you kept for Simon all this while. It's a dangerous time. Be careful." My sister knows. She's into her second marriage.

"Don't worry." I laugh. "Now that I'm finally off it,

there's nothing in the world that would tempt me back on that roller coaster."

"Just be careful," my sister says.

And I do remember her words, though only fleetingly, a day later when I look up to see James Whitby in my office. He flashes his boyish grin, rakes his fingers through his hair. "Look," he says, "I know this is crazy and can only lead to trouble. But I just keep thinking that for someone as sordid as me—I mean, when two people have shared such an *intimate* experience as divorce—I wondered if I could take you out to dinner tonight?" And suddenly I understand why we never learn, why we never have the sense to stay off the roller coaster: because nothing feels so deliriously, dangerously good as that first stupid but trusting leap over the edge.

# SARA LEWIS

# TROUBLE PEOPLE

## FROM SEVENTEEN

∽

ON THE DAY of the season's first football game, there was a pep rally at Alameda High. The three classes competed to be the loudest-cheering grade in the school. The cheer for Ernie Baird's class was "V-I-C-T-O-R-Y, we're the '86 seniors, watch us fly." The cheerleaders on the field were screaming so loud that their faces were red and the veins in their necks stood out. Ernie sat quietly, waiting for the rally to be over and for the lunch period to begin. He was not into sports, and if he had had any school spirit, he would have tried not to act like a jerk about it. Still, for the rest of the day, that stupid cheer rang in his ears as if it were some song he had heard too many times on the radio.

On his way home from school, Ernie stopped at Sanchez's place. Sanchez lived one house down the hill from Ernie and his mother. For five years, since Ernie was twelve, he had been doing chores for Sanchez: getting the mail and feeding the cat while Sanchez was away and gradually taking over the gardening as Sanchez's arthritis got worse. Tomorrow, Sanchez was leaving for New York, so he was going to tell Ernie what to do while he was gone.

Sanchez opened the door before Ernie had a chance to ring the bell. He had on a loose white shirt, khaki pants, and huaraches that squeaked when he walked. Ernie had once bought a pair of huaraches, too, but they hurt, and he didn't have the stamina to break them in.

"First of all," said Sanchez, leading Ernie into the kitchen, "Ted is on a diet." Ted was the cat. "Just give him a half can of Pet Pantry with a small handful of Kitty Crunch mixed in and about a teaspoon of warm water to take the chill off. No Cat Snax and no milk, no matter how much he begs you." Sanchez reached out to stroke Ted, who lay asleep on a kitchen chair. "You little minx," he said.

Sanchez walked into the living room, beckoning Ernie to follow. Like the house where Ernie lived with his mother, Sanchez's had a living room with big sliding glass doors so that you could see all the way down the mountain, into the valley, over a hill, to the freeway, and out to the ocean. Looking out, Sanchez said, "Sometimes, I hate to leave it," and rubbed his hands over his face, as if wiping it clean. He turned again to Ernie and, pointing to the ferns hanging in the window, said, "These, you'll observe, are new. They need a lot of mist." He reached behind the curtain and pulled out a spray bottle, aiming at a fern and squeezing it twice, to demonstrate.

"Okay," said Ernie, "lots of mist for these guys."

Sanchez gave him a nod. "The plants in the bedroom should be watered and fed on Wednesday or so. You remember how to do the fertilizer, right?"

"Sure, I know," said Ernie.

"It won't rain anytime soon, so stick to the regular watering schedule for outdoors. Then there's just the mail."

"Okay. Have a good trip," said Ernie, heading for the door.

"Thanks. And listen. You can use the stereo, but I might bring someone back with me, so neatness counts. Bernice will clean one time, the week I come home, but let's make that an easy day for her, shall we?"

"Right," said Ernie. "I'll make sure I cover my tracks."

Whenever people asked Ernie what he was going to do next year, after he graduated, he said he didn't know yet. But that wasn't quite true. When he'd gone to visit his father in New Mexico last summer, Ernie had asked for a loan to start a business. He wanted to rent a storefront in Santa Cruz to sell T-shirts and fabric silk-screened with his own designs. His dad had said no to the loan, saying that art school or college would be a better idea. Ernie had been mad for a while, but then he'd thought of Sanchez. When Sanchez came back from New York, Ernie planned to ask him for a loan. He had a whole bunch of samples of his work all ready to show Sanchez. Ernie was pretty sure the answer would be yes because Sanchez liked him a lot.

The next day in Government, Ernie was watching Frances Waters. She was probably the reason Mr. Wood was assigning partners for the oral report, rather than letting people choose their own partners, Ernie thought. Frances wore dumpy clothes that made her look middle-aged at seventeen. ("Where does she *get* those sweaters?" "Are those industrial-strength nylons?" Ernie had heard other girls say about Frances.) She had droopy breasts, too, and a little bit of a mustache. She was smart in school. The only thing wrong with that was that she hadn't learned that you didn't have to shoot your hand up in the air every time you knew the answer, and if you knew something that wasn't in the book, you didn't necessarily have to share it with the class. Ernie had his own problems—he was fat—but at least he knew how to behave in a socially acceptable manner, in a way that meant if the class had to pick partners, he would get one.

As if Mr. Wood were punishing him for these thoughts, Ernie got Frances as his partner for the oral report.

Frances slid her desk over next to Ernie's. "I've already thought of a topic," she said. "We can go to the library this week and check the *Readers' Guide* for recent articles." She pulled a notebook marked GOVERNMENT PROJECT out of her book bag. This is going to be intense, Ernie thought. Do I really deserve this?

The topic Frances had picked was the pollution of the beaches of their town by the oil drilling off the coast. Other people wanted that topic, too, but Frances had managed to clear it with Mr. Wood first. The report was only supposed to be fifteen minutes long, and they had a month to work on it. Frances wanted to get started right away.

Saturday, Ernie watered everything inside and out and misted Sanchez's houseplants. Then he cleaned Sanchez's garage. "I wish you'd work that way over here," his mother would say, if she knew what he was doing. Ernie had brought his homework so that he could spend the rest of the day here. He put his U2 album on the stereo. At home, there was no stereo, so Sanchez let Ernie bring his records over when he was taking care of the place.

Sometimes, Ernie toured the rooms, looking at Sanchez's things, always careful to leave them just as he found them. Sanchez had owned an art gallery in New York before he sold it and moved here to retire. He had paintings by several artists whose names Ernie recognized. Sanchez had even bought a couple of pieces from Ernie's mother, who was a potter. He had paid a lot more than she usually got at the People's Craft Center, where she worked part time and sold most of her pieces.

Ernie sometimes looked in the old desk in Sanchez's bedroom and at the piles of letters in its little compartments. He had taken some of the letters out of their envelopes, his heart pounding hard, as if Sanchez would suddenly appear from South America, Europe, or Oakland and catch him. Some of the letters were written on thin, blue paper in Spanish, which Ernie couldn't understand because he took French. Others contained descriptions of new artists and their work and sometimes newspaper clippings.

In Sanchez's closet were some clothes that Ernie wanted to try on: a tuxedo, a cashmere sport coat and a pair of herringbone pants that had been made in England, and a stack of ironed pajamas.

Sometimes, Sanchez brought Ernie presents when he returned from trips. Ernie's favorite was a box of "trouble people" from Guatemala, six tiny figures in a wooden box. At night, you were supposed to take out one doll to represent each of your troubles, according to the Guatemalan Indian tradition. While you slept, the people were supposed to solve your problems. Ernie tried it once when Ted ran away for three days. It worked: Ted came back the next day, skinny but unharmed.

Ernie did more work for Sanchez than he got paid for. Last year, when Ernie planted the rosemary he found in flats behind the garage, Sanchez called him a prince. He said, "You have added years of life to these old knees." Ernie couldn't wait to hear what Sanchez would say when he saw the clean garage.

As soon as he got home, Frances called to ask if Ernie wanted to get together to make an outline for their report. "I think my mom's going out, so I won't be able to use the car," he said.

"I have a car," said Frances. "Where do you live?"

When Frances arrived, Cynthia went to the door. The first thing Frances said when she walked in was "I love your house, Mrs. Baird."

"Call me Cynthia," said Ernie's mother, smiling. "Let me show you around."

There wasn't much to show, Ernie thought, but his mother always stretched this out. She started with the view out the living room window, saying it was the reason she rented this place twelve years ago. Recently, the valley had filled up with houses, a development called Rancho Vallejo. Farther away, Cynthia pointed out, were the offshore oil derricks. "Gradually," she said to Frances, "a lot of ugly lights are appearing where there used to be the most peaceful darkness."

"Geez," said Ernie, rolling his eyes, but they both ignored him.

Cynthia showed Frances every room in the house and took her out to the garage, which she used as her studio. Then Cynthia gave her a slice of pumpkin bread, and Frances asked for the recipe. When there was a slight pause in the conversation, Ernie said, "Hey, pardon me, but if we're not going to work on this report, I might as well split."

As soon as Frances had finished a half-hour description of the work she wanted Ernie to do, she walked over to his mother and said, "It was a pleasure meeting you, Cynthia. I hope you'll be here next time I come over."

Ernie waited until he heard her car start before he shouted, "Next time? *Next* time? You try to be a little nice to someone, let her come over and study, and before you know it, she wants to move in."

"Oh, calm down," Cynthia said.

"You made it worse. If I wanted you to adopt her, Cynthia, believe me, I'd just come out and say it."

"I was just trying to be nice."

"To *her*, yes, very nice. But what about your own flesh and blood? And what happened to Ray? I thought you had a date."

"He canceled." Cynthia had been seeing Ray, on and off, for seven years. He was married, so she could never be sure, until the last minute, whether he would keep a date.

On Career Day, Ernie ditched a senior assembly—a program called Choices in that morning's "Alameda Announcements"—to do some watering over at Sanchez's place. He was out back trimming the wisteria when a car pulled into the driveway. A minute or two later, a guy about Cynthia's age came through the living room doors into the backyard. Ernie froze for a moment, then said, "Hey."

"How ya doin'?" called the intruder. "I'm George Sanchez, Jorge's son." Ernie wouldn't have believed this, except that the man looked exactly like a young Sanchez. "So you're the one who keeps everything looking so nice, huh?" George stretched out his hand for Ernie to shake.

"Ernie Baird. I live up the hill. I work here," said Ernie.

"Well, thanks," said George. "You've done a great job." He paused for a moment, looking around the yard. Then he looked down the hill at some distant point, maybe the antenna of the radio station downtown. He rubbed his face in the same gesture Sanchez had made a few weeks ago. He seemed to be trying to think of something to say. "I'm afraid we've had some bad news," he said finally. "We lost my father a few weeks ago."

"Sanchez?" said Ernie. "He died?"

"Yes. It was very fast, though. He didn't suffer. It was a heart attack. He was on his way to New York. My wife and I were going to meet him at the airport."

Ernie didn't say anything. Sanchez had been dead three weeks. The last time Ernie saw him was almost the last day he was alive.

"Listen," said George, "I'm sure my father appreciated all your work. The place looks great. But for the time being, I'd rather you didn't do anything else, okay? Thanks. Say, do you have a key to the house?"

"Sure I do," said Ernie.

"I'd like to have it, if you don't mind."

Ernie reached into his pocket for the key. "But what about Ted?"

"Ted?"

"His cat. Sanchez's cat. I feed him."

George thought a moment. "Would you like to take him home?"

"Sure, but I couldn't," said Ernie. "My mom doesn't like cats."

George said, "I'll figure out something, then."

"There's one more thing," said Ernie. "I have all my records in the house."

"Okay," said George. "I'll help you get them out."

Ernie got a box from the garage, and they loaded it with albums. Ernie showed him where Ted's food was. "Now," said George, walking Ernie out to the front steps, "how much did my dad owe you?" He reached into his pants pocket.

"Nothing," said Ernie. "He paid me before he left." This wasn't true, but Ernie just wanted to go home now. Halfway down the driveway, he turned around. He wanted to say something else—that Sanchez was the coolest old guy he'd ever known or that the ferns needed to be misted today—but George was already closing the front door.

Cynthia was out in her studio when he got home. It wasn't until Ernie told her about it that the fact of Sanchez's death started to sink in. "I think he died on the plane," he said. Then because he could feel his lips quivering and tears beginning to form in his eyes, he started for the house. As he turned, he suddenly pictured a very young Sanchez, standing with George as a small boy in front of a hamburger stand on a hot beach.

Cynthia said, "I'm so sorry, honey." The sound of her sympathetic voice infuriated Ernie for some reason. He wanted to turn around and tell her to shut up and leave him alone. But he was already crying too hard, so he kept walking and didn't say anything at all.

Frances had done so much research that their presentation lasted over half an hour. Ernie was embarrassed to sit in front of the class with her. He let everyone know this by acting as if he wasn't very familiar with the material, even turning to Frances once and saying, "What am I supposed to say now?" Everyone laughed, and Frances seemed to enjoy turning the pages of his notes for him and pointing to the right spot. The rest of the report was slightly comical, too, with Ernie acting disorganized and a little clownish and Frances behaving like an efficient schoolmarm. They both got As. Ernie was relieved when it was over.

At lunch, Ernie was standing with two other guys, waiting for the cafeteria to open. Frances came over and said, "Let's celebrate finishing our report, okay? Why don't you come over to my house for dinner sometime?"

One of the other guys said, "Pfff," and turned to face the lunchroom windows, covering his smile with his hand.

"Well, maybe, sometime," Ernie said

"How about tonight?" said Frances.

"Tonight isn't the best night for me."

"Thursday night, then?"

"I'm going to be really busy with some things for the next few weeks," said Ernie. "Maybe next month."

"Okay," Frances said and walked quickly toward the library.

When she was out of earshot, Ernie said, "Try me again in my next life," and the other two guys laughed. A few times during the afternoon, he thought, I hope she didn't get too bummed out.

One night the week after Christmas vacation, Cynthia came home early from a date with her boyfriend. Ray was not Cynthia's type, in Ernie's opinion. Besides the fact that he was married, he was a very straight guy, an advertising executive. Ernie couldn't figure out why she had never married his father, Gary, who was a photographer, an artist like Cynthia.

Ernie was making chocolate chip cookies when Cynthia slammed the front door and threw her keys into the ceramic bowl on the hall table. Then she turned on the TV, which was strange, because Cynthia hated TV. Ernie came out of the kitchen to see what was going on. Cynthia was sitting there in the dark. She still had her coat on. "Ray is moving to Chicago," she said. "With his wife."

In the light of the television screen, Cynthia's face looked

blue and a little ghostly. It was wet because she had been
crying. Ernie wanted to dry his mother's face with the dish
towel he was holding. Instead, he said sharply, "Ray is a
creep, anyway. You're better off."

Cynthia leaned her elbow on the arm of her chair and
covered her eyes with her hand. If Ernie hadn't known the
situation and couldn't hear her sobbing, he might have thought
from the way her lips stretched across her teeth that she was
smiling.

The phone rang. It was Frances. "Hi," she said.

"Hello," said Ernie.

"How are you?"

"Fine."

Frances paused, then said, "So what's been happening?"

"Nothing."

"Have you applied to any colleges for next year or
anything?" she asked.

"No," said Ernie.

"Oh. Well, would you like to go to a movie Friday
night?"

"Sorry," said Ernie. "I have a date." This was a lie, but he
had to get rid of her.

"I'm not doing very well, am I?" she said.

The following week, Cynthia stayed home and talked on
the phone a lot. She told the people at the Craft Center that she
had the flu, and as far as Ernie could tell, she didn't go into
her studio, either. When he came home from school in the
afternoons, the morning paper was still in the driveway and
Cynthia was lying on her bed, though he knew there was
nothing wrong with her except that she couldn't stop crying.
She put boxes of tissues in the kitchen, in the car, and on her
dresser, as if she planned to be sad for a long time.

Exactly one week after Ray told her he was leaving, Ernie
came home and found Cynthia practicing typing with a book,
*Ten Days to Better Office Skills,* propped up beside her. The
newspaper was open to the want ads, and several secretarial
jobs were circled.

"Don't you like your job anymore?" Ernie asked her.

Without looking up, Cynthia said, "It's not enough
money."

"I thought you said you'd never work in another office."
Cynthia didn't say anything. "Didn't you tell me that one
time? Cynthia?"

"I changed my mind," she said.

"How come?" said Ernie.

She stopped typing to stare at him hard. "Things are
different now." She said this through clenched teeth, moving
only her lips. "I'm going to do something else. Will that be all
right with you?"

"Excuse me for being concerned," Ernie said as Cynthia
turned back to her typing.

Accidentally, Ernie had just found out something: Ray
had been giving Cynthia money, and she had hidden this from
Ernie. He remembered sometimes seeing Cynthia's checks from
her job and from the sales of her work. It only occurred to him
now that they didn't add up to enough. The rent on their house
had gone up a lot since they moved in. "You're paying for the
view," the landlord always said when Cynthia protested the
increases. "There are cheaper places." To Ernie, it seemed
pathetic to accept money from a creep like Ray just to hang on
to a view.

All at once, it seemed to Ernie that there was a kind of
slimy lower layer beneath the surface of the people and events
that he knew. It had started with Sanchez dying on the air-
plane, and now Cynthia's taking money from Ray was another
part of it. He wondered if everybody else had seen this all
along. On the other hand, he thought, maybe he alone saw how
sleazy even the most normal-looking situation could become.

Cynthia finally got a job working in the office of a group
of lawyers. Every night at five-thirty, she would come home
and go straight to her room to take off her dress and high heels.
She would put on her bathrobe and pad around in her nylons.
Most nights, she didn't feel like making dinner, so Ernie would
make spaghetti or chili. Sometimes, Cynthia wasn't even hungry and would go to bed before nine.

Frances called again, at the beginning of the second semester. "I noticed you're in Wood's class this time, too, and I was
absent today. Did you get the assignment?"

"Yeah, hold on," said Ernie. "Pages 186 to 210. Write a page
about how city regulations affect your everyday life."

"Thanks," said Frances. "You know, you seem kind of down lately. I was wondering, would you like to talk about it?"

"No," said Ernie. "Bye." He hung up.

Sanchez's house remained empty through the spring. Cynthia had heard at work that George and another son were fighting over the place in court. Someone had closed all the curtains in the house. Ernie imagined all the plants inside, hanging on wires from the ceiling, all dead, probably a fire hazard. He wondered about Ted, but he had no way of finding out whether George had gotten him a good home.

This semester, Ernie's last at Alameda High, he had completely lost interest in school. He would write down all the assignments, but no matter how he tried to talk himself into it, when he got home, he couldn't force himself to do his homework. When he was at school, he hoped no one would say anything to him. In class, he hoped his teachers wouldn't call on him. Sometimes, just opening his mouth to talk seemed like too much trouble. When he tried to think about what he was going to do after graduation, his mind went blank.

Lately, Ernie was watching a lot of TV, even soap operas. Since Cynthia was gone all day now, Ernie found himself ditching his last class to come home in time for a show called "City of Dreams." The characters were always dropping in on each other, sitting at kitchen tables with mugs of coffee and talking about their problems. Ernie especially liked it when the people finally revealed terrible secrets, things they had kept hidden for years. He wished that he had a secret that he could tell someone and then feel better. But who would he tell?

One day, Ernie skipped school entirely. He dropped his mother off at work, then drove all the way down to Santa Barbara, where he ate a burrito under a giant tree next to the freeway. Then he drove a little farther and stopped at Rincon to watch the surfers from the road. He wished he could surf. He wanted to sit out there with those guys, wear a wet suit, float on a board, and know that eventually a good wave would come. On the way home, Ernie heard Bruce Springsteen on the radio singing "My Hometown" and had to pull over into the emergency lane to cry and blow his nose. He wondered if he would ever feel at home anywhere.

Close to the end of the school year, Ernie found out he was flunking geometry. His teacher kept him after class one day. "What are your plans for next year?" Mrs. Coehlo asked him.

"I don't have any," said Ernie.

"Why not?"

"I just haven't thought about it very much," he said.

"You know as well as I do that unless you do something drastic, you're going to stay right here at Alameda High." Ernie stared at her with the blankest expression he could produce, hoping she would give up and leave him alone. "Mr. Baird," she continued, "you have only turned in three homework assignments for this class, and you've failed two out of three tests. If you don't turn in three quarters of the homework and raise your test grades, I'm going to have to give you an F. I don't think either one of us would enjoy starting the whole course over again in summer school. We have a problem here, Mr. Baird."

"*We* don't have a problem, Mrs. Coehlo. *You* have finished high school and college. You've got a husband and kids and a job. I'm the one who's in trouble."

He could see Mrs. Coehlo fighting an urge to yell at him. "I'm giving you a chance to get yourself out of trouble. You can continue to do nothing. Or you can turn in the homework between now and two weeks from Friday and take the two tests the following Monday after school. If you need extra help before then, I'm in the teachers' lounge most lunchtimes." She picked up a pile of homework and her attendance book and left him staring at a poster of a Möbius strip on the classroom wall.

That night, Ernie woke up from a dream, turned on his light, and looked around for his box of trouble people. He just wanted to see them again. He took out four of them and laid them on the top of their box. They were dressed in pants or dresses made of strings and scraps of bright fabric. Their hair was made of black sand glued to their heads, and their eyes were painted wide open. "Help," Ernie whispered to them. He picked up one doll and said, "Geometry." Then he put it down, picked up the next one, and said, "My mom." To the third, he said, "A job." He held the last one in the palm of his hand for a moment before he whispered, "Frances Waters."

For the last weeks of school, Ernie started getting up early every morning and staying up late to do geometry problems. At lunch, he worked in the library, sitting in a back corner where no one could see that he was eating—two packs of little doughnuts covered with powdered sugar that he pulled, one by one, out of his backpack. At the end of two weeks, Ernie had finished all the homework he needed in order to pass.

On his way to Mrs. Coehlo's room the afternoon he was supposed to take the tests, Ernie walked past the temporary buildings, where all the language classes were. Frances was there, sitting in her car, listening to a Joni Mitchell tape and putting on makeup. She was looking at herself in the rearview mirror and concentrating so hard that she didn't notice Ernie leaning on a dumpster about fifteen feet away. She put on everything: eye shadow and mascara, stuff to make her cheeks pink, and two colors of lipstick, one on top of the other. She studied the effect from several angles, then spit on a tissue and wiped everything off. Ernie walked away then, thinking that it wasn't really fair to watch what other people did when they felt desperate.

He took the two tests back-to-back while Mrs. Coehlo sat at her desk eating a tuna sandwich and copying grades into a spiral notebook. When he had finished, she marked his tests as he watched—a 71 and an 83. "You did it," she said. Ernie didn't smile or say anything, but he felt glad that he had finally gotten himself out of trouble.

Frances was hanging around near Ernie's locker. She was wearing a flowered dress with puffy sleeves and a low, elasticized neckline. She probably made it herself, Ernie thought. "This is my final offer," she said. "Would you like to go to the senior prom with me?" He could tell by the way she said it that she had practiced to make her voice sound casual. It was a hot day, and Frances had big, wet circles under her arms. "I know these things are stupid," she said. "But we could make it fun. Would you go? Just as a goof?"

"Frances, I can't," Ernie said. "I almost flunked a class.

They wouldn't let me into the prom. I even got a letter about it from the activities office. I would've had to turn in a note from Mrs. Coehlo by last Friday, and she just gave it to me five minutes ago. But I have to be honest with you. I don't dance, and I hate to get dressed up. So even if I hadn't almost flunked geometry, I would have had to say no."

"Right," she said. "I see what you mean. Don't worry. I won't bother you again," she said walking away.

"I really am sorry," Ernie said. But she didn't turn around.

The senior beach party was held the day before graduation. Ernie wondered if getting to go was worth doing all those geometry problems; there was nothing good to eat. Near the hot dogs, Ernie spotted Frances. He was about to duck out of sight when he saw that several football players were teasing her. "Go easy on that champagne, Frances. It goes right to your head, you know," one of them said.

"Here, let me freshen your drink," said another, reaching toward her with a bottle of cold duck. Frances was holding her plastic cup at such an angle that champagne slowly trickled out onto the sand. It took Ernie a few moments to realize that Frances was drunk.

"Okay, guys," Ernie said, "that's enough."

"Oh, look, Frances, it's your hero, Ernie Baird, coming to your rescue."

"Leave her alone, Fremont," said Ernie.

"Sure, Baird, just watch out your girlfriend here doesn't puke all over you."

The group moved away, but an English teacher came over then. "Listen," she said. "The drinking age in California is still twenty-one. Get her out of here, Ernie, before we all get into trouble."

For a second or two, Ernie considered saying that he and Frances were not together. Then he said, "Okay, Miss Jackson. I'll take her home."

Miss Jackson started to walk away, then she turned around and said, "I hope you haven't been drinking, too."

"No way," said Ernie. "Want to smell my breath?"

"Not especially," said Miss Jackson, and she went over to relieve Jenny Rosenburg, who was taking instant photos of Senior Sweethearts for $1.50 apiece.

"Come on, Frances," Ernie said. "We have to go."

Frances sank down onto a picnic bench. "I can't go home," she said. "I'm drunk."

"I see that."

"My father will have a cow," she said and started to cry. Big teardrops rolled down her cheeks, and her face was turning red. "I feel terrible."

"Okay, okay," said Ernie. "You'll feel better in a little while. And you don't have to go home. We can go someplace else. Here." Ernie handed her a napkin to dry her tears, took the cup from her, and led her to Cynthia's car. His mother didn't need it that night; she had gone out with one of the lawyers from her office.

He took Frances to a party he knew about at Robert Crandall's house, in Rancho Vallejo. Crandall's mother had pasted up decorations in the family room—a large cardboard owl wearing glasses and blue silhouettes of a boy and girl in mortarboards. Outside, around the pool, Mrs. Crandall had strung paper lanterns, alternating with fake rolled-up diplomas. Ernie found lawn chairs for himself and Frances. Crandall was walking around in bare feet, faded jeans, and a Seafoam Surf Shop T-shirt. He gestured to the decorations. "Isn't this wild?" he said. "Hey, get yourself some food, Ernie, before the surfers get here and scarf it all up."

When he was gone, Frances said, "Could he tell that I'm drunk?"

"No, I don't think so. I'm pretty sure he couldn't." Then because she looked so sad sitting there, Ernie changed the subject. "So, Frances, what are your plans for the future?"

"College," she said. "I'm going to Cornell. That's back east."

"Oh?" said Ernie. "I have a brilliant career ahead of me also. I got a job at Taco Casa on Mesa Drive."

"You're not going to college?" Frances said.

"Don't look so shocked," said Ernie. "I'll survive. And who can tell? Maybe while I'm spooning beans into tortillas, I'll discover the meaning of the universe." They sat quietly for a few minutes, looking at the pool. The lights were on under the water so that it glowed aqua in the dark. Probably, it was visible from Ernie's house on Sierra Road, where no one was home to see it. "You know," Ernie said, "a friend of mine died this year, and a few other things happened. I guess reality kind of caught me by surprise, sort of sneaked up behind me and bit me on the butt. I used to think I knew exactly what I wanted to do. Now I'm not so sure."

"This year has been hard for me, too," Frances said. "But you probably know that." She looked down at her sandals for a moment. Then she said, "Sometimes, I am so lonely."

A few months ago, Ernie thought, it would have been embarrassing to hear this. Now he knew what she meant. He also felt protected by the fact that she was still a little out of it from the champagne. "Sure you're lonely," he said. "Everybody is. Why do you think people have parties?"

Frances appeared to be considering possible answers to this question. "So they won't have to feel so lonely?" she said uncertainly.

"You're absolutely right," said Ernie. "It's a very common feeling. But you're not lonely right now, are you? This is okay, isn't it, here at this party with me?"

"Yes," she said. "This is okay." A feeble little smile started to form on her lips. "I guess it is."

"I'm glad to hear that," said Ernie. "I feel okay, too, right at the moment."

Ernie got them each a plate of food from the table that Mrs. Crandall had set up in the family room. Then he went to the kitchen to boil some water. He found a jar of instant coffee and made Frances a cup, black, just like they always did on television, even though he knew from driver's ed that nothing makes a person undrunk except the passing of time.

They stayed at the party a couple of hours, until Frances felt sober enough to go home. Ernie even danced with her once, just to cheer her up. Then later, when he dropped her off at her house, he stayed to watch her walk up her driveway, unlock the front door, and flip one hand backward in a wave before he drove away. He couldn't quite figure it out: It wasn't as if now they were friends, exactly; they were more like two people who'd gone through some scary ordeal together—an earthquake or a shipwreck—and survived. He didn't pass any other cars on the way home, and he didn't even turn on the radio. He wanted to preserve the quiet.

The moon was so bright that Ernie went all the way up Sierra Drive without headlights. At the top of the hill, he stopped the car and got out to see if he could find the light of the Crandalls' pool. There were four pool lights on in Rancho Vallejo that night, but Ernie was sure he had picked out the right one.

# TODD LIEBER

# COUNTRY THINGS

FROM THE MISSOURI REVIEW

ॐ

IT WAS THE THIRD WEEK in July, nine days after my thirteenth birthday. My older brother, Cal, and I were walking beans, the temperature up around ninety and humidity just as high, the afternoon sun sharp as a welding torch. I came out of the field and saw our neighbor, Ken Harbison, in his pickup. I figured he wanted Cal, so I waved and started the next row.

"Arrow," he said, "come here."

My name's Aaron, but people call me "Arrow" because I'm built like one. Ken had a thermos of water and gave me a drink. He's not that old—fifty, maybe—but he's got arthritis pretty bad and has a habit of rubbing his hands together and staring at them, which he was doing. I looked past him down the rows we'd done, at the thick, dark beans and the sun-baked dirt stretching to our yard. In the shade of oaks and black walnuts, with the white rail fence around it, our house looked like a little oasis in the heat.

Cal came out of the field. "I swear," he said, "if the wind don't blow the plants around so you can't tell burrs from beans, the sweat rolls in your eyes and you can't see shit anyway."

He raised his shirt to wipe his face, and the muscles across his chest rippled and shone like corrugated steel.

"Boys," Ken said, "you're needed at home."

Well, it could have been any number of things. But I couldn't think which one of them would make his hands shake the way they did on the wheel. He could barely steer us over the culvert.

"I've known you boys since you were born, haven't I," he said. "Your dad and me grew up together."

"What happened?" Cal said.

"Knowed him all his life," Ken said.

Mom ran down the front steps when we pulled in the driveway and threw an arm around each of us. She'd been with the gilts in the farrowing house, and she smelled like pig and had dried afterbirth and iodine stains on her hands. She wasn't crying, but she had been.

Nobody knew what happened. Dad had been hauling big bales home and somehow the tractor wheel must have slipped off the road when he turned onto the highway. Someone passing had seen the tractor and baler trailer in the ditch and found him underneath.

"Where is he?" Cal said.

He was at one of the doctors' offices in town.

"Which one?" Cal said. "Don't you know?"

We were standing in the kitchen, Mom with her back to the sink, where the dishes from dinner were soaking. She'd had her hair under a kerchief, like she always did when she worked, but now she'd taken the kerchief off and was twisting it.

"How the hell can you not know?"

So he made her say it. "He isn't alive, Cal."

She tried to pull us to her again, and I let her hug me, but Cal wouldn't. He banged his fist on the table and the lid jumped off the sugar bowl. He opened a cupboard and slammed it shut. The phone rang and he picked it up.

"What!" he shouted.

He listened to whoever it was for a minute, then handed the phone to Mom and went down the hall to the bathroom.

After that the phone kept ringing until Mom unplugged it, and one neighbor after another, it seemed like, pulled in the driveway. Cal stayed in the bathroom a long time, and when he came out he'd washed and combed his hair. Maud Crutchfield was there then, holding a covered dish in each arm, and Cal got out Mom's folding bridge table and took the dishes from her. He stared at me.

"Quit it," he said. "Get out of that corner and be some help."

But I couldn't. The kitchen felt like 120 degrees, and something was rising and rising in my throat, like it would choke me if I couldn't get out of there. The first moment I thought nobody'd notice, I slipped outside.

I ran as if someone was chasing me, past the barn and the machine shed, down the lane, through the barbed wire, into the corn. In the field, I slowed to a walk and went along the edge until I came to a waterway. Dad had mowed it a couple weeks before and new grass was coming, a fresh green meadow winding up the corn like a river into wilderness. I walked in a ways and sat down. The sun wasn't blazing anymore, and the white sky had started turning blue and pink in the west. A breeze came up and rustled the corn. Some killdeer flew up the waterway to hunt, and I watched the lacy white border fan out under their wings when they swooped to the ground. In a while I could breathe again.

It was almost dark when Mom started calling. Her voice had to go around the corn, so it seemed to come from the other side of the field. It was high and soft, drawing out the syllables: "Ai-ai-rr-un-n, Ai-ai-rr-un-n." It didn't sound like her, but like some other, not even human voice calling me into the corn. Something in me wanted to follow it into the darkness between the rows. I let her call a long time before I started back to the house.

She was standing on the front porch, moths fluttering above her head in the yellow glare of the light.

"Where were you?" she said.

I told her I'd just gone for a walk. She put her arm around me, and we went inside.

Andrea, Cal's girlfriend, was there. Cal was supposed to be in training for football, but a bottle of Dad's whiskey was on the table and they were both drinking it. There was a glass at Mom's place, too. Andrea got up and gave me a hug.

"Oh, Arrow," she said, "I'm so sorry."

Andrea's probably the prettiest girl I've ever seen. She has long, curly hair and a little Dutch mouth that even now I still imagine kissing sometimes. She must have come right from work that night because she was wearing a red dress with straps instead of sleeves over her shoulders. Ordinarily I'd have let her hug me all night if she wanted to, but the whiskey on her breath made me want to get away.

She was sitting in my place, so the only one left was Dad's. I sat on the floor, and nobody said anything about it.

Nobody was saying much of anything. Mom asked if I was hungry and I said no, and a little later she sort of laughed and said she guessed she could plug the phone back in. Around nine-thirty, Ken tapped on the screen door.

"Charlotte?" he said.

Mom asked him to come in, but he wouldn't. The porch light was off and I could barely see his shape through the screen.

"I took care of your chores," he said, "If you need anything, just holler. We're here."

Cal said, "Thanks, Ken," and Mom whispered that she would. It was full dark and the crickets were loud.

I don't remember falling asleep or leaving the kitchen, but the next thing I knew I was in my bed. The sun was bright again, and a hammer was ringing. I got dressed and went outside. Cal was in the yard, under the bale trailer, banging on the front axle.

"Where's Mom?" I said.

"Still asleep. Let her be. I don't think she slept last night."

"Pretty hard to sleep with all this clatter," I said. "What are you doing?"

"Do me a favor. Raise that tongue up." I did, and he banged some more. "God, this son of a bitch is bent," he said.

He was wearing shorts—it was that hot already—and his sneakers and bare legs stuck out from under the trailer, his knees bent and flexed for leverage. The muscles of his calves bulged like footballs, the veins wrapped tight around them. I wondered what he'd do. He didn't *have* to go. He could stay and run the farm—he was old enough and knew enough to do it. Maybe he and Andrea'd get married and she'd move in with us.

He slid out from under the trailer, kicking up gravel. "Christ, it's hot," he said. He walked to the hydrant and I followed him.

"Cal," I said, "what are you going to do?"

"Fix that bastard enough to haul the rest of the hay home."

"I can see that," I said. "I mean what are you going to *do*?"

He spat into the dust and wiped his hands on his shorts. "I'm going to get the rest of that fucking hay home," he said.

So I guess I knew then, though it was a few days later, after the funeral, before I got told. Mom came in my room and sat on the bed. All she and Dad had ever wanted for Cal and me, she said, was for us to be able to choose what we'd like to do, whatever it might be. She reminded me how Cal had dreamed all his life about playing football for Iowa, how he'd worked so hard for it.

"You wouldn't want him to have to give all that up, would you?" she said.

"No," I said, "but what about the farm? What about what I want?"

She didn't answer.

"Will we have to move?"

"No," she said, "we won't have to move. I don't think so."

Both our legs were dangling off the bed, bare feet coming out of blue jeans. Her feet were more calloused than mine. For as long I could remember, she and Dad had worked the farm as partners. All spring they'd be out together in the fields, Mom disking or harrowing, Dad planting behind her. She used to joke that she'd gotten married in June and spent her honeymoon cultivating. But it was what she wanted to do. For all of us to pull together as a family to make it work—that was her and Dad's dream. I didn't understand how she could let Cal leave. I didn't know what she'd do. Or what I would.

"You're awfully quiet," she said. "What are you thinking?"

I didn't tell her. I was kicking my feet back and forth against the bed, and she started kicking hers in step. I changed my timing and she tried to match it and I changed again. She put her arms around my neck.

"Oh, honey," she said. "We'll be all right. You'll see."
But I didn't. I didn't see how she could even *say* that.

All you heard all August, it seemed, was about the
Hawkeyes. The coach, Hayden Fry, came on TV with his Texas
accent and said how great they looked in practice, how Ronnie
Harmon's leg was good as new, and how terrific it was that
Chuck Long had passed up the pros to come back for a fifth
year. Everyone thought they'd win the Big Ten and go to the
Rose Bowl. I got real sick of hearing about them. The Saturday
night of their opening game, I went to my room early.

Mom knocked on the door. "Arrow," she said, "you're
not in bed, are you?"

"Yes."

"You're not watching the game?"

"No."

She opened the door. "You haven't missed a game in
years."

"Well, I'm missing this one."

She stood in the doorway and we stared at each other.
She'd just taken a shower and her blond hair was straight and
wet-dark down her back. "Aaron," she said, finally, "I can't
watch it alone."

I thought how, past years, she'd always make a big batch
of popcorn and Dad would come in from combining or plowing
or whatever he was doing. It took a real emergency for them to
miss a game.

I got out of bed.

"Thank you," she said.

Secretly I was hoping the Hawks would lose, but they
won fifty-eight to nothing. Cal got to play the whole fourth
quarter and almost had a touchdown except he got knocked out
of bounds at the one and next play they gave the ball to
someone else. Mom's eyes were on the screen but for most of
the game her mind wasn't. A couple of times she had to ask me
the score.

When my own school started, I had trouble making myself
go. I knew summer was over, but the weather stayed hot and
dry and even with football, it didn't seem like fall. Some

mornings I couldn't stand the other kids and the teachers, and I'd skip out after first or second period. Mom was in town a lot of days and the farm was still and spooky. The cows were way off in the timber and all the hogs were gone.

The day Mom sent the last gilts to the packing house, I stood behind the truck and watched them go up the loading chute. It hurt every time the trucker buzzed one with his prod.

It didn't seem possible not to hear the clanking of the lids on the hog feeders—that sound I'd heard for as long as I could remember, so constantly day and night I didn't even know I was hearing it until now, when I didn't.

I started spending a lot of time in Dad's workshop. It was the one place on the farm that had been mostly just his, and nobody but me had been in it since the accident. The welder was out beside the corn head, and I could see where he'd been patching it for fall. All his tools were there, some hung up, some just laying around where he'd left them. They were covered with a thin coating of dust that made them seem old and made me think of the really old things I used to find around the farm. Once I'd discovered a whole set of harness, worn but all there, buried in a corner of the barn. I'd asked Dad whose it was, but he didn't know.

Dad made a lot of inventions in that shop. He had an old wood stove and winter nights he'd stay out past midnight tinkering with one thing or another. Every piece of equipment we bought, he had some idea how to make it better, like the disk openers he put on the planter last spring. Once he made a table for my room, all out of horseshoes welded together.

It was odd to stand in the quiet, thinking of his inventions and surrounded by his things. It felt almost as if he was with me, as if because he'd worked so closely with these things and loved them so, they'd taken on part of his spirit.

Maybe I've got some gears that don't mesh, but I believe that can happen to things.

I made it nearly a month before Mom found out about school. We were eating supper on a Wednesday night when out of nowhere she said, "Aaron, why have you been leaving school early?"

She'd been in town all afternoon and still had on the gray

suit she wore when she wanted to seem businesslike. She'd got her hair cut, too, and it looked strange—all short and curly.

"I haven't," I said.

"The principal's office says you have every day this week. And it's not the first time."

I took my plate to the sink.

"Aaron," she said.

So I tried to tell her about time—how it felt out of joint to be in school.

She listened, and while I talked she took my hand. "Sometimes I feel that way too," she said. "Like it's just too impossible to believe. But you have to stay in school."

"I can't," I said.

"Arrow," she said, "this isn't discussable. You can't just leave school."

I didn't say anything. I got up and started for my room.

"Come back," she said. "Sit down."

I did.

"Listen," she said, "how would you like to go up to Iowa City this weekend for the Indiana game?"

"Why?"

"Cal has a ticket for you right behind the bench. You could stay with him in the dorm, meet all the players. Wouldn't that be fun?"

"Who wants to see Indiana," I said. "They stink."

"Oh, Aaron. Don't be this way."

"I just don't want to go."

"Well, you're going," she said. "Whether you want to or not."

She put me on the bus Friday after school, and Cal met me in Iowa City. He had red blotches on his neck like he gets every year from his shoulder pads, but otherwise he looked the same. He was wearing a long-sleeved shirt with the sleeves rolled up and the neck open about halfway down his chest.

"Hey, champ!" He punched me in the arm. Then, while we waited for the driver to find my suitcase, he introduced me to Cindy.

She was tall and blond, with makeup that looked like wax and powdery perfume that made me want to sneeze. She was from Chicago. As we left the station, she put her arm around Cal's waist.

"Who is she?" I asked him, first chance I got. "Does Andrea know?"

"Andy and I"—he held his hand flat and made it shake—"had a little parting of the ways."

I had to sit with her at the game, where she had on even more makeup and perfume and never once got excited. It wasn't a bad game, either. The Hoosiers played better than I thought and might have won if Larry Station hadn't intercepted a pass with a couple of minutes left. Cal only got in a couple of plays. After the game she went out to dinner with us, so I never got to meet Chuck Long or Ronnie Harmon or any of the players. Then Cal dropped her at a party where he was going to meet her later and took me back to his room. That was the first time all weekend we were alone.

His room was bare—no rug, no pictures on the walls, just two chipped dressers, two scuffed desks, two metal beds. We each sat on one of the beds. I guess Mom had told him to talk to me about the farm, because he hadn't before but now he started telling me how Dad had always wanted a better life for us than what he'd had and how he—Cal—had dedicated the season to him and hoped he was somewhere watching and was proud. I wished he'd just shut up about it, but I didn't say anything until he came over and put both hands on my shoulders.

"Arrow," he said, "we all got to stick together now."

I hit him—not hard, just to get his hands away. But he slapped me back hard, across the face. Then he grabbed both my wrists in one hand.

"I can't change what happened," he said. "Neither can Mom. You're old enough to know that."

He went back to his bed.

"I know what you want," he said. "You want me to come home and farm. Don't you know that's a dead life? You think I want to work my ass off sixteen hours a day just to be poor?"

"We aren't poor," I said.

"You don't even know."

I guess I'd started to cry.

"I'm sorry I hit you," he said, "but Jesus, Arrow, I don't know what to say. I don't know what's wrong with you."

"Nothing's wrong with me," I said. "Why don't you just go to your party and leave me alone."

I didn't think he would, but he did. After he left, I lay on that metal bed with the lights out, listening to the thump of a stereo from somewhere and people shouting outside. I couldn't understand him—why he'd want to live in a room like that.

Sunday after I got home, after Mom asked about the weekend, she said she had to have a talk with me. She made herself coffee and we sat in the living room.

"Duane Mott was out yesterday," she said

I said, "No! You can't do that!"

"It's what we have to do."

I'd been seeing the sale bills for as long as I could remember, but I never thought I'd see one for my own farm. I knew how it would start: "To settle the estate of George Blount. . . ." And as clearly as I saw the sale bill in my mind, I saw Dad's machinery and equipment, washed and clean, laid out in straight lines in the yard. I saw the hayracks, loaded with all the old miscellaneous things nobody'd really want but somebody'd buy anyway. I could hear Duane Mott saying, "All right, what else we got to throw in with this chain? How about these hog pans, folks. Who'll give a dollar? Well, then, fifty cents and let's go."

"You got to keep a tractor," I said. "You can't sell both tractors."

She didn't answer. She was leaning toward me, sitting with her knees close together.

"And the cows," I said. "I can take care of the cows."

She was shaking her head, squinting. Her eyes looked bluer than I'd ever seen them.

"And the welder and Dad's tools," I said. "No way you're selling that stuff."

She shook her head harder, her eyes wet and blue spread all over her face. "Please," she said. "Don't."

"You bitch!"

I headed for my room, but she caught me on the stairs. Her fingers dug into my arm.

"Damn it, Aaron," she said, "I've kept the house. And the land. Maybe you don't think that's a lot, but it is. It's a damn lot."

She let me loose. I was sorry I'd cursed her, but I couldn't say so. I went on to my room. It was late afternoon and the autumn sun, like always that time of day, made a warm patch inside my window. I remembered how I used to come home from school and say, "Hi, sun"—as if it were my friend, as if it did that just for me. How stupid. Outside, it made the thin, dry grass in the yard look fat and yellow, but beyond our white fence it couldn't disguise the way the corn had turned pale and brittle, the way the beans without leaves looked scrawny, like birds without feathers—like anything with its fullness gone.

She'd kept the land, she said. Big deal. What was the land to me? It was just itself. It would go on year after year, growing and dying, no matter what I thought or felt or wanted. No matter what anybody did.

Mom started working in town, at some lawyer's office where she'd worked before she and Dad got married. In the mornings we'd ride together to the end of the driveway, sit in the car, and wait for the school bus. We almost never said anything, just listened to the radio until the bus came.

"You don't have to do this, you know," I told her one morning. "I always waited outside before."

All she said was, "I know."

After school, I was working with Ken. Mom had hired him to do our crops, and I was helping. That meant I rode with him in the combine until we had a wagon full, then hauled the load over the culvert to where his wife, Maggie, could auger it into their truck. Then I brought back an empty wagon and rode some more. At night, when I came in, Mom would be out in the shed or the farrowing house with her green notebook, writing down every single thing she was going to sell.

In the afternoons before I went to the field I read what she'd written. Things she'd already set out or hauled to the hayrack had check marks beside them, and every day more lines were filled and there were more checks. I ran from the house to the fields, to the fall-yellow earth covered with leaves, climbed the worn metal ladder of the combine. The ground was solid, the stalks dry, and the sky that crisp October blue that seems it'll last forever. The roaring gears shut everything else from my mind, and I sat in a kind of trance watching plant after plant disappear in front of me.

The corn was easy going, but about the time we switched to beans a big wind came and brought cold and drizzle. It was still October, but you'd never have known. The sky was gray mist and the wind blew the beans over so far Ken had to drive on the south-side row to get them all. His arthritis started acting up, and he'd wince each time he had to turn the combine. Going across the culvert got slippery and scary, and when I got on gravel, mud flew off the tires in chunks as big as the dead coons beside the highway. It was the kind of weather Dad would have stopped in, but Ken kept on. After us, he had a lot of his own fields still to do.

The fourth day of drizzle, the bean straw started tangling in the reel, and every few rounds we had to stop, get down on our knees in the mud, and pull it out. We were doing that when Maggie drove up with Ken's afternoon coffee.

"Isn't it getting kind of useless?" she said.

"Oh, it's messy," Ken said, "but not enough to shut down."

He drank half his coffee, then set the cup on top of the reel and went back to digging at the straw. Maggie watched him.

"What an awful way to combine," she said.

"Got to be done."

He threw the straw behind him in thick slabs matted together with mud. His coffee stopped steaming as the drizzle settled into it. Maggie filled it up and drove away.

Two days before our sale, the drizzle turned white. At first it was just specks, like chaff flying over the reel on a dry, windy day, and we rode along for maybe ten minutes before I asked Ken. "Is that snow?"

"It ain't manna from heaven," he said.

A couple minutes more and there was no mistaking it. Ken turned on the wipers and we plodded ahead, but by the end of the field the wipers weren't keeping up and the reel was plugged solid. He swung the combine around to face the next rows and shut it off. He leaned back, took his gloves off, and rubbed his hands.

"Snow in October," he said. "One year in ten it'll do that. Would have to pick this one."

We sat awhile, watching the muddy ground turn white, the thick, wet flakes settling on the brown stalks. I thought about how many of the pods would crack and fall from the weight, about Ken's own fields.

"What'll you do?" I asked.

That seemed to amuse him. "Depends what *it* does, now, don't you think?"

I felt foolish for asking. I'd heard Dad say enough times that if he ever felt a need to plan ahead he'd choose some other line of work.

Without the heater on it got cold fast in the cab. Ken rolled up his sleeve to see his watch.

"No sense sitting here," he said. "Might as well get that machinery moved out."

I felt like he'd just dumped snow down my back. But he got out of the combine and started walking across the field, and I had no choice but to go.

He threw open the doors to our machine shed and started Dad's small tractor, the 606. He backed it to the plow.

"Hitch me up," he said, and tossed me the pin.

For a minute I stared at him, sitting up in Dad's seat with his gloves on and hood around his face, the snow blowing in on him. Everything inside me wanted to run.

"Come on, Arrow," he said, "hitch me up."

I put the pin in the draw bar and hooked up the hoses. He raised the plow and pulled it out of the shed, took it into the yard and dropped it beside the fence. I unhitched him. He went back for the disk and dropped it beside the plow. Then the field cultivator, the baler, the rake, until every piece of machinery we owned was lined up in the yard.

I hitched every implement and ran along and unhitched it. And while we worked, something happened that I don't know if I can explain. I never forgot what we were doing or what it meant, but for a while it was like I *did* forget, or like it didn't matter. The rhythm of the work got inside me, watching Ken on the tractor, guiding him back to the hitch, trying to be as fast and smooth as I could hooking up, with the snow swirling around us and darkness falling—like we were two men just doing a hard job that had to be done.

We had our sale on a Thursday afternoon, partly to keep

the weekenders from interfering with the serious bidders, partly so Cal could be there. The snow had quit by then, and the sun had come out and melted most of it. It was cold enough that the farmers were wearing sweatshirts and coveralls, but most had their hoods down and coveralls unzipped. It was too wet to work, so we had a good turnout.

I got to stay home from school and Cal came down early, in time for breakfast. He sat with both elbows on the table reading the *Register* sports section.

"Hey," he said. He looked at me just a minute, then back to his paper.

I said, "Hey," and slipped into my chair.

"How does pancakes and sausage sound?" Mom said. She was at the stove, wearing jeans—the first morning in a long time she had.

"I don't care," I said.

"So anyway," Cal said, "my adviser thinks I should switch my major to computer science."

"Is that what you want?" Mom said.

"It's where the jobs are."

They went on talking, about school and computers. Mom told how she was learning to use one at work. I sat and waited for my breakfast, but when the pancakes were ready they felt heavy and dry in my mouth.

"Arrow's been helping Ken with the crops," Mom said.

Cal nodded, "I hear the corn made a hundred sixty bushel."

"Yes," I said. "But the wind blew the beans over pretty good."

"Lost a lot?"

"Not too many." I explained how Ken drove to get them.

"Then it started raining," Mom said.

"We kept on, though," I said, and told how we had to unplug the reel every few rounds.

Cal shook his head. "If it ain't one damn thing, it's another."

"It wasn't that bad," I said. "It got messy, but not enough to shut us down. Till the snow came."

"So how much is left?"

"Probably sixty acres. But it's the bottom ground. We'll probably go over to Ken's next and come back to it after the ground freezes."

"Cost you more beans, won't it?"

"Not much else we can do though," I said, "unless it dries out awful fast."

They were both looking at me, paying attention. I told how risky it felt going over the culvert and how strange it was when it started snowing, how at first I'd thought it was chaff. Before I knew it, I'd finished my breakfast.

Cal opened the sports section again and we talked about the Hawks' game Saturday at Michigan, who was undefeated too. Mom did dishes and sat with us. Nobody said a word about the sale. It felt like a day out of time, like Thanksgiving or Christmas, when everything's different. Or it might have been one of those winter Saturdays when Dad was gone buying cattle and the three of us spent all morning around the kitchen table.

Then about eleven, Duane Mott came. Mom asked him in for coffee, and while he was drinking it a woman from the Medora auxiliary knocked, wanting to know where to set up their lunch trailer. Cars and pickups started parking up and down our road on both sides, and folks strolled around the yard looking over the machinery. Finally Duane put on his cowboy hat, took Mom's green notebook, and went out. Mom and Cal put on their jackets. Mom tied a kerchief around her hair.

"Are you coming?" she said.

I shook my head. She put her hand on my shoulder a minute. Then she and Cal went out.

The first thing Duane auctioned was an old post-hole digger the handle always fell out of. From the kitchen, I couldn't see who bought it or how much it brought. After that he sold a lot of mainly junk off the hayrack, and then, before he went on to the machinery, he got to Dad's tools.

I tried telling myself they were just things—metal, wood, rubber, plastic. They weren't Dad's anymore. It didn't matter who used them or what for. I tried to imagine what would happen to the level and T-square Duane was holding up, one in each hand. Probably they'd end up like the things I sometimes found: that harness, or the garden map someone had penciled inside the door of the old smokehouse, or the shapeless bits of iron we always turned up plowing. Traces of people whose names I didn't even know.

It took Duane almost two hours to sell all the things off the hayrack. Then he sold the rack, and the knot of people trailed him across the yard to the first row of machinery. He sold the hay conditioner in a minute or two. The sale would go fast now, and I was glad. I looked past Duane, over the heads of the bidders, at our cornstalks poking through what was left of the snow. They stretched to where Ken's alfalfa started, and beyond that I could see Crutchfield's house up on the hill, and past that Proudfit's big blue Harvestores against the sky. The land. Someday, I thought, I'll have my own machinery, my own things, to give to it.

Mom and Cal had stayed behind the crowd. Cal was wearing his black-and-yellow Iowa jacket, sitting on the edge of the rack dangling his legs. Mom stood beside him. She was looking in my direction but not at me, not at anything, really, just staring—maybe over the fields, like I'd been. Cal had a piece of pipe he was playing with, tossing it up a little ways then catching it.

I slipped into my coveralls and went out to be with them.

# RICHARD MCCANN

# MY MOTHER'S CLOTHES: THE SCHOOL OF BEAUTY AND SHAME

FROM THE ATLANTIC MONTHLY

∽

LIKE EVERY CORNER HOUSE in Carroll Knolls, the corner house on our block was turned backward on its lot, a quirk introduced by the developer of the subdivision, who, having run short of money, sought variety without additional expense. The turned-around houses, as we kids called them, were not popular, perhaps because they seemed too public, their casement bedroom windows cranking open onto sunstruck asphalt streets. In actuality, however, it was the rest of the houses that were public, their picture windows offering dioramic glimpses of early-American sofas and Mediterranean-style pole lamps whose mottled globes hung like iridescent melons from wrought-iron chains. In order not to be seen walking across the living room to the kitchen in our pajamas, we had to close the venetian blinds. The corner house on our block was secretive, as though it had turned its back on all of us, whether in superiority or in shame, refusing to acknowledge even its own unkempt yard of yellowing zoysia grass. After its initial occupants moved away, the corner house remained vacant for months.

The spring I was in sixth grade, it was sold. When I came down the block from school, I saw a moving van parked at its curb. "Careful with that!" a woman was shouting at a mover as he unloaded a tiered end table from the truck. He stared at her in silence. The veneer had already been splintered from the table's edge, as though someone had nervously picked at it while watching TV. Then another mover walked from the truck carrying a child's bicycle, a wire basket bolted over its thick rear tire, brightly colored plastic streamers dangling from its handlebars.

The woman looked at me. "What have you got there? In your hand."

I was holding a scallop shell spray-painted gold, with imitation pearls glued along its edges. Mrs. Eidus, the art teacher who visited our class each Friday, had showed me how to make it.

"A hatpin tray," I said. "It's for my mother."

"It's real pretty." She glanced up the street as though trying to guess which house I belonged to. "I'm Mrs. Tyree," she said, "and I've got a boy about your age. His daddy's bringing him tonight in the new Plymouth. I bet you haven't sat in a new Plymouth."

"We have a Ford." I studied her housedress, tiny blue and purple flowers imprinted on thin cotton, a line of white buttons as large as Necco Wafers marching toward its basted hemline. She was the kind of mother my mother laughed at for cutting recipes out of *Woman's Day*. Staring from our picture window, my mother would sometimes watch the neighborhood mothers drag their folding chairs into a circle on someone's lawn. "There they go," she'd say, "a regular meeting of the Daughters of the Eastern Star!" "They're hardly even *women*," she'd whisper to my father, "and their *clothes*." She'd criticize their appearance—their loud nylon scarves tied beneath their chins, their disintegrating figures stuffed into pedal pushers—until my father, worried that my brother, Davis, and I could hear, although laughing himself, would beg her, "Stop it, Maria, please stop; it isn't funny." But she wouldn't stop, not ever. "Not even thirty and they look like they belong to the DAR! They wear their pearls inside their bosoms in case the rope should break!" She was the oldest mother on the block but she was the most glamorous, sitting alone on the front lawn in her sleek kick-pleated skirts and cashmere sweaters, reading her thick paperback novels, whose bindings had split. Her hair was lightly hennaed, so that when I saw her pillow- cases piled atop the washer, they seemed dusted with powdery rouge. She had once lived in New York City.

After dinner, when it was dark, I joined the other children congregated beneath the streetlamp across from the turned- around house. Bucky Trueblood, an eighth-grader who had once twisted the stems off my brother's eyeglasses, was crouched in the center, describing his mother's naked body to us elemen- tary school children gathered around him, our faces slightly upturned, as though searching for a distant constellation, or for the bats that Bucky said would fly into our hair. I sat at the edge, one half of my body within the circle of light, the other half lost to darkness. When Bucky described his mother's nip- ples, which he'd glimpsed when she bent to kiss him good- night, everyone giggled; but when he described her genitals, which he'd seen by dropping his pencil on the floor and look- ing up her nightie while her feet were propped on a hassock as she watched TV, everyone huddled nervously together, as though listening to a ghost story that made them fear something dan- gerous in the nearby dark. "I don't believe you," someone said; "I'm telling you," Bucky said, *that's what it looks like.*"

I slowly moved outside the circle. Across the street a cream-colored Plymouth was parked at the curb. In a lighted bedroom window Mrs. Tyree was hanging café curtains. Be- hind the chain link fence, within the low branches of a willow tree, the new child was standing in his yard. I could see his white T-shirt and the pale oval of his face, a face deprived of detail by darkness and distance. Behind him, at the open bed- room window, his mother slowly fiddled with a valance. Be- hind me the children sat spellbound beneath the light. Then Bucky jumped up and pointed in the new child's direction— "Hey, you, you want to hear something really *good*?"—and even before the others had a chance to spot him, he vanished as suddenly and completely as an imaginary playmate.

The next morning, as we waited at our bus stop, he loitered by the mailbox on the opposite corner, not crossing the street until the yellow school bus pulled up and flung open its door. Then he dashed aboard and sat down beside me. "I'm Denny," he said. Denny: a heavy, unbeautiful child, who, had

his parents stayed in their native Kentucky, would have been a
farm boy, but who in Carroll Knolls seemed to belong to no
particular world at all, walking past the identical ranch houses
in his overalls and Keds, his whitish-blond hair close-cropped
all around except for the distinguishing, stigmatizing feature of
a wave that crested perfectly just above his forehead, a wave
that neither rose nor fell, a wave he trained with Hopalong
Cassidy hair tonic, a wave he tended fussily, as though it were
the only loveliness he allowed himself.

What in Carrol Knolls might have been described by someone not native to those parts—a visiting expert, say—as *beautiful*, capable of arousing terror and joy? The brick ramblers
strung with multicolored Christmas lights? The occasional front-
yard plaster Virgin entrapped within a chicken-wire grotto
entwined with plastic roses? The spring Denny moved to Carroll Knolls, I begged my parents to take me to a nightclub, had
begged so hard for months, in fact, that by summer they finally
agreed to a Sunday matinee. Waiting in the backseat of our
Country Squire, a red bow tie clipped to my collar, I watched
our house float like a mirage behind the sprinkler's web of
water. The front door opened, and a white dress fluttered
within the mirage's ascending waves: Slipping on her sunglasses, my mother emerged onto the concrete stoop, adjusted
her shoulder strap, and teetered across the wet grass in new
spectator shoes. Then my father stepped out and cut the sprinkler off. We drove—the warm breeze inside the car sweetened
by my mother's Shalimar—past ranch houses tethered to yards by
chain link fences; past the Silver Spring Volunteer Fire Department and Carroll Knolls Elementary School; past the Polar
Bear Soft-Serv stand, its white stucco siding shimmery with
mirror shards; past a bulldozed red-clay field where a weathered billboard advertised IF YOU LIVED HERE YOU'D BE HOME BY
NOW, until we arrived at the border—a line of cinder-block
discount liquor stores, a traffic light—of Washington, D.C.
The light turned red. We stopped. The breeze died and the
Shalimar fell from the air. Exhaust fumes mixed with the smell
of hot tar. A drunk man stumbled into the crosswalk, followed
by an old woman shielding herself from the sun with an orange
umbrella, and two teenaged boys dribbling a basketball back

and forth between them. My mother put down her sun visor. "Lock your door," she said.

Then the light changed, releasing us into another country. The station wagon sailed down boulevards of Chinese elms and flowering Bradford pears, through hot, dense streets where black families sat on wooden chairs at curbs, along old streetcar tracks that caused the tires to shimmy and the car to swerve, onto Pennsylvania Avenue, past the White House, encircled by its fence of iron spears, and down 14th Street, past the Treasury Building, until at last we reached the Neptune Room, a cocktail lounge in the basement of a shabbily elegant hotel.

Inside, the Neptune Room's walls were painted with garish mermaids reclining seductively on underwater rocks, and human frogmen who stared longingly through their diving helmets' glass masks at a loveliness they could not possess on dry earth. On stage, leaning against the baby grand piano, a *chanteuse* (as my mother called her) was singing of her grief, her wrists weighted with rhinestone bracelets, a single blue spotlight making her seem like one who lived, as did the mermaids, underwater.

I was transfixed. I clutched my Roy Rogers cocktail (the same as a Shirley Temple, but without the cheerful, girlish grenadine) tight in my fist. In the middle of "The Man I Love" I stood and struggled toward the stage.

I strayed into the spotlight's soft-blue underwater world. Close up, from within the light, the singer was a boozy, plump peroxide blonde in a tight black cocktail dress; but these indiscretions made her yet more lovely, for they showed what she had lost, just as her songs seemed to carry her backward into endless regret. When I got close to her, she extended one hand—red nails, a huge glass ring—and seized one of mine.

"Why, what kind of little sailor have we got here?" she asked the audience.

I stared through the border of blue light and into the room, where I saw my parents gesturing, although whether they were telling me to step closer to her microphone or to step farther away, I could not tell. The whole club was staring.

"Maybe he knows a song!" a man shouted from the back.

"Sing with me," she whispered. "What can you sing?"

I wanted to lift her microphone from its stand and bow

deeply from the waist, as Judy Garland did on her weekly TV show. But I could not. As she began to sing, I stood voiceless, pressed against the protection of her black dress; or, more accurately, I stood beside her, silently lip-syncing to myself. I do not recall what she sang, although I do recall a quick, farcical ending in which she falsettoed, like Betty Boop, "Gimme a Little Kiss, Will Ya, Huh?" and brushed my forehead with pursed red lips.

That summer, humidity enveloping the landfill subdivision, Denny, "the new kid," stood on the boundaries, while we neighborhood boys played War, a game in which someone stood on Stanley Allen's front porch and machine-gunned the rest of us, who one by one clutched our bellies, coughed as if choking on blood, and rolled in exquisite death throes down the grassy hill. When Stanley's father came up the walk from work, he ducked imaginary bullets. "Hi, Dad," Stanley would call, rising from the dead to greet him. Then we began the game again: Whoever died best in the last round got to kill in the next. Later, after dusk, we'd smear the wings of balsa planes with glue, ignite them, and send them flaming through the dark on kamikaze missions. Long after the streets were deserted, we children sprawled beneath the corner streetlamp, praying our mothers would not call us—*"Time to come in!"*—back to our ovenlike houses; and then sometimes Bucky, hoping to scare the elementary school kids, would lead his solemn procession of junior high "hoods" down the block, their penises hanging from their unzipped trousers.

Denny and I began to play together, first in secret, then visiting each other's houses almost daily, and by the end of the summer I imagined him to be my best friend. Our friendship was sealed by our shared dread of junior high school. Davis, who had just finished seventh grade, brought back reports of corridors so long that one could get lost in them, of gangs who fought to control the lunchroom and the bathrooms. The only safe place seemed to be the Health Room, where a pretty nurse let you lie down on a cot behind a folding screen. Denny told me about a movie he'd seen in which the children, all girls, did not have to go to school at all but were taught at home by a beautiful governess, who, upon coming to their rooms each morning, threw open their shutters so that sunlight fell like bolts of satin across their beds, whispered their pet names while kissing them, and combed their long hair with a silver brush. "She never got mad," said Denny, beating his fingers up and down through the air as though striking a keyboard, "except once when some old man told the girls they could never play piano again."

With my father at work in the Pentagon and my mother off driving the two-tone Welcome Wagon Chevy to new subdivisions, Denny and I spent whole days in the gloom of my living room, the picture window's venetian blinds closed against an August sun so fierce that it bleached the design from the carpet. Dreaming of fabulous prizes—sets of matching Samsonite luggage, French Provincial bedroom suites, Corvettes, jet flights to Hawaii—we watched Jan Murray's "Treasure Hunt" and Bob Barker's "Truth or Consequences" (a name that seemed strangely threatening). We watched "The Loretta Young Show," worshipping yet critiquing her elaborate gowns. When "The Early Show" came on, we watched old Bette Davis, Gene Tierney, and Joan Crawford movies—*Dark Victory, Leave Her to Heaven, A Woman's Face*. Hoping to become their pen pals, we wrote long letters to fading movie stars, who in turn sent us autographed photos we traded between ourselves. We searched the house for secrets, like contraceptives, Kotex, and my mother's hidden supply of Hershey bars. And finally, Denny and I, running to the front window every few minutes to make sure no one was coming unexpectedly up the sidewalk, inspected the secrets of my mother's dresser: her satin nightgowns and padded brassieres, folded atop pink drawer liners and scattered with loose sachet; her black mantilla, pressed inside a shroud of lilac tissue paper; her heart-shaped candy box, a flapper doll strapped to its lid with a ribbon, from which spilled galaxies of cocktail rings and cultured pearls. Small shrines to deeper intentions, private grottoes of yearning: her triangular cloisonné earrings, her brooch of enameled butterfly wings.

Because beauty's source was longing, it was infused with romantic sorrow; because beauty was defined as "feminine," and therefore as "other," it became hopelessly confused with my mother: Mother, who quickly sorted through new batches of photographs, throwing unflattering shots of herself directly

into the fire before they could be seen. Mother, who drama-
tized herself, telling us and our playmates, "My name is Maria
Dolores; in Spanish, that means 'Mother of Sorrows,' " Mother,
who had once wished to be a writer and who said, looking up
briefly from whatever she was reading, "Books are my best
friends." Mother, who read aloud from Whitman's *Leaves of
Grass* and O'Neill's *Long Day's Journey Into Night* with a
voice so grave I could not tell the difference between them.
Mother, who lifted cut-glass vases and antique clocks from her
obsessively dusted curio shelves to ask, "If this could talk,
what story would it tell?"

And more, always more, for she was the only woman in
our house, a "people-watcher," a "talker," a woman whose
mysteries and moods seemed endless: Our Mother of the White
Silk Gloves; Our Mother of the Veiled Hats; Our Mother of
the Paper Lilacs; Our Mother of the Sighs and Heartaches; Our
Mother of the Gorgeous Gypsy Earrings; Our Mother of the
Late Movies and the Cigarettes; Our Mother whom I adored
and who, in adoring, I ran from, knowing it "wrong" for a son
to wish to be like his mother; Our Mother who wished to
influence us, passing the best of herself along, yet who held the
fear common to that era, the fear that by loving a son too
intensely she would render him unfit—"Momma's boy," "tied
to apron strings"—and who therefore alternately drew us close
and sent us away, believing a son needed "male influence" in
large doses, that female influence was pernicious except as a
final finishing, like manners; Our Mother of the Mixed Messages; Our Mother of Sudden Attentiveness; Our Mother of
Sudden Distances; Our Mother of Anger; Our Mother of Apology. The simplest objects of her life, objects scattered accidentally about the house, became my shrines to beauty, my grottoes
of romantic sorrow: her Revlon lipstick tubes, "Cherries in the
Snow"; her Art Nouveau atomizers on the blue mirror top of
her vanity; her pastel silk scarves knotted to a wire hanger in
her closet; her white handkerchiefs blotted with red mouths.
Voiceless objects; silences. The world halved with a cleaver:
"masculine," "feminine." In these ways was the plainest ordinary love made complicated and grotesque. And in these ways
was beauty, already confused with the "feminine," also confused with shame, for all these longings were secret, and to

control me all my brother had to do was to threaten to expose that Denny and I were dressing ourselves in my mother's clothes.

Denny chose my Mother's drabbest outfits, as though he were ruled by the deepest of modesties, or by his family's austere Methodism: a pink wraparound skirt from which the color had been laundered, its hem almost to his ankles; a sleeveless white cotton blouse with a Peter Pan collar; a small straw summer clutch. But he seemed to challenge his own primness, as though he dared it with his "effects": an undershirt worn over his head to approximate cascading hair; gummed hole-punch reinforcements pasted to his fingernails so that his hands, palms up, might look like a woman's—flimsy crescent moons waxing above his fingertips.

He dressed slowly, hesitantly, but once dressed, he was a manic Proteus metamorphosing into contradictory, half-realized forms, throwing his "long hair" back and balling it violently into a French twist; tapping his paper nails on the glass-topped vanity as though he were an important woman kept waiting at a cosmetics counter; stabbing his nails into the air as though he were an angry teacher assigning an hour of detention; touching his temple as though he were a shy schoolgirl tucking back a wisp of stray hair; resting his fingertips on the rim of his glass of Kool-Aid as though he were an actress seated over an ornamental cocktail—a Pink Lady, say, or a Silver Slipper. Sometimes, in an orgy of jerky movement, his gestures overtaking him with greater and greater force, a dynamo of theatricality unleashed, he would hurl himself across the room like a mad girl having a fit, or like one possessed; or he would snatch the chenille spread from my parents' bed and drape it over his head to fashion for himself the long train of a bride. "Do you like it?" he'd ask anxiously, making me his mirror. "Does it look *real*?" He wanted, as did I, to become something he'd neither yet seen nor dreamed of, something he'd recognize the moment he saw it: himself. Yet he was constantly confounded, for no matter how much he adorned himself with scarves and jewelry, he could not understand that this was himself, as was also and at the same time the boy in overalls and Keds. He was

split in two pieces—as who was not?—the blond wave cresting
rigidly above his close-cropped hair.

"He makes me nervous," I heard my father tell my mother
one night as I lay in bed. They were speaking about me. That
morning I'd stood awkwardly on the front lawn—"Maybe you
should go help your father," my mother had said—while he
propped an extension ladder against the house, climbed up
through power lines he separated with his bare hands, and
staggered across the pitched roof he was reshingling. When his
hammer slid down the incline, catching on the gutter, I screamed,
"You're falling!" Startled, he almost fell.

"He needs to spend more time with you," I heard my
mother say.

I couldn't sleep. Out in the distance a mother was calling
her child home. A screen door slammed. I heard cicadas, their
chorus as steady and loud as the hum of a power line. *He needs
to spend more time with you.* Didn't she know? Saturday
mornings, when he stood in his rubber hip boots fishing off the
shore of Triadelphia Reservoir, I was afraid of the slimy bottom and could not wade after him; for whatever reasons of his
own—something as simple as shyness, perhaps—he could not
come to get me. I sat in the parking lot drinking Tru-Ade and
reading *Betty and Veronica*, wondering if Denny had walked
alone to Wheaton Plaza, where the weekend manager of Port-o'-
Call allowed us to Windex the illuminated glass shelves that
held Lladro figurines, the porcelain ballerina's hands so realistic
one could see tiny life and heart lines etched into her palms. *He
needs to spend more time with you.* Was she planning to dis-
continue the long summer afternoons that she and I spent
together when there were no new families for her to greet in
her Welcome Wagon car? "I don't feel like being alone today,"
she'd say, inviting me to sit on their chenille bedspread and
watch her model new clothes in her mirror. Behind her an
oscillating fan fluttered nylons and scarves she'd heaped, discarded, on a chair. "Should I wear the red belt with this dress
or the black one?" she'd ask, turning suddenly toward me and
cinching her waist with her hands.

Afterward we would sit together at the rattan table on the
screened-in porch, holding cocktail napkins around sweaty glasses

of iced Russian tea and listening to big-band music on the Zenith.

"You look so pretty," I'd say. Sometimes she wore outfits I'd selected for her from her closet—pastel chiffon dresses, an apricot blouse with real mother-of-pearl buttons.

One afternoon she leaned over suddenly and shut off the radio. "You know you're going to leave me one day," she said. When I put my arms around her, smelling the dry carnation talc she wore in hot weather, she stood up and marched out of the room. When she returned, she was wearing Bermuda shorts and a plain cotton blouse. "Let's wait for your father on the stoop," she said.

Late that summer—the summer before he died—my father took me with him to Fort Benjamin Harrison, near Indianapolis, where, as a colonel in the U.S. Army Reserves, he did his annual tour of duty. On the propjet he drank bourbon and read newspapers while I made a souvenir packet for Denny: an airsickness bag, into which I placed the Chiclets given me by the stewardess to help pop my ears during takeoff, and the laminated white card that showed the location of emergency exits. Fort Benjamin Harrison looked like Carroll Knolls: hundreds of acres of concrete and sun-scorched shrubbery inside a cyclone fence. Daytimes I waited for my father in the dining mess with the sons of other officers, drinking chocolate milk that came from a silver machine, and desultorily setting fires in ashtrays. When he came to collect me, I walked behind him— gold braid hung from his epaulets—while enlisted men saluted us and opened doors. At night, sitting in our BOQ room, he asked me questions about myself: "Are you looking forward to seventh grade?" "What do you think you'll want to be?" When these topics faltered—I stammered what I hoped were right answers—we watched TV, trying to preguess lines of dialogue on reruns of his favorite shows, "The Untouchables" and "Rawhide." "That Della Street," he said as we watched "Perry Mason," "is almost as pretty as your mother." On the last day, eager to make the trip memorable, he brought me a gift: a glassine envelope filled with punched IBM cards that told me my life story as his secretary had typed it into the office computer. Card One: *You live at 10406 Lillians Mill Court, Silver Spring, Maryland.* Card Two: *You are entering seventh*

*grade.* Card Three: *Last year your teacher was Mrs. Dillard.*
Card Four: *Your favorite color is blue.* Card Five: *You love the
Kingston Trio.* Card Six: *You love basketball and football.*
Card Seven: *Your favorite sport is swimming.*

Whose son did these cards describe? The address was
correct, as was the teacher's name and the favorite color; and
he'd remembered that one morning during breakfast I'd put a
dime in the jukebox and played the Kingston Trio's song about
"the man who never returned." But whose fiction was the rest?
Had I, who played no sport other than kickball and Kitty-
Kitty-Kick-the-Can, lied to him when he asked me about myself? Had he not heard from my mother the outcome of the
previous summer's swim lessons? At the swim club a young
man in black trunks had taught us, as we held hands, to dunk
ourselves in water, surface, and then go down. When he had
told her to let go of me, I had thrashed across the surface,
violently afraid I'd sink. But perhaps I had not lied to him;
perhaps he merely did not wish to see. It was my job, I felt, to
reassure him that I was the son he imagined me to be, perhaps
because the role of reassurer gave me power. In any case, I
thanked him for the computer cards. I thanked him the way a
father thanks a child for a well-intentioned gift he'll never
use—a set of handkerchiefs, say, on which the embroidered
swirls construct a monogram of no particular initial, and which
thus might be used by anyone.

As for me, when I dressed in my mother's clothes, I
seldom moved at all: I held myself rigid before the mirror. The
kind of beauty I'd seen practiced in movies and in fashion
magazines was beauty attained by lacquered stasis, beauty attained by fixed poses—"ladylike stillness," the stillness of
mannequins, the stillness of models "caught" in mid-gesture,
the stillness of the passive moon around which active meteors
orbited and burst. My costume was of the greatest solemnity: I
dressed like the *chanteuse* in the Neptune Room, carefully
shimmying my mother's black slip over my head so as not to
stain it with Brylcreem, draping her black mantilla over my
bare shoulders, clipping her rhinestone dangles to my ears.
Had I at that time already seen the movie in which French
women who had fraternized with German soldiers were made

to shave their heads and walk through the streets, jeered by their fellow villagers? And if so, did I imagine myself to be one of the collaborators, or one of the villagers, taunting her from the curb? I ask because no matter how elaborate my costume, I made no effort to camouflage my crew cut or my male body.

How did I perceive myself in my mother's triple-mirrored vanity, its endless repetitions? I saw myself as doubled—both an image and he who studied it. I saw myself as beautiful, and guilty: The lipstick made my mouth seem the ripest rose, or a wound; the small rose on the black slip opened like my mother's heart disclosed, or like the Sacred Heart of Mary, aflame and pierced by arrows; the mantilla transformed me into a Mexican penitent or a Latin movie star, like Dolores Del Rio. The mirror was a silvery stream: On the far side, in a clearing, stood the woman who was icily immune from the boy's terror and contempt; on the close side, in the bedroom, stood the boy who feared and yet longed after her inviolability. (Perhaps, it occurs to me now, this doubleness is the source of drag queens' vulnerable ferocity.) Sometimes, when I saw that person in the mirror, I felt as though I had at last been lifted from that dull, locked room, with its mahogany bedroom suite and chalky blue walls. But other times, particularly when I saw Denny and me together, so that his reality shattered my fantasies, we seemed merely ludicrous and sadly comic, as though we were dressed in the garments of another species, like dogs in human clothes. I became aware of my spatulate hands, my scarred knees, my large feet; I became aware of the drooping, unfilled bodice of my slip. Like Denny, I could neither dispense with images nor take their flexibility as pleasure, for the idea of self I had learned and was learning still was that one was constructed by one's images—"*When boys cross their legs, they cross one ankle atop the knee*"—so that one finally sought the protection of believing in one's own image and, in believing in it as reality, condemned oneself to its poverty.

(That locked room. My mother's vanity; my father's highboy. If Denny and I, still in our costumes, had left that bedroom, its floor strewn with my mother's shoes and handbags, and gone through the darkened living room, out onto the sunstruck porch, down the sidewalk, and up the street, how would we have carried ourselves? Would we have walked boldly, chattering extravagantly back and forth between ourselves, like drag queens refusing to acknowledge the stares of contempt that are meant to halt them? Would we have walked humbly, with the calculated, impervious piety of the condemned walking barefoot to the public scaffold? Would we have walked simply, as deeply accustomed to the normalcy of our own strangeness as Siamese twins? Or would we have walked gravely, a solemn procession, like Bucky Trueblood's gang, their manhood hanging from their unzipped trousers?

(We were eleven years old. Why now, more than two decades later, do I wonder for the first time how we would have carried ourselves through a publicness we would have neither sought nor dared? I am six feet two inches tall; I weigh 198 pounds. Given my size, the question I am most often asked about my youth is "What football position did you play?" Overseas I am most commonly taken to be a German or a Swede. Right now, as I write this, I am wearing L. L. Bean khaki trousers, a LaCoste shirt, Weejuns: the anonymous American costume, although partaking of certain signs of class and education, and most recently, partaking also of certain signs of sexual orientation, this costume having become the standard garb of the urban American gay man. Why do I tell you these things? Am I trying—not subtly—to inform us of my "maleness," to reassure us that I have "survived" without noticeable "complexes"? Or is this my urge, my constant urge, to complicate my portrait of myself to both of us, so that I might layer my selves like so many multicolored crinoline slips, each rustling as I walk? When the wind blows, lifting my skirt, I do not know which slip will be revealed.)

Sometimes, while Denny and I were dressing up, Davis would come home unexpectedly from the bowling alley, where he'd been hanging out since entering junior high. At the bowling alley he was courting the protection of Bucky's gang.

"Let me in!" he'd demand, banging fiercely on the bedroom door, behind which Denny and I were scurrying to wipe the makeup off our faces with Kleenex.

"We're not doing anything," I'd protest, buying time.

"Let me in this minute or I'll tell!"

Once in the room, Davis would police the wreckage we'd

made, the emptied hatboxes, the scattered jewelry, the piled skirts and blouses. "You'd better clean this up right now," he'd warn. "You two make me *sick*."

Yet his scorn seemed modified by awe. When he helped us rehang the clothes in the closet and replace the jewelry in the candy box, a sullen accomplice destroying someone else's evidence, he sometimes handled the garments as though they were infused with something of himself, although at the precise moment when he seemed to find them loveliest, holding them close, he would cast them down.

After our dress-up sessions Denny would leave the house without good-byes. I was glad to see him go. We would not see each other for days, unless we met by accident; we never referred to what we'd done the last time we'd been together. We met like those who have murdered are said to meet, each tentatively and warily examining the other for signs of betrayal. But whom had we murdered? The boys who walked into that room? Or the women who briefly came to life within it? Perhaps this metaphor has outlived its meaning. Perhaps our shame derived not from our having killed but from our having created.

In early September, as Denny and I entered seventh grade, my father became ill. Over Labor Day weekend he was too tired to go fishing. On Monday his skin had vaguely yellowed; by Thursday he was severely jaundiced. On Friday he entered the hospital, his liver rapidly failing; Sunday he was dead. He died from acute hepatitis, possibly acquired while cleaning up after our sick dog, the doctor said. He was buried at Arlington National Cemetery, down the hill from the Tomb of the Unknown Soldier. After the twenty-one-gun salute, our mother pinned his colonel's insignia to our jacket lapels. I carried the flag from his coffin to the car. For two weeks I stayed home with my mother, helping her write thank-you notes on small white cards with black borders; one afternoon, as I was affixing postage to the square, plain envelopes, she looked at me across the dining room table. "You and Davis are all I have left," she said. She went into the kitchen and came back. "Tomorrow," she said, gathering up the note cards, "you'll have to go to school." Mornings I wandered the long corridors alone, separated from Denny by the fate of our last names, which had cast us into different homerooms and daily schedules. Lunchtimes we sat together in silence in the rear of the cafeteria. Afternoons, just before gym class, I went to the Health Room, where, lying on a cot, I'd imagine the Phys. Ed. coach calling my name from the class roll, and imagine my name, unclaimed, unanswered to, floating weightlessly away, like a balloon that one jumps to grab hold of but that is already out of reach. Then I'd hear the nurse dial the telephone. "He's sick again," she'd say. "Can you come pick him up?" At home I helped my mother empty my father's highboy. "No, we want to save that," she said when I folded his uniform into a huge brown bag that read GOODWILL INDUSTRIES; I wrapped it in a plastic dry-cleaner's bag and hung it in the hall closet.

After my father's death my relationship to my mother's things grew yet more complex, for as she retreated into her grief, she left behind only her mute objects as evidence of her life among us: objects that seemed as lonely and vulnerable as she was, objects that I longed to console, objects with which I longed to console myself—a tangled gold chain, thrown in frustration on the mantel; a wineglass, its rim stained with lipstick, left unwashed in the sink. Sometimes at night Davis and I heard her prop her pillow up against her bedroom wall, lean back heavily, and tune her radio to a call-in show: "*Night-caps, what are you thinking at this late hour?*" Sunday evenings, in order to help her prepare for the next day's job hunt, I stood over her beneath the bare basement bulb, the same bulb that first illuminated my father's jaundice. I set her hair, slicking each wet strand with gel and rolling it, inventing gossip that seemed to draw us together, a beautician and his customer.

"You have such pretty hair," I'd say.

"At my age, don't you think I should cut it?" She was almost fifty.

"No, never."

That fall Denny and I were caught. One evening my mother noticed something out of place in her closet. (Perhaps now that she no longer shared it, she knew where every belt and scarf should have been.)

I was in my bedroom doing my French homework, dreaming of one day visiting Au Printemps, the store my teacher spoke of so excitedly as she played us the Edith Piaf records that she had brought back from France. In the mirror above my desk I saw my mother appear at my door.

"Get into the living room," she said. Her anger made her small, reflected body seem taut and dangerous.

In the living room Davis was watching TV with Uncle Joe, our father's brother, who sometimes came to take us fishing. Uncle Joe was lying in our father's La-Z-Boy recliner.

"There aren't going to be any secrets in this house," she said. "You've been in my closet. What were you doing there?"

"No, we weren't," I said. "We were watching TV all afternoon."

"*We*? Was Denny here with you? Don't you think I've heard about that? Were you and Denny going through my clothes? Were you wearing them?"

"No, Mom," I said.

"Don't lie!" She turned to Uncle Joe, who was staring at us. "Make him stop! He's lying to me!"

She slapped me. Although I was already taller than she, she slapped me over and over, slapped me across the room until I was backed against the TV. Davis was motionless, afraid. But Uncle Joe jumped up and stood between my mother and me, holding her until her rage turned to sobs. "I can't, I can't be both a mother and a father," she said to him. "I can't do it." I could not look at Uncle Joe, who, although he was protecting me, did not know I was lying.

She looked at me. "We'll discuss this later," she said. "Get out of my sight."

We never discussed it. Denny was outlawed. I believe, in fact, that it was I who suggested he never be allowed in our house again. I told my mother I hated him. I do not think I was lying when I said this. I truly hated him—hated him, I mean, for being me.

For two or three weeks Denny tried to speak with me at the bus stop, but whenever he approached, I busied myself with kids I barely knew. After a while Denny found a new best friend, Lee, a child despised by everyone, for Lee was "effeminate." His clothes were too fastidious; he often wore his cardigan over his shoulders, like an old woman feeling a chill.

Sometimes, watching the street from our picture window, I'd see Lee walking toward Denny's house. "What a queer," I'd say to whoever might be listening. "He walks like a *girl*." Or sometimes, at the junior high school, I'd see him and Denny walking down the corridor, their shoulders pressed together as if they were telling each other secrets, or as if they were joined in mutual defense. Sometimes when I saw them, I turned quickly away, as though I'd forgotten something important in my locker. But when I felt brave enough to risk rejection, for I belonged to no group, I joined Bucky Trueblood's gang, sitting on the radiator in the main hall, and waited for Lee and Denny to pass us. As Lee and Denny got close, they stiffened and looked straight ahead.

"Faggots," I muttered.

I looked at Bucky, sitting in the middle of the radiator. As Lee and Denny passed, he leaned forward from the wall, accidentally disarranging the practiced severity of his clothes, his jeans puckering beneath his tooled belt, the breast pocket of his T-shirt drooping with the weight of a pack of Pall Malls. He whistled. Lee and Denny flinched. He whistled again. Then he leaned back, the hard lines of his body reasserting themselves, his left foot striking a steady beat on the tile floor with the silver V-tap of his black loafer.

# THOMAS MCGUANE

# A MAN IN LOUISIANA

## FROM SHENANDOAH

∽

THAT WINTER, Ohio Exploration had its meeting at the Grand Hotel in Point Clear, Alabama. Barry Seitz went along as special assistant to Mike Royce, the tough, relatively young president of Ohio Exploration. Barry knew spot checks could happen anytime and as this was his first job that could go anywhere, he memorized everything. The range of subjects ran from drilling reports in various oil plays in the Southeast to orthodontic opinions concerning Mike Royce's impossibly ugly daughter. It was Royce's thought that the girl's dentist was "getting the teeth straight, all right, but blowing her profile." Barry was to "mentally note" that Mike Royce wanted to get together some three- and four-year-old snapshots of the girl and arrange a conference with the dentist. Barry didn't envy the dentist. The girl had inherited her father's profile and would always be a rich little bulldog.

The winter meeting was going to be shortened and therefore compressed because Mike Royce had just decided that he hated the South. So, everyone was on edge and the orthodontic issue seemed quite inflamed the longer Royce contemplated his daughter's profile. Barry could see the pressure forming in his boss's face as he stared past the crab boats making their way across the dead slick bay. Barry arranged to have some pictures same-day delivered and he was with his boss when he thumbed through the snapshots. "I could shit," said Royce from a darkening face. "These kids around here have straight teeth and their folks can't change a light bulb."

A number of the things that Mike Royce said were irritating to Barry and when Royce was angry he expressed everything in a blur of exposed teeth that made part of Barry think of self-defending. But Barry saw himself on the cusp of failure or success. At thirty, a backward move could be a menace to his whole life; and while he knew he wouldn't be in Royce's employ forever, he wanted to stay long enough to learn oil lease trading so that he could go out on his own. Once he was free he could do the rest of the things he wanted, have a family, tropical fish, remote control model airplanes. The future was an unbroken sheen to Barry requiring only irreversible solvency. One of Barry's girlfriends had called him yellow. She went out with the morning trash. Having your ducks in a row does not equal yellow. Barry was cautious.

On the last day of their stay at the Grand Hotel in Point Clear, Alabama, Mike Royce rang for Barry. Barry went down to his room and found Royce in a spotted bathrobe, his blunt feet hooked on the rungs of his chair, staring at the photographs of his daughter arranged chronologically. The little girl's square head did seem to change imperceptibly from picture to picture though Barry could not tell the influence of hormones from the influence of orthodontic wire. From left to right, the child did seem to be losing character. In picture one she was clearly a vigorous young carnivore; and by picture seven she seemed insipid, headed nowhere. It seemed a lot to blame on the dentist who, Mike Royce pointed out, would be on the carpet Monday first thing. Barry wanted what Mike Royce wanted. So, Barry wanted those teeth right.

Now Royce turned his attention to Barry. He did not ask Barry to sit down but seemed to prefer to regard him from his compressed posture in his bathrobe.

"Billy Hebert," he said. "Remember him?" He was spot checking a mental note.

"Lake Charles," said Barry.

"That's right, a feature player in that deal down there. Now Billy's main lick, for fun, is to hunt birds—" He reached Barry a slip of paper. "That dog is in Mississippi. I want you to get it and take it to Billy in Lake Charles."

"Very well."

"If you remember back, we need to be doing something out of this world for Billy. Anyway, chop chop."

Barry could see the rows of private piers from Royce's window. A few people had gone out carrying crab traps, towels, radios. They seemed to mock Barry's dog-hauling mission with their prospects. But it was better than hearing about the girl's teeth.

A late fall haze from the paper mills outside Mobile hung on the water. The causeway bore a stream of Florida-bound traffic. Bay shrimpers plied the slick and playoff games sounded from every window of the resort. (He knew cheery types lined up in the lobby for morning papers.) It wasn't that Barry had less a sense of fun than anyone else. He had once alienated a favorite ladyfriend by yelling, "Whee!" during sex. But when riding mowers hummed with purpose on a December day in the Deep South, it seemed cruel and unusual to have to haul a dog from Mississippi to a crooked oil dealer in Louisiana.

The road to the small town in Mississippi on Royce's note wound up from the coastal plain past small cities and shanty towns. Barry ate at a drive-in restaurant next to an old cotton gin and drove up through three plantations that lay along the Tombigbee in what had been open country of farms and plantations. Arms of standing water appeared and disappeared as he soared over leggy trestles heading north. Barry began to be absorbed by his task. Where am I? he thought. He liked the idea of hauling a dog from Mississippi to Louisiana and didn't feel at all demeaned by it as he had back at the Marriott. He passed a monument where the bighearted Union army had set General Nathan Bedford Forrest free; and he felt giddily—no matter how many GTOs and pizza trucks he passed—that he was going back into time, toward Okolona and Shiloh. It seemed every third house had a fireworks stand selling M80s and bottle rockets; and every fifth house was a Baptist Church. O, variety! he thought, comparing this to Ohio.

He reached Blue Wood, Mississippi, shortly after noon

and stopped at a filling station for directions to the house of Jimmy F. Tippett, the man who had advertised the dog. Hearing his accent, the proprietor of the filling station, a round-faced man in coveralls, asked Barry where he came from.

"Chillicothe, Ohio."

The man looked at Barry's face for a moment and said, "Boy, you three-fo' mile from yo' house!"

He took a dirt road out past a gas field, past a huge abandoned WW II ammunition factory and abandoned rail spur. Blue Wood had the air of an old western town with its slightly elevated false-front buildings. Half the stores were abandoned and the sidewalks had three or four Negroes as the sole pedestrians. Barry drove slowly past the hardware store where a solitary white man gripped his counter and stared through the front door waiting for customers. Barry didn't think of this man's somber domination. "My God," he murmured. He couldn't wait to grab that bird dog and run. The teeth of Mike Royce's daughter were behind him, familiar and secure.

Jimmy F. Tippett's house was on the edge of a thousand-acre sorghum field. It was an old house with a metal roof and a narrow dogtrot breezeway. Because of its location, Barry thought it had a faint seaside atmosphere. But above all it spoke of poorness to Barry, and dirty stinking failure; his first thought was, How in the world did this guy lay hands on any dog Mike Royce would buy? Hunching over in the front seat after he'd parked, Barry gave way to temptation and opened Royce's envelope with a thumbnail. Inside was two thousand dollars in crisp hundreds. This, thought Barry, I've got to see.

He got out of the car, walking around the back of it so he could use it as a kind of blind while he looked things over. There were great big white clouds in the direction past the house and a few untended pecan trees. There had been a picket fence all around but it looked like cattle or something had just walked it down into the ground. Here and there a loop of it stood up and the pickets were weathered of most of their white paint and shaped at their ends like clubs in a deck of cards. Barry tried vainly to relate this to his career. In fact, how would Mike Royce and his accountants view this trip? He guessed it would have to be Travel and Entertainment.

The pattern of shadows on the screen door changed and

Barry interrupted his thought to recognize that one of the shadows must now be Jimmy F. Tippett. So he strode up to the house, gulping impressions, and said, "Mr. Tippett, is that you?"

"Yes, sir," came a voice.

"I'm Barry Seitz. I represent Mr. L. Michael Royce. I'm here about a dog."

The screen opened and inside it stood a small man about sixty years of age, in khaki pants and starched white shirt. He had an auto insurance company pen holder in his pocket and a whistle around his neck. His face was entirely covered by fine dark wrinkles. A cigarette hung from the corner of his mouth. He looked Barry over as though he were doing a credit check. "Tippett," he said. "Come in."

Barry walked in. It appeared that Tippett lived entirely in one room. "I can't stay but a minute. I've got to get this dog to Louisiana."

"Have a seat," said Tippett. Barry moved backward and slipped into a chair. Tippett watched him do it. "I'll get the whiskey out," said Tippett. "Help you unwind."

"I'm quite relaxed," said Barry defiantly but Tippett got down a bottle from a pie safe that held the glasses, too.

"You want water or Sem Up?" asked Tippett.

"Neat," said Barry.

"You what?"

"Just straight would be fine," Barry said. Tippett served their whiskey and sat down next to his television set. His drink hand moved slightly, a toast. Barry moved his. It was quiet.

"You go to college?" asked Tippett.

"Yes," said Barry, narrowly avoiding the words "Ohio State." "And you?" he asked. Tippett did not answer and Barry feared he'd taken it as a contemptuous question. Nevertheless, he decided not to go into anything long about college being a waste of time. In fact, Barry had a sudden burst of love for his old college. He felt a small ache looking around the bare room for days of wit and safety before he'd been out and about on unfathomable missions like this one. Dogs, tooth pictures, oil crooks, a secure future. Tippett was humming a tune and looking around the room. I know that tune, thought Barry, it's

"Yankee Doodle Dandy." You bastards fired on our flag first. Fort Sumter.

"What's that song you're whistling?"

"Oh, a old song."

"Really! I sort of remember it as a favorite of mine."

"That's nice. Yes, sir, that's nice. Some of these songs nowadays, why I don't like them. They favor shit to me." There was a worn-out shotgun in the corner, boots, a long rope with a snap on it.

"Let's have a look at this famous dog," said Barry.

"Ain't famous."

"Expensive."

"Expensive? I get about twenty-five cents an ar to wuk the prick."

Tippett whistled through his teeth and a pointer came in from the next room on his belly and laid his head on Tippett's knee. "There he is—Old Bandit."

"He's good-looking," said Barry.

"He get better lookin when you turn him aloose. He'll slap find birds. He a gentleman's shooting dog De Ville. Use a section bean field in five minute. Fellow need enough country for a dog like Bandit. Bandit a foot dog, a truck dog, and a horseback dog. Bandit everything they is. He broke to death but he'll run off on a fool, now."

Barry had caught up on the word *gentleman*. A gentleman's dog. He could see all this, somehow, in the words of the ardent old Tippett. He looked at fidelity writ large in the peaceful bird dog's anciently carved head and was entirely unable to picture the kind of fool he'd run off on. This was a landowner's dog, he sensed, and he mildly resented having to pack him to Louisiana.

"I wish I owned this dog," said Barry.

"I do, too," said Tippett, staring once again at L. Michael Royce's money. "This any good?" he asked, holding it up. Barry just nodded. He wanted to say Royce was an asshole. He was entirely in the world of Tippett, feeling the senselessness of trading the money for Bandit. Now the atmosphere was heavy with the idea of lost dog.

A long silence followed and Barry felt that there had formed a kind of intimacy. This man had something that he and Royce and the man in Louisiana wanted; but now he had gone over to the other side. When he took the dog to the car on a lead, Tippett said, "I was sixty-six in August. I'll never have another dog like that." When he went to the house, he didn't pet Bandit; he never looked back.

Barry started down the road with Bandit on the seat beside him as he went back through the town of Blue Wood. The huge clouds he had noticed driving to Tippett's had seemed to enlarge with the massive angular light of evening; and the empty buildings of Blue Wood looked bombed out and absolutely derelict. A man was selling barbecue from an outdoor smoker. Barry stopped and ate some pork and slaw while he looked at the four-way roads trailing off into big fields. He thought, I'd like to give that dog a whirl. The man rolled down the lid on the smoker.

"Like anything to drink?"

"Sem Up," said Barry. He had decided he would run Bandit.

Barry drove alongside the vast soybean field with its tangle of stalks and curled leaves and long strips of combined ground. There were hedgerows of small hardwoods wound about with burdocks and kudzu. Some of the fields had gas wells and at one county road corner there was a stack of casing pipe and a yellow backhoe as battered as an army tank. When the road came to an end, the bean fields stretched along a stream course and over low rounded hills as far to the west as Barry could see. This is it, he thought, and stopped.

Bandit stirred and whined when the engine shut off. He sat up and stared through the windshield at the empty space. It made Barry apprehensive to not quite understand what riveted his attention so. I wish I had more information, he thought. A little something more to go by. Nevertheless, he turned Bandit loose and thought for the short time he saw him that Tippett was right, that he got prettier and prettier, in his burning race over the horizon. He was gone. It was as though Mike Royce towered up out of the Mississippi horizon to stare down at Barry in his rental car. Clutching the orthodontic photographs and Barry's employment contract.

He got out and started running across the bean field. He ran so fast and uncaringly that the ground seemed to rise and fall beneath him as he crossed the hills. He hit a piece of soft, ploughed ground and it sapped his strength so quickly he found himself stopped, his hands gripping his knees. "Oh, Bandit," he cried out, "Come back!"

Just before dusk, he came through a grove of oak on the edge of a swamp. A cold mist had started up in fingers toward the trees; and at their very edge stood Bandit on point, head high sipping the breeze, tail straight as a poker, in a trance of found birds. Barry thought he cried out to Bandit but he wasn't sure and he knew he wished he wouldn't frighten him into motion. He walked steadily in Bandit's direction. He stood at his work not acknowledging him. When he was about a hundred feet away, the covey started to flush. He froze as birds roared up like brown bees and swarmed into the swamp. But Bandit stood still and Barry knew he had him. He admired Tippett's training in keeping Bandit so staunch and walked to the dog in an agony of relief. Good Bandit, he said and patted his head, Bandit's signal to go on hunting: He shot into the swamp.

The brambles along the watery edge practically tore his clothes off. His hands felt sticky from bloody scratches. By turns he saw himself strangling Royce, Tippett, and the man in Louisiana. He wondered if Royce would ever see him as a can-do guy again. From Cub Scouts on he had had this burden of reliability and as he felt the invisible dog tearing it away he began to wonder why he was running so fast.

He reached higher ground and a grove of hickories with a Confederate cemetery, forty or fifty unknown soldiers. He sat down to rest among the small stones, gasping for air. What he first took to be the sound of chimes emerging distantly from the ground turned out to be his own ringing ears. It occurred to him that some of the doomed soldiers around him had gone to their deaths with less hysteria and less terror than he had brought to the chase for this dog. Maybe it wasn't just the dog, he thought, and grew calm. Maybe it was that little bitch and her crowned teeth.

It was dark and Barry gave himself up to it. A symphonic array of odors came up from the ground with the cooling night and he imagined the Confederate bones turning into hickory trees over the centuries. Shade, shelter from the wind, wood for ax handles, charcoal for barbecue. Sem Up. Bones.

But, he thought, standing, that dog isn't dead yet; and he resumed his walk. He regained open country somehow and walked in a gradual curve that he thought would return him to his car. He thought his feet remembered the hills but he wasn't sure and he didn't care. His eyes recorded the increasing density of night until he could no longer see the ground under him. The moon rose and lit the far contours of things but close up the world was in eclipse. In a while, he came to the edge of a pond. Only its surface could be seen like a sheet of silver hanging in midair. As he studied it, trying to figure out how to go around, the shapes of horses materialized on its surface. He knew they must be walking the bank but the bank itself was invisible and the only knowledge of horses he had was the progress of their reflection on the still water. When the horses passed, he walked toward the water until he saw his own shape. He watched it disappear and knew he'd gone on around.

Back in the bean field, Barry felt a mild wave of hysteria pass over him once more, one in which he imagined writing a memo to Royce about having been knee-deep in soybean futures, much to report, et cetera, et cetera, by the way couldn't seem to lay hands on Louisiana man's dog et cetera, et cetera. Hope dogface girl's teeth didn't all fall out. More later, yrs, B. After which, he felt glumly merry and irresponsible.

When he got to his car, it occurred to him that this had all happened a couple of miles from Tippett's house. No great distance for a hyena like Bandit. So he drove over there where he found the house unlighted and silent. He walked to the door. A bark broke out and was muffled. Barry knocked. The door opened and Tippett said, "I thought you went to Louisiana."

"Hand him over," said Barry.

"Come in," said Tippett. Barry walked into the empty room. Tippett had a loose T-shirt on and his pants were held by the top button only. Barry looked all around and saw nothing. He felt uncertain.

"Didn't Bandit come back?"

Tippett didn't answer. He just sat down and poured from the whiskey bottle that was right where he'd left it earlier.

"You lose that dog?" he asked. Something tapped across the floor in the next room. He doesn't want to go to Louisiana, he thought, and he surely doesn't want to go with me. A wave of peace came over him.

"Yeah, I did," said Barry, rising in his own esteem. The old man studied him closely, studied his face and every little thing he did with his hands. Barry raised his glass to his lips, thinking only of the movement and the whiskey. He quit surveying the old man's possessions and wondering what time it was somewhere else.

"What do you suppose would make a trained dog just go off and leave like that?" Barry asked.

The old man made a sound in his throat, almost clearing it to speak something which must not be misunderstood. "Son," he said, "anything that'll eat shit and fuck its own mother is liable to do anything." The two men laughed as equals.

Barry thought of the men down in the Confederate grave-yard. He considered the teeth of Mike Royce's daughter and his own "future." Above all, he thought of how a dog could run so far that, like other things, it never came back.

# SUE MILLER

# INVENTING THE ABBOTTS

## FROM MADEMOISELLE

∽

LLOYD ABBOTT WASN'T the richest man in our town, but he had, in his daughters, a vehicle for displaying his wealth that some of the richer men didn't have. And, more unusual in our midwestern community, he had the inclination to do so. And so, at least twice a year, passing by the Abbotts' house on the way to school, we boys would see the striped fabric of a tent stretched out over their grand backyard, and we'd know there was going to be another occasion for social anxiety. One of the Abbott girls was having a birthday, or graduating, or coming out, or going away to college. "Or getting her period," I said once to my brother, but he didn't like that. He didn't much like me at that time, either.

By the time we'd return home at the end of the day, the tent would be up and workmen would be moving under the cheerful colors, setting up tables and chairs, arranging big pots of seasonal flowers. The Abbotts' house was on the main street in town, down four or five blocks from where the commercial section began, in an area of wide lawn and overarching elms. Now all those trees have been cut down because of Dutch elm disease and the area has an exposed, befuddled air. But then it

165

was a grand promenade, nothing like our part of town, where the houses huddled close as if for company; and there probably weren't many people in town who didn't pass by the Abbotts' house once a day or so, on their way to the library for a book, or to Woolworth's for a ball of twine, or to the grocery store or the hardware store. And so everyone knew about and would openly discuss the parties, having to confess whether they'd been invited or not.

My brother, Jacey, usually had been, and for that reason was made particularly miserable on those rare occasions when he wasn't. I was the age of the youngest daughter, Pamela, and so I was later to be added to the usual list. By the time I began to be invited to the events under the big top, I had witnessed enough of the agony which the whimsicality of the list cost my brother to resolve never to let it be that important to me. Often I just didn't go to something I'd been invited to, more than once without bothering to RSVP. And when I did go, I refused to take it seriously. For instance, sometimes I didn't dress as the occasion required. At one of the earliest parties I attended, when I was about thirteen, I inked sideburns on my cheeks, imagining I looked like my hero of the moment—of several years actually—Elvis Presley. When Jacey saw me, he tried to get my mother not to let me go unless I washed my face.

"It'll look worse if I wash it," I said maliciously. "It's India ink. It'll turn gray. It'll look like dirt."

My mother had been reading when we came in to ask her to adjudicate. She kept her finger in the book to mark her place the whole time we talked, and so I knew Jacey didn't have much of a chance. She was just waiting for us to leave.

"What I don't understand, John," my mother said to Jacey—she was the only one who called him by his real name—"is why it should bother you if Doug wants to wear sideburns."

"*Mother*," Jacey said. He was forever explaining life to her, and she never got it. "This isn't a costume party. No one else is going to be *pretending* to be someone else. He's supposed to just come in a jacket and tie and dance. And he isn't even wearing a tie."

"And that bothers you?" she asked in her gentle, high-pitched voice.

"Of course," he said.

She thought for a moment. "Is it that you're ashamed of him?"

This was hard for Jacey to answer. He knew by my mother's tone that he ought to be above such pettiness. Finally, he said, "It's not that I'm ashamed. I'm just trying to protect him. He's going to be sorry. He looks like such a jerk and he doesn't even know it. He doesn't understand the *implications*."

There was a moment of silence while we all took this in. Then my mother turned to me. She said, "Do you understand, Doug, that you may be the only person at this party in artificial sideburns?"

"Yeah," I answered. Jacey stirred restlessly, desperately. He could see where this was heading.

"Do you understand, honey, that your sideburns don't look real?" Her voice was unwaveringly gentle, kind.

Well, I had thought they might almost look real, and this news from someone as impartial as my mother was hard to take. But the stakes were high. I nodded. "Yeah," I said.

She pressed it. "That they look, really, as though you'd drawn them on?"

I swallowed and shrugged. "Yeah," I said again.

She looked hard at me a moment. Then she turned to Jacey. "Well, darling," she said. "It appears he does understand. So you've really done all you can, and you'd better just go along and try to ignore him." She smiled, as though to try to get him to share a joke. "Just pretend you never saw him before in your life."

Jacey was enraged. I could see he was trembling, but he had boxed himself in with his putative concern for my social welfare. I felt the thrill of knowing I was causing him deep pain.

"Mother," he said, as though the word were a threat. "You don't understand *anything*." He left the room, slamming the door behind him.

My mother, who never discussed the behavior of one of us with the other, didn't even look at me. She bowed her head in the circle of lamplight and continued to read her book. I left too, after a moment, and was in my room when I heard Jacey hurtling past my door and down the stairs again. His rage had been feeding on itself and he was yelling almost before he got into her presence. "Let me tell you something, Mom. If you let him go to the party like that, I'm not going. Do you hear me? I'm not going." His breathing was audible to me from the top of the stairs—he was near tears—but my mother's answer, which was long, was just a murmur, a gentle flow of her voice for awhile. And though he ran out of the house afterward, slamming the front door this time, he was at the party when I got there later. He was dancing and following my mother's advice to pretend he didn't know me.

The reason my entry into his social world, particularly the Abbott part of it, was so painful, so important, to my brother was that he had already fallen in love with their family, with everything they stood for. In an immediate sense, he was in love with the middle Abbott girl, Eleanor. She wasn't the prettiest of the three, but she seemed it. She was outgoing and sarcastic and very popular; and Jacey wasn't the only boy at Bret Harte High trying to close in on her. He spent a long time on the phone each evening talking either to her or about her to girlfriends of hers who seemed to manage her social life through messages they would or wouldn't take for her. He was with her whenever he could be after school and on weekends. But here he was at a disadvantage because he, like me, had a part-time job all through high school, which the other boys in our circle of friends didn't. In this difference between us and the others we knew socially lay, I think, a tremendous portion of the appeal Eleanor Abbott had for my brother.

My father was one of the few in Haley who had died in the Second World War, killed by American bombs actually, while being held prisoner by the Germans. Most of the fathers of our friends had had large enough families by the time America got involved that they didn't go. But my father enlisted when Jacey was two and I was on the way. He died only a few months before my birth, and my mother brought us back to live with her parents in Haley, the small town in Illinois where she'd grown up.

I can't remember my Grandfather Vetter well—he had a heart attack when I was still quite small—but Grandma Vetter was as important as a second parent throughout my childhood. She died when I was ten. We had just sat down to dinner one night when she said, "I think I'll just lie down for a little while," as though that were what everyone did at the beginning of a meal. My mother watched her walk down the hallway to her room on the first floor, and then went directly to the telephone and called the doctor. Grandma Vetter was dead by the time he arrived, stretched out on the bed with her dress neatly covering her bony knees. I remember thinking that there was some link between the way she looked, as though she *were* just resting and would get up any minute, and the way the table looked, every place neatly set, every plate heaped with food, as though we would sit down any minute. I was very hungry, and looking at the table made me want to have my dinner, but I knew I shouldn't care about the food at a time like this—my mother and brother were crying—and I was ashamed of myself.

Throughout my childhood my grandmother preferred Jacey to me—he was a more polite, conscientious boy—and this left my mother and me with a special bond. She was, as I've indicated, incapable of overt favoritism, but she told me later that my infancy provided her with a special physical comfort after my father's death, and I often felt a charge of warmth and protectiveness from her when my grandmother was critical of me, as she often was, in one way or another.

My mother was the only woman in our circle who worked. She taught second grade at the Haley Elementary School, moving to third grade the years Jacey and I would have been her pupils. And, as I've said, we boys worked too, starting in seventh and eighth grade, mowing lawns and delivering papers. By our senior year of high school, each of us had a salaried part-time job, Jacey at the county hospital, I at a drive-in in town. It wasn't that others in our world led lives of great luxury—few besides the Abbott girls did. Our home, the things we did, the kinds of summer trips we took, were much like those of our friends. But my brother and I provided ourselves with many of the things our friends' parents provided them with, eventually even paying most of our own way through college. We were "nice" boys, ambitious boys, but there was a price for our ambition.

Somehow we must have understood too, and yet didn't question, that although our lives were relatively open—we could number among our friends the richest kids, the most popular kids—our mother's mobility in Haley was over. She was single, she needed to work. These facts constituted an insurmountable social barrier for her. Yet it seems to me I barely noticed her solitude, her isolation from the sociable couples who were the parents of my friends. And even if I had noticed it, I wouldn't have believed it could have a connection to the glorious possibilities I assumed for my own life.

Because of our relative poverty, our lives were full of events which were beyond the experience of our friends, but which then seemed only adventurous and exciting to me. For instance, coming back from a car trip to California one summer, we ran out of money. My mother stopped in Las Vegas with a nearly empty gas tank and about three dollars' worth of change in her purse, and won over two hundred dollars—more than enough to get home on—with her second quarter in the slot machine. That kind of thing didn't happen to friends of ours, and somehow, as a result, their mothers seemed more childish to me, less capable, less strong. I thought there was no one else like my mother.

But Jacey yearned for everything she, he, we, were not, and in his senior year of high school, he particularly yearned for Eleanor Abbott.

I'm finally able to see now that at least a part of my passionate embrace of the role of rebel in high school had to do with a need to leap over the embarrassment I could not, out of loyalty to my mother, let myself feel about all those aspects of our lives which I was slowly beginning to perceive as difficult or marginal. I *did* think the Abbott girls and their endless parties ostentatious, ridiculous; but in addition, some private part of me yearned, angrily, for the ease and gracefulness of their kind of life, their sure sense of who they were and how they fit in, as much as Jacey yearned overtly for it.

At the time, though, I thought his yearning, particularly his yearning for Eleanor, was shallow and contemptible. She was a year ahead of me in high school, but even I knew she wasn't smart. In fact, she was in biology with me because she'd flunked it the first time around. I couldn't understand what attracted him to her, especially since I knew she hung around at least as much, and perhaps more—because he was so often busy with his job—with three or four other senior boys.

One summer afternoon, though, the last summer before Jacey went off to college, the drive-in where I worked closed early because the air-conditioning was out of order. I came straight home, elated to have an unexpected day off. My mother had gone up to Chicago for a few days to visit a college friend, and I expected Jacey might still be sleeping, since he was working the night shift as an orderly at the county hospital. I was hot, and I felt like celebrating my release from routine, so I charged down the basement stairs two at a time to raid the big freezer. My mother kept it stocked with four or five gallons of various flavors of ice cream. As I opened the case and leaned into the cool, sweet darkness the freezer seemed to exhale up at me, I heard a rustling noise from the front part of the basement, a whisper. I shut the freezer slowly, my heart thudding, and moved silently toward the doorway. I don't know what I expected—thieves, perhaps—but it wasn't what I saw in the few seconds I stood in the doorway before my brother shouted, "No!" and I turned away. He and Eleanor Abbott were naked on the daybed set up near the wall of the coal bin, and Eleanor Abbott was sitting on him. He was in the process of reaching up with his body to cover hers from view when I looked at them. The light in the basement was dim and they were in the far corner—it was like looking at silvery fish in an unlighted aquarium—but the vision lingered with me a long time, clear and indelible.

I left the house immediately—got my bike out of the garage and rode around aimlessly in the heat all afternoon. By the time I came home, it was twilight and my brother was gone. I went down to the basement again. I went into the front room and I lay down on the daybed. I turned my face into its mildew-smelling cover, and imagined that I was breathing in also the rich, mysterious odor of sex.

I remember being less surprised at my brother than I was at Eleanor Abbott. I thought about the three or four other boys she went out with—some of them more seriously than with my brother, I knew from gossip at school. The possibility arose that Eleanor Abbott was having sex, not just normal sex as I'd been able to imagine it with girls I knew, but that she was actually *sitting* on all of the boys she went out with. The possibility arose that Eleanor Abbott, whom I'd seen as utterly vacuous, utterly the conventional rich girl, was a bigger rebel than even I was, in my blue jeans and secret cigarettes, in the haircut I now modeled on James Dean's.

My brother never mentioned what I'd seen, and the silence seemed to increase the distance between us, although I felt a respect for him I'd never entertained before. I saw that even his life could contain mysteries unguessed at by me.

He went away to college that fall on a partial scholarship. I saw Eleanor Abbott around school. Sometimes she'd smile at me in the halls or say hello, especially when she was with friends. I felt that I was somehow comical or amusing to her, and I felt at those moments genuinely exposed, as though what she seemed to think of me was all I really was—a joker, a poser. I discovered, too, that she dominated my fantasy life completely, as she perhaps knew when she'd laugh and throw her head back and say, "Hello, Doug," when we met. Once I actually walked into a door as she passed.

She went to college the next year, to a women's college in the East. My brother mentioned her several times in letters to my mother, letters she read aloud to me. He said that he'd gone to visit her, or had her to Amherst for the weekend. I don't know what visions this conjured for my mother—she never offered her opinion on any of the Abbotts except to say once that Lloyd Abbott had been "kind of a dud" as a young man—but for me images of absolute debauchery opened up. I could hardly wait to be alone in my room. I found these images nearly impossible, though, to connect with my breathing brother when he came home at Christmas or Easter, ever more trig, ever more polished.

Eleanor didn't come home at the Easter break, I remember, and Jacey seemed to have no trouble finding other women to hang around with. This shocked me, his betrayal of her, in a way that her earlier presumed betrayal of him did not. It seemed, as hers had not, cynical. Hers I had romanticized as wildness, pure appetite.

Sometime in early May I was sitting at the dining room table doing homework, when the phone rang. My mother was in the kitchen, and she called, "I'll get it." She came out to the telephone stand in the hall. Her voice, after the initial hello, was cool and polite, so I assumed it was some social acquaintance of hers and went back to my chemistry. She was silent on the phone a long time, and then she said, sharply and angrily, "No, that's impossible." Her tone made me look up. She had turned her back to me, as though to shield me from whatever was going on. After another, shorter silence, she said, "No, I'm sorry. I can't do that. If you have something to say to my son, you'd better talk to him yourself." I started to stand, my heart thudding, thinking of the various misdeeds of the last weeks, the last months. I ran around at the time with a small gang of misfits, and we specialized in anonymous and, we thought, harmless acts of vandalism—like setting a car upside down on its owner's front lawn, or breaking into the school cafeteria and urinating into the little cartons of orange juice.

"That's right," my mother said stiffly. "I'm very sorry." And she hung up.

After a moment she turned and saw me still standing there, looking, I'm sure, terrified and puzzled. Her worried face relaxed. She laughed. "Sit down, darling," she said. "You look as though you're about to meet your maker."

She came into the dining room and put her hands along the back of the chair opposite me. "That wasn't even about you. It was Joan Abbott, about John." The vertical line between her eyebrows returned. "I'm going to ask you one question, Doug, and if you have no idea, or don't want to answer, just tell me."

I nodded.

She looked down at her hands, as if she was ashamed to be doing what she was about to do. "Is there any sense, do you think, in which John has—oh, I don't know, it sounds ridiculous—*corrupted* Eleanor Abbott? Led her astray?"

My mind was working in several directions at once, trying to reconstruct the phone call, trying to figure out what the answer to the question might really be, trying to figure out how much I wanted to tell her, and if I told her anything, how to put it.

"Well, I know he's made love to her," I blurted finally. She looked startled only for a second. I could feel a deep flush rise to my face. "But not because he's *talked* about it." She nodded, I think, approvingly. "But—I would have said that Eleanor was pretty much in charge of her own life. I mean, she had lots of boyfriends. That she slept with, I think. Even in high school." By now I was talking down to my chemistry book. "I mean, I think he liked her more than she liked him. Not that she didn't like him. I mean, I don't know," I said.

"I see," my mother said. I looked up at her. Suddenly she grinned at me and I felt the pinch of love for her that came only occasionally at this stage of my life. "Well, that was clear as a bell, Doug."

That June, Pamela Abbott, who was in my class, had a tent party to celebrate our graduation. I had been eagerly anticipating seeing Eleanor there, telling her I was going to Harvard in the fall, trying, as I see now, the appeal of my conventional success where the romance of my rebel stance had failed. My brother had been home for a week but he hadn't mentioned her, and some secret, competitive part of me hoped she was done with him, that she would turn to me for the intensity she hadn't found in him.

There was no sign of Eleanor. I danced with her sister once and asked about her; she simply said that Eleanor couldn't make it. But what I heard from others in the course of the evening, in little knotted whispers, was that Eleanor had in some sense broken with her family. Run away somehow. She'd flunked or dropped out of school (something no boy in our world, much less a girl, would ever do), and had taken a job as a waitress or a dancer or an airline stewardess, depending on who told the story.

When I got home that night, I saw the light on in my brother's room. I went and stood awkwardly in his doorway. He was reading in bed, the lower part of his body covered with a sheet, the upper part naked. I remember looking at the filled-in grown-up shape of his upper body and momentarily hating him.

"Thought I'd report on the Abbott party," I said.

He set his book down. "I've been to the Abbott party," he said, and smiled.

"Well, everyone was there, except you."

"I'm surprised you still go," he said.

"I'm surprised you don't," I said.

"I wasn't asked."

"Oh," I said, with, I hoped, a question in my voice.

"I'm *persona non grata* there," he said flatly.

After a pause, I said, "Eleanor wasn't there, either."

"M-mm," he said. "Well, I'm not surprised."

"I heard she'd left school," I said.

"I heard that too," he answered.

"What's she doing now?" I asked.

"She hasn't told me," he said.

"So you're not in touch with her," I asked.

"No, I've outlived my usefulness to Eleanor." I was surprised to hear the bitterness in his voice.

"How were you *useful* to her?"

"I should imagine that would be easy enough to figure out."

I didn't know what to say.

"I mean," he said, "even aside from the little scene in the basement."

I shook my head, confused and embarrassed.

"Look," he said. "Eleanor was looking for a way not to be an Abbott, to get away from that whole world. And it turns out that it takes a lot to get away. It's not enough that you sleep around with boys from your world. But when you start fucking boys from across the *tracks*—" he said. He was agitated. He sat up, throwing back the covers, and got out of bed. He walked to the dresser and lit a cigarette.

"You mean she was sleeping with guys—like Prohaska or something?" I tried not to look at his nakedness.

He stood leaning on the dresser. He inhaled sharply on the cigarette and then smiled at me. "No, I mean she was sleeping with me. And she made sure her parents found out about it."

I was silent for a moment, unable to understand. "But *we're* not from across the tracks," I said.

He cocked his head. "No?" he asked. "Well, maybe I'm not talking about literal tracks."

"I don't believe that," I said after a pause. "I don't believe in what you're talking about."

He shrugged. "So don't believe in it," he said. He carried the cigarette and an ashtray back to bed with him, covered himself again.

I persisted. "I mean, we're just the same as them. We're just as good as they are."

He smiled. "Ask the Abbotts about that."

"The Abbotts," I said, with what I hoped was grand contempt in my voice, forgetting for the moment my eagerness to attend Pamela's party.

"Okay. Ask Mom. Ask her about how well *she's* lived in Haley all these years. Ask her whether she's as good as anyone else around here." Then, as though something in my face stopped him, his expression changed. He shrugged. "Maybe I'm all wet," he said. "Maybe you're right." He tapped an ash into the ashtray. "I mean, this is America after all, right?"

I stood in the doorway a minute more. "So what do you think Eleanor is doing?" I finally asked.

"Look, I don't care what she's doing," he said. He picked up his book, and after a few minutes I left.

I went to Harvard in the fall, as did Pamela Abbott— though in those days we still called her part of it Radcliffe. The year after that my brother moved to Cambridge to study architecture at Harvard. Gingerly we began to draw closer together. We still occupied entirely different worlds, mine sloppy and disorganized, his orderly and productive. I thought it emblematic of this that I was so utterly unattracted to the women he preferred. They were neat, wealthy, Waspy and, to me, asexual. I was drawn to ethnic types, women with dark skin, liquid black eyes, wild hair. But I had none. My wild women were abstracts, whereas Jacey had a regular string of real women in and out of his apartment; and I could never look at them, with their tiny pained smiles, without thinking of Eleanor perched on top of my brother in the damp basement the day I wanted ice cream.

We both continued to go home each summer to be with my mother, and it was the summer following his first year in Cambridge, the summer before my junior year, that Jacey fell in love with the oldest Abbott sister, Alice.

Alice had been a year ahead of him in high school, had

gone to a two-year college somewhere, and then married. She was arguably the prettiest of the sisters, the most conventional, and if she hadn't been older than he was at a time when that constituted a major barrier, she was probably the one my brother would have been attracted to in the first place. If he had fallen in love with her back in high school, I think their courtship might have proceeded at a pace slow enough, tender enough, so that her parents might ultimately have been reconciled to it; the issue of our marginal social status might have been overcome if it hadn't been combined with Eleanor's sexual precocity, if Alice had come first.

But Alice had married someone else, someone acceptable, and had two children. And now she was back home, something having happened to her marriage. The children were preschoolers; and I was startled once that summer to walk past the Abbotts' house and see a tent set up in the backyard with balloons and streamers floating in the protected air beneath it. I heard children's shouts, someone crying loudly, and I realized that the cycle had begun again for the Abbotts. That if Alice stayed at home, their house, their largesse, would dominate the social world of another generation of Haley children.

I don't know where Jacey met Alice—there certainly were enough people in whose homes they might have bumped into one another—and I can't imagine how he explained himself to her in the context of what her family thought had gone on between him and Eleanor, but he began to see her secretly that summer, arranging to go to the same parties, to meet accidentally. I went out with Pamela every now and then without having any romantic interest in her; we mostly commiserated on how dull Haley was, talked about places around Boston we missed; and she told me about Jacey and Alice.

I said I didn't believe her.

"Alice told me," she said.

"But secretly?" I asked.

"She's afraid of my parents," Pamela said.

"But she's a grown woman, with children. I mean, she's been married, for God's sake."

"Oh, that," Pamela said contemptuously.

"What do you mean, 'Oh, that'?" I asked.

"That was practically an arranged marriage," she said.

"They think that Alice has peanut shells for brains or something, so they sort of suggested after she graduated that maybe it was time to tie the old knot, and they sort of suggested that Peter was the one she ought to do it with. Or they just waxed so enthusiastic about him or something that she just did it."

"I don't believe it," I said. I thought of my own mother—how conscientiously she had left Jacey and me free to make our own choices and decisions in life. "No one could be that miserable."

She shrugged. "Look, Alice is the good one, and Eleanor was the bad one, and I'm the one who sort of gets off the hook. I don't know how it got set up that way, but that's the way it works."

We sat in silence for a minute. "What do you hear from Eleanor?" I asked.

She looked at me sternly. "I don't," she said.

I'm not sure that Jacey even slept with Alice that first summer. From what little he said about her, and from what I knew via Pamela, Alice was feeling fragile since the end of the marriage and tentative about getting involved with someone supposedly as dangerous as Jacey. But it was striking to me back in Cambridge that year that he stopped seeing other women. The seemingly endless parade in and out of his apartment stopped; and I was the one, finally, who had women.

I only had two, but it was enough to perplex me thoroughly. I was very involved with theater groups at Harvard; I'd been in one production or another practically nonstop since midway through my freshman year. Now, as a junior, I was getting lead roles; and the exotic women I'd dreamed of having, theatrical women who ringed their eyes with black pencil, were interested in me. But somehow both my romances fell flat, didn't seem as gripping as the roles I played; or even as the tense, delicate relationship Jacey was now maintaining by mail with Alice. Though he wouldn't really talk about Alice with me, about what she was like or what they did together, I knew he was determined to have her, to rescue her the following summer, and I watched it all impatiently.

The summer started and then progressed somewhat as the first one had. There were the frequent phone calls, the arranged meetings. But then Jacey brought Alice to our house.

I suppose they had problems finding places to go together privately, and they finally decided they had no alternative. At first it was when my mother was away, off on her annual trip to a college classmate's in Chicago. I was sitting in the living room, watching television, and I heard them come in. I looked up to see Alice, then Jacey, going upstairs. I could hear the murmur of their voices off and on through the night after I went to bed, and the sounds of their lovemaking, but it didn't bother me as it might have if it had been Eleanor. They left sometime in the dead of the night.

He brought her to the house every night my mother was gone, and we never spoke of it. I don't know what they did in the weeks after my mother's return, but in mid-August, he brought Alice to the house when my mother was home. She didn't hear them come in. She was in the backyard watering the plants; and then for a while I could hear her moving around the kitchen. At about ten o'clock, though, she crossed to the bottom of the stairs and stopped, hearing their voices. Then she came into the dining room, where I was.

"Who's upstairs with John?" she asked.

"I think it's Alice Abbott," I said.

"Oh," she said. "How long is she likely to stay?"

"I don't know," I said. "But I wouldn't stay up and wait for her to leave."

The next morning I didn't have breakfast at home. From the time I woke I could hear Jacey and mother talking in the kitchen, their voices floating out the open windows in the still summer air, hers steady, kind, and his impassioned, occasionally quite clearly audible. From what he said, I could tell she felt he needed to make his courtship of Alice open. It even seemed she was trying to get him to move out if he wanted to sleep with Alice, perhaps rent a room somewhere. As I left the house, he was saying, "But it's because I do love her, Mother. It couldn't be more different from Eleanor. Eleanor was just an *idea* I had."

I went to the new shopping mall just outside of town and had six honey-dipped doughnuts. I sat next to Evan Lederer—I'd known him in high school—and we talked about summer jobs. Evan was doing construction with a crew working on the interstate, and he had an even, bronze tan to show for it. As we stood together at the cash register, he said, "I hear your brother's taking out Alice Abbott."

"Is that right?" I said.

He grinned and punched my arm.

I don't know what my brother and mother agreed on, but he didn't move out and he didn't, to my knowledge, ever bring Alice to the house again. And then, just before he was to go back to Cambridge and reclaim his apartment from a subletter who was leaving early, it was over. Her parents had found out and simply said no, and apparently Alice didn't have the strength or the financial independence to defy them.

There were several days of phone calls, when my mother and I sat shut in the kitchen or our respective rooms, trying not to listen to Jacey's desperate voice rising and falling, attempting to persuade Alice that it could work if she would just make the break.

And then even the calls stopped, and he just stayed in his room until his job ended and he could leave. And that's literally how he did it. He came home from his last day of work, took a shower, and started loading up his car. My mother tried to persuade him to stay overnight and start the trip the following morning, but he argued that he'd have to drive through at least part of one night anyway, and it might as well be at the beginning of the trip. "Besides," he told her, "the sooner I get out of this fucking town the better."

It shocked me to hear my brother swear in front of my mother, mostly because I took it as an indicator of how deeply lost he was in his own misery; we simply never used that kind of language when she was around. She seemed to put the same construction on it I did, though. Without missing a beat, she said, "Well, of course you feel that way. Would you like me to make you some snacks for the road?"

When he left, she stood looking after his car for a long time. I went up onto the front porch, but she didn't follow. Finally I called to her, "Are you coming in, Mom?" And she turned and began to climb the stairs. I had a sudden revelation then of my mother's age. She had always looked the same age to me—simply *older*—but in that moment she looked as tired as

Grandma Vetter had when she told us that she was just going to lie down for a bit.

We had a fairly silent dinner, and afterward, over coffee, she said to me, "Do you think your brother will be all right?"

"Well, he's not going to do anything stupid to himself, if that's what you mean."

"That's not what I mean," she said, her quickly raised hand dismissing even the possibility of that.

"I know," I said. I felt ashamed. Then, impulsively, I said, "I just wish he'd never met the Abbott family."

She sighed. "If John hadn't met the Abbotts, he'd have had to invent them, one way or another. There is no end of Abbotts in the world, if that's what you need. And he just needs that somehow." She picked up the chipped yellow cup and sipped her coffee. "Well, really, I know how."

I was startled. "What do you mean, you know how?"

She sat back in her chair wearily and looked at me. She shook her head slowly. "I think John had a hard time, a terrible time, with the way you both grew up, and it made him want—oh, I don't know. Not money, exactly, but kind of the sense of place, of knowing where you belong, that money can give you. At least in a town like Haley." She shrugged. "And that, the way he grew up, that was my fault."

I answered quickly. "No it wasn't, Mom. If he feels that way, it's his responsibility. I mean, I grew up however he did, and that's not the way I feel."

"Yes, but you're different from John."

I started to protest again, but she lifted her hand to silence me. "No, listen. I can explain it." Then she sighed again, as if coming around to some central, hard truth. "You know that after Charlie—your father's—death, I was just—I was just a mess. I hurt so badly that some mornings I'd be crying before I even woke up. And then I had you." She looked up at me. "And poor old John, well, he just got lost in there. I just didn't have anything left for him."

She shook her head. "He was such a sad sack kind of kid anyway. He'd always been jumpy and intense, even as a baby. I just couldn't settle in and be loving to him. He was too nervous. Whereas *you*—" She smiled at me. "You just slept and smiled and nursed. When you were a toddler, I had to pin a sign on the back of your shirt saying, 'Don't feed this child,' because you'd go around the neighborhood and everyone would just give you things.

"And I swear, as I remember it, I spent weeks just sleeping with you in bed after you were born. I got dressed for meals, but that was about it. Otherwise I'd sleep and sleep and sort of come alive just to nurse you or change you. I just couldn't believe Charlie wasn't coming back. I was twenty-four years old." Her face was blank, remembering things I couldn't understand.

She cleared her throat. "And John just floated away from me. My mother was right there, you know, and terribly concerned about me, and she sort of took him over. That was what she felt she could do for me. I can remember early on sometimes I'd hear him crying or calling for me, and then I'd hear her, and after a while he'd stop, and I'd be *glad*. I'd just hold you and go back to sleep. Or more like a trance, it really was. I'll never forgive myself."

I wanted to comfort her. "But he loved Grandma Vetter," I said. "I mean, he ended up getting a lot out of that."

"Well, yes, I think he did, but in the meantime, making that shift from me to her was terrible for him. And I'm not so sure having my mother as a substitute was so good for him. I mean, she was born in another century. All her values and rules, while they're perfectly good ones, were ones that sort of—stiffened John, fed *that* side of who he was. And I, I knew that he, much more than you, needed to learn to relax, to be playful. But I just didn't, couldn't, help him." She twirled her cup slowly in its saucer. "And then I was working and he was so good and reliable, and you were the one always in scrapes."

I felt a pang of something like guilt. "But he turned out fine, Mom. He turned out great."

"Oh, I know he did, darling, but I'm talking about something else. I'm talking about why John struggles so hard to have certain things in his life. Or even certain people."

I frowned at her, not sure I understood.

"I let him go, Doug, don't you see?"

I shook my head, resolute on her behalf.

She looked at me for a moment. Then suddenly she said, "All right, I know. I'll tell you. It's like the time, I remember, I was driving you boys back from somewhere—Oh, I know where it was. It was that time—I'm sure you don't remember, you were so little—but we'd been out East to visit your Dad's folks, and we were coming home through Sandusky. We were going to stop at my great-aunt's for the night. Viola. She's dead a long time now. And I just couldn't find it. I tried for about an hour and a half, but nothing was where it was supposed to be by my directions. And so I finally just pulled over—I was so aggravated—and I said out loud, 'Well, that's it. We're lost.' And I was so busy looking at these directions and maps and things that I didn't notice John for a few minutes. But when I finally looked at him—Well, I've never seen a child so terrified. I asked him what the matter was and he said, 'You said we were *lost*!' And suddenly, by the way he said it, I knew he thought I'd meant lost in a sort of fairy-tale sense—like Hansel and Gretel, or someone being lost for years in a forest. Never getting home. Starving to death. I remember feeling just terrible that he had so little faith in me. In my ability to protect him."

She shook her head and smiled ruefully. "You know, most kids his age—he was five or six, I think—don't think they're lost as long as they've got their mother with them. But I knew right then that I'd lost John. Just lost him." She shook her head again.

After a moment I said softly, "I think he'll be all right, Mom."

"Oh, I know he'll be all right, honey," she cried. "I know it! That's what breaks my heart." And for the first time in my memory since Grandma's death, I saw my mother cry.

I went over to Jacey's apartment more frequently that fall than I had in the past. I had a sense of him as a trust that my mother had placed in me. I'm not sure what made for the conviction that she had never spoken about me to him as she'd spoken about him to me, but I felt secure in it. And I felt she'd somehow asked me to help her pay a debt to Jacey that she, and therefore perhaps I too, owed him.

It didn't make much difference to our relationship, because Jacey simply wouldn't speak to me about anything intimate; but in fact, I liked the order and the quiet in his carefully furnished apartment. On Sundays, I almost always bought English muffins and the *Times* and walked over there. We'd sit quietly all morning, eating and going through the paper, occasionally reading aloud or commenting on some story.

But as the fall wore on, I found more and more, when I dropped over unexpectedly, that he'd come to the door in a bathrobe or towel and tell me that it wasn't a good time. He never smiled or suggested in any of the ways some of my friends might have that it was because there was a woman inside, but I knew that's what it was, and I was happy for him; though a little surprised after the intensity of his feeling for Alice. But it was clear to me, by now, that Jacey was a lover of women, that he needed and enjoyed their company in a way that some men don't—perhaps, I remember speculating then, because of my mother's painful turning away from him when he was a young child. That he was again able to be interested in women seemed to me a sign of health, and I wrote my mother that Jacey was, as I put it, "beginning to go out a bit," though he hadn't actually spoken to me about it.

He invited me to early dinner one Friday in late October. Early, because he was doing something later on. It was a cold, rainy night, and I remember a sense of nostalgia swept over me as I walked the short distance to his apartment, stumbling occasionally over the bumps in the rain-slicked brick sidewalks. I was in the throes of another dying romance, powerfully disappointed because the woman I thought I had loved was so much more mundane than I had originally conceived of her as being. Jacey had made a fine meal—scallops and salad and a very good wine. We had several cups of coffee afterward, and I remember thinking how thoroughly in charge he was of his own life, wondering how many years it would take before I would be able to know what shape I wanted to give my life, let alone do anything about it. He went into his study to get some slides he wanted to show me, and the doorbell rang.

"Shall I get it?" I asked.

"Sure," he called back.

A woman stood under the porch light, wearing a poncho,

her head bent down, her face lost in the shadow of her hood. As I opened the glass door, she raised her head. It was Pamela Abbott. She looked startled, but her voice was smooth. "Hello, Doug," she said.

I said hello. For a few confused moments, I thought that she'd somehow come to my brother's apartment to see me; but as I followed her in, I realized this couldn't be, that it was, of course, John she had come for. Even then I couldn't make my mind work to understand it reasonably.

Jacey greeted her coolly and took her coat, shaking it away from him several times before he hung it up. She sat down at the table, and I joined her. He was standing. He asked her if she wanted some coffee. She shrugged. "Sure, if you're having some."

While he was in the kitchen, I felt compelled to make talk. "So, Pamela," I said. "What's up?"

She shrugged again.

"I mean, God," I said, feeling more and more like an idiot, "I'm really sweating out this *facing life* business. Trying to decide what in hell I'm going to do next year, you know?" She looked steadily at me and didn't respond. "Do you have any idea what you're going to do?"

"I don't know," she said. "I'll probably go to New York and get a job in publishing, I think."

"God, that sounds exciting. But it's rough, isn't it? I mean, to get a job?"

"I don't know. My father has a couple of connections. I don't think it'll be too hard to get some shit lower-level thing."

Jacey was standing in the doorway now, a cup of coffee in his hand. "And then climb the ladder, using his connections all the way," he said sharply. I looked at him, but his face was blank. He walked over to her and set the coffee in front of her. She shrugged again. She looked at him as he went back to his seat. I watched her watching my brother, and saw that she was frightened of him. I realized that I should have left as soon as she arrived, that she was what my brother was "doing" later. We sat in silence for a minute. Jacey lit a cigarette and the smell of sulfur and burning tobacco hung in the little room.

"Well," he said suddenly to Pamela. His voice was still sharp. "Do you want to go to bed?"

She looked quickly at me and then away. After a moment she raised her shoulders. "Sure," she said without emotion, as though accepting some punishment. He stood up. She stood up. I stood up. I was trying to meet my brother's eye, and it seemed to me that for a second I did; but his gaze slid quickly sideways. He walked out of the room first, and she followed him, without looking at me again.

I left the apartment immediately. My heart was pounding in my ears. I walked down to the black river in the rain, across the Western Avenue bridge and all the way up to the boathouse on the other side, trying to understand what my brother was doing to himself, to Pamela, to me. He who was so private, who kept his life and emotions so masked, had exposed himself and Pamela to me, had shown me how contemptuously he could treat her, how despicable he could be. He who had felt used, I know, by Eleanor; and who, I could guess, had felt abused by Alice, was now doing both to Pamela. It seemed to me like a violation of everything I would have said he believed in. And I felt slapped that he had asked me to witness it all, as though he were exposing also my pretensions to understand anything about life.

I was cold and drenched by the time I got home. I took a long shower, grateful that both of my roommates were out, and went to bed early. I lay awake for a long time, thinking about Jacey, about myself, about how we had grown up.

I didn't get in touch with my brother or go to his apartment again for several weeks. Finally he called. It was a Sunday. He said he'd gotten the *Times* and made breakfast and he wondered if I wanted to come over. I said okay, not enthusiastically; and then I said, "Will there be just the two of us?"

"Yes," he said. "That won't happen again."

It was cold outside, gray. The trees were nearly stripped of leaves and I had the sense of winter coming on. John had a fire going in his fireplace and had set breakfast out on the coffee table. I was, for once, repelled by the orderliness. I wondered if I'd ever see my brother in a spontaneous moment. I swallowed some of his good coffee.

"I wanted to apologize," he said.

"Oh," I said.

"What I did was wrong."

"Did you tell that to Pamela?" I asked.

"What business is that of yours?" he said, flaring suddenly. Then he looked away, into the fire for a moment. We were sitting side by side on the couch. "Yes," he said tiredly. "You're right. And I did say it to her. I'm not seeing her anymore. I wanted you to know that." Then he slouched lower in the couch and started to talk. He told me that Pamela had come over unexpectedly almost as soon as school started. It upset him to see her and he had a lot to drink while she was there, as she did. He said she did most of the talking, about her family, about Alice, about Eleanor. She seemed eager to align herself with him against her parents. She told him that they were stupid, rigid. Worse, they were cruel. She said that they had destroyed Eleanor and were destroying Alice; that she was the only daughter smart enough to see the process, the pitfalls on the one hand of resisting too hard, or, on the other hand, of caving in. She called her father a tyrant, a bastard. She said that Jacey couldn't imagine the kinds of things said about him, about our family, in their house.

And then, drunk, she said how wonderful she'd always thought he was; how much she admired him; how much she wanted him. She thought they ought to sleep together.

Drunk too, and angry, he had done it. Then he had passed out, and in the morning she was gone. He said he had thought that that was probably it, that she'd seen herself as fulfilling some part of what he called her "Abbott destiny" by having him as a lover.

But she kept coming over, and he kept sleeping with her. He said he knew it was wrong, that he didn't even like her really. But that in some ways it was like having Alice again, and it was like getting back at her too. And so he just kept doing it.

He got up and poked the fire. He sat down again, this time on the floor. "And then I began to feel *used* again," he said. "It was crazy; I was using her too. But I began to feel that somehow I was just—some bit actor in some part of their family drama. She kept telling me she loved me; and I just kept getting more and more cruel to her. More angry." He looked at me suddenly. "I guess inviting you over was a way of seeing how much she'd take, how low she'd go." He turned away again. "I was pretty far gone too, in some kind of rage I'd lost control over. But finally I just said I wouldn't see her anymore. I was trying to be kind, but it ended up being a pretty ugly scene. Lots of tears and yelling."

I thought of Pamela, so flip, so sure of herself. "Did she not want to stop?"

He shrugged. "She claims she's in love with me. She threatened to tell Alice we were lovers if I wouldn't see her anymore."

"God!" I said. "Think she will?"

He shook his head. "I don't know. She may. I'm hoping it'll seem so uselessly cruel that she'll decide not to. But it's her family. And I took that risk when I slept with her. And there won't be anything more between me and Alice anyway, so maybe it'd be for the best. Maybe it'd confirm all the terrible things her father has to say about me, and make things easier for Alice."

"That's pretty magnanimous of you," I said.

He looked at me and smiled. "Not entirely. I'd like to be able to let go of her. It's been hard. I mean, I've been in love with her for a year and a half and I've slept with her maybe ten times. And I never will again. She still writes to me all the time, even though I can't answer. That kind of stuff. I mean, maybe it's part of the whole thing. Why I slept with Pamela in the first place. To push that possibility away forever."

We talked on into the late afternoon, sometimes about other things—his work, my theatrical ambitions—but we'd always circle back to Alice and Pamela. When it began to get dusky, Jacey got up and turned the lights on. I stretched. I told him I had to go. I took the theater section of the *Times* and headed back to Adams House.

That was the end of my brother's involvement with the Abbott girls. He told me a few Sundays later that he thought Pamela must have said something to Alice or to her family, because the letters abruptly stopped, but otherwise we didn't speak of them again. I went home the following summer and he stayed in Cambridge. He had a drafting job with a little design company. Alice was still living at home and I saw her a few times during the summer. At first I didn't recognize her. She'd put on at least twenty-five pounds. She didn't say hello to me, but I didn't really expect her to. In fact, as if by some unspoken agreement, we each pretended not to know the other when our paths crossed.

In the fall I moved to New York. I saw Pamela there occasionally, for a few years. We still had friends from college in common. She was an assistant editor at a good publishing house, and I was trying to get any kind of acting job. We'd talk when we met, a little edgily. She'd ask about Jacey, and I'd ask about Alice and Eleanor, as if they were vague acquaintances, and not a part of who we both were. She was in touch with Eleanor again, but Eleanor refused to see the family at all. She was a stewardess, and she loved it, loved to travel, Pamela said. Alice lived at home and let her parents run her children, her life. Pamela went home every now and then for a few days, which was about as long as she could stand it, she said.

Our only really difficult conversation was our last one, when I had to tell her that Jacey had gotten married. She looked pained for the smallest fraction of a second, and then the tough smile reemerged. "Well, I assume that whoever it is is rich."

"Why do you assume that?" I asked. In fact, Jacey's wife, an architect too, did have some money, perhaps even as much as the Abbotts had. But I knew enough now to know that that really wasn't rich. And Jacey seemed happy no matter what.

"Isn't that the only kind of girl he's ever been interested in?" she asked jauntily. "Hasn't he been trying to marry *up* since about the day he had his first erection?"

There were so many levels on which her remark offended me—the insult about Jacey's intentions, the implied insult about his, and therefore my, social class—that I wasn't able to choose at which level I wanted to respond. I answered quickly, almost without thinking, "Why do you assume that for him to have married one of you would be to marry up?"

She looked at me for a moment with her mouth open, and then she turned away.

I didn't see her again before I moved to Chicago. I wanted

to be nearer my mother, who wasn't well, and I'd gotten a good job with a repertory company there.

My mother got worse over the next three years—she had cancer—and I often went down and spent two or three weeks in the old house with her when there were breaks in my work. One summer night we were driving past the Abbotts' and the tent was up again. Dance music swelled out on the summer air. The band was playing "Blowin' in the Wind" to a bouncy fox-trot rhythm. My mother looked over at the soft yellow lights, the moving figures. "Imagine a child of Alice's being old enough to dance," she said. And I recalled, abruptly, that she had known all the Abbotts, all the children in town, really, as second-graders. That in some sense we remained always young, always vulnerable in her vision. She didn't think of the pain we'd all caused each other.

She died in the early winter of that year. I went down frequently in the fall. We sat around at home in the evenings, often drinking a fair amount. She'd lost so much weight by then that she was, as she called herself, a cheap drunk; and we seemed to float back easily into the comfortable, desultory intimacy we'd had when I was home alone with her in high school. Once she asked me what came next for me in life. I asked her what she meant. "Oh, I don't know, darling," she said. "You just seem so content, I wonder if this is really—*it* for you."

"I don't know," I said honestly. I felt, at the moment, so peaceful that it wouldn't have bothered me if it was. "It seems to me I've chosen the right profession, certainly. I'm really much better at pretending than at being. You know, I used to have such contempt for Jacey, for what he wanted out of life, for the kinds of women he went after. But in fact he always really went after things. And he suffered with it, but he's all right in the end. I like him. Whereas I haven't done that. I'm happy, but—Well, that's all that really counts, I guess. I am happy. I'm actually very happy."

"I know what you mean," she said. "I've been happy too, and glad I didn't have the messes that some of my friends made of their lives. But sometimes I've worried that I lived a little like a nun, you know. Sort of a *pinched* life, in the end."

We sat. The only sound was the occasional faint noise of the old house shifting somewhere slightly in the cold fall air.

Then I said, "Why didn't you ever remarry, Mother? Surely there were possibilities."

"Fewer than you'd think," she said. "Everyone always thinks things are more possible than they are. I mean, single men don't stay in Haley if they've got any starch. Who was there my age who was eligible? Drew Carter was always around, but he's a washout. And now there's a few old widowers who smell like their dogs." She laughed. "I'm getting mean," she said. "And then I was a schoolteacher for all those years. You don't meet men in a job like that. No, the only time I ever met anyone was in Chicago, a friend of Beatrice Goulding's. I used to go up and visit him every summer, stay with him for five or six days. Surely you remember that. I always told you I was staying with Beatrice." I nodded. I remembered those visits. "He was a wonderful man. Wonderful." And then, with that deft way my mother had of casting the entire story she was telling in a new light, she said, "A little boring, but really, very wonderful."

"Well, why didn't you marry him? Move us all up there?"

"Oh, I couldn't have done that to John," she said instantly. "He'd had such a terrible early childhood, and he was so happy at that stage. Remember? He was playing ball and had a good job and was chasing around after that middle Abbott girl. No." She shook her head. "All this life in Haley had gotten to be too important to him then. I can't imagine having asked him to give it up. I never would have forgiven myself. No, it was better for me to go on as I had been. And besides, I was still really in love with Charlie. With my memory of him. And I've enjoyed my life. I have," she said wistfully.

"Well, it's not over yet," I said.

But it nearly was. Jacey came out for the eight or ten days before she died. We took care of her at home, as she'd wanted, with a visiting nurse to help us. She was very uncomfortable the last few days, though not in actual pain, and I think we were both relieved when her struggle stopped, when we didn't have to listen to her trying to breathe anymore in the night.

There wasn't really a funeral, because she'd been cremated and because she didn't want a service. She had requested that we have a hymn sing, and she had written down three or four of her own favorites she wanted us to be sure to do. Jacey and I discussed the plans the morning after she'd died. We were washing the last of her dishes, putting things away in the kitchen. "Isn't it like her," he said, tears sitting in his eyes, "to want to control even the way we let her go." He shook his head in proud amazement, and I thought how differently we knew her, understood her.

So we gathered, around twenty or so of her friends, mostly women, and Jacey and I, and some young people who were former students; and sang "Guide Me, O Thou Great Jehovah" and "Fight the Good Fight" and "Amazing Grace" and "For All the Saints." It seemed so insufficient, as any service does, I suppose, that we went on singing too long to compensate, and Jacey and I were both hoarse the next day.

But there were still things to pack up, and so we went to the old center of town to get some boxes. It was a cold, bright day, and the town looked small and shabby in the raw light, as though nothing important could ever have happened there. We were loading the trunk and the backseat of the car in front of the liquor store, when I saw a woman walking toward us down the street whom I recognized instantly as Mrs. Abbott. She didn't look very different from the way she had at all those parties. Her hair, dyed now, I suppose, was still a pale arranged blond; her lipstick was a girlish pink. She saw Jacey, and I could tell that for a moment she was thinking of walking past us without acknowledging us; her step wavered marginally. But then she made some internal decision and approached. Jacey saw her and straightened up. We both assumed, I think, that she would speak to us of our mother's death, which is what every conversation we'd had in the last few days had started with.

But whether she didn't know what we were both in town for, or whether her own emotions of the moment drove it out of her mind, that's not what she spoke of. A brilliant social smile flickered quickly across her face and was gone. Then, standing an uncomfortable distance from us on the sidewalk, she made for a minute or two the kind of small talk she'd made all those years ago under the tents in her backyard—a comment on the weather, on how we'd changed, on how busy young people's lives were, they could hardly ever get home anymore. As she spoke she nodded repeatedly, an odd birdlike motion of her head. There was an awkward silence when she finished—I know I couldn't imagine what an appropriate response would be—and then she said with brittle cheer to Jacey alone, "Well, I've no more daughters for you." And as though she'd been talking about his loss rather than her own, she smiled again, and walked on.

For a moment we stood motionless on the sidewalk, watching her diminishing figure. Then I turned to Jacey, expecting, I suppose, some comment, and ready to be angry along with him, on his behalf. Instead he bent down and started again to load the empty boxes that would hold my mother's belongings into the car, as though what Mrs. Abbott had just said and done had all happened years before, with the rest of it, when he was a child.

# BHARATI MUKHERJEE

# THE MIDDLE MAN

FROM PLAYBOY

§

THERE ARE ONLY two seasons in this country, the dusty and the wet. I already know the dusty and I'll get to know the wet. I've seen worse. I've seen Baghdad, Bombay, Queens—and now this moldering spread deep in Mayan country. Aztecs, Toltecs, mestizos, even some bashful whites with German accents. All that and a lot of Texans. I'll learn the ropes.

Forget the extradition order; I'm not a sinful man. I've listened to bad advice. I've placed my faith in dubious associates. My first American wife said, "In the dog eat dog, Alfred, you're a beagle." My name is Alfie Judah, of the once illustrious Smyrna, Aleppo, Baghdad—and now Flushing, Queens—Judahs.

I intend to make it back.

This place is owned by one Clovis T. Ransome. He reached here from Waco with fifteen million in petty cash hours ahead of a posse from the SEC. That doesn't buy much down here—a few thousand acres, residency papers, and the right to swim with the sharks a few feet off the bottom. Me? I make a living from things that fall. The big fat belly of Clovis T. Ransome bobs above me like whale shit at high tide.

The president's name is Gutierrez. Like everyone else, he has enemies, right and left. He is on retainer from men like Ransome, from the *Contras*, maybe from the *Sandinistas* as well.

The woman's name is Maria. She came with the ranch or with the protection; no one knows.

President Gutierrez's country has definite possibilities. All day I sit by the lime-green swimming pool, sun-screened so I won't turn black, going through my routine of isometrics while Ransome's *Indios* hack away the virgin forests. Their hate is intoxicating. They hate gringos—from which my darkness exempts me—even more than Gutierrez. They hate in order to keep up their intensity. I hear a litany of president's names, Hollywood names, Detroit names—Carter, *chop*, Reagan, *slash*, Buick, *thump*—bounce off the vines as machetes clear the jungle greenness. We spoke a form of Spanish in my Baghdad home. I understand more than I let on.

In this season, the air's so dry it could scratch your lungs. Bright-feathered birds screech, snakeskins glitter, as the jungle peels away. Iguanas the size of wallabies leap from behind macheted bushes. The pool is greener than the ocean waves, cloudy with chemicals that Ransome has trucked over the mountains. When toads fall in, the water blisters their skin. I've heard their cries.

Possibilities, oh, yes.

I must confess my weakness: women.

In the old Baghdad when I was young, we had the hots for blondes. We'd stroll up to the diplomatic enclaves just to look at women. Solly Nathan, cross-eyed Itzie, Naim, and me. Pinkish flesh could turn our blood to boiling lust. British matrons with freckled calves, painted toenails through thin-strapped sandals, the onset of varicose veins, the brassiness of prewar bleach jobs—all of that could thrill us like cleavage. We were twelve and already visiting whores during those hot Levantine lunch hours when our French masters intoned the rules of food, rest, and good digestion. We'd roll up our fried flat bread smeared with spicy potatoes, pool our change, and bargain with the daughters of washerwomen while our lips and fingers still glistened with succulent grease. But the only girls cheap enough for boys our age with unspecified urgencies were swamp Arabs from Basra and black girls from Baluchistan, the broken toys discarded by our older brothers.

Thank God those European women couldn't see us. It was comforting at times just to be natives, invisible to our masters. *They* were worthy of our lust. Local girls were for amusement only, a dark place to spend some time, like a video arcade.

"You chose a real bad time to come, Al," he says. He may have been born on the wrong side of Waco, but he's spent his adult life in tropical paradises, playing God. "The rains'll be here soon, a day or two at most." He makes a whooping noise and drinks Jack Daniel's from a flask.

"My options were limited." A modest provident fund I'd been maintaining for New Jersey judges had been discovered. My fresh new citizenship is always in jeopardy. My dealings can't stand too much investigation.

"Bud and I can keep you from getting bored."

Bud Wilkins should be over in his pickup any time now. Meanwhile, Ransome rubs Cutter over his face and neck. They're supposed to go deep-sea fishing today, though it looks to me as if he's dressed for the jungle. A wetted-down hand towel is tucked firmly under the back of his baseball cap. He's a Braves man. Bud ships him cassettes of all the Braves' games. There are aspects of American life I came too late for and will never understand. It isn't love of the game, he told me last week. It's love of Ted Turner.

His teams. His stations. His America's Cup, his yachts, his network.

If he could be a clone of anyone in the world, he'd choose Turner. Then he leaned close and told me his wife, Maria—once the mistress of Gutierrez himself, as if I could miss her charms or underestimate their price in a seller's market—told him she'd put out all night if he looked like Ted Turner. "Christ, Al, here I've got this setup and I gotta beg her for it!" There *are* things I can relate to, and a man in such agony is one of them. That was last week, and he was drunk and I was new on the scene. Now he snorts more J.D. and lets out a whoop.

"Wanna come fishing? Won't cost you extra, Al."

"Thanks, no," I say. "Too hot."

The only thing I like about Clovis Ransome is that he doesn't snicker when I, an Arab to some, an Indian to others, complain of the heat. Even dry heat I despise.

"Suit yourself," he says.

Why do I suspect he wants me along as a witness? I don't want any part of their schemes. Bud Wilkins got here first. He's entrenched, doing little things for many people, building up a fleet of trucks, of planes, of buses. Like Ari Onassis, he started small. That's the legitimate side. The rest of it is no secret. A man with cash and private planes can clear a fortune in Latin America. The story is, Bud was exposed as a CIA agent, forced into public life, and made to go semipublic with his arms deals and transfer fees.

"I don't mind you staying back, you know. It's Bud she wants to poke."

Maria. I didn't notice Maria for the first few days of my visit. She was *here*, but in the background. And she was dark, native, and I have my prejudices. But how shall I say—is there deeper pleasure, a darker thrill than prejudice squarely faced, suppressed, fought against, and then slowly, secretively surrendered to?

Now I think a single word: adultery.

On cue, Maria floats toward us out of the green shadows. She's been swimming in the ocean; her hair is wet; her big-boned, dark-skinned body is streaked with sand. The talk is, Maria was an aristocrat, a near–Miss World whom Ransome partially bought and partially seduced away from Gutierrez, so he's never sure if the president owes him one or wants to kill him. With her dark hair and smooth, dark skin, she has to be mostly Indian. In her bikini, she arouses new passion. Who wants pale, thin, pink flesh, limp, curly blond hair, when you can have lustrous browns, purple-blacks?

Adultery and dark-eyed young women are forever entwined in my memory. It is a memory, even now, that fills me with chills and terror and terrible, terrible desire. When I was a child, one of our servants took me to his village. He wanted me to see something special from the old Iraqi culture. Otherwise, he feared, my lenient Jewish upbringing would later betray me. A young woman, possibly adulterous but certainly bold and brave and beautiful enough to excite rumors of promiscuity, was that day stoned to death. What I remember now is the breathlessness of waiting as the husband circled her, as she struggled against the rope, as the stake barely swayed to her writhing. I remember the dull *thwock* and the servant's strong fingers shaking my shoulders as the first stone struck.

I realize I am one of the very few Americans who know the sound of rocks cutting through flesh and striking bone. One of the few to count the costs of adultery.

Maria drops her beach towel onto the patio floor, close to my deck chair, and straightens the towel's edge with her toes. She has to have been a dancer before becoming Ransome's bride and before Gutierrez plucked her out of convent school to become his mistress. Only ballerinas have such blunted, misshapen toes. But she knows. To the right eyes, even her toes are desirable.

"I want to hear about New York, Alfred." She lets herself fall like a dancer onto the bright-red towel. Her husband is helping Eduardo, the houseboy, load the jeep with the day's gear, and it's him she seems to be talking to. "My husband won't let me visit the States. He absolutely won't."

"She's putting you on, Al," Ransome shouts. He's just carried a case of beer out to the jeep. "She prefers St. Moritz."

"You ski?"

I can feel the heat rising from her, or from the towel. I can imagine as the water beads on her shoulders how cool her flesh will be for just a few more minutes.

"Do I look as though I ski?"

I don't want to get involved in domestic squabbles. The *Indios* watch us. A solemn teenager hefts his machete. We are to have an uncomplicated view of the ocean from the citadel of this patio.

"My husband is referring to the fact that I met John Travolta in St. Moritz," she says defiantly.

"Sweets," says Ransome. The way he says it, it's a threat.

"He has a body of one long muscle, like an eel," she says.

Ransome is closer now. "Make sure Eduardo doesn't forget the crates," he says.

"O.K., O.K.," she shouts back. "Excuse me." I watch her corkscrew to her feet. I'm so close I can hear her ligaments pop.

Soon after, Bud Wilkins roars into the cleared patch that serves as the main parking lot. He backs his pickup so hard against a shade tree that a bird wheels up from its perch. Bud lines it up with an imaginary pistol and curls his fingers twice in its direction. I'm not saying he has no feeling for wildlife. He's in boots and camouflage pants, but his hair—what there is of it—is blow-dried.

He stalks my chair. "We could use you, buddy." He uncaps a beer bottle with his teeth. "You've seen some hot spots."

"He doesn't want to fish." Ransome is drinking beer, too. "We wouldn't want to leave Maria unprotected." He waits for a retort, but Bud's too much the gentleman. Ransome stares at me and winks, but he's angry. It could get ugly, wherever they're going.

They drink more beer. Finally, Eduardo comes out with the crate. He carries it bowlegged, in mincing little half-running steps. The fishing tackle, of course. The crate is dumped into Bud's pickup. He comes out with a second and a third, equally heavy, and drops them all into Bud's truck. I can guess what I'm watching. Low-grade arms transfer, rifles, ammo, and maybe medicine.

"*Ciào, amigo*," says Bud in his heavy-duty Texan accent. He and Ransome roar into the jungle in Ransome's jeep.

"I hope you're not too hungry, Alfie." It's Maria calling from the kitchen. Alfred to Alfie before the jeep can have made it off the property.

"I'm not a big eater." What I mean to say is, I'm adaptable. What I'm hoping is, let us not waste time with food.

"Eduardo!" The houseboy, probably herniated by now, goes to her for instructions. "We just want a salad and fruit. But make it fast. I have to run into San Vincente today." That's the nearest market town. I've been there; it's not much.

She stands at the front door, about to join me on the patio, when Eduardo rushes past, broom in hand. "*¡Vaya!*" he screams.

But she is calm. "It must be behind the stove, stupid," she tells the servant. "It can't have made it out this far without us seeing it."

Eduardo wields his broom like a nightstick and retreats into the kitchen. We follow. I can't see it. I can only hear desperate clawing and scraping on the tiles behind the stove.

Maria stomps the floor to scare it out. The houseboy shoves the broom handle into the dark space. I think first, being a child of the overheated deserts, giant scorpions. But there are two fugitives, not one—a pair of ocean crabs. The crabs, their shiny purple backs dotted with yellow, try to get by us to the beach, where they can hear the waves.

How do mating ocean crabs scuttle their way into Clovis T. Ransome's kitchen? I feel for them.

The broom comes down—thwack, thwack—and bashes the shells in loud, succulent cracks. *Ransome, gringo*, I hear.

He sticks his dagger into the burlap sacks of green chemicals. He rips, he cuts.

"Eduardo, it's all right. Everything's fine." She sounds stern, authoritative; the years in the presidential palace have served her well. She moves toward him, stops just short of taking his arm.

He spits out, "He kills everything." At least, that's the drift. The language of Cervantes does not stretch around the world without a few skips in transmission. Eduardo's litany includes crabs, the chemicals, the sulphurous pool, the dead birds, and snakes and lizards.

"You have my promise," Maria says. "It's going to work out. Now I want you to go to your room; I want you to rest."

We hustle him into his room, but he doesn't seem to notice his surroundings. His body has gone slack. I hear the name Santa Simona, a new saint for me. I maneuver him to the cot and keep him pinned down while Maria checks out a rusty medicine cabinet.

He looks up at me. "You drive *Doña* Maria where she goes?"

"If she wants me to, sure."

"Eduardo, go to sleep. I'm giving you something to help."
She has water and a blue pill ready.

While she hovers over him, I check out his room. It's
automatic with me. There are crates under the bed. There's a
table covered with oilcloth. The oilcloth is cracked and grimy.
A chair by the table is a catchall for clothes, shorts, even a
bowl of fruits. Guavas. Eduardo could have snuck in caviar,
imported cheeses, Godiva candies, but it's guavas he's chosen
to stash for siesta-hour hunger pains. The walls are hung with
icons of saints. Posters of stars I'd never have heard of if I
hadn't been forced to drop out. Baby-faced men and women.
The women are sensuous in an old-fashioned, Latin way, with
curvy lips, big breasts, and tiny waists. Like Maria. Quite a
few are unconvincing blondes, in that brassy Latin way. The
men have greater range. Some are young versions of Fernando
Lamas; some are in fatigues and boots, striking Robin Hood
poses. The handsomest is dressed as a guerrilla, with all the
right accessories: beret, black boots, bandoleer. Maybe he'd
played Ché Guevara in some B-budget Argentine melodrama.

"What's in the crates?" I ask Maria.

"I respect people's privacy," she says. "Even a servant's."
She pushes me roughly toward the door. "So should you."

The daylight seems too bright on the patio. The bashed
shells are on the tiles. Ants have already discovered the flat-
tened meat of ocean crabs, the blistered bodies of clumsy toads.

Maria tells me to set the table. Every day, we use a lace
cloth, heavy silverware, roses in a vase. And every day, we
drink champagne. Some mornings, the Ransomes start on the
champagne with breakfast. Bud owns an air-taxi service and
flies in cases of Épernay, caviar, any damned thing his friends
desire.

She comes out with a tray. Two plates, two fluted glasses,
*chèvre* cheese on a bit of glossy banana leaf, water biscuits.
"I'm afraid this will have to do. Anyway, you said you weren't
hungry."

I spread a biscuit and hand it to her.

"If you feel all right, I was hoping you'd drive me to San
Vincente." She gestures toward Bud Wilkins's pickup truck. "I
don't like to drive that thing."

"What if I don't want to?"

"You won't. Say no to me, I mean. I'm a terrific judge of character." She shrugs, and her breasts are slower than her shoulders in coming down.

"The keys are on the kitchen counter. Do you mind if I use your w.c. instead of going back upstairs? Don't worry, I don't have horrible communicable diseases." She laughs.

This may be intimacy. "How could I mind? It's your house."

"Alfie, don't pretend innocence. It's Ransome's house. This isn't *my* house."

I get the keys to Bud's pickup and wait for her by the bruised tree. I don't want to know the contents of the crates, though the stenciling says FRUITS and doubtless the top layer preserves the fiction. How easily I've been recruited, when a bystander is all I wanted to be. The Indians put down their machetes and make signs to me: *Hi, Mom, we're number one.* They must have been watching Ransome's tapes. They're all wearing Braves caps.

The road to San Vincente is rough. Deep ruts have been cut into the surface by army trucks. Whole convoys must have passed this way during the last rainy season. I don't want to know whose trucks; I don't want to know why.

Forty minutes into the trip, Maria says, "When you get to the T, take a left. I have to stop off near here to run an errand." It's a strange word for the middle of a jungle.

"Don't let it take you too long," I say. "We want to be back before hubby gets home." I'm feeling jaunty. She touches me when she talks.

"So Clovis scares you." Her hand finds its way to my shoulder.

"Shouldn't he?"

I make the left. I make it sharper than I intended. Bud Wilkins's pickup sputters up a dusty rise. A pond appears and around it shacks with vegetable gardens.

"Where are we?"

"In Santa Simona," Maria says. "I was born here, can you imagine?"

This isn't a village, it's a camp for guerrillas. I see some women here, and kids, roosters, dogs. What Santa Simona is is

a rest stop for families on the run. I deny simple parallels.
Ransome's ranch is just a ranch.

"You could park by the pond."

I step on the brake and glide to the rutted edge of the
pond. Whole convoys must have parked here during the rainy
season. The ruts hint at secrets. Now, in the dry season, what
might be a lake has shrunk to a muddy pit. Ducks float on
green scum.

Young men in khaki begin to close in on Bud's truck.

Maria motions to me to get out. "I bet you could use a
drink." We make our way up to the shacks. The way her
bottom bounces inside those cutoffs could drive a man crazy. I
don't turn back, but I can hear the unloading of the truck.

So: Bud Wilkins's little shipment has been hijacked, and
I'm the culprit. Some job for a middle man.

"*This* is my house, Alfie."

I should be upset. Maria has turned me into a chauffeur.
You bet I could use a drink.

We pass by the first shack. There's a garage in the back
where there would be the usual large cement laundry tub.
Three men come at me, twirling tire irons the way nightsticks
are fondled by Manhattan cops. "I'm with her."

Maria laughs at me. "It's not you they want."

And I wonder, *Who* was she supposed to deliver? Bud,
perhaps, if Clovis hadn't taken him out? Or Clovis himself?

We pass the second shack, and a third. Then a tall guerrilla
in full battle dress floats out of nowhere and blocks our path.
Maria shrieks and throws herself on him and he holds her face
in his hands, and in no time they're swaying and moaning like
connubial visitors at a prison farm. She has her back to me. His
big hands cup and squeeze her halter top. I've seen him somewhere. Eduardo's poster.

"Hey," I try. When that doesn't work, I start to cough.

"Sorry." Maria swings around, still in his arms. "This is
Al Judah. He's staying at the ranch."

The soldier is called Andreas something. He looks me
over. "Yudah?" he asks Maria, frowning.

She shrugs. "You want to make something of it?"

He says something rapidly, locally, that I can't make out.

She translates, "He says you need a drink," which I don't believe.

We go inside the command shack. It's a one-room affair, very clean, but dark and cluttered. I'm not sure I should sit on the narrow cot; it seems to be a catchall for the domestic details of revolution—sleeping bags, maps and charts, an empty canteen, two pairs of secondhand army boots. I need a comfortable place to deal with my traumas. There is a sofa of sorts, actually a car seat pushed tight against a wall and stabilized with bits of lumber. There are bullet holes through the fabric, and rusty stains that can only be blood. I reject the sofa. There are no tables, no chairs, no posters, no wall decorations of any kind, unless you count a crucifix. Above the cot, a sad, dark, plaster crucified Jesus recalls his time in the desert.

"Beer?" Maria doesn't wait for an answer. She walks behind a curtain and hefts a six-pack of Heineken from a noisy refrigerator. I believe I am being offered one of Bud Wilkins's unwitting contributions to the guerrilla effort. I should know it's best not to ask how Dutch beer and refrigerators and 1957 two-tone Plymouths with fins and chrome make their way to nowhere jungle clearings. Because of guys like me, in better times, that's how. There's just demand and supply running the universe.

"Take your time, Alfie." Maria is beaming so hard, it's unreal. "We'll be back soon. You'll be cool and rested in here."

Andreas manages a contemptuous wave; then, holding hands, he and Maria vault over the railing of the back porch and disappear.

She's given me beer, plenty of beer, but no church key. I look around the room. Ransome or Bud would have used his teeth. From his perch, Jesus stares at me out of huge, sad Levantine eyes. In this alien jungle, we're fellow Arabs. You should see what's happened to the old stomping grounds, *compadre*.

I test my teeth against a moist, corrugated bottle cap. It's no good. I whack the bottle cap with the heel of my hand against the metal edge of the cot. It foams and hisses. The second time, it opens. New World skill. Somewhere in the back of the shack, a parakeet begins to squawk. It's a sad, ugly sound. I go out to the back porch to give myself something to do, to maybe snoop. By the communal laundry tub, there's a cage, and inside the cage, a mean, molting bird. A kid of ten or twelve teases the bird with bits of lettuce. Its beak snaps open for the greens and scrapes the rusty sides of the bar. The kid looks defective, dull-eyed, thin but flabby.

"Gringo," he calls out to me. "Gringo, gum."

I check my pockets. No Dentyne, no Tums, just the plastic cover for spent traveler's checks. My life has changed. I don't have to worry about bad breath or gas pains turning off clients.

"Gringo, Chiclets."

The voice is husky.

I turn my palms outward. "Sorry, you're out of luck."

The kid leaps on me with moronic fury. I want to throw him down, toss him into the scummy vat of soaking clothes, but he's probably some sort of sacred mascot. "How about this pen?" It's a forty-nine-cent disposable, the perfect thing for poking a bird. I go back inside.

I am sitting in the H.Q. of the guerrilla insurgency, drinking a Heineken, nursing my indignation. A one-armed man opens the door. "Maria?" he calls. "*Prego.*" Which translates, indirectly, as "The truck is unloaded and the guns are ready and should I kill this guy?" I direct him to find Andreas.

She wakes me, maybe an hour later. I sleep as I rarely have, arm across my eyes, like a Bedouin, on top of the mounds of boots and gear. She has worked her fingers around my buttons, pulls my hair, my nipples. I can't tell the degree of mockery, what spillover of passion she may still be feeling. Andreas and the idiot boy stand framed in the bleaching light of the door, the boy's huge head pushing the bandoleer askew. Father and son, it suddenly dawns. Andreas holds the birdcage.

"They've finished," she explains. "Let's go."

Andreas lets us pass, smirking, I think, and follows us down the rutted trail to Bud's truck. He puts the birdcage in the driver's seat and, in case I miss it, points at the bird, then at me, and laughs. Very funny, I think. His boy finds it hilarious. I will *not* be mocked like this. The bird is so ill fed, so cramped and tortured and clumsy, it flutters wildly, losing more feathers merely to keep its perch.

"*Viva la revolución*, eh? A leetle gift for helping the people."

No, I think, a leetle sign to Clovis Ransome and all the pretenders to Maria's bed that we're just a bunch of scrawny blackbirds and he doesn't care who knows it. I have no feeling for revolution, only for outfitting the participants.

"Why?" I beg on the way back. The road is dark. "You hate your husband, so get a divorce. Why blow up the country?"

Maria smiles. "Clovis has nothing to do with this." She shifts her sandals on the birdcage. The bird is dizzy, flat on its back. Some of them die, just like that.

"Run off with Andreas, then."

"We were going to be married," she says. "Then Gutierrez came to my school and took me away. I was fourteen and he was Minister of Education. Then Clovis took me away from him. Maybe you should take me away from Clovis. I like you, and you'd like it, too, wouldn't you?"

"Don't be crazy. Try Bud Wilkins."

"Bud! Wilkins is, you say, dog meat." She smiles.

"Oh, sure," I say.

I concentrate on the road. I'm no hero; I calculate margins. I could not calculate the cost of a night with Maria, a month with Maria, though for the first time in my life, it was a cost I might have borne.

Her voice is matter-of-fact. "Clovis wanted a cut of Bud's action. But Bud refused, and that got Clovis mad. Clovis even offered money, but Bud said, 'No way.' Clovis pushed me on him, so he took, but he still didn't budge. So—"

"You're serious, aren't you? Oh, God."

"Of course I am serious. Now Clovis can fly in his own champagne and baseball games."

She has unbuttoned more of the halter, and I feel pressure on my chest, in my mouth, against my slacks, that I have never felt.

All the lights are on in the villa when I lurch Bud's pickup into the parking lot. We can see Clovis T. Ransome, very drunk, slack-postured, trying out wicker chairs on the porch. Maria is carrying the birdcage.

He's settled on the love seat. No preliminaries, no questions. He squints at the cage. "Buying presents for Maria already, Al?" He tries to laugh.

"What's that supposed to mean?" She swings the cage in giant arcs, like a bucket of water.

"Where's Bud?" I ask.

"They jumped him, old buddy. Gang of guerrillas not more'n half a mile down the road. Pumped twenty bullets in him. These are fierce little people, Al. I don't know how I got away." He's watching us for effect.

I suspect it helps when they're in your pay, I thought, and you give them Ted Turner caps.

"Al, grab yourself a glass if you want some Scotch. Me, I'm stinking drunk already."

He's noticed Bud's truck now. The emptiness of Bud's truck.

"That's a crazy thing to do," Maria says. "I warned you." She sets the cage down on the patio table. "Bud's no good to anyone, dead or alive. You said it yourself, he's dog meat." She slips onto the love seat beside her husband. I watch her. I can't take my eyes off her. She snakes her strong, long torso until her lips touch the cage's rusted metal. "Kiss me," she coos. "Kiss me, kiss, kiss, sweetheart."

Ransome's eyes are on her, too. "Sweets, who gave you that filthy crow?"

Maria says, "Kiss me, lover boy."

"Sweetie, I asked you who gave you that filthy crow."

I back off to the kitchen. I could use a shot of Scotch. I can feel the damp, Bombay grittiness of the air. The rains will be here, maybe tonight.

When I get back, Ransome is snoring on the love seat. Maria is standing over him, and the birdcage is on his lap. Its door is open and Clovis's fat hand is half inside. The bird pecks, it raises blood, but Clovis is out for the night.

"Why is it," she asks, "that I don't feel pride when men kill for me?"

But she does, deep down. She wants to believe that Clovis, mad, jealous Clovis, has killed for her. I hate to think of Maria's pretty face when Clovis wakes up and remembers the munitions are gone. It's all a family plot in countries like this, revolutions fought for a schoolgirl in white with blunted toes. I, too, would kill for her.

"Kill it, Alfie, please," she says. "I can't stand it. See, Clovis tried, but his hand was too fat."

"I'll free it," I say.

"Don't be a fool—that boy broke its wings. Let it out and the crabs will kill it."

Around eleven that night, I have to carry Ransome up the stairs to the spare bedroom. He's a heavy man. I don't bother with the niceties of getting him out of his blue jeans and into his pajamas. The secrets of Clovis T. Ransome, whatever they are, are safe with me. I abandon him on top of the bedspread in his dusty cowboy boots. Maria shan't want him tonight. She's already told me so.

But she isn't waiting for me on the patio. Maybe that's just as well. Tonight, love will be hard to handle. The dirty glasses, the booze and soda bottles, the Styrofoam-lidded bowl we used for ice cubes are still on the wicker-and-glass coffee table. Eduardo doesn't seem to be around. I take the glasses into the kitchen. He must have disappeared hours ago. I've never seen the kitchen in this bad a mess. He's not in the villa. His door has swung open, but I can't hear the noises of sleeping servants in the tropics. So, Eduardo has vanished. I accept this as data. I dare not shout for Maria. If it's ever to be, it must be tonight. Tomorrow, I can tell, this cozy little hacienda will come to grief.

Someone should go from room to room and turn out the lights. But not me. I make it fast back to my room.

"You must shut doors quickly behind you in the tropics or bugs get in."

Casually, she is unbuttoning her top, untying the bottom flaps. The cutoffs have to be tugged off, around her hips. There is a rush of passion I have never known, and my fingers tremble as I tug at my belt. She is in my giant bed, propped up, and her breasts keep the sheet from falling.

"Alfie, close the door."

Her long thighs press and squeeze. She tries to hold me, to contain me, and it is a moment I would die to prolong. In a frenzy, I conjugate crabs with toads and the squawking bird, and I hear the low moans of turtles on the beach. It is a moment I fear too much, a woman I fear too much, and I yield. I begin again, immediately, this time concentrating on blankness, on burned-out objects whirling in space, and she pushes against me, murmuring, "No," and pulls away.

Later, she says, "You don't understand hate, Alfie. You don't understand what hate can do." She tells stories; I moan to mount her again. "No," she says, and the stories pour out. Not just the beatings; the humiliations. Lending her out, dangling her on a leash, like a cheetah, then the beatings for what he suspects. It's the power game, I try to tell her. That's how power is played.

Sometime around three, I wake to a scooter's thin roar. She has not been asleep. The rainy season must have started an hour or two before. It's like steam out there. I kneel on the pillows to look out the small bedroom windows. The parking lot is a mud slide. Uprooted shrubs, snakes, crabs, turtles are washed down to the shore.

Maria, object of my wildest ecstasy, lies inches from me. She doesn't ask what I see. The scooter's lights weave in the rain.

"Andreas," she says. "It's working out."

But it isn't Andreas who forces the door to my room. It is a tall, thin Indian with a calamitous face. The scooter's engine has been shut off and rain slaps the patio in waves.

"*Americano*." The Indian spits out the word. "Gringo."

Maria calmly ties her halter flaps, slowly buttons up. She says something rapidly and the Indian steps outside while she finds her cutoffs.

"Quickly," she says, and I reach for my pants. It's already cold.

When the Indian returns, I hear her say, "Jew" and "Israel." He seems to lose interest. "*Americano?*" he asks again. "Gringo?"

Two more Indians invade my room. Maria runs out to the hall and I follow to the stairs. I point upward and try out my Spanish. "Gringo is sleeping, drunk."

The revolution has convened outside Clovis's bedroom. Eduardo is there, Andreas, more Indians in Ted Turner caps, the one-armed man from Santa Simona. Andreas opens the door.

"Gringo," he calls softly. "Wake up."

I am surprised, truly astonished, at the recuperative powers of Clovis T. Ransome. Not only does he wake but he sits, boots on the floor, ignoring the intrusion. His Spanish, the first time I've heard him use it, is excellent, even respectful.

"I believe, sir, you have me at a disadvantage," he says. He scans the intruders, his eyes settling on me. "Button your fly, man," he says to me. He stares at Maria, up and down, his jaw working. He says, "Well, sweets? What now?"

Andreas holds a pistol against his thigh.

"Take her," Ransome says. "You want her? You got her. You want money, you got that, too. Dollars, marks, Swiss francs. Just take her, and him"—he says, pointing to me—"out of here."

"I will take your dollars, of course."

"Eduardo—" Ransome jerks his head in the direction, perhaps, of a safe. The servant seems to know where it is.

"And I will take her, of course."

"Good riddance."

"But not him. He can rot."

Eduardo and three Indians lug out a metal trunk. They throw away the pillows and start stuffing pillowcases with bundles of dollars, more pure currency than I've ever seen. They stuff the rest inside their shirts. What it must feel like, I wonder.

"Well, Señor Andreas, you've got the money and the woman. Now what's it to be—a little torture? A little fun with me before the sun comes up? Or what about him—I bet you'd have more fun with him. I don't scream, Señor Andreas, I warn you. You can kill me, but you can't break me."

I hear the safety clicking off. So does Clovis.

I know I would scream. I know I am no hero. I know none of this is worth suffering for, let alone dying for.

Andreas looks at Maria as if to say, "You decide." She holds out her hand and Andreas slips the pistol into it. This seems to amuse Clovis Ransome. He stands, presenting an enormous target. "Sweetie—" he starts, and she blasts away, and when I open my eyes, he is across the bed, sprawled in the far corner of the room.

She stands at the foot of their bed, limp and amused, like a woman disappointed in love. Smoke rises from the gun barrel, her breath condenses in little clouds and there is a halo of condensation around her hair, her neck, her arms.

When she turns, I feel it could be any of us next. Andreas holds out his hand, but she doesn't return the gun. She lines me up, low, genital level, like Bud Wilkins with a bird, then sweeps around to Andreas and smiles.

She has made love to me three times tonight. With Andreas today, doubtless more. Never has a truth been burned so deeply in me, what I owe my life to, how simple the rules of survival are. She passes the gun to Andreas, who holsters it, and they leave.

In the next few days, when I run out of food, I will walk down the muddy road to San Vincente, to the German bar with the pay phone. I'll wear Clovis's Braves cap and I'll salute the Indians. "Hi, Mom," I'll say.

"Number one," they'll answer. Bud's truck has been commandeered, along with Clovis's finer cars. Someone in the capital will be happy to know about Santa Simona, about Bud, Clovis. There must be something worth trading in the troubles I have seen.

# TIM O'BRIEN

# THE THINGS THEY CARRIED

FROM ESQUIRE

ᔕ

FIRST LIEUTENANT JIMMY CROSS carried letters from a girl named Martha, a junior at Mount Sebastian College in New Jersey. They were not love letters, but Lieutenant Cross was hoping, so he kept them folded in plastic at the bottom of his rucksack. In the late afternoon, after a day's march, he would dig his foxhole, wash his hands under a canteen, unwrap the letters, hold them with the tips of his fingers, and spend the last hour of light pretending. He would imagine romantic camping trips into the White Mountains in New Hampshire. He would some-times taste the envelope flaps, knowing her tongue had been there. More than anything, he wanted Martha to love him as he loved her, but the letters were mostly chatty, elusive on the matter of love. She was a virgin, he was almost sure. She was an English major at Mount Sebastian, and she wrote beautifully about her professors and roommates and midterm exams, about her respect for Chaucer and her great affection for Virginia Woolf. She often quoted lines of poetry; she never mentioned the war, except to say, Jimmy, take care of yourself. The letters weighed ten ounces. They were signed "Love, Martha," but Lieutenant Cross understood that Love was only a way of signing and did not mean what he sometimes pretended it meant. At dusk, he would carefully return the letters to his rucksack. Slowly, a bit distracted, he would get up and move among his men, checking the perimeter, then at full dark he would return to his hole and watch the night and wonder if Martha was a virgin.

The things they carried were largely determined by necessity. Among the necessities or near-necessities were P-38 can openers, pocket knives, heat tabs, wristwatches, dog tags, mosquito repellent, chewing gum, candy, cigarettes, salt tablets, packets of Kool-Aid, lighters, matches, sewing kits, Military Payment Certificates, C rations, and two or three canteens of water. Together, these items weighed between fifteen and twenty pounds, depending upon a man's habits or rate of metabolism. Henry Dobbins, who was a big man, carried extra rations; he was especially fond of canned peaches in heavy syrup over pound cake. Dave Jensen, who practiced field hygiene, carried a toothbrush, dental floss, and several hotel-size bars of soap he'd stolen on R&R in Sydney, Australia. Ted Lavender, who was scared, carried tranquilizers until he was shot in the head outside the village of Than Khe in mid-April. By necessity, and because it was SOP, they all carried steel helmets that weighed five pounds including the liner and camouflage cover. They carried the standard fatigue jackets and trousers. Very few carried underwear. On their feet they carried jungle boots—2.1 pounds—and Dave Jensen carried three pairs of socks and a can of Dr. Scholl's foot powder as a precaution against trench foot. Until he was shot, Ted Lavender carried six or seven ounces of premium dope, which for him was a necessity. Mitchell Sanders, the RTO, carried condoms. Norman Bowker carried a diary. Rat Kiley carried comic books. Kiowa, a devout Baptist, carried an illustrated New Testament that had been presented to him by his father, who taught Sunday school in Oklahoma City, Oklahoma. As a hedge against bad times, however, Kiowa also carried his grandmother's distrust of the white man, his grandfather's old hunting hatchet. Necessity dictated. Because the land was mined and booby-trapped, it was SOP for each man to carry a steel-centered, nylon-covered flak jacket, which weighed 6.7 pounds, but which on hot days seemed much heavier. Because you could die so quickly, each man carried at least one large compress bandage, usually in the helmet band for easy access. Because the nights were cold, and because the monsoons were wet, each carried a green plastic poncho that could be used as a raincoat or groundsheet or makeshift tent. With its quilted liner, the poncho weighed almost two pounds, but it was worth every ounce. In April, for instance, when Ted Lavender was shot, they used his poncho to wrap him up, then to carry him across the paddy, then to lift him into the chopper that took him away.

They were called legs or grunts.

To carry something was to "hump" it, as when Lieutenant Jimmy Cross humped his love for Martha up the hills and through the swamps. In its intransitive form, "to hump" meant "to walk" or "to march," but it implied burdens far beyond the intransitive.

Almost everyone humped photographs. In his wallet, Lieutenant Cross carried two photographs of Martha. The first was a Kodachrome snapshot signed "Love," though he knew better. She stood against a brick wall. Her eyes were gray and neutral, her lips slightly open as she stared straight-on at the camera. At night, sometimes, Lieutenant Cross wondered who had taken the picture, because he knew she had boyfriends, because he loved her so much, and because he could see the shadow of the picture taker spreading out against the brick wall. The second photograph had been clipped from the 1968 Mount Sebastian yearbook. It was an action shot—women's volleyball—and Martha was bent horizontal to the floor, reaching, the palms of her hands in sharp focus, the tongue taut, the expression frank and competitive. There was no visible sweat. She wore white gym shorts. Her legs, he thought, were almost certainly the legs of a virgin, dry and without hair, the left knee cocked and carrying her entire weight, which was just over one hundred pounds. Lieutenant Cross remembered touching that left knee. A dark theater, he remembered, and the movie was *Bonnie and Clyde*, and Martha wore a tweed skirt, and during the final scene, when he touched her knee, she turned and looked at him in a sad, sober way that made him pull his hand back, but he would always remember the feel of the tweed skirt and the knee beneath it and the sound of the gunfire that killed

Bonnie and Clyde, how embarrassing it was, how slow and oppressive. He remembered kissing her good-night at the dorm door. Right then, he thought, he should've done something brave. He should've carried her up the stairs to her room and tied her to the bed and touched that left knee all night long. He should've risked it. Whenever he looked at the photographs, he thought of new things he should've done.

What they carried was partly a function of rank, partly of field specialty.

As a first lieutenant and platoon leader, Jimmy Cross carried a compass, maps, code books, binoculars, and a .45-caliber pistol that weighed 2.9 pounds fully loaded. He carried a strobe light and the responsibility for the lives of his men.

As an RTO, Mitchell Sanders carried the PRC-25 radio, a killer, twenty-six pounds with its battery.

As a medic, Rat Kiley carried a canvas satchel filled with morphine and plasma and malaria tablets and surgical tape and comic books and all the things a medic must carry, including M&Ms for especially bad wounds, for a total weight of nearly twenty pounds.

As a big man, therefore a machine-gunner, Henry Dobbins carried the M-60, which weighed twenty-three pounds unloaded, but which was almost always loaded. In addition, Dobbins carried between ten and fifteen pounds of ammunition draped in belts across his chest and shoulders.

As PFCs or Spec 4s, most of them were common grunts and carried the standard M-16 gas-operated assault rifle. The weapon weighed 7.5 pounds unloaded, 8.2 pounds with its full twenty-round magazine. Depending on numerous factors, such as topography and psychology, the riflemen carried anywhere from twelve to twenty magazines, usually in cloth bandoliers, adding on another 8.4 pounds at minimum, fourteen pounds at maximum. When it was available, they also carried M-16 maintenance gear—rods and steel brushes and swabs and tubes of LSA oil—all of which weighed about a pound. Among the grunts, some carried the M-79 grenade launcher, 5.9 pounds unloaded, a reasonably light weapon except for the ammunition, which was heavy. A single round weighed ten ounces.

The typical load was twenty-five rounds. But Ted Lavender, who was scared, carried thirty-four rounds when he was shot and killed outside Than Khe, and he went down under an exceptional burden, more than twenty pounds of ammunition, plus the flak jacket and helmet and rations and water and toilet paper and tranquilizers and all the rest, plus the unweighed fear. He was dead weight. There was no twitching or flopping. Kiowa, who saw it happen, said it was like watching a rock fall, or a big sandbag or something—just boom, then down—not like the movies where the dead guy rolls around and does fancy spins and goes ass over teakettle—not like that, Kiowa said, the poor bastard just flat-fuck fell. Boom. Down. Nothing else. It was a bright morning in mid-April. Lieutenant Cross felt the pain. He blamed himself. They stripped off Lavender's canteens and ammo, all the heavy things, and Rat Kiley said the obvious, the guy's dead, and Mitchell Sanders used his radio to report one U.S. KIA and to request a chopper. Then they wrapped Lavender in his poncho. They carried him out to a dry paddy, established security, and sat smoking the dead man's dope until the chopper came. Lieutenant Cross kept to himself. He pictured Martha's smooth young face, thinking he loved her more than anything, more than his men, and now Ted Lavender was dead because he loved her so much and could not stop thinking about her. When the dust-off arrived, they carried Lavender aboard. Afterward they burned Than Khe. They marched until dusk, then dug their holes, and that night Kiowa kept explaining how you had to be there, how fast it was, how the poor guy just dropped like so much concrete. Boom-down, he said. Like cement.

In addition to the three standard weapons—the M-60, M-16, and M-79—they carried whatever presented itself, or whatever seemed appropriate as a means of killing or staying alive. They carried catch-as-catch-can. At various times, in various situations, they carried M-14s and CAR-15s and Swedish Ks and grease guns and captured AK-47s and Chi-Coms and RPGs and Simonov carbines and black-market Uzis and .38-caliber Smith & Wesson handguns and 66 mm LAWs and shotguns and silencers and blackjacks and bayonets and C-4 plastic explosives. Lee Strunk carried a slingshot; a weapon of last resort, he called it. Mitchell Sanders carried brass knuckles. Kiowa carried his grandfather's feathered hatchet. Every third or fourth man carried a Claymore antipersonnel mine—3.5 pounds with its firing device. They all carried fragmentation grenades—fourteen ounces each. They all carried at least one M-18 colored smoke grenade—twenty-four ounces. Some carried CS or tear-gas grenades. Some carried white-phosphorus grenades. They carried all they could bear, and then some, including a silent awe for the terrible power of the things they carried.

In the first week of April, before Lavender died, Lieutenant Cross received a good-luck charm from Martha. It was a simple pebble, an ounce at most. Smooth to the touch, it was a milky-white color with flecks of orange and violet, oval-shaped, like a miniature egg. In the accompanying letter, Martha wrote that she had found the pebble on the Jersey shoreline, precisely where the land touched water at high tide, where things came together but also separated. It was this separate-but-together quality, she wrote, that had inspired her to pick up the pebble and to carry it in her breast pocket for several days, where it seemed weightless, and then to send it through the mail, by air, as a token of her truest feelings for him. Lieutenant Cross found this romantic. But he wondered what her truest feelings were, exactly, and what she meant by separate-but-together. He wondered how the tides and waves had come into play on that afternoon along the Jersey shoreline when Martha saw the pebble and bent down to rescue it from geology. He imagined bare feet. Martha was a poet, with the poet's sensibilities, and her feet would be brown and bare, the toenails unpainted, the eyes chilly and somber like the ocean in March, and though it was painful, he wondered who had been with her that afternoon. He imagined a pair of shadows moving along the strip of sand where things came together but also separated. It was phantom jealousy, he knew, but he couldn't help himself. He loved her so much. On the march, through the hot days of early April, he carried the pebble in his mouth, turning it with his tongue, tasting sea salts and moisture. His mind wandered. He had difficulty keeping his attention on the war. On occasion he would yell at his men to spread out the column, to keep their eyes open, but then he would slip away into daydreams, just pretending, walking barefoot along the Jersey shore, with Martha, carrying nothing. He would feel himself rising. Sun and waves and gentle winds, all love and lightness.

What they carried varied by mission.

When a mission took them to the mountains, they carried mosquito netting, machetes, canvas tarps, and extra bug juice.

If a mission seemed especially hazardous, or if it involved a place they knew to be bad, they carried everything they could. In certain heavily mined AOs, where the land was dense with Toe Poppers and Bouncing Betties, they took turns humping a twenty-eight-pound mine detector. With its headphones and big sensing plate, the equipment was a stress on the lower back and shoulders, awkward to handle, often useless because of the shrapnel in the earth, but they carried it anyway, partly for safety, partly for the illusion of safety.

On ambush, or other night missions, they carried peculiar little odds and ends. Kiowa always took along his New Testament and a pair of moccasins for silence. Dave Jensen carried night-sight vitamins high in carotin. Lee Strunk carried his slingshot; ammo, he claimed, would never be a problem. Rat Kiley carried brandy and M&Ms. Until he was shot, Ted Lavender carried the starlight scope, which weighed 6.3 pounds with its aluminum carrying case. Henry Dobbins carried his girlfriend's panty hose wrapped around his neck as a comforter. They all carried ghosts. When dark came, they would move out single file across the meadows and paddies to their ambush coordinates, where they would quietly set up the Claymores and lie down and spend the night waiting.

Other missions were more complicated and required special equipment. In mid-April, it was their mission to search out and destroy the elaborate tunnel complexes in the Than Khe area south of Chu Lai. To blow the tunnels, they carried one-pound blocks of pentrite high explosives, four blocks to a man, sixty-eight pounds in all. They carried wiring, detonators, and battery-powered clackers. Dave Jensen carried earplugs. Most often, before blowing the tunnels, they were ordered by higher command to search them, which was considered bad news, but by and large they just shrugged and carried out orders. Because he was a big man, Henry Dobbins was excused

from tunnel duty. The others would draw numbers. Before
Lavender died there were seventeen men in the platoon, and
whoever drew the number seventeen would strip off his gear
and crawl in headfirst with a flashlight and Lieutenant Cross's
.45-caliber pistol. The rest of them would fan out as security.
They would sit down or kneel, not facing the hole, listening to
the ground beneath them, imagining cobwebs and ghosts, whatever was down there—the tunnel walls squeezing in—how the
flashlight seemed impossibly heavy in the hand and how it was
tunnel vision in the very strictest sense, compression in all
ways, even time, and how you had to wiggle in—ass and
elbows—a swallowed-up feeling—and how you found yourself
worrying about odd things—will your flashlight go dead? Do
rats carry rabies? If you screamed, how far would the sound
carry? Would your buddies hear it? Would they have the
courage to drag you out? In some respects, though not many,
the waiting was worse than the tunnel itself. Imagination was a
killer.

On April 16, when Lee Strunk drew the number seventeen, he laughed and muttered something and went down quickly.
The morning was hot and very still. Not good, Kiowa said. He
looked at the tunnel opening, then out across a dry paddy
toward the village of Than Khe. Nothing moved. No clouds or
birds or people. As they waited, the men smoked and drank
Kool-Aid, not talking much, feeling sympathy for Lee Strunk
but also feeling the luck of the draw. You win some, you lose
some, said Mitchell Sanders, and sometimes you settle for a
rain check. It was a tired line and no one laughed.

Henry Dobbins ate a tropical chocolate bar. Ted Lavender
popped a tranquilizer and went off to pee.

After five minutes, Lieutenant Jimmy Cross moved to the
tunnel, leaned down, and examined the darkness. Trouble, he
thought—a cave-in maybe. And then suddenly, without willing
it, he was thinking about Martha. The stresses and fractures,
the quick collapse, the two of them buried alive under all that
weight. Dense, crushing love. Kneeling, watching the hole, he
tried to concentrate on Lee Strunk and the war, all the dangers,
but his love was too much for him, he felt paralyzed, he
wanted to sleep inside her lungs and breathe her blood and be
smothered. He wanted her to be a virgin and not a virgin, all at

once. He wanted to know her. Intimate secrets—why poetry? Why so sad? Why that grayness in her eyes? Why so alone? Not lonely, just alone—riding her bike across campus or sitting off by herself in the cafeteria. Even dancing, she danced alone—and it was the aloneness that filled him with love. He remembered telling her that one evening. How she nodded and looked away. And how, later, when he kissed her, she received the kiss without returning it, her eyes wide open, not afraid, not a virgin's eyes, just flat and uninvolved.

Lieutenant Cross gazed at the tunnel. But he was not there. He was buried with Martha under the white sand at the Jersey shore. They were pressed together, and the pebble in his mouth was her tongue. He was smiling. Vaguely, he was aware of how quiet the day was, the sullen paddies, yet he could not bring himself to worry about matters of security. He was beyond that. He was just a kid at war, in love. He was twenty-two years old. He couldn't help it.

A few moments later Lee Strunk crawled out of the tunnel. He came up grinning, filthy but alive. Lieutenant Cross nodded and closed his eyes while the others clapped Strunk on the back and made jokes about rising from the dead.

Worms, Rat Kiley said. Right out of the grave. Fuckin' zombie.

The men laughed. They all felt great relief.

Spook City, said Mitchell Sanders.

Lee Strunk made a funny ghost sound, a kind of moaning, yet very happy, and right then, when Strunk made that high happy moaning sound, when he went *Ahhooooo*, right then Ted Lavender was shot in the head on his way back from peeing. He lay with his mouth open. The teeth were broken. There was a swollen black bruise under his left eye. The cheekbone was gone. Oh, shit, Rat Kiley said, the guy's dead. The guy's dead, he kept saying, which seemed profound—the guy's dead. I mean really.

The things they carried were determined to some extent by superstition. Lieutenant Cross carried his good-luck pebble. Dave Jensen carried a rabbit's foot. Norman Bowker, otherwise a very gentle person, carried a thumb that had been presented to him as a gift by Mitchell Sanders. The thumb was dark brown, rubbery to the touch, and weighed four ounces at most. It had been cut from a VC corpse, a boy of fifteen or sixteen. They'd found him at the bottom of an irrigation ditch, badly burned, flies in his mouth and eyes. The boy wore black shorts and sandals. At the time of his death he had been carrying a pouch of rice, a rifle, and three magazines of ammunition.

You want my opinion, Mitchell Sanders said, there's a definite moral here.

He put his hand on the dead boy's wrist. He was quiet for a time, as if counting a pulse, then he patted the stomach, almost affectionately, and used Kiowa's hunting hatchet to remove the thumb.

Henry Dobbins asked what the moral was.

Moral?

You know. *Moral.*

Sanders wrapped the thumb in toilet paper and handed it across to Norman Bowker. There was no blood. Smiling, he kicked the boy's head, watched the flies scatter, and said, It's like with that old TV show—Paladin. Have gun, will travel.

Henry Dobbins thought about it.

Yeah, well, he finally said. I don't see no moral.

There it *is*, man.

Fuck off.

They carried USO stationery and pencils and pens. They carried Sterno, safety pins, trip flares, signal flares, spools of wire, razor blades, chewing tobacco, liberated joss sticks and statuettes of the smiling Buddha, candles, grease pencils, *The Stars and Stripes*, fingernail clippers, Psy Ops leaflets, bush hats, bolos, and much more. Twice a week, when the resupply choppers came in, they carried hot chow in green Mermite cans and large canvas bags filled with iced beer and soda pop. They carried plastic water containers, each with a two-gallon capacity. Mitchell Sanders carried a set of starched tiger fatigues for special occasions. Henry Dobbins carried Black Flag insecticide. Dave Jensen carried empty sandbags that could be filled at night for added protection. Lee Strunk carried tanning lotion. Some things they carried in common. Taking turns, they carried the big PRC-77 scrambler radio, which weighed thirty pounds with its battery. They shared the weight of memory. They took up what others could no longer bear. Often, they carried each other, the wounded or weak. They carried infections. They carried chess sets, basketballs, Vietnamese-English dictionaries, insignia of rank, Bronze Stars and Purple Hearts, plastic cards imprinted with the Code of Conduct. They carried diseases, among them malaria and dysentery. They carried lice and ringworm and leeches and paddy algae and various rots and molds. They carried the land itself—Vietnam, the place, the soil—a powdery orange-red dust that covered their boots and fatigues and faces. They carried the sky. The whole atmosphere, they carried it, the humidity, the monsoons, the stink of fungus and decay, all of it, they carried gravity. They moved like mules. By daylight they took sniper fire, at night they were mortared, but it was not battle, it was just the endless march, village to village, without purpose, nothing won or lost. They marched for the sake of the march. They plodded along slowly, dumbly, leaning forward against the heat, unthinking, all blood and bone, simple grunts, soldiering with their legs, toiling up the hills and down into the paddies and across the rivers and up again and down, just humping, one step and then the next and then another, but no volition, no will, because it was automatic, it was anatomy, and the war was entirely a matter of posture and carriage, the hump was everything, a kind of inertia, a kind of emptiness, a dullness of desire and intellect and conscience and hope and human sensibility. Their principles were in their feet. Their calculations were biological. They had no sense of strategy or mission. They searched the villages without knowing what to look for, not caring, kicking over jars of rice, frisking children and old men, blowing tunnels, sometimes setting fires and sometimes not, then forming up and moving on to the next village, then other villages, where it would always be the same. They carried their own lives. The pressures were enormous. In the heat of early afternoon, they would remove their helmets and flak jackets, walking bare, which was dangerous but which helped ease the strain. They would often discard things along the route of march. Purely for comfort, they would throw away rations, blow their Claymores and grenades, no matter, because by nightfall the resupply choppers would arrive with more of the same, then a day or two later still more, fresh watermelons and crates of ammunition and sunglasses and woolen sweaters—the resources were stunning—sparklers for the Fourth of July, colored eggs for Easter. It was the great American war chest—the fruits of science, the smokestacks, the canneries, the arsenals at Hartford, the Minnesota forests, the machine shops, the vast fields of corn and wheat—they carried like freight trains; they carried it on their backs and shoulders—and for all the ambiguities of Vietnam, all the mysteries and unknowns, there was at least the single abiding certainty that they would never be at a loss for things to carry.

After the chopper took Lavender away, Lieutenant Jimmy Cross led his men into the village of Than Khe. They burned everything. They shot chickens and dogs, they trashed the village well, they called in artillery and watched the wreckage, then they marched for several hours through the hot afternoon, and then at dusk, while Kiowa explained how Lavender died, Lieutenant Cross found himself trembling.

He tried not to cry. With his entrenching tool, which weighed five pounds, he began digging a hole in the earth.

He felt shame. He hated himself. He had loved Martha more than his men, and as a consequence Lavender was now dead, and this was something he would have to carry like a stone in his stomach for the rest of the war.

All he could do was dig. He used his entrenching tool like an ax, slashing, feeling both love and hate, and then later, when it was full dark, he sat at the bottom of his foxhole and wept. It went on for a long while. In part, he was grieving for Ted Lavender, but mostly it was for Martha, and for himself, because she belonged to another world, which was not quite real, and because she was a junior at Mount Sebastian College in New Jersey, a poet and a virgin and uninvolved, and because he realized she did not love him and never would.

Like cement, Kiowa whispered in the dark. I swear to God—boom-down. Not a word.

I've heard this, said Norman Bowker.

A pisser, you know? Still zipping himself up. Zapped while zipping.

All right, fine. That's enough.

Yeah, but you had to see it, the guy just—

I *heard*, man. Cement. So why not shut the fuck *up*?

Kiowa shook his head sadly and glanced over at the hole where Lieutenant Jimmy Cross sat watching the night. The air was thick and wet. A warm, dense fog had settled over the paddies and there was the stillness that precedes rain.

After a time Kiowa sighed.

One thing for sure, he said. The Lieutenant's in some deep hurt. I mean that crying jag—the way he was carrying on—it wasn't fake or anything, it was real heavy-duty hurt. The man cares.

Sure, Norman Bowker said.

Say what you want, the man does care.

We all got problems.

Not Lavender.

No, I guess not, Bowker said. Do me a favor, though.

Shut up?

That's a smart Indian. Shut up.

Shrugging, Kiowa pulled off his boots. He wanted to say more, just to lighten up his sleep, but instead he opened his New Testament and arranged it beneath his head as a pillow. The fog made things seem hollow and unattached. He tried not to think about Ted Lavender, but then he was thinking how fast it was, no drama, down and dead, and how it was hard to feel anything except surprise. It seemed unchristian. He wished he could find some great sadness, or even anger, but the emotion wasn't there and he couldn't make it happen. Mostly he felt pleased to be alive. He liked the smell of the New Testament under his cheek, the leather and ink and paper and glue, whatever the chemicals were. He liked hearing the sounds of night. Even his fatigue, it felt fine, the stiff muscles and the prickly awareness of his own body, a floating feeling. He enjoyed not being dead. Lying there, Kiowa admired Lieutenant Jimmy Cross's capacity for grief. He wanted to share the man's pain, he wanted to care as Jimmy Cross cared. And yet when he closed his eyes, all he could think was boom-down, and all he could feel was the pleasure of having his boots off and the fog curling in around him and the damp soil and the Bible smells and the plush comfort of night.

After a moment Norman Bowker sat up in the dark.

What the hell, he said. You want to talk, *talk*. Tell it to me.

Forget it.

No, man, go on. One thing I hate, it's a silent Indian.

For the most part they carried themselves with poise, a kind of dignity. Now and then, however, there were times of panic, when they squealed or wanted to squeal but couldn't, when they twitched and made moaning sounds and covered their heads and said Dear Jesus and flopped around on the earth and fired their weapons blindly and cringed and sobbed and begged for the noise to stop and went wild and made stupid promises to themselves and to God and to their mothers and fathers, hoping not to die. In different ways, it happened to all of them. Afterward, when the firing ended, they would blink and peek up. They would touch their bodies, feeling shame, then quickly hiding it. They would force themselves to stand. As if in slow motion, frame by frame, the world would take on the old logic—absolute silence, then the wind, then sunlight, then voices. It was the burden of being alive. Awkwardly, the men would reassemble themselves, first in private, then in groups, becoming soldiers again. They would repair the leaks in their eyes. They would check for casualties, call in dust-offs, light cigarettes, try to smile, clear their throats and spit and begin cleaning their weapons. After a time someone would shake his head and say, No lie, I almost shit my pants, and someone else would laugh, which meant it was bad, yes, but the guy had obviously not shit his pants, it wasn't that bad, and in any case nobody would ever do such a thing and then go ahead and talk about it. They would squint into the dense, oppressive sunlight. For a few moments, perhaps, they would fall silent, lighting a joint and tracking its passage from man to man, inhaling, holding in the humiliation. Scary stuff, one of them might say. But then someone else would grin or flick his eyebrows and say, Roger-dodger, almost cut me a new asshole, *almost*.

There were numerous such poses. Some carried themselves with a sort of wistful resignation, others with pride or stiff soldierly discipline or good humor or macho zeal. They were afraid of dying but they were even more afraid to show it.

They found jokes to tell.

They used a hard vocabulary to contain the terrible softness. *Greased*, they'd say. *Offed, lit up, zapped while zipping*. It wasn't cruelty, just stage presence. They were actors and the war came at them in 3-D. When someone died, it wasn't quite dying, because in a curious way it seemed scripted, and because they had their lines mostly memorized, irony mixed with tragedy, and because they called it by other names, as if to encyst and destroy the reality of death itself. They kicked corpses. They cut off thumbs. They talked grunt lingo. They told stories about Ted Lavender's supply of tranquilizers, how the poor guy didn't feel a thing, how incredibly tranquil he was.

There's a moral here, said Mitchell Sanders.

They were waiting for Lavender's chopper, smoking the dead man's dope.

The moral's pretty obvious, Sanders said, and winked. Stay away from drugs. No joke, they'll ruin your day every time.

Cute, said Henry Dobbins.

Mind-blower, get it? Talk about wiggy—nothing left, just blood and brains.

They made themselves laugh.

There it is, they'd say, over and over, as if the repetition itself were an act of poise, a balance between crazy and almost crazy, knowing without going. There it is, which meant be cool, let it ride, because oh, yeah, man, you can't change what can't be changed, there it is, there it absolutely and positively and fucking well *is*.

They were tough.

They carried all the emotional baggage of men who might die. Grief, terror, love, longing—these were intangibles, but the intangibles had their own mass and specific gravity, they had tangible weight. They carried shameful memories. They carried the common secret of cowardice barely restrained, the instinct to run or freeze or hide, and in many respects this was the heaviest burden of all, for it could never be put down, it required perfect balance and perfect posture. They carried their reputations. They carried the soldier's greatest fear, which was the fear of blushing. Men killed, and died, because they were embarrassed not to. It was what had brought them to the war in the first place, nothing positive, no dreams of glory or honor, just to avoid the blush of dishonor. They died so as not to die of embarrassment. They crawled into tunnels and walked point and advanced under fire. Each morning, despite the unknowns, they made their legs move. They endured. They kept humping. They did not submit to the obvious alternative, which was simply to close the eyes and fall. So easy, really. Go limp and tumble to the ground and let the muscles unwind and not speak and not budge until your buddies picked you up and lifted you into the chopper that would roar and dip its nose and carry you off to the world. A mere matter of falling, yet no one ever fell. It was not courage, exactly; the object was not valor. Rather, they were too frightened to be cowards.

By and large they carried these things inside, maintaining the masks of composure. They sneered at sick call. They spoke bitterly about guys who had found release by shooting off their own toes or fingers. Pussies, they'd say. Candyasses. It was fierce, mocking talk, with only a trace of envy or awe, but even so, the image played itself out behind their eyes.

They imagined the muzzle against flesh. They imagined the quick, sweet pain, then the evacuation to Japan, then a hospital with warm beds and cute geisha nurses.

They dreamed of freedom birds.

At night, on guard, staring into the dark, they were carried away by jumbo jets. They felt the rush of takeoff. *Gone!* they yelled. And then velocity, wings and engines, a smiling stewardess—but it was more than a plane, it was a real bird, a big sleek silver bird with feathers and talons and high screeching. They were flying. The weights fell off, there was nothing to bear. They laughed and held on tight, feeling the cold slap of wind and altitude, soaring, thinking *It's over, I'm gone!*—they were naked, they were light and free—it was all lightness, bright and fast and buoyant, light as light, a helium buzz in the brain, a giddy bubbling in the lungs as they were taken up over the clouds and the war, beyond duty, beyond gravity and mortification and global entanglements—*Sin loi!* they yelled, *I'm sorry, motherfuckers, but I'm out of it, I'm goofed, I'm on a space cruise, I'm gone!*—and it was a restful, disencumbered sensation, just riding the light waves, sailing that big silver freedom bird over the mountains and oceans, over America, over the farms and great sleeping cities and cemeteries and highways and the Golden Arches of McDonald's. It was flight, a kind of fleeing, a kind of falling, falling higher and higher, spinning off the edge of the earth and beyond the sun and through the vast, silent vacuum where there were no burdens and where everything weighed exactly nothing. *Gone!* they screamed, *I'm sorry but I'm gone!* And so at night, not quite dreaming, they gave themselves over to lightness, they were carried, they were purely borne.

On the morning after Ted Lavender died, First Lieutenant Jimmy Cross crouched at the bottom of his foxhole and burned Martha's letters. Then he burned the two photographs. There was a steady rain falling, which made it difficult, but he used heat tabs and Sterno to build a small fire, screening it with his body, holding the photographs over the tight blue flame with the tips of his fingers.

He realized it was only a gesture. Stupid, he thought. Sentimental, too, but mostly just stupid.

Lavender was dead. You couldn't burn the blame.

Besides, the letters were in his head. And even now, without photographs, Lieutenant Cross could see Martha playing volleyball in her white gym shorts and yellow T-shirt. He could see her moving in the rain.

When the fire died out, Lieutenant Cross pulled his poncho over his shoulders and ate breakfast from a can.

There was no great mystery, he decided.

In those burned letters Martha had never mentioned the war, except to say, Jimmy, take care of yourself. She wasn't involved. She signed the letters "Love," but it wasn't love, and all the fine lines and technicalities did not matter.

The morning came up wet and blurry. Everything seemed part of everything else, the fog and Martha and the deepening rain.

It was a war, after all.

Half smiling, Lieutenant Jimmy Cross took out his maps. He shook his head hard, as if to clear it, then bent forward and began planning the day's march. In ten minutes, or maybe twenty, he would rouse the men and they would pack up and head west, where the maps showed the country to be green and inviting. They would do what they had always done. The rain might add some weight, but otherwise it would be one more day layered upon all the other days.

He was realistic about it. There was that new hardness in his stomach.

No more fantasies, he told himself.

Henceforth, when he thought about Martha, it would be only to think that she belonged elsewhere. He would shut down the daydreams. This was not Mount Sebastian, it was another world, where there were no pretty poems or midterm exams, a place where men died because of carelessness and gross stupidity. Kiowa was right. Boom-down, and you were dead, never partly dead.

Briefly, in the rain, Lieutenant Cross saw Martha's gray eyes gazing back at him.

He understood.

It was very sad, he thought. The things men carried inside. The things men did or felt they had to do.

He almost nodded at her, but didn't.

Instead he went back to his maps. He was now determined to perform his duties firmly and without negligence. It wouldn't help Lavender, he knew that, but from this point on he would comport himself as a soldier. He would dispose of his good-luck pebble. Swallow it, maybe, or use Lee Strunk's slingshot, or just drop it along the trail. On the march he would impose strict field discipline. He would be careful to send out flank security, to prevent straggling or bunching up, to keep his troops moving at the proper pace and at the proper interval. He would insist on clean weapons. He would confiscate the remainder of Lavender's dope. Later in the day, perhaps, he would call the men together and speak to them plainly. He would accept the blame for what had happened to Ted Lavender. He would be a man about it. He would look them in the eyes, keeping his chin level, and he would issue the new SOPs in a calm, impersonal tone of voice, an officer's voice, leaving no room for argument or discussion. Commencing immediately, he'd tell them, they would no longer abandon equipment along the route of march. They would police up their acts.

They would get their shit together, and keep it together, and maintain it neatly and in good working order.

He would not tolerate laxity. He would show strength, distancing himself.

Among the men there would be grumbling, of course, and maybe worse, because their days would seem longer and their loads heavier, but Lieutenant Cross reminded himself that his obligation was not to be loved but to lead. He would dispense with love; it was not now a factor. And if anyone quarreled or complained, he would simply tighten his lips and arrange his shoulders in the correct command posture. He might give a curt little nod. Or he might not. He might just shrug and say Carry on, then they would saddle up and form into a column and move out toward the villages west of Than Khe.

# RACHEL PASTAN
# UNDERGROUND

FROM THE GEORGIA REVIEW

ᴒ

IT WAS, APPARENTLY, a small dinosaur, only about five feet high. It had soft, vegetation-grinding teeth, but its claws were dangerous. No one knew for certain how old it was, which makes some doubt that it was ever really a dinosaur at all—many believe it was merely an abnormally large lizard, or one of those crocodiles flushed into the city's sewer system. Lisa, however, insisted it was a dinosaur, a real one. If anyone would know, she would, and she said she never doubted it.

An assortment of doors opened off the basement corridors. Some led to cool, soundproofed music rooms, others to darkrooms pungent with the smells of chemicals, and a few to huge, dusty laundry rooms, scattered with odd socks. Most of the rooms, however, were scarcely bigger than closets. Many of them were locked, their uniform surfaces revealing nothing about what lay within.

Lisa walked up and down the dark corridors, trying an occasional handle. She hardly noticed whether it turned, whether a deserted room opened itself to her, or if it did, what lay inside.

Once, as Lisa had walked back and forth almost until dawn, an opened door revealed a couple making love. Startled out of her somnambulant revery, Lisa uttered a confused "Oh!" and shut the door with a bang. She continued to walk on, but she stopped every few minutes, startled all over again by the vision that sprang repeatedly before her eyes: the two lovers active in what she considered her personal and secret domain. The faces turned toward her in a kind of frightened reproach, a sudden frozen tension in the naked limbs. The expression of the eyes stayed most vividly in her mind—a little fearful, but somehow essentially calm and unsurprised. As if the eyes knew she would discover them eventually, as if the eyes had been silently waiting to meet her particular gaze. She did not absorb the whole image until after she had shut the door, did not realize until she was halfway down the corridor that it had been two women she had seen through the open door.

Lisa was a junior in college, but for weeks she had not been going to classes. Studying seemed pointless to her, the material irrelevant to any living she had ever planned to do. Papers were worse—there was nothing to say that had not been said. If she could not be original, she would not write at all. She watched TV instead. After a few days, even the effort of rising from the bed to change the channel seemed phenomenal.

Only at night could she rouse herself. That was when, ghostlike, she haunted the basement. She liked thinking of the people who lay curled in their beds above her as she walked. She liked being the only one in the vast expanse of the dormitory who was in motion.

It is the dinosaur, of course, that bewilders people—the physicality of it that they disbelieve. Of course, when Lisa touched it, and when she remembered it afterwards, she thought less about the unknown than about the familiar. She had touched (so it seemed to her) something out of a nearer past, part of the exhilarating adventure world of childhood. When she was young she had seen so many dinosaur movies—trembling with excitement in the darkened theater, palms sticky, clutching at the warm, skinny arm of the girl in the seat beside her—that the following mornings in church she had imagined the apocalypse as the work of a celestial dinosaur-of-God, gnashing its yellow teeth and flashing its all-seeing red eyes in a vivid image of the Lord's final vengeance.

It was almost always quiet in the basement, and it seemed deserted that night when Lisa, in blue jeans and a loose white camisole, moved barefooted through the must-smelling corridors. No spiders scuttled across the dusty floors. No moth fluttered against the flickering light bulbs, shaded only with grime, that dotted the flaking ceiling. She could see herself walking like one of the black-and-white ghosts on the television set that had become the focus of her life.

She thought about the bishop who was a friend of her grandfather. Once, when her family had been traveling somewhere, they had spent the night in the bishop's house in Philadelphia. Late at night, looking for the bathroom, she had mistakenly opened the door to his study. Through the first crack she could see his profile, glowingly illuminated by the lamp behind him. It was not his features, however, so much as his strong neck that attracted her attention, straining determinedly over the large book that lay open on the table in front of him. His hands clutched at each other in his lap, and his whole posture indicated a tense questioning, as though his life were condensed into this cosmic yet concrete inquiry for which he expected, at any moment, like a man next to a radio clutching the stub of a lottery ticket, to discover the solution. Yet he had seemed, too, Lisa remembered, as though he doubted whether he was actually up to the whole thing.

This, Lisa felt uneasily, was the way she now studied her television screen.

She really hadn't had the TV that long—only since early in the fall. It had been a cool day, she recalled. She had walked slowly along the sunny side of the street, not noticing the way the light fell in bright patches on the sidewalk, not noticing the dark-haired man who brushed against her in the crowd and smiled apologetically. She merely hummed quietly and drifted along.

Eventually, on a side street, she came upon a small yellow house. Its narrow front yard was filled with sagging tables displaying an assortment of household objects, each one marked with a little tag.

A youngish woman with dark hair stood behind the tables. Wearing dirty blue jeans and a loose yellow sweater, she looked tired but cheerful, with agreeable features. What Lisa noticed most, however, was the way that the woman held her hands definitively, almost pugnaciously, in her pockets.

Lisa stopped in front of the tables and glanced over an eggbeater, a clock radio, an electric mixer. The next table had a toaster oven, a Waring blender, and an electric can opener—all left over from a decade when such things were in fashion. She looked again at the woman, who shifted her weight comfortably from foot to foot but kept her hands in her pockets.

"The clock radio is almost new," the woman said.

Lisa picked it up and looked at it. She switched it on and a burst of folk music issued forth, melancholy, a little tinny but soothing. They stood in silence for a minute or two, listening to the music. Small clouds rushed across the sun before the pursuing wind, causing a rapid alteration of light and shadow to fill the little yard.

"Almost new," the woman repeated.

Lisa switched it off. "I already have a clock," she said, putting it back on the table.

There was another silence as the woman looked at Lisa curiously. "Are you a student?" the woman asked at last.

Lisa nodded.

The woman nodded back. "I know how it is," she said, turning toward the front steps. "Come on into the house—I've got just the thing for you."

Lisa followed, wondering how the woman was going to manage the door with her hands in her pockets, but she just pulled them out calmly and opened it. Lisa trailed behind, leaving the row of appliance-covered tables unattended in the suddenly sun-flooded yard.

In her mind, now, Lisa was moving again through the hallways of the yellow house. When her hand brushed against the damp concrete walls of the basement, she thought they were the white plaster ones in the north of the city. As she opened a door into another part of the basement, she felt she was entering the bright kitchen with pots hanging on hooks from the walls. And at last, stepping carefully along a slightly inclined ramp, she ascended the narrow stairway opening out into a large attic room.

The room was dimly lit by a single window, below which, on the floor, lay a mattress, neatly covered with a blue sheet. In front of it sat a small black-and-white TV set, its bent antennae arcing gracefully toward the window. The scarcity of light, the minimum of furniture, the roughness of the floor, and the room's situation at the top of the building—all made the place seem, to Lisa, a kind of sanctuary, a sacred retreat from the world.

The woman sat down on the mattress, leaned back on her elbow, and looked sadly at the blank television screen. She raised her hand to run it absentmindedly across her collarbone. She looked up at Lisa, and then down to the floor, and then up at Lisa again.

Lisa was fascinated by the woman's uncovered hands. They moved rapidly but gracefully now, as if they wanted to make the most of their time out of the confining pockets of her jeans.

"Sit down," the woman said, lifting her eyes from the blank screen to Lisa's face and holding them there with a fixed gaze.

Lisa made herself stop remembering.

She stood still in the middle of the hallway, the thick dust on the floor tickling her feet. She rubbed her eyes with the heels of her hands until the gray corridor went blurry. She listened to the steady hum from the water pipes. Now she noticed a strong, acrid smell hovering in the damp air. It was like a combination of sap, lemons, and autumn leaves. Lisa stood even stiller, smelling it.

She remembered the smell of the woman's skin in the yellow house, in the attic—the fragrant saltiness of it, the freshness of it as Lisa sat down beside her on the blue-sheeted mattress. She remembered how the woman had shifted her eyes again, had looked away from Lisa, out of the window at the clouds hurrying across the sky. Lisa remembered how relieved she had felt, and also how deserted, when the woman's focus changed.

It was very still in the attic.

"So," the woman said at last, her eyes on the busy, unexceptional clouds.

"Yes?"

The woman turned her head slowly from the window, past the TV set, and settled her gaze on Lisa again. She raised herself from her elbow and reached out, very slowly, to touch the television. She ran her fingers slowly along the screen, caressing it. Her hands were like feathers. "Do you want it?" the woman asked.

Standing in the basement, Lisa heard a sound. *There should be no sound*, she thought. *There should be no one here but me.* She felt a wave of nausea as she remembered that other nocturnal discovery. *Please*, she thought, *let there be no one here but me.*

When Lisa had said nothing, as if unsure what the question meant, the woman had repeated: "Do you want it? Do you want the TV?"

"I don't know," Lisa said slowly. "What would I do with a TV?"

The woman shrugged. She pulled at her short hair with her hands. "It belonged to a friend of mine," she said. "She used to watch it when she was in school. So all the academics wouldn't rot her brain."

Lisa did not respond. The woman continued to watch her steadily. Lisa looked at the blank screen as though it might come to life.

There was definitely a faint noise coming from some other part of the basement. It was a click, like an animal setting a clawed foot on the concrete floor, and it echoed through the corridors. Lisa's heart began to beat fast. Another click echoed, and then another.

Lisa remembered how frightened she had been, initially, at the complete blankness of the television screen. Anything could appear there—anything. As she watched it in the empty attic, next to the woman she did not know and whose facial expression she could not read, the screen seemed to return her gaze ironically, as if to reply *Yes, anything.* ANYTHING.

The clicks got louder, coming at more regular intervals. It was some sort of animal, she was sure, perhaps some large dog that had made its way into the depths of the building and gotten shut in. *What else could it be?* she thought. At least, judging by the sounds, it probably wasn't a man with a knife. In her worst fears it was a wolf, but she knew that a wolf couldn't get down into the basement. *It must be somebody's dog,* she thought. *And yet,* she almost didn't let herself think, *the smell isn't like a dog's.* The smell was stronger now. *Whatever it is,* she thought, *it's getting closer.*

In her memory, she saw the woman's hands moving gracefully along the blue sheet, tracing patterns.

"What's your name?" the woman asked.

"Lisa."

The woman began to trace the letters of the name on the little stretch of blue between them.

The sounds got closer and closer, and the sap-and-lemon smell got stronger. Lisa was dizzy from it, and from fear, but she was sure it was a dog—it couldn't be anything but a dog—so she stayed where she was. Her feet were beginning to sweat against the dusty floor. The clicks came ever louder. *That's a huge dog,* she thought. Her mouth was dry. The clicks echoed so loudly that Lisa couldn't hear her own voice as she cried out, "Hello?" And then, through the din of the unknown, fiercely echoing clicking, she was back in her own mind again, back in her memory, seeing the woman's hand slowly tracing the invisible letters. The light fingers nearly reached her thigh at the apex of the *A*, and then withdrew a little. They began again.

Lisa watched, twitching her own fingers without knowing it as they lay in her lap. This time, as the hand finished the graceful *S*, it ran out of room. It traced the *A* slowly on the side of Lisa's leg. Lisa drew in her breath sharply. The fingers finished the *A*, and then rested lightly on Lisa's thigh. She felt as if she were exploding from the inside.

And then, when the sound of the clicking feet and the closeness of the smell were so overpowering that she thought she was actually going to faint, when her mind was so filled with a feeling like mist and damp sand that she could hardly keep the present separate from memory, could hardly remember where she was standing, could barely remember what it was that the fear was—at the instant when she was feeling, as if it were just then happening, the caress of the woman's feather-soft hand on her tense thigh, feeling her own palm moving out of her warm lap to cover it, feeling the two hands rubbing lightly across each other, the woman's other hand reaching forward and touching her thin white shirt, falling from her collarbone to cover her breast, and her own hand reaching out to the woman, the woman's breath caressing her face, her lips open to meet the other's lips—just at that very moment when she was remembering all this, the thing, the other presence, rounded the corner with its footsteps ringing deafeningly, and stopped in its tracks.

With a shock she recognized it.

The small dinosaur stood almost upright on its back legs, balancing itself with the powerful tail which lay in a graceful curve across the floor. It was a dusky, gray-green color in the dim light. Its small beaked snout looked, when tilted to the side as it was now, inquisitive. She thought she must have seen it in some movie once, since she recognized it so distinctly, but with the living presence of it staring her in the face, she couldn't remember when. It looked at her with dark eyes that seemed almost humanly penetrating. They were far from the fishy quality the camera gave to dinosaurs' eyes in the movies.

She took a step in its direction. It stood still. This stillness frightened her more than the threat of violence. She took another step.

She was convinced the dinosaur was watching her with curiosity. She felt its eyes calling her forward. She thought the gray-greenness of its body was like the sea. She noticed how, as it stood sturdily on its back legs and tail, its small front limbs seemed to float lightly in the air.

As she took one step after another toward the still dinosaur, she thought with certainty that she could tell, as if it were already a memory, what it would be like later.

She imagined she was walking toward her own bed. When she reached it in her mind, she pulled the covers up around her, leaned back against the wall, and looked at her television. The screen was like a mirror, reflecting her calm face and her calm gray eyes. She held her breath.

Lisa couldn't remember any time in the past year, at least, when her image in any mirror had looked so calm. Examining her eyes, rediscovering the old curves of her face, she felt an overwhelming sense of freedom and control come over her, breaking wavelike, tangible, sanely cool, over her warm body.

She took another step. The closer she moved to it, the more familiar it became. It seemed warm, too—not an image, not an overgrown chameleon, but another species altogether, watching as well as warm. A warm, watching animal that knew her and that she knew. She took another step, and then another, and she noticed that she was breathing more calmly now, and she stepped again and again, and her footsteps echoed a little in the corridor, and she watched the dark eyes watch her, and she stepped, and she was enveloped in the warm, autumn smell, and as she stepped she reached out her hand, and the dinosaur reached out toward her, and at the moment when she touched the creature she heard the water rushing in the pipes above her, and the creature's smell became her own smell, and she closed her eyes, not to shut it out, but the way some people close their eyes when they make love, because the smell and the touch and the knowing are enough.

# ELIZABETH TALLENT

# MIGRANTS

## FROM THE PARIS REVIEW

∽

SISSY ISN'T A small-town girl at heart—only through a steady refusal of circumstances, luck and love, to align themselves her way. Two years ago, Sissy's mother left Iowa with her boyfriend for L.A.; now they manage a trailer park of unpaved lanes and old palms whose lowest branches are dead, dry fans. Sissy's father sells the big Rain Cats, irrigation sprinklers that pivot around fields cut circular to accommodate them, the air above the pipes stunned with heat, the winter wheat below abruptly glistening, so that a long shadow seems towed by the sprinklers across a solid light-tan plane. Immediately below the pipes is the dividing line, drawn slowly forward, between drenched and parched, with the crossed wheat turning dark in a sharp stretch and throwing off a thin, prismatic spume, or entire moving rainbows no bigger than birds' wings. Someday, Rafer says in his sales pitch, all of this will be run by computers, and in a far field the linked arms of Rain Cats will spring to life whether anyone is there to see them or not.

Just after Sissy's junior year of high school, Rain Cat relocated Rafer to Wheaton, Colorado, and paid for the Mayflower van. Sissy left a boyfriend Rafer didn't know about;

Rafer left a bowling-alley waitress Sissy did. His new territory
is vast and marginal, dusty fields of wheat, alfalfa, soybeans,
and sugar beets worked by wetbacks and owned by farmers
who are barely making it and already have too much capital tied
up in obsolete heavy equipment—the kind of men, Rafer says,
who shyly tap toothpicks from the plastic dispenser beside the
cash register when they finally pay for the cup of coffee they
nursed all morning long, and whose own fathers were so poor
they cut the eyes from potatoes, planted the eyes, and boiled
the potatoes to feed their families. All spring in Wheaton,
where she knows no one and nobody seems to be under forty
anyway, Sissy has been lonely; all spring Rafer has been on the
road. Once when she thought she was cracking up, he warned
her long-distance, "Sissy, it's a good thing I'm gone. If I wasn't
gone, would I be making sales?" More gently, "Don't you
know I go through this all week because I want a future for
you?" Gentlest of all, "You're not going to grow up into one
of those women who thinks the world owes them a living."

"Daddy, don't talk like that." Because she knew he meant
her mother.

"We're in this together, aren't we? You just want to keep
your head. I know that I can count on you."

Rafer says she shouldn't live for the weekends, but on
Saturday nights they eat steak in a restaurant and he tells her
about his week. Sunday mornings they take Joe, Rafer's dog,
and his old .22, and drive out to one of the arroyos where a
million shattered bottles lie, and Rafer steadies her arm while
she shoots chips of glass, and sometimes dimes, from the
eroded wall. She likes the way the dust floats up and smokes
away. When they come home her hair is always lighter, her
shoulders sunburned, and she cooks dinner for them both. Joe
licks Rafer's face to wake him up, weekend mornings, and
Rafer lifts Joe's floppy ear and sings into it as if it's a microphone, until Joe growls.

Sissy stops her bicycle at a windmill far out in the grasslands—stops as if windmill water, scummed with algae the dead
landlocked green of pool-table felt, has some faint connection
to clear Rain Cat water; stops as if Rafer, wherever he is, can
feel her stopping. Though there seems to be no wind, the

windmill blades keep turning, and blades of shadow switch with light on Sissy's face. The heat pausing on her cheek is pleasant, though she's almost sure the part in her hair is burning, her forehead and nose flecking with more ugly sharp freckles. Now that she's resting, the gloss of sweat, absent throughout the long bike ride, pricks her shaved armpits—a feeling like the beginning of a rash. A mourning dove lands on the holding tank's rim, peers at Sissy, fails to see her, and flutters to the ground, which is rutted by thousands of sun-baked cattle tracks, hoping to find a track that still cradles an inch of sour water. It used to puzzle her that the birds wouldn't bathe in the holding tank, but then she figured it out—it is impossible for a dove to drown in a cattle track.

She tips her bicycle up and walks it back to the highway, studying low bluffs that fade backward into a line of identically eroded, shades-paler bluffs; under the shadows of small moving clouds, the bluffs seem to be folding and unfolding. Between her and them lie a hundred miles that are nothing but empty. After that a thousand miles, and after that L.A. Ah, she hates it here. *Hates* it. From dry weeds drawn into the bicycle spokes, a hail of grasshoppers patters against her bare legs. When their wings flick open, oval dapples form glaring eyes precise down to the fawn iris and darker pupil. The eyes wink out as the grasshoppers fasten again onto trembling grass, and Sissy looks behind her at the bicycle's snaking track. All that way for what? For nothing.

But the highway radiates a tarry heat different from the heat of the grass, and exchanging one for the other is a relief. For an hour, by the watch loose on her sweating right wrist, she is the only moving thing in that landscape. Stranded on the horizon is a peaked farmhouse, gray with weather, its frame sides narrow as shutters closed against noon. This farmhouse has always depressed Sissy. She shakes her head, the bicycle wobbles dangerously, and from behind there is a blare of sound, rusty but convincing. Astonished, she looks over her shoulder to find a gypsy line of junk cars, moving probably at thirty miles an hour, so that, as they very gradually gain on her, she can drink it in: the candied sweetness of hot car paint, a whiff of burning engine oil, and the cigarette smoke of the drivers, who are all young Spanish men; the charred doors wired shut with coat hangers, windshields that are cobwebs of fracture sealed by a graffito of yellowed tape; other windows ballooning with wet shirts or hung with rag-tag, brilliant bits of underwear; grandmothers sleeping in the improvised shade of diapers flapping as they dry. Sissy loves them for having appeared behind her, out of nowhere. The dusty dashes hold groves of plastic saints, and rosaries wag from the rearview mirrors. A child sucking on its fist pushes aside a pair of fluttering panty hose and gazes out at her. Another child pushes up beside the first, yawns widely, peels up a damp T-shirt, and shyly scratches a scarred chest. Sissy, too, feels shy. She is so exposed on the bicycle. They're migrants, she knows, up from Mexico for the summer. That too is cause for shyness, because the migrants who camp and work in the fields around Wheaton are shunned by the Anglos. Rafer has told her some cruel things he's seen.

The grown women all seem to be sleeping, many with children sprawled across their laps. Sleeping children look so much hotter than sleeping adults, Sissy thinks; they look as if they've fainted, their hands loose and their hair stuck to their foreheads. She laughs when a passing car shows the soles of two tiny bare feet resting flat against a window rolled halfway up. The heels are black. Gusts of real heat hit Sissy between the cars. She feels she belongs with them now, and doesn't like falling behind. She chooses a Cadillac with scorched fins and burnt-out taillights, and tires herself in keeping alongside it; she wonders whether the driver, who never once glances sideways, has speeded up a little to lose her, and then she wonders at the enraged alarm she feels, knowing that he has. It is a brief battle. The Cadillac noses gently, very gently, into her lane, and she is forced to slow onto the shoulder. She feels flat amazement: Why did he do that? The Cadillac eases back into line, and the cars are gone. The highway's two lanes go desolate, the silence extremely definite. She sees a Coke bottle someone threw from a window. The bottle is rolling down the yellow line above its own delicately coasting shadow, to a hollow tone that seems to come from far away.

In Wheaton's post office there is a clerk, nearsighted Mr. Cox, who loves twiggy young trees fresh from the nursery, and Sissy likes him for that, though he is old and often cranky.

Sprinklers fret across the dozen new dogwoods staked along the sidewalks, their slim trunks bandaged in gauze like the legs of colts. "Good for you, Coxy," Sissy says to herself. In fact, according to Rafer, Mr. Cox is less hostile to wetbacks than post office clerks in the surrounding small towns, and on Saturdays the migrants can be found, in from the fields, patiently waiting for Mr. Cox to hand them the money orders necessary to convey their entire paychecks home to Mexico. The ruined cars that passed Sissy three weeks ago in the grasslands are lined up now along the yellow curb in front of the post office. She glances into an ancient Chevrolet with a corroded hood; an empty baby bottle, its nipple dented with fine teethmarks, is nested upright in a child's torn sneaker. She shoulders open the glass door, and the men inside, scarcely turning, make way for her so subtly that she sees only their neatly shaven napes, sunburned even through the darkness of the skin, and the backs of thin white shirts showing the ghosts of undershirts. There is a good, sharp barbershop smell. She stands, biting her lower lip, while the line dissolves away from her, the men gravitating toward a wall of wanted posters, making it seem that there is something irresistible and natural in their attraction to this wall.

Mr. Cox, squinting up from his scales, sees her alone. "Well, Sissy," he says. "This is a pleasure. Come on up."

"I can't, Mr. Cox," she says. "I was last in line."

He aims around himself a mole's assessing squint, suddenly exposed to light. "No line left, Sissy."

"But there was."

"Yes," he assents, "I guess there was. You may as well take advantage."

"That's exactly it, Mr. Cox."

"What's exactly what?"

"If I came straight to you, I'd be taking advantage." She nods to the wall of wanted posters, but she means the men, and he knows she means the men.

Mr. Cox looks moleishly amused. "Did you see my trees, Sissy?"

"They're great trees. I like dogwoods. You did all of that?"

"Nobody else was about to," he says sourly. She has

offended him. With Mr. Cox it always happens so fast. Where she has offended, Sissy has always felt an instant need to appease, and this, though nothing else would have, gets her to the counter, where she must hand over her letter to her mother, aware, suddenly, that she is being watched. She examines the backs of the silent men from the corner of her eye. One is leaning against the counter, not having removed himself as far as the others from her exchange with Mr. Cox. Rafer said that one of the migrants speaks a wary but quite good English, and stays by the counter all day, using the post office pen on its chain of chrome beads to fill in the money-order forms for the others, who speak only Spanish. Rafer guessed that in Mexico he had been a teacher. Now, though she is not absolutely sure she is right about who he is, she smiles, the smile divided lightly between Mr. Cox and the young migrant, and falling on no one. Mr. Cox, unbemused, gives an economic lick to her stamp, and strikes it onto the letter's corner with his fist. "In here all day," he says, leaving off the *I've been* because he knows she knows that, "I forget what English is supposed to sound like. This all you came in for, Sissy? *One* stamp? We have these with wildflowers on 'em. I got the first sheets and thought of you."

She shakes her head.

"I thought you'd like 'em," he complains. "See?"

"You're busy," she says, to remind him of the migrants' silence.

"Always am, Sissy," he says. "Don't let it fool you that there's usually nobody in here. Nice to see you. Did you like those trees of mine?"

"Very much," she says.

"*Bueno hay*," he says to the young teacherlike migrant. "Let's get this damn operation underway again, *que no*?"

The migrant fingers the glossy pen at the end of its chain and pulls a fresh set of papers near. "O.K.," he says politely. Mr. Cox squints at the migrant and the pen with moleish rue, his mouth shut grimly. Sissy senses he dislikes this daylong appropriation, by the young teacher, of U.S. Postal Service property.

Dead, the jackrabbit lies with its legs stretched out behind it and its chin pillowed on the leaf of a wild gourd, halting the trembling of that one wide, insect-frayed leaf, though the other leaves still rock along the rabbit's back and past its outflung heels, showing here and there, within the pointed shadows the leaves cast against each other, the hot yellow trumpet of a flower. A bloody cowlick is hardening at the base of the rabbit's skull, and a stray ant searches the pads of its extended forefoot, where the claws indent the coarse fur in snug stitches, each claw a pale husk with a curved marrow of compacted dust grains. Joe shudders beside Sissy with the intensity of the effort required to *stay;* he yawns and begins to pant. Tears fall from his tongue straight to the ground, where the dust pops into craters quick as those holes that percolate in wave-wetted sand. His ears are laid back, his eyes anxiously narrowed in the guilty look of a dog who is waiting for a human to perform some minor but necessary task. She whistles, willing Joe to glance at her, but he continues to stare at the rabbit in the leaves. His sense of what is right is as severe and unswerving as his gaze: she can not shoot something and leave it to the crows.

She squats to draw the rabbit out by its hind legs, the smudged leaf, as the rabbit's head slides from it, springing up with an injured jack-in-the-box wobble. She tears a leaf away and wipes the ants from the rabbit's fur, trying to get them all, because they're red ants, and can sting. For some reason, she is being gentle. As she holds it, smearing its chest with the leaf, the rabbit has a silken-slack weight.

"All right, Joe," she says, and bends for the .22. "Is that what you wanted?" He only yawns foxily and trots away, looking back just often enough to make sure they're still a pair, that he doesn't get so far ahead that she feels abandoned: She is a responsibility Rafer has left with him. They are roughly a mile from the pickup, which she left on the highway's shoulder, and to get there they will cross a pair of irrigation ditches separated by an expanse of eroded furrows and wild grass dyed a starchy, faintly pink tan by the summer. Joe leaps the first irrigation ditch with several feet to spare, then circles back and wades into the massed reflections of the cattails on the bank. He drinks noisily, water striders skating between his legs, and once he snaps at a dragonfly. Sissy crosses above him on a bridge that is a single rocking plank. She lays the rabbit on the far end, puts the gun down, and takes off her sneakers. The dark water folds itself around her ankles and her reflection melts downstream in idle zebra stripes. The wind makes all of the reeds on the bank bend together, into each other, with a sound like slapping. She arches her feet and spreads her toes as wide as they will go. She examines her freckled arms for fleas from the rabbit. She shot it out of the worst sort of boredom, because it sat up in the field in front of her when Joe wasn't in the way, and she is sorry for it now. The rabbit's eye made a neat brown marble of a target, smaller than a chip of glass in the arroyo wall. This is Sunday, and Rafer was supposed to have been home last night; so it is almost sure he will be coming in tonight, and she can beg pearly garden potatoes and carrots from her neighbor, and slice them for a stew.

When she lifts her feet out, they feel silky, as if with algae, though they're quite clean. Joe looks up, water running from his jaws and chest. She picks up the gun, lifts the rabbit, and hastily changes her grip: its legs have stiffened, and the hocks resist her grasp in knuckly points, like a pair of dice. Joe is out of the water and far ahead, not even troubling to look over his shoulder this time, and she doesn't even try to keep up. The rabbit's head swings, upside down, past the arched tips of dry grasses.

Cautiously, she avoids a prickly pear that has occupied the peeling basin of an ancient tractor tire; some of the prickly pear's pads are engraved with zigzags of tire tread. In front, Joe gives two short, sharp barks—of warning—as she moves into the deep cattails of the second ditch's bank. She comes out beside Joe, who is sitting quite still on the steep bank, and together they look down at the young migrant who has been bathing there. The man cups his genitals in his hands and stares up at her, amazed and wild. Only after a shocked silence does she remember the gun in her hand and the rabbit she holds by its heels. She lets the rabbit slide slowly into the reeds, which fan-closed over it, and then kneels in studied slow motion, still facing the migrant, to lay the gun behind her, within reach but on the ground. She stays like that—very nearly kneeling, very nearly at eye level with the man in the stream.

His eyes are large, his lips drawn away from his teeth in a fear so extreme it seems unreal to her. She tries to think whether she has ever really frightened, really terrified, anyone in her life before, and knows that she hasn't—not like this, and not even close. A thin white shirt is pinned like a kite in the cattails behind him. He had wanted to keep it dry, or air his sweat from the cloth, and this is a revelation of his fastidiousness, of something as private as his nakedness. She loves the half-floating, half-sagging shirt. She shakes her head softly, meaning it as an apology to him. She wants to apologize for coming so suddenly through the reeds, for forgetting the gun, for the way Joe is watching him, a strict surveillance. For everything. He must have understood what she wanted, because he says—oddly, perhaps even ironically, but with a certain sweetness—"*Mil gracias.*" It is a phrase she has always liked. A thousand is so many, so generous.

Then, startled at seeing what—distracted by his nakedness—she hadn't seen before, she is sure that she knows him, that he is the schoolteacher from the post office. It is so quiet that she can hear the water running between his thighs. "*De nada,*" she says. It is nothing.

It isn't nothing. She has seen in his face how scared he was, and she watches the significance of this dawn on him. He bends forward until the water laps across his flat belly. It is an awkward position, but his body to the chest is hidden from her. He is still cupping himself, under the water. She can see his hands dimly.

"Do you speak any English?" she says.

His hair is dripping into his eyes, and he no longer wishes to look at her; it is as if he has an answer, and is deliberately, warily withholding it. She likes the clean line of his cheekbone, the gravely downcast glance, but there is something mocking and set about his dark upper lip, where the mustache is a feathery trace. He looks over his shoulder to his shirt. She understands that this means she should now back away; she should let him get his shirt. She almost wants, so silently instructed, to do so, yet she wants—it is so exquisitely clear what she wants that she can't, for the fraction of an instant, condemn herself for wanting it—to watch him rise from the water.

Joe releases them from the game of statues. He laps noisily from the ditch and sniffs at the young migrant, who holds out his hand shyly. Joe ignores the hand. It is tipped up slightly, the cunning fingers curled and at ease, the palm a grid of old cuts, some healed, others healing. The man begins to make coaxing noises, musical little whimpers. Coins of light reflected from the current float over his dark shoulders like minute spotlights. His chest, when he extends his arm, is adazzle. He smiles to himself at the dog's stubbornness. She knows that he will never, if he can help it, look at her again. He knows something is wrong with her from the way she is just standing there, but he doesn't know what it is, or how to free himself of her.

"You could talk to me if you wanted," she says. "Please? *Por favor*? You don't understand. I've heard you. I know you."

She tries to think if there is anything else she can say. There isn't. There simply isn't. She doesn't know any more Spanish. The man in the stream whines gently, like a dog.

That night, to make up for having been gone longer than he'd warned her he would be, and for whatever else it is that is wrong (something is), Rafer drives her the forty miles north to Cheyenne for a movie. She watches the red taillights of the car before them blink and elide into the corner of his eye like a tear swept sideways by the wind. Then the red light vanishes and his eye is clear and dark until another set of taillights appears in it. She wonders where, in the unlit fields stretching away from the highway, the young migrant is, and what his life will be like after this. Rafer takes her hand in the dusk of the theater before the movie begins, rubs their two sets of knuckles along the armrest, and whispers, "This was a long way to come for a movie. You ought to feel properly grateful," and though for a moment she is, she does feel that, she whispers back, "Daddy, I want a bus ticket to L.A."

# LEIGH ALLISON WILSON
# MASSÉ

FROM HARPER'S

ﻬ

THE TRUTH IS it's not much of a city. When I moved in two years ago, all I knew about it was from a Chamber of Commerce brochure I got free at the courthouse. WELCOME, it said, TO THE BIG CITY IN THE LITTLE VALLEY BY THE LAKE. I had six suitcases in the back of my car and $350 and a good reason for leaving the place I'd left. For a woman like me, that's all people need to know. You start explaining things too much, you start giving heartfelt reasons for this and for that, and then nothing becomes clear and people don't trust you and you start looking at your life from bad angles. I like things clear. But the truth is it's not much of a city, not much of a valley, and you have to drive five miles to get to the lake. These are simple facts.

In the brochure they said the population was twenty thousand, but it is really closer to sixteen or seventeen. One problem is that most of the Chamber of Commerce live outside town, in big houses on the lake, and so maybe they don't come into the city much, to get the accurate head count. One thing I'm good at is counting. On Sunday nights at the local P & C, the average customer head count is twenty-six; on weekdays it is fifty-four after five o'clock. I can tell you the price of leaded

250

gas at ten different stations, the price of unleaded at seven of them. Anytime you get good at something, it's because of a habit; counting things is just a habit with me. Last week I counted twelve geese heading for Canada in two perfect lines, a perfect V, and twelve is enough to prove that spring is coming. You can sometimes live a good life figuring angles and counting things, if you're in the habit of it.

What I've done for the last two years is, I drive a UPS truck during the day and I play pool at night. I have had some trouble lately, but not because of the UPS or the pool. You might think that these are things that women don't do—drive trucks for a living, that is, and play pool—but I do them, and so you probably just don't know enough women. Take into account enough numbers, anything is possible. Phineas says that the opposite is true, that given enough numbers nothing is possible, but he is a bartender who doesn't like crowds. Very little he says makes any sense. I've been seeing him off and on for the past six months, mostly off.

I met him, as I said, about six months ago, when all the trouble started. It was November, but a clear day, and the wind was gusting to forty miles per hour. I know because I listen to the radio in my truck. Every street I drove down that day had hats in the air, like a parade, from all the wind. This is what you could call an economically depressed town, which means that everybody in it is depressed about money, so I remember that November day's weather in particular. It was the only time I have ever seen anything like a celebration on the streets, all those hats in the air and everybody running after them, their faces as red and distorted as any winning crowd on television. I do not own a television, but all the bars have them. There are thirty-three bars in this city, and only nine have regulation pool tables. This is just a fact of life.

That day I was behind in my deliveries, although mostly I am punctual to a fault. I have a map of the city inlaid like a tattoo in my mind—where the easy right-hand turns are, where the short lights are, where the children play in the streets and thus become obstacles. I had to memorize the map in the Chamber of Commerce brochure to get the job, but anyone can tell you that maps like that are useless to a good driver. Maps are flat, cities are not. Obstacles are everywhere, but the good driver knows where they are and how to avoid them. Picture the city as a big pool table, right after the break in eight ball. Your opponent's balls surround you, like seven stop signs all over the table. You must deliver the goods in a timely fashion. Knowing the correct angles is everything. The simple truth is I know all the angles in this town. But that day I was behind in my deliveries and Danny, the dispatcher, kept coming over the radio, kidding around.

"You're late, you're late," he said. "Frankly, I'm appalled. Frankly, your ass is in a slingshot." He was in his silly-serious mood, jazzing around with the radio, bored to death with his job. He used to be a big shot on some high school football team in the city, but that was years ago, and although he is still a huge, bruised-looking man, the only big shots in his life now come from bars. He drinks too much is my meaning, but in a town like this that goes without saying.

"It's the wind," I told him, clicking the mike. "It's the wind and about fifty zillion hats. I'm not kidding, there's exactly a hundred fifty hats out here today."

"Ignore 'em," he said. "Run 'em down," he said. His voice came out high and crackly, as though any minute he might burst into weird, witchlike laughter. Radios do this to everybody's voice.

"What's the matter with you?" I asked, but I could tell that he'd already signed off, was already kidding around with another truck, his big body hunched over the radio back at the office, surrounded by boxes and handcarts and no windows anywhere. Danny's life is highly unclear. Once I tried to teach him pool, to show him a few straightforward things about the game. He handled the cue stick the way lips handle a toothpick, all muscle and no control, then he tried a crazy massé shot that was all wrong for the situation and ended up tearing the felt of the table. Finesse and control are the names of the game in pool, but he would have none of it. They kicked him out of the bar. I ran the table twelve straight games after he left and picked up about seventy dollars—a very good night for me.

I made my last delivery at about four o'clock, the wind buffeting the truck every yard of the way. Usually I am punctual, but the fact is the elements are an important factor in any driving job. That day the wind was a factor. For another thing, there is always the customer factor. If your customer is in a hurry, he just grabs a pen or pencil and lets it rip; you get an unclear address and end up wasting precious minutes. My advice is, always use a typewriter. That way there is nothing personal to get in the way of the timely execution of your business. Chaos is no man's friend, clarity is everything.

I parked the truck in the lot at four-thirty, tied up some loose ends inside the office, then went outside to my car. It is a '73 navy Impala with a lot of true grit. Most people picture a good car and they think of bright color or sleek line or some other spiffy feature. This is all wrong. The best part of a good car, what makes it a good car, is its guts: pistons that never miss a beat; a carburetor so finely tuned it is like a genius chemist, mixing air and gasoline as if from beakers; a transmission that works smoothly, the gears meshing like lovers. This Impala has guts; even Phineas says so. I drove home and on the way counted smokestacks, eight of them, all rising above town in the shape of cigars stuck on end. Then something strange happened.

I was driving past the pet shop where I buy fish, only six blocks from my apartment. Up ahead the street was empty as an old Western set except for a few newspapers, seized by the wind, that tented up in the air, then fell and lay flat on the pavement. Along the sidewalks on both sides telephone poles stretched way into a distance I couldn't quite see. Maybe being late that day had me all worked up. I don't know. But I began to imagine bank shots with my car. I began to figure out at exactly what angle I would have to hit a telephone pole in order to bank the car across the street and into the pole on the other side. Then I began to do it with buildings—double banks into doorways, caroms off two fireplugs and into a brick wall, a massé around a parked car and into the plate glass of the corner drugstore. By the time I parked at my apartment, the knuckles of my hands were pale on the wheel.

Overhead, slightly distorted by the windshield, I could see Mrs. McDaniels, my landlady, leaning over the second-floor railing of my apartment building, her eyes magnified by bifocals and staring straight down, it seemed, onto my knuckles. I put my hands in my lap and stared back at her. She is a businesslady, never misses a trick; she calls all of us tenants her "clientele," just as if she were the madam of a whorehouse. The apartment building looks like one of those ten-dollar-a-night motels—two stories with lines of doors opening onto a common walkway that has a wrought-iron railing down the length of it. But Mrs. McDaniels runs a tight ship, no monkey business.

"Have you tried goldfish?" she called down when I got out of the car. "My sister says she has goldfish you couldn't kill with a hammer."

"I think so, I don't know," I called back. My hands were shaking so much I had to put them in the trouser pockets of my uniform, fisting them up in there. When I got up to the second floor, I began it again, this time with Mrs. McDaniels—I figured I'd have to put a lot of left English on my body in order to graze Mrs. McDaniels and whisk her toward the right, into the doorway of my apartment. I brought out a fist with my keys in it.

"You're late," she said, her eyes large and shrewd as a bear's. "Are you drunk or what?"

I quit listing sideways, then jiggled the keys. "No," I told her. "Just a dizzy spell. It's from sitting down all day. All the blood goes to my butt or something."

"Goldfish," she said, sniffing the air around me until, apparently satisfied, she moved to the side so I could get to my door. "Well?" she asked, and she asked it again, "Well?" For a moment I thought Mrs. McDaniels wanted to shake my hand, then I noticed the Baggie of water between her fingers. In it two goldfish held themselves as rigid and motionless as dead things. And they might as well have been, because I knew right then that they were doomed.

"I don't know," I told her, opening the door with one arm so that she could go inside ahead of me. "I think I tried goldfish first thing."

Once inside the room Mrs. McDaniels began to war with herself. She prides herself on being someone who is easygoing and friendly with her tenants, but when she gets inside your apartment, she can't help herself. Those eyes behind the glasses glaze over with suspicion, search for holes in the plaster, gashes in the parquet. My apartment is one large room, with a kitchenette and a bathroom off it, a couch, a card table, three chairs, a bed, a dresser, and a fish tank. She went directly over to the couch, studying my new poster of Minnesota Fats.

"You're fixing the place up," she said suspiciously.

"I used the special glue, Mrs. McDaniels. It doesn't peel the paint."

"Oh!" she cried. "I don't mind at all, not at all. Not *me*." I could see that good humor and business were tearing Mrs. McDaniels apart, but finally business won out and she pulled a top corner of the poster away from the wall. It came away cleanly, just as the advertisement for the glue had predicted, though after that the corner bent over and didn't stay stuck anymore. "Silly me," she cried gaily. She was in high spirits now. "I really like that poster."

For a year and a half I had lived in the apartment without anything on the walls. Every time Mrs. McDaniels came inside, she'd say, "You live like a transient, just like a transient." And I always said, "I like things neat." And I did. But this Minnesota Fats poster caught my eye. In it Fats is crouched over the cue ball, looking into the side pocket, which is where the camera is. You don't see the side pocket, you just see Fats looking squint-eyed at you, looking at you as if he knew a pretty good trick or two. And he does. The poster cost me two-fifty but was worth every penny.

"I think I tried goldfish about a year ago," I told her. "They didn't last."

"You never know," she said. "I think these guys are winners." She held up the Baggie and studied the fish for flaws. I did not bother to look at them; I knew. They were already as good as dead.

When I first moved in, the fish tank was the only piece of furniture in the room, if you can call a fish tank furniture. The tenant before me had skipped out on his rent but had left the tank as a kind of palliative gesture. Inside there was even a fish, still alive, roaming from one end of the tank to the other. It was rat-colored, about three inches long, with yellow freckles all over its sides—an ugly, sour-looking fish. I called it The Rockfish. After a month or so, I got to thinking maybe it was lonely, maybe loneliness had made it go ugly and sour, and so I went down to the pet store for some companions to put into the tank. The guy there gave me two angelfish—two pert, brightly colored fish that he said got along famously with each other and with just about anybody else. I put them in with The Rockfish and waited for something to happen. The next day I thought to look in the tank, but there was no sign of the angelfish, not a trace, just The Rockfish patrolling all the corners. After that I tried every kind of fish in the pet store— guppies, gobies, glassfish, neons, swordtails, even a catfish bigger than The Rockfish. They all just vanished, as if the tank had pockets. Mrs. McDaniels became obsessed when I told her about it. From then on nothing would do but that we find a fish good enough to go the distance in the tank. We didn't know whether The Rockfish was a male or a female or some sort of neuter, but we tried everything again: hes, shes, its, they all disappeared. Soon I wished I had never told Mrs. McDaniels anything about it, because I could tell she was beginning to associate me with the fish. She started dropping hints about what a man could do for a woman around the house, about how a woman like me could use a good man to straighten out her life. I just told her I already had all the angles figured, thank you, and that a good man wasn't hard to find if you were looking for one, which I wasn't.

"Listen," said Mrs. McDaniels, shaking the Baggie. "My sister says these guys don't know the meaning of death. They're right from her own tank. She should know."

"She should," I said, "but frankly, Mrs. McDaniels, I think they're dead meat."

"When are you settling down?" she asked absently. She was bent over the tank, flicking the glass in front of The Rockfish, her glasses pressed right up against it. I wondered then, because it seemed strange, whether Mrs. McDaniels's eyes, magnified by the glasses and the glass of the tank, whether her eyes might look huge as billiard balls to The Rockfish. No mistake, it had to be a strange sight from that angle. "Here's hoping," she said. Then she dumped the goldfish in. They floated for a few seconds, eye to eye with The Rockfish, but then they seemed to glance at each other and, before you could blink, the both of them shot down the length of the tank and huddled behind a piece of pink coral, sucking the glass in the corner for all they were worth.

"They know," I said. "One look and they knew."

"Look at the bright side," she said. "Nothing's happened yet."

"Not yet. But nothing ever happens when you're looking. It waits till you're at work or shopping or daydreaming or something—that's when it all happens."

"A big girl like you," she said, giving me the once-over. "Ought to be married is what you ought to be."

"Thanks for the fish, Mrs. McDaniels." I showed her to the door.

"Listen. Keep me posted. My sister says they're tough buggers, says they can eat nails."

"I'll keep you posted," I said, then I shut the door. For some reason, I began to snicker like crazy as soon as Mrs. McDaniels left. I went over to the tank, snickering, but The Rockfish only hung in the middle, sedate and ugly as sin. The two goldfish were still sucking away in the corner. I had to lie down on the bed to keep from snickering. For a few minutes I thought maybe I was having a heart attack. There were these pins and needles in my arms and legs, this pain in my chest, but then it all went away after a while. I lay like a stick on the bed, trying to get some sleep, counting my breaths to relax a little. Maybe being late had me worked up. Usually I got through work at two in the afternoon, home by two-thirty, but that day I was all off. I couldn't relax and I kept thinking about how I couldn't, which of course just made things worse and aggravated me and gave me the feeling I was in a fix for good. I got to thinking, then, that my life was going to take a turn for the bad, that somehow I would be off-balance and out of step for the rest of whatever was coming. Across the room I could see the unclear, rat-colored shape of The Rockfish swimming the length of the tank, banking off the far walls, then swimming back again at the same latitude, back and forth, patrolling. And I wondered, to keep from snickering, to ward off the heart attack, I wondered if it knew I was watching. Did it know I kept count of things going on in the tank? Did it know I had all its angles figured, its habits memorized? Did it think I'd almost masséd my car around a fireplug and into a telephone pole? Did it think I was a friend?

\*       \*       \*

I slept like a dead man, because I didn't wake up until around ten-thirty that night, my neck twisted at an odd, painful angle. The only light in the room came from the phosphorescent green glow of the fish tank. Mrs. McDaniels must have switched the tank light on earlier, because I almost never did. It gave me the creeps, as if the tank were the window onto some obscene green world where the tiniest ripple had profound ramifications, the kind of world you always suspect might happen to you suddenly, like Kingdom Come, if you lost all your habits. You lose your habits, and then you can kiss everything you've gotten good at good-bye.

I got out of bed, but things were still off somehow; the feeling of things gone wrong was like a fur on my tongue. Usually I got home at two-thirty, ate something, then slept until about ten o'clock, when business at the pool tables got going good. But that day I'd overslept and was late to begin with, and I knew as if I'd been through it before—which I hadn't—that trouble was just beginning. All I did was grab my keys and I was out of the apartment, almost sprinting to my car. Outside the wind grabbed hold, but I tucked my chin against it until I was inside the car, gripping the wheel and breathing hard. I figured by hurrying I could get a jump on whatever might come next, though when trouble comes, mistake number one is hurrying. I knew that, but I hurried just the same.

On the way to the bar I kept my mind on driving, no funny business. There are nine bars in this town with regulation pool tables, and I always go to a different one each night, until I have to start over again. That night I was due for a bar called The Office, which is a nice enough place if you can stand seeing typewriters and other office equipment hanging on the walls. Oddly enough, it is a favorite hangout for secretaries during cocktail hours. They seem to like the idea of getting drunk surrounded by the paraphernalia of their daily lives. At night, though, the clientele switches over to factory workers and middle-level management types—supervisors, foremen—and you can pick up a nice piece of change. All the way to The Office I kept myself rigid as a fence post. Only one thing happened. I was passing the button factory, a big yellow building with two smokestacks that went at it all the time, burning bad buttons maybe. It struck me, as I passed, that those smoke-stacks looked a lot like pool cues aimed right for the sky—that's all I thought, which was strange, but nothing to knock you off balance. Nothing like banking your car off buildings. I'd even begun to think I could relax a little by the time I got to the bar.

Because The Office is situated among gas stations and retail stores, it gave off the only light on the block except for occasional streetlamps. The plate glass in front glowed yellow like a small sunset surrounded by nothing at all and out in the middle of nowhere, the kind of sunset people plan dream vacations around, and a sure recipe for disappointment. For a moment I thought better of the whole thing, almost turned around and went home, but the fact of the matter was, I knew that if I did all was lost, because once you gave in you kept on giving in. A habit is as easily lost and forgotten as hope for a better shake in things. So I went on into the bar.

As soon as I got inside I thought it would be all right. The two tables were busy, mostly guys in blue work shirts rolled up to the elbows, holding the cues like shotguns. It was promising because anyone in town recognized the blue work shirts. They came from the nuclear power plant up on the lake, the one that might or might not ever get built, which meant they had money and didn't much mind throwing it away on a fifty-fifty possibility. I had played a foreman from the power plant once, a year before, and during the course of the game he explained that even though the job was dangerous half the time, the money they got was the real health hazard. "More of our men die from drunk driving," he said, "than from touching the wrong wire," and he said it in a proud, fisty sort of way. He was an electrical engineer from east Tennessee, where he said anything that happened had to happen big or else nobody noticed it from one valley to the next. I took him for twenty dollars, then he got unfriendly. But that's the way with those guys: They see a woman playing pool and they automatically assume a fifty-fifty chance, usually more. Then they get un-friendly when they see you've got a good habit. They just don't know enough women. Numbers count.

In The Office, to get to the pool tables you have to finesse your way through about twenty tables full of people who have had too much to drink. Cigarettes, flitting through the air on the tail end of a good story, are obstacles, and so are wayward elbows and legs. One sure sign that you're drunk is if you're in somebody's way. But I got through that part. I made a beeline for Bernie, who was chalking his cue at the second table, the good table, the one with a roll you could figure.

"You are tardy," he said in his formal way, still chalking his cue. Sometime during his life, Bernie was a schoolteacher: astronomy. On certain nights he'd take you outside and point out the constellations, his old nicotine-stained fingers pointing toward the stars. He knew his stuff. And he knew pool, too, except for a tendency to grow passionate at the least provocation, a tendency that combined with old age and Jack Daniel's was ruining his game. Given a population of sixteen or seventeen thousand, Bernie was the only rival I had in town. But we never played together, sometimes never saw each other for weeks; we just appreciated the habits we'd both gotten into.

"You are tardy," he repeated, giving me a dark look. "And the stars are out tonight." He meant that people were spending money like nobody's business.

"I think it's the wind," I told him. "I think there's something funny in the wind."

"Ha!" Bernie cried. He put down the chalk and picked up his cigarette, puffing on it. Then, in a cloud of smoke, he wheeled around to the table, brought up his cue, and nailed the eight ball on a bank into the side pocket, easy as you please. It threw his opponent all off. His opponent had on a blue work shirt that was either too small for him on purpose or else was the biggest size they had: His muscles showed through the material as though he were wearing no shirt at all. On the table only one ball was left, sitting right in front of a corner pocket, and by the look on the guy's face you could tell he'd figured he had the old man on the run, the game sewn up. What he didn't know was that Bernie's opponents in eight ball always had only one ball left on the table. But the guy was a good sport and paid his ten dollars without muscling around or banging his cue on the floor. Sometimes with your big guys chaos is their only response to losing. It is just a fact of life.

"That is that," Bernie said, putting the ten in his wallet. "The table is all yours."

"Where you going?" Bernie always stayed at the tables until about midnight, and if he was around, I just watched and took pointers, waiting for him to get tired and go home before I got busy. Usually I took over where he left off. "It's only eleven," I said, "and you say the stars are out."

"I have a granddaughter coming in on the midnight train." He made a face that meant he was tickled pink, the corners of his mouth stretched and stained with a half million cigarettes. "All pink and yellow, like a little doll. She can point out Venus on the horizon with her eyes shut. A beautiful girl. You should meet her."

"Maybe I will."

"Seven years old and she knows the difference between Arcturus and Taurus. For Christmas last year, do you know what she told her mother she wanted? Guess what she wanted."

"A pool cue," I said, which was exactly what I would have asked for.

"No, you are insane. A telescope! She said she wanted to get close to the sky, close enough to touch it. She's no bigger than a flea and she asks for a telescope!" Bernie slapped his palms together, then sidled closer. "Between us, she is a genius, has to be. My granddaughter, a genius."

"You must be proud of her," I said. All of a sudden I wanted Bernie out of the bar. His very breath smelled like trouble. Then I noticed his shot glass of Jack Daniel's was missing from the stool he usually kept it on; he was sober as a judge. I wanted Bernie gone.

"Oh, she is going places, I can feel it. I can *feel* it!" He slapped his palms together again, bouncing on his feet a little, then he swung toward the men in the work shirts and opened his arms enough to include me in the sweep of them. "Gentlemen, I leave you with this young lady as my proxy. Do not be fooled by her gender." He looked at me appraisingly. "Do not be fooled by the uniform. She can handle herself."

"Thanks, Bernie," I said, but I didn't look at him then, and I didn't look at him when he left. Instead I looked at all the guys in blue work shirts. At first they each one had an expression of irritation and rebellion: They didn't like the idea of me usurping command of the table just because the winner knew me. And I didn't blame them, except that the next expression on each of their faces was a familiar one.

"All right, George, you're up," one of them said. "Take her and then let's us get serious," he said, which was exactly what I had expected from their expressions. I could read these guys like a brochure. Any other night I would have grinned and aw-shucked around, leading them on a little bit. I might have even offered to wait my turn, humbling myself to the point of idiocy, until they said, "No, you go on, honey," gallantry making idiots of them, too. That night, though, something was wrong with me. For one thing, the whole day had been all wrong. For another, seeing Bernie sober and giddy as a billy goat really threw me. I hadn't known he had a granddaughter or a daughter or even a wife. I'd never seen him sober. Something about it all set me going again. I imagined flinging myself headlong into the knot of blue work shirts, sending them all flying to the far corners of The Office, like a good break.

"O.K., little lady," said the one named George, winking and grinning to his friends. "Let's see how you deliver." He could not contain himself. "Did you hear that? Did you hear what I just said? I said, I asked her, 'Let's see how you deliver.'"

They all snorted, stamping their cues on the end of their boots, and I regretted not changing out of my uniform. It was a bad sign because I'd never worn it to the bars before, just one result of hurrying trouble. You never knew when somebody might take a wild hair and try to mess up your job, somebody with a poor attitude toward losing and a bad disposition and a need for spreading chaos. I felt dizzy for a minute, as though I'd been submerged in water and couldn't make the transition.

"Winners break," George said. Now he was all business, ready to get the game over with so he could play with his friends. He strutted around, flexing his work shirt. Most nights, when I had the break, I would try to sink a couple, then leave the cue ball in a safe position, ducking my chin and smirking shamefacedly, as though I'd miscalculated. The point is, never let the guys waiting in line see that your game in no way depends on luck; it scares them if you do, shrinks their pockets like a cold shower, so to speak. But that night I was crazy, must have been. George went into an elaborate explanation of how he had to go to the bathroom but would be back before

his turn, how I'd never even know he was gone. I said, "Five
bucks." He rolled his eyes comically, performing for his friends,
then said it was all right by him. "You're the boss, Chuck,"
he said. I don't know what got into me. Before George was out
of sight, I broke and sank two stripes. Then I hammered in the
rest of them, taking maybe three seconds between each shot.
By the time old George could zip up his pants, I'd cleared the
table.

"Fucking-A," said one of George's friends.

"Whoa," another one said. "Holy whoa."

It was a dream, that whole game was a dream. I had read
somewhere that a sure sign of madness was when life took on a
dreamlike quality, when you started manipulating what you
saw as easily as you manipulate dreams. Those pins and needles
came back into my feet, prickly as icicles. George came back,
too. I figured the night was over. They would all get pissed off
and quit playing and begin to attend to their beers. But—
surprise—they ate it up, practically started a brawl over who
was up next. It wasn't anything you could have predicted. I
guess it pumped them up with adrenaline, or else with a kind of
competitive meanness, because for the rest of the night they
banged the balls with a vengeance. They were none too polite,
and that's a fact. Whatever happened during those games happened in a dream. A wad of five-dollar bills began to show
through the back pocket of my uniform trousers. The guys in
blue work shirts were like a buzzing of hornets around me,
their faces getting drunker and redder every hour.

Near closing time, around two in the morning, George
came back for a last game. I'd been watching him play on the
other table, and even with the handicap of a dozen beers he
could run five or six balls at a time, which is not embarrassing
for bar pool. But there was real hatred on George's face, sitting
there like a signpost. All those beers had loosened his features
until his eyebrows met in a single, straight-edged line, the kind
of eyebrows the Devil would have if he had eyebrows. Some
men just can't get drunk without getting evil, too. I suggested
we call it a day, but George would have none of it. He
swaggered around, foulmouthed, until I said all right just to
shut him up.

"Fucking dyke," he said, loud enough for me to hear. I

kept racking the balls. He was the one who was supposed to rack them, but now I didn't trust him to rack them tightly.

"I said," he said, a little louder, "fucking *dyke* in a uniform." He was drunk—and I should have known better—though, as I've said, that day was the beginning of trouble. One rule of pool is never get emotional. You get emotional and first thing you know, your angles are off, your game is a highly unclear business.

"Asshole," I told him. "Fucking *asshole* in a uniform." My hands shook so much I gripped my cue as if it were George's neck. I am not a grisly or violent person, but there you go.

"Just play, for God's sake," said one of his friends. They were all grouped around the table, their faces as alike and featureless as the balls in front of them. I imagined that their eyes were the tips of cues, blue, sharp, nothing you wanted pointed in your direction.

"Radiation mutant," I said. "Rockfish." Then I broke. Sure enough, emotion had its effect. None of the balls fell.

"Fifty bucks, you pervert," George said, rippling those eyebrows at me. "No, make it a hundred." All that beer was working up some weird, purplish coloration into his cheeks.

They say that during important moments time goes by more slowly, elongates somehow just when you need it most. It is a falsehood. Time goes slowly when you're utterly miserable, or when you might be about to die, and both are situations any sane person would want to go by quickly. When you really need it, time isn't there for you. I wanted to study the table for a while, get myself under control and ready. I wanted to go outside and have somebody point out the constellations, show me the difference between Taurus and Arcturus. I wanted somebody to give me a fish that didn't die in the tank. I wanted somebody, anybody, to tell me that I was living a good life, that my habits were excellent, that I was going places.

"This is all she wrote, Chuck," George said, leaning over the table like a surgeon. It looked grim, not because the spread was all in George's favor—which was true—but because I had gotten emotional. Nothing was clear anymore, not the angles, not the spin, nothing. My cue stick might just as well have been a smokestack.

"Shit!" George cried, and he slammed a beefy hand against his beefy thigh.

He'd run the table except for the eight ball, leaving me with some tricky shots—stop signs all over the table. By now everyone in The Office stood around the table, watching, belching, not saying a word. I thought about what Minnesota Fats would do, how Fats would handle the situation, but all I saw was that corner of the poster, unstuck and curled ominously over Fats's head. I wondered what would happen if I picked up each of my balls and placed them gently in the pockets, like eggs into Easter baskets. Crazy, I must have been crazy.

The first couple of shots were easy, then it got harder. I banked one ball the length of the table, a miraculous shot, though it left the cue ball in an iffy position. I made the next one anyway. After each shot I had to heft the stick in my hand, get the feel of it all over again, as if I were in George's league, an amateur on a hot streak. Finally the game came down to one shot. I had one ball left, tucked about an inch and a half up the rail from the corner pocket, an easy kiss except that the eight ball rested directly in the line of the shot. There was no way I could bank the cue ball and make it.

"All she wrote," George said, "all she by God *wrote!*"

I hefted my cue stick for a massé, the only thing left to do.

"Oh, no," cried George. "No you don't. You might get away with that shit in lesbo pool, but not here. You're not doing it here. No, sir. No way."

"Who says?" I asked him, standing up from the table. I was sweating a lot, I could feel it on my ribs. "Anything goes is my feeling."

"Bar rules." George appealed to his friends. "Right? No massé in bar rules. Right? Am I right?"

"Phineas!" somebody called. "Phineas! No massé on the tables, right?"

Phineas came out around the bar, rubbing his hands on an apron that covered him from the neck to the knees. He had short, black, curly hair and wore round wire-rimmed glasses, the kind of glasses that make people look liberal and intelligent somehow. He looked clean and trim in his white apron, surrounded by all those sweaty blue work shirts. For a minute he just stood there, rubbing his hands, sizing up the table.

"What's the stake?" he asked philosophically.

"Hundred," George said. He was practically screaming.

Phineas puckered his mouth.

"Well," he said, drawing the sound out. Maybe he was buying time. Maybe he was leading them on. Or maybe he was a bartender who didn't like crowds and didn't like crowds asking for his opinion—which is exactly what he is. "Anything goes," he said. "Anything goes for a hundred bucks is my opinion."

"I'll remember this," George said, snarling, his purple face shaded to green. "You prick, I'll remember this."

"Fine," said Phineas, almost jovially. He folded his arms across that white apron and looked at me. He might have winked, but more likely he was just squinting, sizing me up.

"Massé on the ten into the corner," I said stiffly, formally, the way Bernie would have done. Anybody will tell you, a massé is ridiculous. You have no real cue ball control, no real control period. You have to bring your stick into an almost vertical position, then come down solidly on one side of the cue ball, which then—if you do it right—arcs around the obstacle ball and heads for the place you have in mind. It is an emotional shot, no control, mostly luck. And anytime you get yourself into the position of taking an emotional shot, all is pretty much lost. I hefted the cue stick again, hiked it up like an Apache spearing fish. Then I let it rip. The cue ball arced beautifully, went around the eight ball with a lot of backspin, then did just what it was supposed to do—kissed the ten on the rail. The trouble was, it didn't kiss the ten hard enough. The ball whimpered along the rail about an inch, then stopped short of the pocket. A breath would have knocked it in, but apparently nobody was breathing.

"That's all she wrote," I told Phineas. He just smiled, looking liberal and intelligent behind his glasses.

The upshot was, George won the game. I'd left the cue ball in a perfect position for making the eight in the side pocket. Any idiot could have made that shot, and George was no idiot, just a drunken jerk. He even got friendly when I paid him his money, wanted to take me home, his breath hot and sour as old beer. But then Phineas stepped in, cool as you please, and said that *he* was going home with me. Between the two there was no choice: I told Phineas to meet me out front at my car. "A '73 navy Impala," I told him. It was not that unusual, even though the day had me off balance. I'd had a couple of guys over to my apartment before, after the bars closed, the kind of thing where in the morning you find yourself clenching the pillows, hoping they don't use your toothbrush or something. Even if I did see those guys again, their faces would mean no more to me than the faces of former opponents in a pool game.

The wind had died, nothing moved when I went out to the car. On the way to my apartment Phineas told me about how he hated crowds, how there was nothing possible with those kinds of numbers. I told him numbers counted, but he didn't argue the point. Then he told me how nice my car was. "True grit," I said. "Nothing spiffy, just good guts." He put his hand on my thigh. We rode like that for a long time. When we passed the button factory, I told him about the smokestacks looking like pool cues. Then, for some reason, I told him about driving my car into telephone poles, banking it off buildings.

"You shouldn't get all out of control over a game," he said. After that I didn't tell him anything else, pretended I was concentrating on his hand against my thigh.

Inside my apartment I didn't turn on the lights. The green glow of the fish tank let me see all I wanted to see, maybe more. Phineas, of course, went right for the tank, which was what everybody did when they came into my apartment.

"How come you only have two fish?" he wanted to know.

"That one there, with the yellow freckles. It kills everything I put in there. Wait and see. In the morning that other one won't be there. It's a shark," I said.

"No kidding," he said, peering in at The Rockfish. "Really? A shark?"

"No. It's just an it. A killer it."

Phineas straightened up. "What's your name?"

"Janice," I said.

"At least in this town it's Janice," I said, revealing myself a little, although I wasn't about to go into heartfelt reasons for this and that. It didn't matter because then he kissed me, hard, standing there in front of the fish tank. In a minute or so, he broke away.

"You can play your ass off in pool, Janice," he said. He began to unbutton his shirt. It was flannel, which matched his glasses somehow; the apron he'd left back at the bar. I took off the trousers of my uniform, then he kissed me again, his hands down low.

"You look real nice," he said. "Out of uniform, as it were." He laughed, and I laughed, too, in a strange kind of way.

After that I was on the couch with him on top of me. He got busy. I put my hands on his back, but he did all the work. The whole time I was thinking, my head to one side, staring into the fish tank. I was thinking that maybe I would leave town. Maybe I would pack up my car and move and get around my trouble that way. I could leave the fish tank, skip out on the rent, just like the guy before me had done. Let The Rockfish chew its own gristle, I thought, let Mrs. McDaniels drop hints to somebody else. The Rockfish was patrolling the tank, whipping beside the lone goldfish like terror on the move, and the goldfish sucked madly on the glass in the corner, behind the pink coral, wriggling whenever The Rockfish swept by. It struck me as the saddest thing I'd ever seen. Then I began it again, with Phineas this time. I imagined he was performing a massé on me, several massés, coming down hard on one side and then the other, one emotional shot after another, only I wasn't going anywhere. I must have snorted, because Phineas worked harder all of a sudden.

"Feel it?" he said, or asked, whispering, and I could tell that he'd come to a crucial moment. "Can you feel it?" And I said, "Yes," I said, "Yes, yes, I can feel it," but I couldn't. I shifted slightly to make things easier, but I couldn't feel a thing, not a thing—nothing.

# ABOUT THE AUTHORS

ᔓ

Gail Galloway Adams was born in Texas and is completing a doctorate in American studies from Emory University. "Inside Dope" received the 1986 Texas Institute of Letters Short Story Award. Her poetry and fiction have appeared in *The American Review*, *The Georgia Review*, and *The North American Review*. She lives in Morgantown, West Virginia, with her husband and son and is a lecturer at West Virginia University.

Margaret Atwood is the author of over twenty books of poetry, fiction, and nonfiction. She is perhaps best known for her six novels, *The Edible Woman*, *Surfacing*, *Lady Oracle*, *Life Before Man*, *Bodily Harm*, and the bestselling *The Handmaid's Tale*. "The Whirlpool Rapids" is from her most recent book of stories, *Bluebeard's Egg*.

Russell Banks is the author of *Continental Drift*, *The Relation of My Imprisonment*, and *Success Stories*. He has been awarded a Guggenheim, a National Endowment for the Arts, and a Fulbright fellowship and his fiction has received numerous prizes and awards. He lives in Brooklyn and teaches in the writing program at Princeton University.and at New York University.

Charles Baxter's fiction and poetry have appeared in many periodicals. He has published two books of short stories, *Harmony of the World* and *Through the Safety Net*, and a novel, *First Light*, has just been published by Viking. He teaches at Wayne State University in Michigan.

Robert Cohen lives in New York City. His fiction has appeared in *Ploughshares, Iowa Review, Massachusetts Review*, and *Ascent*. This story is excerpted from his recently published first novel, *The Organ Builder* (Harper & Row).

Mary Gordon is the author of three novels, *The Company of Women, Final Payments*, and *Men and Angels*. Her most recent book is *Temporary Shelter*, a collection of stories. A graduate of Barnard College, she now lives in upstate New York with her husband and two children.

Amy Herrick is a graduate of the Iowa Writers' Workshop and has published stories in *TriQuarterly, Kenyon Review, The Random Review*, and *Schlaflos*. She was the recipient of a 1985 G. E. Younger Writers' Award.

Janette Turner Hospital, an award-winning novelist, was born in Australia. She divides her time between Boston (she is Visiting Writer-in-Residence at M.I.T.) and Kingston, Ontario, where she now lives. Her novels, *The Ivory Swing, The Tiger in the Tiger Pit*, and *Borderline*, were published internationally. Her short stories have appeared in a number of magazines, and a collection entitled *Dislocations* was recently published by McClelland & Stewart in Canada.

Sara Lewis's stories have appeared in *The New Yorker, The Mississippi Review*, and *Seventeen*. She and her husband live in Massachusetts, where she is writing her first novel.

Todd Lieber lives on a small farm near Indianola, Iowa, where he is a professor of English at Simpson College. He has an MFA from the University of Arizona. Other recent stories have appeared in *Ms., Kansas Quarterly*, and *Yale Review*, and he is just finishing a first novel about rural America.

Richard McCann is working on a first novel for Viking/Penguin. He is the author of a book of poems, *Dream of the Traveler*

(Ithaca House). His work has appeared in *The Atlantic Monthly, Virginia Quarterly Review*, and *Shenandoah*, among others. He has been the recipient of a Fulbright fellowship in 1982–1983 as well as fellowships from Yaddo, MacDowell, and The Virginia Center for Creative Arts.

Thomas McGuane is the author of several highly acclaimed novels, including *The Sporting Club; The Bushwacked Piano*, which won the Richard and Hilda Rosenthal Award of the American Academy and Institute of Arts and Letters; *Ninety-Two in the Shade*, which was nominated for the National Book Award; *Panama; Nobody's Angel; Something to Be Desired*; and *An Outside Chance*, a collection of essays on sport. He lives in Montana.

Sue Miller has published stories in *Ploughshares, The Atlantic Monthly, The North American Review, Mademoiselle*, and other magazines. The story included here is the title story of a collection, *Inventing the Abbotts* (Harper & Row). Miller lives in Cambridge, Massachusetts, with her husband and son and teaches at Boston University. Her novel, *The Good Mother*, was published in 1986. She is currently working on a second novel.

Bharati Mukherjee last year saw the paperback reissuing of two novels, *The Tiger's Daughter*, and *Wife*, as well as the publication of a nonfiction collaboration with Clark Blaise, *The Sorrow and the Terror*, on the Air India bombing of 1985. Her last book of stories, *Darkness*, was published in 1986, and a new collection is forthcoming from Grove. She teaches writing at Columbia University.

Tim O'Brien is the author of *If I Die in a Combat Zone, Northern Lights, The Nuclear Age*, and *Going After Cacciato*, which won the 1979 National Book Award in fiction. His stories have appeared in *Esquire, The Atlantic Monthly, Shenandoah, Massachusetts Review*, and *Redbook*. He is currently working on a fifth book.

Rachel Pastan's work has appeared in *The Georgia Review* and *The Mississippi Review*. She lives in Cambridge, Massachusetts. "Underground" is her second published story.

Elizabeth Tallent is the author of *Museum Pieces*, a novel, and a collection of stories, *Time with Children*. She lives in Nevada.

Leigh Allison Wilson's first book, *From the Bottom Up*, won the Flannery O'Connor Prize for Fiction in 1983. Her stories have appeared in *Harper's, Mademoiselle, The Georgia Review*, and *Grand Street*, among others. She lives in upstate New York, where she is working on a book of stories.

## ABOUT THE EDITOR

George E. Murphy, Jr. is the editor of *Tendril* Magazine, an independent literary journal, and is the editorial director of Wampeter Press, Inc. He is the author of a book of poems, *Rounding Ballast Key* (Ampersand Press, 1985), and a children's book, *Teddy: A Christmas Story*. He is also the editor of two anthologies, *The Poets' Choice: 100 American Poets' Favorite Poems*, and (with poet/biographer Paul Mariani) *Poetics: Essays on the Art of Poetry*. In 1983, he won the New York Contemporary Press Poetry Prize. In 1985, he was awarded the Joseph P. Shaw Award from Boston College for distinguished contributions to contemporary literature. And in 1987 he was given a poetry fellowship to the Bread Loaf writers' conference. He currently lives in Key West and is working on a novel and compiling *The Key West Reader: An Historical Literary Anthology*.